Dale Mayer

Knock, knock…

Book 5

Psychic Visions

KNOCK, KNOCK...
Dale Mayer
Valley Publishing
Copyright © 2012

ISBN: 1927461715
ISBN-13: 978-1927461716

DEDICATION

This book is dedicated to my four children who always
believed in me and my storytelling abilities.
Thank you!

ACKNOWLEDGMENTS

Knock, Knock… wouldn't have been possible without the support of my friends and family. Many hands helped with proofreading, editing, and beta reading to make this book come together. Special thanks to my editor Pat Thomas.

I thank you all.

Chapter 1

There is no revenge so complete as forgiveness.
...Josh Billings

Ice hit her first. Inside and out.

Shay Lassiter woke to find goosebumps marching across her cold skin in the early morning. She tugged up the chocolate brown duvet she'd thrown off sometime in the night but even that didn't account for the cold filtering slowly through her waking consciousness. The rest of her brain screamed at her to wake up all the way. *Something was off.*

Morris, the ever-present ghost of her beloved childhood pet, snuggled up close. She didn't understand the miracle of his existence, but she rejoiced in it every day. The deep purr rumbled at her shoulder making her smile. She was thankful his gentle blue ball of energy sat on her bed most days. She rarely saw him in physical form, but he was always there in spirit – offering immeasurable comfort. Most times, the sound of his engine powered through the small room. That oversized orange tabby had been the size of a small car, but had a diesel truck motor for an engine.

The purr shut off.

Shit.

Her internal alarm finally kicked in as the bedding pressed down on her, confining, where moments before it had been comforting. She threw the duvet back, springing from bed, her heart pounding. A clammy film coated her skin. *What the hell was wrong?*

She spun around, searching her darkened bedroom for the cause of the unease settling deep in her soul.

There was no one there with her.

Last night, she'd gone to sleep without a problem. That was surprising because she'd had an argument with her fiancé, Darren, before going to sleep. And it had been a bad one, making her doubt their relationship...again. But still, she knew that discord hadn't created this type of response. Her psyche often chose the wee hours of the morning to wake her up and chew away at her, but she'd never woken up quite like this. Shivering, she looked down at her cami and boy shorts to see the hairs rising on her smooth skin. Her teeth chattered as she ran to check the thermostat in her room. It was normal.

Of course it was. It *should* be warm; it was summertime.

She ran back to bed and huddled against her headboard with her duvet high up on her chest.

Shay?

Stefan Kronos spoke, his familiar voice swept through her mind, calming her. He must have heard her silent distress in the night. *Stefan? Something's wrong. Only I can't see what it is.*

I'll check it out.

The emptiness in her mind told her Stefan had left. God, she didn't know what she'd do without him. He didn't always respond this quickly, but her psychic friend always knew when something was wrong.

Then she heard *it*...

The click of her front door opening...then closing. Something moved across her living room floor.

She had an intruder.

Alarm swept through her. *Oh no.* The door had been locked. She'd double-checked it before going to bed. There's no way anyone could get in.

Unless they had a key.

Shay? Get out of the apartment. Stefan's sharp voice sliced through her frozen state. *There's a rogue energy heading toward you.*

Too late, she whispered in her mind. *It's too late. He's inside already. Call for help, Stefan. Hurry!*

Hide. I'm getting help.

"Shay? Oh, hi, honey. I hadn't expected you to be awake." Her fiancé stood at her bedroom doorway, a crooked smile on his face. Darren held up a key in his hand. It gleamed in the slice of moonlight creeping through her drapes. Dressed all in black, he cut an elegant figure. His handsome good looks and confidence had been part of what attracted her to him in the first place.

Relief swamped her. "Oh thank God," she murmured and closed her eyes. Her rigid spine relaxed. There was nothing to worry about after all. Feeling much better and slightly foolish, she opened her eyes and smiled warmly at him. So happy to see him after their fight and her initial panic.

It's just Darren, Stefan.

Silence in her mind.

Darren? he asked in a flat voice. *Your fiancé?*

Yes. She gave a small deprecating laugh.

Shay? Then...why the fear?

Her eyes widened. Good question. "Darren, why are you here at this hour?" She glanced at the clock. "It's two in the morning." She stared at him, confused, as something else registered – finally. "And where did you get the key?"

He shifted away from the door, his smile widening. But there was something off about that twist to his lips. A little too tight, and an odd glow added to the toothy shine. "When you wouldn't give me a key, I decided to have one made up on my own."

She blinked. That didn't make any sense. Did it? No. It was wrong. She tossed back her long brown hair, trying to clear her head. And wished her roiling stomach would calm. She couldn't seem to think straight.

"Why? I don't understand."

His lips quirked. He tossed the key on the bed. "I know. But I figured that I had to do something. After all, we're fighting more lately. Not making up the same. It's as if we're on the verge of a break up."

"Oh, I don't think—"

"Stop." He held up his hands. "You know you don't look at our relationship quite the same anymore. Neither do I." His hands dropped and he shook his head. "You also know you've been spending more time on that damn Children's Hospital project than ever. Even when I said I didn't like it."

Oh shit. He was breaking up with her. But then why get a key made? And of course she spent a lot of time on that project. It was special. The kids were special. He knew that.

Didn't he?

Why was nothing making any sense right now?

Stefan whispered through her mind. *Shay, something's wrong. What's happening?*

She stared at Darren. *I don't know.*

To her fiancé, she said, "I don't understand."

"I know you don't. That's okay. I can explain." He walked over and sat down at the edge of her bed. "It's too bad, though. You're a beautiful lady. Inside and out."

"Thank you, I think?" Shay might be confused, but some truths were making their way inside. He'd had a key to her home made without her permission and he had let himself into her apartment in the middle of the night. Like Stefan had said, something was wrong.

And now she was starting to feel more than a little nauseous. And, she felt...slower. Her mind sluggish. As if she were in shock. Or hurt... But she wasn't. She gazed down at her arms and the rest of her body. She felt weak, faint even, but not like she was injured in any way.

"You don't get it, do you, Shay?"

She stared up at him, puzzled. "No. And I'd appreciate it if you'd explain. This isn't very funny."

"No, it isn't. You ruined all my plans."

She tilted her head and tried to focus. "Plans?"

"Yes, plans." Looking relaxed and at ease, he crossed one leg over the other and then clasped his hands over his knees. "See. I need money. Lots of money."

Feeling foolish and spaced out, she asked, "Why?"

He smiled, a knowing smile. "For lots of things." He tilted his head and looked at her steadily. "Are you feeling okay?"

She tried to swallow, her tongue thick, unwieldy. "I don't know. I feel a bit...weird, actually."

"That's all quite normal. I'm making it easy on you."

Normal. What was *normal* about any of this? "I...I don't understand."

He gave an exaggerated sigh. "No, I don't suppose you do. So let me make this simple." He stood and walked over to the window. "I need money. You have money. And, if we were together, that wouldn't be a problem. On top of your personal fortune, you control an amount that's unbelievably large. See, that's really attractive. Plus, taking you to bed isn't exactly a hardship." He leered at her. "In fact, that part has been sheer fun. I figured I was in clover. We were engaged—"

"Still are, I thought."

His smile didn't quite reach his eyes. "So you say. See, I understand the female mind. I know that you aren't as happy as you were. And once that thread of discontent starts, it only gets worse. Our fight tonight was about moving up the wedding day.

But you didn't want that. You're hesitating. And that means you have doubts. And doubts are dangerous because they could mean the end of my plans – and make me very unhappy." He moved the blinds slightly. "I can't have that."

He sighed. "I thought I could save you... I have to admit that even now I'm having doubts..." He cocked his head and stared at her. She could barely see a softening in his features. A pondering. A weighing of options.

Then he straightened, stuck out his chin and shook his head. "No. It has to be this way." The moonlight shone in through the crack between the blinds. "Too bad though; you showed such promise."

Shay closed her eyes as his words and tones filtered through the growing fog in her brain.

Stefan, Dear God, I need help.

It's coming. Stay with me.

I don't know if I can. I don't know what's happening.

Nothing good! Damn it, I told you there was someone better out there for you.

She'd have laughed if she could. Instead a strange lassitude had filled her veins, mixed into her bloodstream. *I can't think.*

The buzz of Stefan's thoughts disturbed the clouds fogging her mind.

Shay, read his energy. Shay? Shay! Damn it, stay with me. You need to read his energy.

She didn't want to. It was difficult. She could barely understand Stefan's instructions. Something about Darren's energy. Her head lolled to the side. "What did you do to me?"

"Well, I'm punishing you, of course. Actually it's not that much of a punishment. If I thought I could control you, I'd keep you around, but I can't. The decision has been made." He paused and tilted his head. "You're strong, you know. Not as strong as me, of course, but still strong."

He hesitated; his gaze turned inward as if listening to an inner voice. Then sighed and shook his head. "No. I can't change my plans. If you ever found out what you could do with all that strength... If you could be trained to use it properly... But no. You aren't trainable. I've seen that already." He walked around the bed, studying her. "It's almost over. See? This is a nice way to go. Just fall asleep and you'll be gone. But of course, everyone resists it. Too bad. So sad. Everyone keeps clinging to their pathetic little lives even when that point is long gone."

Then she got it. *Oh God.*

"You're going to kill me?" The fog deepened. She struggled to push it back. To find clarity. To find answers. To find a way out of this hell.

Stefan had said, 'Read his energy.' Not an easy task. The fog thinned slightly, a small victory, and she tried to shift her vision to see Darren's energy.

As she'd done when things became serious between them. It was almost instinctive self-preservation to do so. She'd discovered he had a few anger issues, a few regrets, some energy heading into his past. A few walls saying he had a few secrets, but nothing to make her feel like she should delve deeper into the core of the man.

And now she realized her mistake. When it was too late to do anything about it.

She'd believed what she'd seen. The façade he'd presented. And had missed seeing him for who he really was. On the inside.

He was talking again, preening. "You live out your days worrying about what to do with all that lovely money. Oh poor you. You were so focused you never even saw who came knocking on your door. Didn't really see me. Not as I am inside. Only as I wanted you to see me."

She closed her eyes and opened her senses. With her fading strength, it was easier to function entirely on a soul energy level. The physical form was so much harder to sustain and control as it failed around her.

Clouds of dark black, sickly green energy surrounded him. Like a hard shell, it protected him on the inside, while he… *While he what?*

She couldn't see clearly enough. Fog rolled in. She blinked several times, trying hard to understand. There was a long cord from his root chakra to…the bed. And then to her. *He'd connected a cord to her.*

That connection, in itself wasn't the issue. Most people had hooks or cords into others, but not like this one.

Stefan's voice murmured deep in her psyche. *Stay with me, Shay. The cops will be there within minutes.*

Too late, she whispered. *His energy… It's sick. Deep, dark, diseased. Dying. Stefan, see it for yourself. I can see him. The real him. He's been hiding all this time. Somehow masking who he really was.*

And that betrayal hurt. So much. She'd loved Darren. Had planned to marry him and bear his children. She had planned to link her life with this man, who now stood so separate from her, watching her die by his own intent. Dear God. How had this happened? How had she not seen the man for who he was?

Because he could hide himself. And his personality is what's sick. He's not dying. You are!

Her thoughts drifted, scattered. *How is he doing this? I feel so weak. It's as if he's draining my very soul.* She couldn't hold a focus. She understood in theory what Stefan had said…but reality felt distant. Like this was happening to someone else.

He's opened your heart chakra. Draining your energy in a torrential wash. He's going to syphon you dry.

She pondered that bit of information. She should be upset about it. Should probably care. But it was hard to connect the information to its logical outcome – to use it.

You have to do something, urged Stefan. *Don't fight it. Embrace him with love. Start from that power position. Remember, energy is everywhere. You cannot be drained if you remember that universal energy flows through you at all times.*

She blinked at the tidbits of understanding as they filtered in.

Know that I am here. Part of you. As he drains you, I'm refilling you with love.

She couldn't move, she couldn't do anything but exist, caught in a war between life and death.

How?

Open your crown chakra to the universal energy. Create a spinning loop between your chakras to build power. But protect yourself; don't let him see you turn the tide of the energy flow. I will start it for you, but you have to help yourself.

His words penetrated slower than the energy. By the time she understood what Stefan meant, she was working on her crown chakra, opening it. She already felt the effects and, bolstered by the rise in her own energy, she immediately picked up the pace, refilling her body, enlivening her soul.

Don't feed the anger. Feed the love. Feel the power in the loving energy. Feel it strengthen you on all levels. You don't have to be his victim.

I can make him my victim. She had to admit, a part of her loved that idea.

Don't. It will change you. It will be something you will never forget. We need to find another way.

There isn't one. We can't hold him off forever, she whispered. *And how else can anyone stop him? Or others like him?*

Stefan's silence gave her the answer. She could stay in this unlimited loop, or she could do something about it. Something lethal. What choice was there? She had to do something before Darren realized what was happening. Shay focused on funneling more and more universal energy though her body, creating a swirling vortex within her. Gaining strength. Gaining purpose. Gaining determination for what was to come.

"How many have you killed?" she whispered, letting her eyes close weakly. He needed to believe she was dying. That he'd won. And she needed to know the extent of the damage he'd inflicted on those around him. To know she was doing the right thing in destroying him.

Darren stepped closer to hear her question. "How many? Is that what you asked?"

"Yes." She kept her eyes closed, focused on the energy pouring through her, gathering, waiting for the right time.

He laughed. "So many. It's really easy once you understand how. The biggest trick is hiding what I'm doing until I'm ready for people to know. Like you. You're very intuitive. Very astute. I had to be especially alert, in your case. It was good for a while. Kept me on my toes. But tonight I deposited a nice fat check you were kind enough to write out for me." He laughed. "Oh, you don't remember writing me a check, do you? That's okay. I'm great at forging signatures, too. I stole the checks awhile ago... It's not like you'll need them after today."

"How many?" Her voice gained a desperate strength. She needed to know. Even one death was too many. If he'd killed other people, she'd have no problem doing what needed to be done. She'd have to. He had to be stopped before he went on to kill again.

In the far distance, she heard sirens.

"Isn't that nice? You're curious. You can't stop the process now, you know. I chose Friday on purpose. No one will find you until Monday. When you don't show up for work, they will come looking." He glanced around the bedroom. "It's really too bad. I'd so hoped that this would be my forever home." He chuckled. "Odd to think I'm still using that childhood phrase. So few would understand it."

"How many?" she insisted, her voice stronger as anger stirred dangerously close to the surface. She had to keep herself in check. Had to keep her anger reined in. She had to take him out the right way. Or her actions would be impossible to live with.

He laughed. "Dozens, over the years."

Dozens. And with that, she knew there was no one else, no other way to stop him. He had ways of killing people that no one would ever know. That no one would ever understand. That no one would be able to prove. He had to be stopped. And there were so few people capable to do that.

She was one of them. Stefan was another.

Stefan. I need all you can channel my way.

I'm open and pouring. Do it. We can't hang on like this for much longer.

She opened her eyes and stared at the man she'd once loved. Now, her heart was filled with loathing for what he'd done – she hated him with a passion that fed her actions like she'd never felt before. But she had to find a way past that to the core of love from one human being to another. She had to come from a soul level.

She could do that.

"Darren."

He looked up at her, a sarcastic smile on his face. "What's the matter, Shay? Aren't you going to plead for your life?" he said mockingly.

She made it look agonizingly difficult to raise her arm and motion him closer. And to make that arm drop down weakly to the bed. He thought he'd almost drained her dry and had no idea what she could do. Good. She just needed him a little closer.

He sat down on the bed with his hip pushing up again her thigh. Now, if she could only reach… Her arm trembled with effort as she stretched it out and placed her hand on his chest. Right over his heart.

Barely holding the building energy force back, she asked, *Stefan, Are you ready?*

"What did you want to say, dearest Shay?" Darren's mocking voice floated through the room, surrounding her. Filling her. Firing her actions.

She opened up her swirling vortex. In her mind, she said to Stefan, *Now.*

She looked Darren in the eyes and whispered, "Go to hell."

She channeled the vortex to jettison the stream of loving soul energy forward to his heart – the actual organ – with all the energy that she could manage. With all the caring she could find.

He gasped once, his eyes going wide.

Shock and disbelief flashed livid on his face. Understanding lit the deep depths of his gaze. But it was too late for him to act. His opportunity was gone before he ever saw it.

Or, maybe, it wasn't.

Even as his eyes darkened, a firestorm of energy ricocheted through his heart chakra and back into her, burning though her palm as some type of fireball lit the room.

Something else – *someone else* – had joined the fray. And combined, they were stronger, more powerful and…desperate…to survive.

Shay poured energy, opening herself up to the universe and channeling everything she could access into the fight.

Stefan. What's happening?

I don't know. Another element has been added. Possibly another person…

Then we can't win, she cried out in pain and frustration. *That's two against two. And they have the advantage. How do we save this?*

Look out!

A small blue fireball leapt from her bed and flew into the energy torrenting through her hand.

No! Shay cried out.

It was too late. Morris, her ghostly feline, had joined the fight – and turned the tide as his loving, protective energy joined hers. There was a momentary pause, as if both sides were re-evaluating the balance of power, and then a deep purr sounded from the center of the maelstrom.

The space beneath her hand exploded.

Shay was thrown back against the headboard.

Darren was flung to the floor.

Regaining her wits, Shay scrambled to her feet to look over the edge of the bed.

Darren's features had frozen, his mouth open in a horrible rictus of terror, and like a tidal wave after it has lashed a beach and receded back out to the ocean, the color had slipped from his skin – leaving a gray wasteland behind.

But he was still alive.

Her heart squeezed tighter. Pain and shock rippled through her.

His eyes dimmed.

And that's when she saw it. A second light inside. A second awareness? A second person? A different part of Darren? How? Was he manipulated? Possessed? Or was this the other 'something' that had joined the fray?

She cried out, *Stefan, look!*

But it was too late to stop the process.

A deep sigh whispered from Darren's chest one last time, and his eyelids dropped closed.

He was dead.

Chapter 2

Almost one year later...on a Saturday evening...

Shay walked into the packed ballroom, a fixed smile on her face. Her heart beating nervously in her chest. This was their big day.

She'd been waiting a long time to meet Roman Chandler. They had become acquaintances via email years ago, initially connecting over their grandfathers' mutual friendship, and then they became friends...close friends. And now...? She didn't know what they were. But, despite her last bad experience, she hoped.

If she had doubts about whether she was ready for a relationship again, she shoved them down and out of sight. She wanted to be ready. She could be ready. She had to be ready. Roman wasn't likely to wait. Her stomach somersaulted at the thought.

I haven't gone there since Darren...

She dismissed that thought. She'd take it slowly this time. Make sure she knew exactly what she was getting into before diving in too deep.

Still, no matter the confused and wounded state in her heart, she was totally excited to meet Roman in person. She already knew his twin brother Ronin, a detective with the Portland Police Department, but on a more professional basis. Of course, their grandfathers were best friends so it only made sense that their families would rub up well against each other.

Only Roman hadn't lived in Portland for years. He'd just recently moved back.

She didn't think he knew she was coming to the reception tonight. Then she couldn't put it past Bernice to have told him in confidence – she'd been trying to match the two of them for a long time. This charity event was Bernice's baby.

The ballroom was stuffed with people – mostly couples.

Who said being tall was a disadvantage? At almost 5' 9" without heels, Shay appreciated the view all the time, but in her toe-crushing stilettos, she was really enjoying being able to see over the heads of the others gathered here. With subdued classical music in the background, the many crystal chandeliers and ornate draperies and exquisite paintings provided a perfect backdrop to tonight's event.

Bernice Folgrent, of Folgrent's Foundation, never did anything small.

The noise and ambiance had the urgent tempo of schmoozing, smooching and the what-the-hell, the-booze-is-free atmosphere. A typical high-powered business reception for a big name charity foundation with hush-hush conversations, secretive smiles, handshakes and private deals. Millions of dollars would cross hands tonight and she, for one, was glad of it. There were so many in need.

Still, this function was so not her choice. But as the trustee for her family's foundation, she had to attend all sorts of these events, and she was as comfortable here as in the animal shelter where she helped out. One just had to remember the animals *here* were more dangerous. Plus, she could be proud of herself – she was neither a boardroom broad nor a high roller's arm candy. Thank God for that.

But no matter her personal preferences, tonight was a necessity and a delight. She'd come at Bernice's request. At eighty plus – and the number in that plus was a well-guarded secret – Bernice was a force to be reckoned with. When she wanted two people to meet, you had to either follow along or leave the continent. And even *that* might not save you.

Besides it was Roman who Bernice wanted Shay to meet... She didn't know that the two of them had been corresponding for a long time already...

"Shay!"

Shay pivoted smoothly to see a beautifully dressed older woman bearing down on her. Shay grinned. Bernice, dressed in gold brocade and evening gloves, only needed a cigarette holder to complete the old-time elegant picture. Still, despite her glamorous packaging, she was not to be misunderstood or underestimated, particularly when, like Shay, she also controlled millions of dollars.

For most people, it was a case of be nice to Bernice or face the dragon. Thankfully, Shay had known Bernice since she was a little girl and Shay had no need of Bernice's money because she controlled millions of her own. Besides, Shay loved the grande dame but that didn't make her blind to the old woman's machinations.

Bernice wrapped her in a smothering hug, her thickly made-up face passing discretely close to Shay's cheek as she kissed the air. "Darling, you look simply fabulous."

Shay smiled. "Thanks, Bernice. You're looking pretty stylish yourself."

"Of course, my dear," Bernice said comfortably. "The only difference between us is that I need hours to look like this – you do it naturally." She smirked. "And of course, I know what to *do* with my looks." She winked outrageously.

Shay laughed. Bernice wasn't going to change at this stage of her life. One either accepted her or avoided her. And Shay always had a soft spot for her.

"Come along now. There is this stunning man you have to meet."

"Oh, but—"

"No buts. You have to get out on the scene again. No more hiding away. Roman is the perfect person to catch your interest. You need to balance business with pleasure…and you need to spend more time with the *right* animals." Bernice nudged Shay, nodding her head in the direction of two men conversing off to the side.

"You're incorrigible."

"And you're too reclusive. Come on. Life is for living. Men are for loving." She motioned toward the two men. "I'd take those two any day." Bernice gave her a smug smile. "In fact, I took on a pair like them not all that long ago."

"Whoa." Shay held up her hand. "I so don't need to know. No more extolling your escapades, please. I still haven't recovered from your last titillating story."

"Now if only they'd do you some good. You have to forget about that dweeb fiancé of yours that died so tragically. He was never the man for you. You changed, and not for the better, when you were with him. Such a terrible thing to watch."

Shay turned to Bernice in shock. Inside, she was still struggling with Bernice calling Darren a dweeb. Bernice prided herself on keeping up with the younger set, but it still sounded so wrong to hear that word come out of the older woman's mouth. Or maybe it just sounded wrong when used in connection with her ex-fiancé? The man had been a lot of things, but he was not inept and geeky. Too much the opposite in fact. But he *had* died tragically.

Thankfully.

"What do you mean, *I changed*?"

"Oh my Lord, you became this dishrag, ready to wipe his nose and fetch his coffee. Don't you realize how much better you are than that?"

"I did *not* act like that." She couldn't stop the outrage that whipped through her. "Bernice, that's not fair. I loved him."

"Of course you did, my dear. That's the only reason anyone tolerated him in the first place." She barreled through the crowd. A crowd that parted magically as people understood it was *Bernice* that wanted to get past. Several times Shay murmured a polite 'thank you' as people stepped out of the way. Bernice had no such inclination.

She walked a path, accepting the magical bowing out of the way as her due.

"The man was a user," Bernice tossed back. "You need someone to light your fires, not squash them before they get a chance to catch. You're such a firecracker in every area but your damn love life. And we're going to fix that."

Shay put on the brakes. "No way. Bernice. Stop."

Not only did Bernice not listen, she doubled back to Shay, snagged her arm and tugged her forward – nicely of course. Everything Bernice did was nice, but there was also enough steel behind her actions to make her a formidable opponent.

Damn.

Shay plastered a laughing smile on her face while catching up to Bernice. "Stop pulling me," she whispered to Bernice.

"Then stop dragging your heels!" Bernice sent her an admonishing look. "I know you're here for other reasons, but you'll have to make time for this. I won't be around forever, you know. Soon, I'll be cha-chaing my way downstairs."

"Ha, even the devil doesn't want you down there with him. You'd order him around for all eternity."

Bernice spun on her heels, her eyes suddenly desperate, frail. She lowered her voice. "Don't joke about the devil. And don't ever, ever make a deal with him. You never know who he has working for him. Some people are just evil."

Whoa! What had gotten into Bernice?

Casting Shay a warning glance, Bernice glanced around furtively. Then she whispered, "I'm serious. You, more than anyone, should understand what I mean." Bernice turned and dragged Shay forward again.

Shay groaned. What was Bernice talking about? Had she gotten another nasty email? She'd been plagued by several lately. Typical Bernice had tossed them off as unimportant. As just expressions of discontent by those who wanted money and weren't going to be getting any. But that brushing off, itself, was unusual for Bernice. She had a tendency to bring in lawyers and scare off potential lawsuits.

Running foundations was big business, and drumming up new money was a constant challenge. These receptions were cornerstones of that process.

Shay was part of the same world. Dealt with the same driven – and sometimes desperate – people. She had her own methodology for finding the shysters and removing them from the honest applicants for her own foundation. And because they shared similar challenges and experiences, Bernice and Shay often compared notes and worked closely on joint projects. Their assistants also stepped in to help resolve problems on each other's projects. It helped to have that type of close working relationship. They watched each other's backs.

"Roman, darling. Here is the young woman I adore as if she were my own." Bernice reached out, latching onto the arm of a tall, suited gentlemen. She tugged him around and pointed to Shay. "Isn't she gorgeous? Just like I promised."

Oh lord. Shay groaned inside. Bernice really hadn't needed to make a public spectacle of this meeting. But why was she surprised? This was typical Bernice.

"Shay, this is Roman Chandler, the grandson of my dearest friend, Gerard Chandler."

Heads had turned at Bernice's loud introduction and color stroked up Shay's neck as she fought back her embarrassment. She should be used to it. But wasn't.

Still, she faced Roman, kept her plastered-on smile in place and lifted her gaze to his.

And sucked in her breath.

The look in his eyes. It was so...intimate. So knowing...as if he knew her...all of her, inside and out. And as if he liked what he knew.

They'd emailed. Chatted. Though they'd corresponded for a few years, over the last year they had built a friendly almost...intimate...relationship over the Internet and phone. And they had talked – like really talked. Theirs was a relationship she hoped would grow. But she'd never *met* him before. Hadn't shared everything with him. She didn't know him – not in the way he seemed to know her.

The heated look in his eyes unnerved her...and yes...intrigued her.

And she had to admit...sparked an answering awareness.

Shay had no illusions about her looks, regardless of Bernice's constant matchmaking attempts. She was too tall for many men, was slim, with milk chocolate brown shoulder-length hair and a largish mouth, and instead of symmetry, her nose was slightly crooked and one eyebrow was slightly off line. All minor in the scheme of things but those same flaws had given her terrible, angst-ridden moments through her teenage years. Now she could brush off the negative thoughts as they came and even though she could get her nose fixed, it no longer mattered to her.

According to the look in Roman's eyes, her flaws didn't matter to him now either. Of course he'd seen pictures of her. But that wasn't the same thing as this. She secretly had high hopes about Roman, but she'd never expected this level of appreciation from him right off.

When he spoke, his voice held both promise and familiarity. "Hello, Shay. I'm delighted to finally meet you." He glanced at Bernice, standing beside them both with a smug, knowing look on her face.

"Hello, Roman." *Did he look at all women as if they shared special memories?* She so badly wanted to ask. Instead, she said, "How nice to meet *you*." She paused then added, "Finally."

His gaze deepened to midnight blue, and he smiled. That wide movement of his lips released her from the intensity of his gaze. She could breathe easy again.

"This is so much better than email," he murmured, "and you are so much better looking in person than in photos."

Under Roman's midnight blue gaze, Shay's stomach churned with unanswered questions and delight. She wanted to take a more in-depth look at his energy, but thought she'd better save her strength for when a deeper reading might be needed.

A strange sound had her turning to face Bernice, her hostess and mentor.

Bernice opened her mouth to speak when she suddenly stopped, an odd look on her face. Her breath sucked in so loudly, Shay leaned closer in concern. "Bernice? Are you all right? What's the matter?"

Silence.

Shay studied her old friend, but Bernice's face had turned ashen, her eyes locked on something behind Shay's back. Shay twisted around to look, but the only thing behind her was a wall. A blank wall.

Turning back around, and seeing no change in her friend, she said, "Bernice, talk to me. You're scaring me."

Bernice's breathing turned ragged, stuttered then almost appeared to stop. Her features locked in place yet her chest rose and fell in a natural movement.

The hairs on the back of Shay's neck rose.

Jesus, she must be having an attack of some kind. "We'll get you some help. Can you talk to me? Can you tell me what's wrong?"

Roman bent to study Bernice's face. "I'll get a doctor." He took off.

Bernice's mouth worked. Still, no sound came out.

Silently, Shay willed Roman to hurry. But from the looks of it, he wasn't going to be fast enough. She raised her hand to call for help when her arm was grabbed. She stared, surprised to see Bernice's bronzed nails cutting into her soft skin.

"Bernice?" Shay rubbed the papery skin on the back of Bernice's fingers with gentle soothing strokes. "Hang on. Help is coming."

From a distance, she could hear rapidly approaching footsteps. *Thank God. Please let her friend be all right.*

Worried, Shay stared into Bernice's eyes, and Bernice stared back. Her gaze dark. Bottomless. Blind. Shay's heart squeezed in fear. "Bernice. Damn it, stay with me. Please talk to me if you can."

Shay willed Bernice's eyes to return to normal. Willed them to blink. To move. To do *something*.

Then *something* else happened. Inside, deep inside, Bernice blinked. A clear movement that Shay could see and understand.

Except for one thing.

On the surface, Bernice's eyelids never moved.

***

Roman Chandler stood off to one side of the ballroom entrance as the paramedics moved the stretcher out through the foyer and into the ambulance. It was certainly a different world out here than the expensive event going on behind him.

Damn. He'd found Bernice was a good friend and benefactress to the people. 'My people,' as she'd say. To see the old fighter brought low by age and sudden change in health was a blow most people here would struggle with – one that would make them look at their own health and wellbeing. She was formidable. Creating stress and tension and love and affection with a few words, a flick of her hand and the flash of her smile.

He hoped whatever was wrong would turn out to be minor but given Bernice's age – well…she hadn't looked good. He'd already called his grandfather and given him the news. His grandfather would no doubt make it to the hospital before the ambulance did. He'd been there for Bernice for over thirty years. That wasn't going to change now.

His thoughts drifted back to the woman who stood beside him, the woman Bernice had just introduced him to…the woman who had intrigued him since their first email. Now he knew his gut reaction was right about Shay.

Shay was…dynamite. Everything he'd hoped for. Hell, he couldn't have hoped for this… He hadn't even known this kind of connection could exist, let alone was something to *hope* for. She'd entered the ballroom with an attitude that caught every man's attention. He knew because he'd watched them all turn to mark her progress.

She had to be almost as tall as him, in heels. And every inch was smoothly muscled and as delectable as any woman he'd seen. And he'd seen plenty. And learned that the inside rarely matched the package.

That he'd *recognized* the delicate line of her neck, the smooth curve of her shoulder, the delicate bones of her wrist, had shocked him. The level of familiarity and desire he felt for her, terrified him. And delighted him. The recognition could *not* be explained away by the plethora of email conversations and a few pictures.

He'd been painting her for years. A delight that had him open to making that initial contact. Since then...well, she'd worked her way into his life, his psyche...even his dreams. Some days she was all he could think about. He'd been looking forward to this meeting for months.

Still his reaction to finally meeting her shook him to the core. From the moment he laid eyes on her this evening he'd wanted her. He'd known that already on an intellectual level. She was so damn interesting. But to have the physical person match his fantasies...well, that's when he'd been deluged by an overwhelming sense of recognition. Not just a superficial knowing, but an understanding of her at a deep, visceral level. It was as if he knew her for who she was, really was. Without the trappings of society, the painful past, the solitary existence he knew she lived. He just knew Shay.

And she wouldn't be happy that he knew as much as he did about her life. She liked her privacy. She would likely blame Bernice and their grandparents... And it's true, they'd started his interest in Shay – at least initially. After that. Well, he was no fool...

He'd almost frozen with shock when she spoke to him. Her voice had been a surprise. Light, cool. Whatever else she was, life, vibrant life, swirled inside. She presented as calm and poised, but that calm exterior in no way hid the richness of the woman on the inside. When she spoke, the artist in him wished he knew how to capture that rich throaty fullness and knew his medium would be lacking if he tried. The sensual promise of her voice sent shivers down his spine and straight to his loins.

And that's the woman he wanted to get to know better. Needed to get to know more.

His paintings didn't do her justice.

The artist in him tried to memorize her details. Like a video camera snapping off stills, he tried to capture the special essence that made up this remarkable woman. He could only hope that later, much later, he'd remember some of what he'd seen and recorded in his mind.

His grandfather had warned him about Bernice's matchmaking surprise tonight. And Roman was grateful. Bernice didn't have a good history as a matchmaker, but she was hell on wheels when she had an agenda.

She'd thrown Callie at him years ago, hadn't she? Look how well that had turned out. *Not.* Still he'd been young and infatuated with his young wife. He couldn't blame Bernice for his own lack of judgment. Callie had been too free-spirited to stick faithfully to one man – even her husband. The divorce had been painful with the list of her flings including names of several of his friends.

Callie was part of *his* history. A part he didn't want to revisit. A mistake he didn't want to repeat. Along with the bullet that had ended his police work. Now he specialized in Internet security. Even had his own company.

This time he knew better.

And he knew Shay had her own history to get over.

Besides, without that painful breakup and change of career, he'd never have returned to the passion of his youth – painting. And he couldn't imagine how empty his life would be now without that constant creative need and drive washing through him.

Moreover, his emotional breakup with Callie had endowed his work with a new edge. But those post-breakup pieces were nothing compared to the work he churned out now. Somewhere along the line, he'd become fixated on his current series and hadn't managed to paint it out of his system. Though he'd tried.

Maybe now, he understood why.

"Excuse me." A man walked around him, making Roman aware that he stood in the middle of the elaborate front entrance, holding back the crowd as he stared down the curved driveway.

He hoped Bernice was all right, if only for his grandfather's sake. He'd be devastated to lose her. His grandfather was getting on in years and wasn't as resilient as he once was.

Another reason for his return to his hometown. To be closer to his family.

It had been time.

***

In the too-silent silence, Shay and the rest of the hushed crowd watched the paramedics efficiently load Bernice into the ambulance and drive away with siren blaring and lights flashing.

Bernice had been a larger-than-life presence for so long; Shay couldn't imagine the void she'd have in her life if Bernice died. She shouldn't think so negatively, but it was hard not to. Shay *knew* what lively, life-giving energy looked like. Their last conversation had been so strange. And Shay knew what at-the-edge-of-death energy looked like. Bernice's energy now indicated that she'd lived well past the best-by date.

And it hurt to think that Bernice might not bounce out of bed and give Shay royal hell for sleeping alone – again. Shay looked for the man Bernice had all but pushed in her direction.

Roman had stood off to one side, casual, concerned and competently keeping the crowd back. Many of those who had gathered had disappeared inside by now.

Shay appreciated that.

Still, whatever she'd seen deep in Bernice's eyes during the episode made her suspicious. She needed to find out just what that double set of eyes had meant...if anything.

She had to do what she could to find out. She stepped back into the ballroom. Despite the thinning masses there were still too many people around for her to do much by way of finding answers. Regardless, she opened her senses and studied the sea of colors swirling through the crowd. Emotions rippled outward as everyone absorbed details and dealt with the crisis in their midst.

She couldn't avoid hearing the words whispering outward as each person's thoughts swirled around them, carried on their energy. Even though she normally saw more images than words, right now, in this crisis, these thoughts damn near screamed in the ether.

Is that Bernice?

The old dame is finally coming to the end of the road.

Oh dear, I hope she'll be okay.

The world won't be the same without her.

About time that old bat bit it.

The last thought had Shay spinning around and pinning a look on a young, rakish-looking man standing off to one side. She studied him, half recognizing him. Still there wasn't any real negativity rolling off him. His energy was more like that of a disgruntled nephew who was hoping he'd be getting something from the will...but wouldn't be, and he *so* knew it.

Shay dismissed him as unimportant, and let her gaze continue to roam, still hearing the whispered thoughts like dull noise in the background. Studying those standing around her, she let her gaze zip past Roman and came to a sudden stop. She slowly retraced the short distance to Roman's aura and studied it.

Her heart slammed into her chest, and she gasped.

He was a man of power. Psychic power.

Like Darren.

But she didn't know what kind of power. It could be anything. And she didn't know if he knew. Many didn't.

Roman turned to look at her, as if just becoming aware of her interest, and raised an eyebrow in concern. He took a half step toward her. She gave a tiny panicked shake of her head and averted her gaze. It was only her strength of will that stopped her from backing away from him. She desperately tried to control her breathing. When she could, she stole another glance at Roman's energy.

And her heart stalled.

Part of him was shielded. Behind a protective wall. She couldn't read him. He could be anyone in there. He could be a good guy...or another bad one.

And for all she knew he could be just like Darren, her dead fiancé who'd tried to kill her.

***

Knock, knock...?

Hi Shay. There you are. Too bad you can't hear me. Standing in the middle of the chaos as usual. Did you enjoy the show? I made sure you got a front row seat.

And you have no idea I even exist. Just the way I like it.

See, or don't see me...it doesn't matter. I'm still special. I can get inside people's auras and sneak into the part of their consciousness they don't like to see. That they hide or bury. The parts that exist but that can't be acknowledged – even from themselves. I can make my hosts do things. Not too much yet. And not for very long, but I'm getting better. Stronger.

You might ask, what's the difference between me and a serial killer? The serial killer gets his hands dirty.

I don't.

And the difference between me and the guy I'm stepping into is...nothing. Because under our skin we all want the same thing. Even you, Shay.

I'm just one of the few that found out how to do it. It's taken time, and a lot of effort, but I'm getting better all the time. Now I don't have to be beside the person; I don't even have to be in the same building. Actually, at this point in my evolution, soon I won't even have to be in the same fucking city. I'll have mastered this technique and can live anywhere. Any way I want.

It's not about money. I can get all I want. It's not about prestige. I could have that too if I so choose. No. This is about the essential building block of our lives. The piece that makes or breaks a person. The piece that says who they really are. What's that piece, you might ask?

It's called power.

Power is all I want and I have lots, but now…now I have the capability to take your power, too. And add to mine. Why would I do that to you?

Easy. You took something very special from me.

And for that, Shay, you will pay.

But not to worry. There are a few other people I plan to meet with first. We'll see each other around.

Oh, my mistake.

No, you won't!

But I'll see you.

Chapter 3

Late Saturday evening...

Once in the elevator, on the way up to her apartment, Shay phoned the hospital for an update on Bernice, only to be told there was no improvement and the doctors were still with her. It didn't look good. She'd immediately called her grandfather to update him on Beatrice's condition. She'd learned he was already at the hospital. Shay offered to join him.

He'd been almost incoherent and inconsolable but ultimately wanting to be alone with his beloved. Bernice was a huge part of their lives.

Shay hoped Bernice would pull through, but given her age... Still it was shock. She'd been indomitable for years with a spine of steel and a body meant for lusty horizontal dancing. Of course, she'd relied on frequent surgeries to keep her in as decent shape as modern medicine allowed. The what and how of all that was a secret between Bernice and her doctor.

Speaking of secrets, Shay remembered Bernice's comment about making a deal with the devil. She wished she understood what she meant by that.

There was no mythical devil in Shay's world. All people were capable of doing evil things, but few thrived on it. Those that did were...the worst. She had experiences with a different reality, giving her insights that well and truly locked her mind to a whole different belief system. One where evil was an all-too-common occurrence. And where dead wasn't necessarily dead.

Shay walked into her Portland apartment later and kicked off her shoes. The waterfront view called to her troubled soul, promising to ease and sooth her tattered nerves. But first she wanted to be comfortable. She changed out of her evening wear into cami and pants, then walked back into her kitchen where she popped the cork on an open bottle of wine. She poured herself a glass and with that in hand, she walked out to the small garden deck to sit under the stars. She needed this space.

It had been a long day.

The stars shone bright in the clear sky, easing the pain slightly. Her life would be forever changed. Bernice had been a huge influence and would be dearly missed.

When her tattered nerves calmed, Shay checked in with Stefan – her friend, her mentor, her apprentice. Who'd have thought she'd have anything to teach the incredibly gifted psychic? Not her.

But he'd convinced her she had something to offer.

She could do some energy tricks and he told her those had value.

And you do, he said in her mind, interrupting her musing. *Stop second-guessing yourself.*

Too tired to bother, she answered back readily. *I'm going to call you on the phone. Hang on.* She picked up the phone and dialed his number. "Hey. Bernice had an attack of some kind. A stroke, maybe. I don't know. It was weird the way it happened. She's at the hospital right now, but I don't know how she is."

"You do, but you don't want to look that close."

That was true. She didn't. Some things she didn't want to know.

"Yes." Shay hesitated. Stefan, like her, had seen too much of the world. "Something else happened at the same time. I want to shrug it off, but—"

"But you can't. So tell me."

Haltingly, she refocused her thoughts and explained the weird sense that someone else had stared – no, blinked – out at her from Bernice's gaze.

"And this wasn't a possession?"

"No. There was no sensation that anyone took her body, took her over in any way. At least that I could sense at the time. Except that damn gaze, as if someone else was looking out at the world from within her head. It was beyond freaky." She took a deep breath. "It was almost like what I saw *that night*."

"*That* night?" he asked.

"Yes. When Darren died." A half-choking laugh escaped. "No, it couldn't be anything to do with him... That's crazy."

"Hmmm."

"What do you think is happening?" She knew he was going to ask her to check and, damn it, she didn't want to. She didn't want to delve into the dark and see the boogeyman tonight.

"I'm not sure. I'll have to ponder it." His voice faded slightly. She smiled and settled back, realizing Stefan was off in his psychic realm, disappearing into the mist like only he could.

Having a psychic in your life meant adjusting to new privacy rules.

She shivered. Being psychic made you who you were. Every aspect of your life was affected. You just didn't always like *how*. None of her 'regular' friends knew of her abilities. And she preferred it that way.

It was hard to find anyone who could understand. For that reason, she didn't see her friendship with Stefan ever lessening. Changing, perhaps, as each grew and developed, but their connection would never stop. They couldn't sever it if they wanted to. And they didn't. Connected on the ethers as they were, it felt as if they were psychic twins. And if that concept didn't blow a person's mind, then nothing would.

Now she was used to the connection, and she appreciated the closeness of someone's life mirroring hers. Thankfully, they were not exactly the same, but enough alike so she didn't feel alone – anymore.

And she knew it was the same for Stefan.

Stefan was a special friend. He was not her lover, but they had a friendship in the deepest sense. Something most men would say was impossible. But most women would be envious of such a relationship. And Stefan wasn't gay.

She'd asked the stunningly handsome man early on in their relationship and his answering look of horror had kept her laughing for days. Even now the memory made her grin.

Another time he'd told her his partner was living her life, unaware that he was there waiting. And that Shay herself was doing the same thing. He told her if she'd look harder, she'd find the truth of his words.

The thing is, she saw too damn much as it was. Why would she want to look any closer?

"Stefan?" she said cautiously, not wanting to pull him free if he wasn't ready to return to this reality.

"I'm here. Just trying to see what's going on with Bernice."

Shay straightened. "What do you see?"

"Not sure. Her body is almost gone. Lots of energy filling the room right now. Her soul is free and wandering the room. It just doesn't feel...right, though."

"That's hardly scientific." She almost laughed. The two of them used their senses the way other people used facts and logic. "You know how the rest of the world would react to your statement?"

"Good thing they don't know about it then, isn't it? There are several people in Bernice's room."

"Is my grandfather there?" In her heart, she hoped so. Pappy had been holding a lost-love candle for Bernice for decades. He'd loved her and lost her, according to him, and Bernice was a once-around type of gal. So far no male had managed to hang onto her. Pappy was just one in a long line of discarded lovers. She wondered if Bernice had any idea how many broken hearts she'd left behind.

"Maybe you should go to the hospital. She's fading quickly."

"I'm not sure I want to be there when she passes."

"She wants *you* there."

Damn. Shay really didn't want to go. Not just because of the whole hospital thing, but there was the death thing. And then there was also the whole Pappy thing.

"She's calling for you."

Shay stood up, asking sharply, "She's awake?"

"No."

"She's calling on the ethers for you," Stefan murmured.

"What?" Shay gasped. "How is that possible? I never heard her."

"She's struggling to be heard. She is new to this. But she knows. She's always known about you."

***

Shay, now in jeans and t-shirt, walked across the hospital parking lot, all her psychic guards solidly locked in place. Like most people gifted with psychic abilities, she hated these institutions. The veil between life and death was thin here. Those overly affected by liminal places had to strengthen their walls to stop the emotions from creeping into their own psyches. Then, of course, there were the walking, talking, living ghosts in every hallway.

The new wing on the children's hospital that Shay's foundation was funding was different. The energy lighter, brighter. Livelier. Innocent. And ghost-free – so far.

Other psychics saw the ghosts themselves, whereas Shay saw the ghost of the person's energy. A slight but important difference.

She read, saw, understood energy.

The auric energy. Someone's chakra energy. The way a person used that energy. The way their body used its energy to function and to heal. Not a very useful skill to most people, but to some people, who wanted the information she could provide, she could be a little *too* useful. And had learned to keep her mouth shut.

If anyone needed to know what a person did with their money, for example, she could find out. Or if someone needed to know if someone else was trustworthy. Or how stable someone was mentally… These were things she could tell with a degree of certainty. She knew, to her own regret, that she wasn't infallible. That when it had counted most, she'd been fooled the same as everyone else.

Hence the need to ensure the secrecy regarding her talents and her joy in the relationship she had with Stefan. He knew and he cared…for her. Not about what she could do for him. Or what information she could supply. Or how she could use that information to his advantage.

He told her there was a group of similar-minded people, all with…abilities like hers. She'd met a few. And probably would enjoy meeting the ones she hadn't. When Stefan said that day would come, she'd smiled.

She entered the hospital entrance and took the right turn down the empty hallways. It had been a tough day already and she didn't think she'd like the way the night would end. Bernice's attack had sent all thought of Roman from her head – at the time. Now however…

The thought of his wall made her cringe.

Shay also knew that having a protective wall didn't make him a sociopath. It made him someone with something to hide. The *what* of the something was what concerned her.

He'd made his interest in her clear, and prior to walking into that room, she'd been crystal clear about him too. Now…she had to ask some hard questions. And she had to reconcile the overwhelming attraction she'd felt between them, that inner knowing that said he was worth it, with the fear that a relationship with him could end badly.

She didn't want to go down that road again.

Her abilities should have shown her who the real Darren was – at least enough to have sent her running in the opposite direction.

Only she'd seen *nothing* wrong in his energy.

Instead she'd let herself be lulled into a false sense of security, sucked into the new love relationship and all the giddiness that state offered. Sure, they'd had problems. Truthfully, there had been times she'd had her doubts about the major step she agreed to take – marriage wasn't for the faint of heart. But she'd put her doubts down to first-time wedding jitters.

Until that night when he'd entered her home unannounced and she'd realized it was too late.

After the mess had finally ended, she'd gone into a full-blown crisis over her ability to accurately see the energy of those closest to her. Always looking for what she might have missed. She'd locked down her feelings and that had created huge trust issues for herself and others.

But was that fair to Roman?

No. But trust, once crushed, was hard to offer again.

In Darren's case, she'd tried to read him and had seen only what he wanted her to see. In Roman's case, she'd read him and had seen the damn wall. And had nearly bolted. What was he hiding? And did it matter?

The long hospital hallway finally ended. She turned the corner and entered Bernice's private room.

"Shay, I'm so glad you made it in time." Her grandfather stood at Bernice's bedside, cradling her pale, limp hand in his. Even after all this time, his love, open and hurting, shone from deep inside his puppy-dog eyes. "She's failing, my dear. I fear she won't last long." Pappy's rheumy gaze zeroed in on Shay sorrowfully. "I'd hoped she'd wake up, at least one more time, but it appears she'll go off gently in the night."

"And maybe that's the best way, Pappy." Shay wrapped an arm around her beloved grandfather's frail shoulders and squeezed. "We don't want her to suffer."

He shook his bowed head, the corner of his lips trembling. "No. We don't."

"Well, Charles. Has there been any change?" Gerard Chandler walked into the private hospital room, disrupting their moment. He and her grandfather were old friends, and both were Bernice's lovelorn suitors. Shay smiled at Gerard and saw the same ravaging grief as on Pappy's face.

"No. She hasn't moved a muscle, unfortunately." Pappy patted Bernice's hand. "Shay just arrived in time to say good-bye."

"Good. Now she can tell us herself what happened last night." Gerard took up the matching position to Pappy's on the far side of Bernice's bed, glaring at her as if Bernice's condition was all Shay's fault. "Roman explained, but we need to hear it from you."

Knowing that both elderly men needed to hear every scrap of information she had, she went over the evening's events. "That's all I know," she lied. "Dr. Fitzpatrick, who was on hand at the gathering, looked after her, and the paramedics arrived very quickly."

She waited a beat, swallowing to moisten her dry throat. "There was nothing I could do to help her," she said, her voice thick with emotion. She said this more for herself than for them. "There was nothing anyone could do."

There was no point telling them what she'd seen in Bernice's eyes at the end. They wouldn't understand. Hell, she didn't understand.

Pappy nodded, reached out one hand and patted her shoulder. "Of course, my dear. I know you did everything you could. It's just her time. And soon, it will be ours."

"Speak for yourself," Gerard grumped. "I'm not ready to kick off."

"I don't think Bernice was either." Shay smiled at the memory. "Just moments before she collapsed, she urged me to start living again. She looked and acted normal. Was our typical, vibrant, life-loving Bernice."

Both men nodded.

Pappy said, "She was unique. Everyone knew and loved her."

The way he spoke, using the past tense, showed an acceptance of what was coming. She opened her psychic vision to see how Bernice's energy was doing and barely stifled a gasp. There was a skin of energy lying heavy and pale on top of her body...as if Bernice's astral body lay on top of her physical body. Shay tracked the pale energy upward to Bernice's face. It lay in peaceful repose as if asleep. That was all good. The end would be soon.

Also good was that the silver cord that connected her astral body to her physical body was thin and weak. Almost ready to be severed. Except a tiny thread wafted around the room. She tried to trace it and found a mass of light gently shimmering energy by the window ledge.

Bernice.

Or what was left of Bernice – her astral soul might be a better way to put it. It was more ghostlike than an astral projection. More ghostlike than those walking on the ethers. This was Bernice as she was ready to depart. And there was still a sparkle to her. A luminescence she'd appreciate. Shay had to smile. Even in transition, Bernice would shine.

And Shay could just imagine Bernice trying to raise a little hell on the other side.

She let her gaze wander the room, looking for a way to interact with Bernice's energy without being noticed. She couldn't guarantee that Bernice would respond; she might not be cognizant in this state – most weren't.

If only she could get the two men to leave the room.

As if on cue, Gerard's phone rang. Pappy snapped at him for disturbing Bernice's solitude.

"It's Roman," Charles said. "He's just arrived. Come out in the hallway. We need to discuss Bernice's arrangements."

Pappy stiffened. "She's not gone yet!"

But Pappy trundled toward the door. The two men stood in the doorway, their heads bent together.

And the cell phone call gave Shay a wonderful idea. She pulled hers out and held it to her ear. She walked over to the window as if to make a call. Bernice's energy wobbled as Shay approached.

As if speaking into the phone, Shay asked in a quiet voice, "Bernice, are you there?"

The glowing mass smiled as if lit from inside. With more of an impression than actual gestures, Shay heard Bernice's voice. *I wanted to tell you something.* She paused. *But I've forgotten what it was.*

"Is this related to what you were trying to say last night?"

Could an astral person pale any more? Shay watched in fascination as Bernice's form wavered before her.

"Bernice?" she whispered. "What's the matter?"

In a horrible repeat of the night before, Bernice froze. She stared at Shay and her mouth opened as if to speak, only no sounds were heard – physically or psychically.

Shay leaned closer, afraid Bernice would disappear before she could get the information she needed. "Bernice, please. Tell me what's going on."

Bernice seemed to make an effort to pull herself together; her form firmed and then wavered. *I love them both, you know. Don't let them suffer more than necessary when you sort this out, my dear.*

"Sort what out? Bernice, I don't understand." Shay tried to keep her voice down but her hushed whisper resounded through the room.

"Shay, are you okay?" Pappy called out behind her.

Shay turned to smile reassuringly at Pappy.

Concerned, he made as if to walk toward her.

She waved him back. "I'm fine, Pappy." She held up her phone as if to say she was still in a conversation. He nodded and turned back to Gerard then stepped out into the hallway to talk to someone else.

Relieved, Shay turned back to Bernice to find her…gone.

She spun around.

Bernice lay still, her skin even more gray and transparent than before. And the pale mist that had hung over her head was no longer there. Blue veins pulsed slowly up her hand and arm. Bernice had gone back into her body, but judging by the sounds of the raspy breathing she didn't rest easy. Shay doubted Bernice would last the hour.

"Bernice?" she whispered, leaning over the old woman. "Please, can't you tell me anything more?"

There was no answer, only the rasping that sounded overly loud in the silence.

Pappy walked over, his hand gently going to Shay's shoulder. "It's almost over."

Gerard walked to the far side of Bernice's bed. He picked up Bernice's right hand, holding it gently. He whispered lovingly, "Go, my dear. Stay safe. Until we meet again."

Indeed, as if she'd heard him, Bernice's chest rose once more, stretching to the extent her rib cage would allow and then sagged downward for the last time.

Then there was only silence.

Pappy choked, his hand patting the back of Bernice's faster than before. His shoulders hunched. He whispered so softly Shay almost missed his words. "Good-bye, my love. Good-bye."

Shay had to wonder about a woman who kept these two men so in love with her that they'd never resented being alone for all these years.

And they didn't resent it. They'd always felt blessed to spend time with her. Even though they were no longer lovers. Even now as she lay dying.

Poor Bernice… And poor Shay. Tears welled at the corner of her eyes. She'd loved Bernice – a larger-than-life presence that no one could ignore. She'd been a lovely friend, a trusted confidant and an exceptional woman. Her legacy would live on for decades. Bernice had done such good works.

A huge hole was opening in Shay's heart. She'd known this day would come. But she wasn't ready to let her surrogate mother go.

She'd always been there for Shay. And Shay's life would be so much emptier now.

A commotion at the door had Shay turning around. Roman walked in, and his suit did not hide the beautiful animal beneath. He attracted her like no other, though she knew better than to respond.

She deliberately turned her attention back to Bernice to give herself a few moments to compose herself. The attraction for Roman scared her even as he intrigued her. And Bernice, who'd been trying to set them up, would probably scold her for being afraid. Bernice would tell her wake up and live a life full of joy and experience. And she'd already said Roman was worth the chance.

And if Shay was wrong about his wall, and what could be hidden behind it, he could be the other half of her heart. And she'd have missed her chance.

Stefan had tried to explain energy and love to her. He had a leading theory about energy blends and music with color combinations. Not having been interested at the time, and having sworn off relationships, she hadn't delved any deeper, but damn if Roman didn't have her dredging her brain for little bits and pieces of Stefan's sage advice. And she'd come up empty. She'd have to ask Stefan later. And take his gentle ribbing as payment.

"I'm glad you're here, Roman. Bernice has just passed on." Gerard spoke quietly from the other side of the bed.

Shay stayed at Pappy's side, waiting for him to regain control of himself and finish his good-byes.

"Hard to believe she's gone." Roman's voice was respectful, calm. She studied him under her lashes feeling the same familiar tug. He was awfully collected. As if he had more insight into the daily life and death in a hospital than she'd first suspected. But then he had been a cop.

40

"She's been such a big part of my life." Gerard's voice trembled ever so slightly.

"Let me know when you're ready to go home." Roman's dark chocolate voice slid down Shay's spine, seeming to linger on every bone before stroking lower.

Christ. She closed her eyes and mentally zipped up her chakras to keep him from going deeper. He could be lethal.

Thank God he didn't know what he was doing to her libido. *Or did he?* She snuck a glance at him, and found him staring directly at her.

"Shay? How are you doing?" Once again, that smooth, caring voice stroked her blood.

She swallowed hard, gave him a polite smile. "I'm fine. Thanks. It's Pappy who's just lost one of his best friends."

Roman cocked his head, that intense gaze locking hers in place. "Wasn't Bernice a friend of yours too?"

She smiled wryly. "Bernice was a force of her own. She was a very good friend. But she was one of Pappy's best friends." She sniffled. "And she will be dearly missed by all of us."

Roman's deep golden brown eyes warmed, smiled. "Isn't that the truth? There aren't many Bernices left in the world."

"There won't ever be another Bernice." Pappy spoke for the first time. He glanced over at Shay. "Give me a moment, will you?"

Happy to give him the time he needed, Shay nodded and walked to the door, motioning the other two men to leave in front of her. "Let's give him privacy."

Gerard shook his head, saying, "I'll stay with him. We both have things to say to her."

With a last glance at Pappy, who nodded, Shay and Roman turned and walked out.

"Hard to believe those two are good friends," Roman said, glancing back to the two men huddled together at Bernice's side.

"Especially when they've loved the same woman for as long as they have."

Roman gaze zipped back to her. "Sounds like you don't approve."

"I'm not sure I do," she answered coolly. "Pappy has been at her side for decades, waiting and hoping for her to change her mind. Almost like a favorite puppy dog, hoping for a pat on his head."

"And, from my understanding, she made it clear she wouldn't change her mind."

"True enough." Shay turned to study the two older men and whispered, "It feels like the passing of an era right now."

The two older men hugged each other while Roman and Shay looked on. Then, first the one, and then the other, bent to kiss Bernice's cheeks.

Using the moment of silence, Shay switched her vision to search the room, on the off chance that Bernice was still there. It happened sometimes. That people stayed close to their bodies after death. Close to what they knew. She searched carefully. And there was no sign of Bernice – in any form.

"What are you looking for?" Roman asked, his voice reeking with curiosity.

She started. "I don't know, just looking at the private rooms." God, that was lame. She raised an eyebrow at him.

A smile played at the corner of his mouth. His gaze, direct and determined, held hers. "And now that we have a few moments of privacy, I have another question for you."

"Oh." Shay stared are him, waiting.

That gaze, that could be so warm and caring, deepened to one that was dark and penetrating. "Why are you afraid of me?"

Oh shit.

✳✳✳

Roman walked into his loft drained. The evening at the hospital had been emotionally charged with Bernice's passing.

42

Gerard and Charles had loved that woman, with a deep abiding love that Roman had never dreamed existed.

Grateful for this piece of calm and serenity within the city, Roman walked out onto his large waterfront deck and breathed deeply of the fresh evening air.

He'd just come home from dropping off his grandfather. He'd hated to leave him alone, but the older man insisted he wanted to grieve on his own. In truth, Roman also wanted the time to think. To think about Shay.

She'd been so caring, so loving with her grandfather. He respected that. Actually he loved that about her. The work she did, the people she chose to help. He had known about that, and who she was, before they met. But he hadn't *known* her – not like this. In fact, he was liking everything he was learning.

Needing the connection, Roman walked into his studio and stared at the latest sketch. He glanced at an earlier one on the wall. Not good enough for showing, but something about the colors made the hanging one special. Like many of the early pictures, he had been compelled to add pale blue in the picture. Like gentle smoke.

He'd fought against adding it, but it seemed the pictures weren't complete until he'd added a blue swirl. For that reason, he often incorporated the blue into the flowing design of the draping material or gown.

Then about a year ago, that insistence had eased, the blue was still there, but it was no longer as prominent.

For a long time he'd wondered about that compulsion to add blue, then decided it had to be part of his artistic growth. As he looked at his current picture, he realized that there was a thin blue film over the figure in the painting, like the brush had whispered a faint blush of blue. It created only the slightest of shimmers.

Done in midnight black, Shay's long, elegant back faced him with her hair drifting across the canvas. The picture stopped at the chin line. His own preference. He wanted to do a full body with her beautiful facial features but so far had resisted. Something had stopped him. He didn't know what or why. While the pictures remained only of her form, then he could fool himself to believe she was *only* his model.

If he did break down and add her face – something he knew he couldn't do yet – he'd be telling the world who she was…and how important she was to him. By creating her full image for all eternity, he would be acknowledging Shay was his muse.

And that would change things.

His muse was a living, breathing thing to him. A relationship he lived with daily.

And if he acknowledged she was his muse, he'd be acknowledging that she was not only necessary in his world but she was his passion.

He swallowed hard. *Could that be?*

And if she was his passion...it was a short hop to considering...acknowledging he wanted her to become his partner, his other half...his one true love.

Still that was a step he hadn't taken. Yet.

✳✳✳

The next morning on the other side of town…

Why was his neighbor coming down his walk? David Cummings lowered the gas can nozzle into the small tank of his lawnmower when Melanie Sergeant called out his name. She tugged her poodle toward him.

David swore under his breath. His wife often teased him that he mowed his lawn every Sunday morning from April to October, like clockwork, as particular about his lawn as the teeth of the patients in his dental practice.

And that meant his neighbors knew where and when to find him. Most of the time that was fine.

Just not today. Today was special. And he didn't have time to chitchat. He hoped Melanie wasn't selling any more chocolate bars for the school she taught at. He just didn't have time today.

He planned to takeDiane to brunch and surprise her with a cruise to Scotland. Five kids and she deserved it. Hell, he deserved it, too. She'd likely cry when she found out. Hell, he might too. Thirty-five years together and still going strong. Damn he was a lucky man.

And he could survive a chat with his neighbor for a few minutes.

"'Morning, Melanie. How are you doing this beautiful weekend?"

As Melanie walked closer, he realized there was something different about her. She looked normal, but... His throat tightened and instinctively he wanted to back away from her. He swallowed hard and resisted. That was foolish. He pasted a smile on his face.

"I'm doing great. It's a lovely day, isn't it?" She gave him a bright smile then a frown appeared on her forehead, and her eyes darkened.

Like really dark.

"Are you okay?" He stepped toward her, and as he did, her eyes sharpened, and went almost black. That was wrong.

He forced himself closer, if she needed help... He wasn't a physician, but he knew enough to give basic CPR. Though his skin was creeping, and his head...

What was wrong with his head?

He blinked. Then blinked again. What was wrong with her eyes?

The light was off. Surely that must be this sudden headache. And the pain stabbing through his chest. Stabbing and stabbing. He could hardly breathe. He opened his mouth to speak, but the only sound that came out of his mouth was a name.

"Angela."

His wife. The love of his life. Angela. He held onto the thought and the image of her as the pain accelerated. He dropped to his knees, then slid sideways to the grass. Damn. Please let this not be a heart attack. The doctors had warned him, but...

Melanie was leaning over him, a look of horror on her face. And her eyes, wide, brown... normal again. How? What?

Then she was screaming and running with her dog to the house, and he was staring at the sky. The pain lower now. In his chest. And he knew he was going to die and would not make it to Scotland.

Suddenly Angela was bending over him, tears running down her beloved face. "Hang on, David, don't you dare die. Damn it, I love you. I need you."

He opened his mouth. It hurt to breathe, much less talk. But if he didn't say it now... "Love you." he choked out. His chin trembled as he fought against the pain, as if it were a live thing inside him—not like any death that he'd ever imagined—and he managed one smile and one more word. "Yes."

Then the pain took him and he cried out. She squeezed his hand and cried out, "David I love you."

I love you back.

And then the pain stopped, and there was nothing.

Chapter 4

Monday morning...

Monday morning dawned bright and clear. But Shay was still tired and confused and chose to take refuge from the crazy weekend by checking out the large animal sanctuary, Exotic Landscape. This was one of her pet projects funded by her foundation. These animals, all kinds and sizes, needed help...and Shay was a sucker for kids and animals. Interestingly enough, Tabitha, who ran the operation, was like Shay...psychic.

Shay'd always loved going there, but this last year she'd damned near lived there. It was a place she could rest, drop her barriers and relax.

And there was another reason to go to the sanctuary – she could use the healing calm for herself right now. And it was Shay's way to get her animal fix. Something she'd needed since Morris's disappearance a year ago.

The animals, of course, required a whole different level and kind of energy care. They didn't hide, manipulate or deceive. Each animal had a happiness or health level that was easy to see. Shay always walked through to make sure they were doing okay. Of course, Tabitha did that regularly. And under her care, the animals thrived here.

Tabitha worked Tuesday to Saturday. Once the two women, of similar age, found each other, and discovered what the other had been hiding from the world, they had become fast friends.

After all, they could communicate on the same level.

They couldn't hide anything from the other – for that same reason. It had taken years to solidify the trust, but once they'd found a comfort level, the relationship gave them immeasurable peace.

Tabitha barreled into her office and plunked down on the single visitor's chair. "Okay, give."

Shay rolled her eyes. "I thought this was your day off?"

Tabitha grinned. "It is. So? No trying to change the subject. What's with you and the hunk?"

"Hunk?" Shay asked dryly, trying to marshal her thoughts, knowing it was hard to hide anything from her friend.

"That's how you think of him so that's what I know." The heat climbed Shay's face, and Tabitha chuckled. "And I am delighted for you."

"Hey, it's nothing."

Tabitha tilted her and let out a heavy sigh of disgust. "It's me, remember. You wanted to meet this guy."

"Yeah, well… It's not so simple." Leaning back, she shared what had been going on and what she knew. "Besides, there's lots of weird stuff going on in my life right now."

"Have you looked at him closer?"

"Only briefly. He's got a big wall up. But I don't get the impression he's like that with other people, just me. There's something he doesn't want me to know. And that scares me." Shay stared at her old friend. "And because I know there's something there—"

"You're scared to have anything to do with him." Tabitha nodded. "But that reaction is just common sense. Still you can't compare everyone you meet to the asshole, Darren. And even if there is something else there...it doesn't have to mean that he's out to harm you. It could mean anything."

"I know, but—"

"But you're avoiding going any deeper just in case," Tabitha finished for her. "There's that fear factor again.

Shay dropped her gaze to study the stack of papers on her desk.

"It's difficult."

"And yet, don't you want to know for sure?" Tabitha prodded.

Shay stared at her in astonishment. "But that's the problem. I won't ever truly *know*. I'll look, assume what I see is what's there, and wonder ever after if he is camouflaging what he's doing, like Darren did. Darren could make his energy look *so* normal on the outside, yet he was something *so* different on the inside. He could change his energy so I'd never suspect." She shrugged. "So why bother trying with Roman? Why torment myself wondering if what I'm seeing is real or not?"

"That doesn't make sense, you know that? You'll torment yourself if you never take the chance to find out." Tabitha shook her head. "You're going to wonder anyway."

"I know." Shay sighed. That's what Stefan said."

✳✳✳

Shay strode into her office Monday morning and sat down in her leather executive chair. She'd come in early enough to be alone – or so she'd hoped. There was something about having the space to herself before the day officially began...

But today that wasn't to be.

Jordan, her assistant, raced in behind her, discarding her coat and purse on the way. When she had Shay's attention, she said, "Oh my God! Did you hear the news?"

Oh no.

Dread coiled inside. *Was this about Bernice's death? Or something else?* Hadn't she had enough bad news already? "I don't know. There's been a lot happening. What news are *you* talking about?" she countered, flipping through the stack of folders on her desk

"It's about David Cummings. He's dead." Jordan brought today's mail to Shay's desk and sorted it in front of her.

Shay looked at Jordan and blinked. Her gaze latched onto the silver, cascading rings lining Jordan's ear. Surely that much weight, if not the incessant clanging as the rings banged against each other, had to give Jordan a headache? With difficulty Shay focused on what Jordan had been trying to tell her. *"Who?"*

"You know. The guy with the application you just approved. We were about to send him a check. For the dental center on 46th Street, Westside Dental... The one that does dental surgery for the kids?"

Shay struggled to put that proposal to the name. She remembered the dental shelter. They'd been funding it for a couple of years. "Sorry, I don't remember that name. That's tough on his family and colleagues."

"We were dealing with Max Charter, and then he moved to the Eastside, and Dr. David Cummings took over the management of this one." Jordan raised an eyebrow. "*He's* the guy that died."

Ah. Now that wasn't good for the dentist or for the Center. Still things like this happened, and they had to deal with it. "That's sad. I presume there is someone stepping in to take over from David?"

"Oh sure. We'll make sure that the new manager is briefed before the money is sent over," said Jordan as she started making notes on a pad of paper she produced out of nowhere – an ability that continually amazed Shay.

Jordan was always organized. She could put her fingers on the files Shay wanted within minutes and usually knew what Shay needed on a day-to-day basis as well. Shay had another older woman, Rose, working in the general office handling the phones and clerical duties but she couldn't begin to compete with Jordan's super organization. On the other hand, Rose handled people with a finesse that smoothed much of Jordan's abruptness.

"Briefing the new manager is a good idea." Shay thought about the amount of funding, winced and forced herself to ask, "Do we know how David Cummings died?"

"Collapsed while mowing his lawn," Jordan said with relish. "They are probably doing an autopsy right now."

Shay rolled her eyes. "They don't do autopsies for every case."

"No?" Jordan looked crestfallen. "That's too bad."

"How do you figure?" Shay stared at her assistant curiously.

"Well, they might make a mistake without it." Jordan shrugged. "Everyone deserves an autopsy to find out the truth."

What? Shay stared at her young assistant in surprise. Rose walked in just then, her subdued navy skirt and blouse a peaceful contrast to Jordan's bright colors. Then her unruffled middle-age personality was hugely calming beside Jordan's youthful bubbliness.

"You know..." Jordan said helpfully. "What if people murder other people and leave no trace? It would be easy to make a murder look like an accident or heart attack."

"It would *not* be easy to do that," Rose said as she brought a stack of folders to Shay's desk. "In fact, I'd imagine a certain amount of skill would be required to dupe the police and medical profession."

With a tinkling headshake, Jordan said, "It happens all the time."

"I don't even want to know how you know that." Shay shook her head.

Jordan laughed. "TV, of course. There are awesome crime shows these days. And even more awesome websites. They show everything."

Rose groaned and disappeared into the outer office.

"And that's so helpful for the budding criminal element, I'm sure," Shay said. "Bring me the Westside Dental file will you? I want to make sure that the situation is monitored carefully before the payment is sent."

"Sure." Jordan bustled off. Her energy bustled about in a smart, attentive manner, just like her personality. Shay shook her head. She'd done her research before hiring Jordan, and there hadn't been any surprises in the last year. She was hard working, honest and reliable. Friendly puppy material, with dynamite organization skills. Those qualities alone, made her valuable. Jordan's energy was always alert and sharp as she went through her day, assessing what needed to be done and deciding when to do it.

If Shay could, she'd hire another dozen like her. Because she'd proven to be so competent, Shay had given Jordan more and more responsibility, and so far her assistant handled it well.

Workers like Jordan were hard to find.

Projects to fund, were not. Unfortunately.

There was never enough money to help everyone, so Shay focused on helping as many children and animals as she could through her foundation. She hated to turn down good causes, but she did when they were run by rotten people. Her psychic skills allowed her to read people's energy to see that much. The good-hearted but totally inept. The liars and the cons. And those with the know-how, plus the skills, to do what needed to be done.

But this death didn't ring her 'happy trigger.' That had nothing to do with her own compassion and caring, but because she knew people and what they were capable of doing to each other – and that made her naturally suspicious.

There was a lot of money at stake. The Lassiter Foundation – and by extension, Shay – controlled millions of dollars. It was up to her to make sure the funds were used properly. She left energy markers with each application she personally approved, and then once a month, she went through and checked out how the money was used.

It took time. The more applications, the more time was required. Occasionally, the news hadn't been good. She'd used a private investigator several times and had a couple of detectives on speed dial to prove what she could sense energetically. She ensured the system worked.

This case raised all kinds of alarms. But apparently this man had died at home. Was this significant?

Time to hit redial and find out.

Just as she pulled out her cell phone, Jordan raced back in. Her wide-eyed look had Shay stalling on the call. "What's the matter?"

"There's a man here to see you. His name is Roman Chandler." She gave an appreciative motion with her hands. "He says he has an appointment, but I don't have him in the books. He also said to ask you."

Shay sighed. "He doesn't have an appointment. But he's the kind that thinks he doesn't need one. Send him in; he knows you're talking to me."

Jordan's expressive face flushed bright red. "Oh. Sorry, I never thought of that."

"It doesn't matter. I spoke with him last night."

A big smirk wreathed her assistant's face. "Oh, last night, huh? That's awesome. He's hot. What a great pair you'll make."

Shay groaned. "Jordan, stop. We didn't go out on a date. We were at the hospital. Bernice passed away last night."

Jordan gasped in horror.

Shay nodded. "Exactly. Now just send him in, please."

"Sure. I am so sorry about Bernice." Jordan went as if to leave, but not before winking at her. "You should still go for it. It's about time, you know."

"About time for what?" Roman stood in the open doorway.

Jordan gasped, her face flushing bright pink again. She shot Shay an apologetic look and raced out.

"Nothing that pertains to you," Shay said smoothly as she stood up to face him. *Drat.* This man's appearance could make the earth move, and she hadn't even noticed because even from a distance, he'd already rocked her foundation.

Sneaking a quick glance, she checked out his energy. Dark greens strode up and down over his body in a calm, controlled manner. That figured. The healer, the moneymaker and the cop.

Gerard ran a huge company dealing with prosthetics and hospital equipment, things along that line, but he was getting old and needed help now. Roman told her he'd created Internet Security Corp after leaving law enforcement. *Could he do both?* Or would he sell his own company to help his grandfather?

That Roman came wrapped up in the best damn package she'd seen in a long time was a bonus.

Now if she could just reconcile that wall of his...

"Take a seat." She motioned for him to step in further. "What can I do for you?" She sat back down and crossed her hands serenely in front of her and waited.

"We didn't finish our discussion last night."

She gaped at him. "Really? You came to my office to ask me why I'm nervous around you? Scared of you?"

"I don't want you to feel that way." He tilted his head, his gaze intent. "I'd like to ask you out to dinner and if you're nervous..."

Oh boy. She hadn't expected that. Yet she should have. It was a natural step for the two of them to take, but...

"I've surprised you." He grinned, a boyish smile that revealed the charmer. "Sorry."

"Yes, you did surprise me," she hedged, not knowing what to say.

"So just say yes." He paused. "Please. I've been looking forward to deepening our relationship from the moment I moved here. Saturday hardly counted."

Flustered, she willed the heat wave to stop its climb up her throat. The intense silence grew thick as she felt Roman's scrutiny. It took more will than she'd had to use in a long time, but she kept her smile firmly in place. Inside...was another story.

She took another peek at this energy. *Wow*. His aura was contained. The energy circulated in a soothing manner.

Then he smiled, and she was almost ready to forget about his shields. And that made him very dangerous. But she watched, fascinated as a slow dawning awareness of her on a whole different level took over his whole face. Shivers of delight whispered through her.

"So what is your answer?"

She stared at him, trying to figure out what to say. Did she want to go out with him? Yes. Should she? She totally should not. She opened her mouth to refuse, only to hear herself say, "Yes."

"Good." He stood up. "Friday night?"

She tossed her hair back and sighed. What had she done? "I don't know when Bernice's funeral is scheduled. It could be earlier than Friday, but if not—"

"Let's make it Saturday evening so we're sure." He walked to the door. "I'll get back to you about the funeral arrangements."

And just like that he was gone.

"OMG. You're going on a date with him." Jordan practically danced through the room like a teenager. "He's gorgeous. Oh my. Where are you going and what are you going to wear?"

Wear? She had no idea. Five days was a long time away. Anything could happen.

***

Roman walked out of Shay's building and down the block toward his own office – or rather, his grandfather's office. The traffic beeped by in a confusion of noise. The sidewalks were full. He stepped into the fast morning crowd and a typical business day in the downtown core. And so not where he wanted to be. He wanted to be working his own business and doing his art.

If only the dynamite CEO for Chandler Inc hadn't quit. And it could take a long time to replace him. Roman's help was supposed to be temporary, but...

On the upside, it would keep him here. Give him time to get to know Shay better. But he could do that without coming to his grandfather's company on a daily basis. It hurt to think about his grandfather getting older. That one day he might not be here.

Roman's mind shifted gears. Bernice, Charles and Gerard had been inseparable for as long as he could remember. And over the last year, each had filled him in on Shay's life in bits and pieces. He knew about her lousy fiancé, his death, her isolation.

Bernice had said Shay was 'different.' Had some unusual skills. He'd pressed her for more information, but she'd clammed up. He'd often wondered what those skills could be. Maybe she was a belly dancer? A magician...? He had asked Ronin about Shay, but not even his twin was willing to share – said Roman would find out, in due time. And he'd told Roman to keep an open mind.

Whatever the hell that meant.

Then again, Ronin knew some interesting people, Dr. Maddy for one. Roman had re-evaluated some of his beliefs after meeting her through a fundraiser. Dr. Maddy had introduced him to a whole new world of paranormal theories, and he had to admit, he supported her children's project when he could.

There were so many people in need.

Did Shay have skills similar to Maddy's? Ronin had just smiled when asked. He had a cop's brain and strong intuition. And knew when to keep his mouth shut.

And Ronin also knew Stefan Kronos. Someone Roman would love to get to know. Not for his apparent otherworldly abilities – Roman wasn't at all sure about those – but for his art. Stefan's work was talked about...everywhere, and yet, somehow he remained a mystery.

That whole psychic thing was unbelievable to many people. There was enough proof – measurable results, like Dr. Maddy's – to keep Roman's doubts at bay. He thought most of what people talked about was garbage, but something about her and the results she'd achieved, just couldn't be explained away. There was media talk, too, about psychics working with the police to solve missing persons and serial killer cases. If psychics could help catch assholes like that, Roman was all for them.

As soon as he entered his grandfather's reception room, Celia, his grandfather's office manager, spoke from behind her monitor. "Roman, your grandfather has been calling you constantly since you left. You forgot your cell phone again, didn't you?"

"Sometimes, I just like to be without it for a while." In fact, the more he painted, the less he wanted to be connected to the world twenty-four-seven.

"If you say so." She shook her head. "Please call him. It will save my stress levels."

He walked into his office, sat down and reached for the phone. "Hello, Grandfather. Yes, the arrangements are being made. Yes, everything will be ready for Bernice's funeral on Friday."

Silence, then his grandfather gave his two cents worth. "Harumph. If you already knew what I was going to say, why did you call me back?"

Rolling his eyes, Roman sat back and stared up at the ceiling. "So that you would know that I know. Stop worrying. Bernice will go to rest in fine style."

"So long as Charles doesn't go changing anything. Damn, that man has been calling me constantly."

Roman grinned. "You two have talked a half-dozen times a day for decades. Today isn't going to be any different."

"I know." A tired sigh wove through the line. "We're sure going to miss her."

"And yet, you still have each other."

"And you have no one. Why aren't you married with a family of your own?"

Roman groaned silently. Since he'd returned to Portland, his grandfather hadn't quit harping on Roman's single status. "I was married, remember?"

"That was a childhood romance. It lasted what...two years? Then divorce. Bet you don't even remember her name," barked his grandfather. "Young kids these days... You don't know what marriage is anymore."

There wasn't much Roman could say to that. Not anything that he hadn't said a dozen times before. "When I find the right woman, I'll get married again. Until then, I'll just enjoy my single status."

"Ha. When was the last time you went on a date? You're always working."

Finally he had something new to add. "That's not true. I'm going on a date on Saturday night. I'm taking a young woman out for dinner."

"Do I know her?" Grandfather asked suspiciously.

"Yes, you do. It's Shay."

"Ah." His grandfather chuckled. "That would make Bernice happy. She always thought the two of your should meet. She spoke highly of Shay's business acumen – and for Bernice that was something. But a couple of times, I sensed she wanted to say more about her but she always stopped herself before saying what was on her mind."

That fit. Bernice wouldn't likely have said too much to his grandfather. Grandfather's comments were nothing if not pointed. He said at his age, he shouldn't have to hold back for fear of offending anyone. Still this behavior hadn't just started. He'd been very vocal all his life.

"Where are you taking her?"

"Not sure yet. I haven't had a chance to try out too many places here."

"Take her to the Sandors. Great seafood."

"Maybe." Except all the patrons there were Grandfather's age. Roman had actually hoped to take her dancing. He didn't know if she danced or not, but with that body she was probably a natural. And he sure wouldn't mind holding her in his arms for a little while.

And he didn't know what she was hiding, but she was hiding something.

And he wanted to find out exactly what.

***

Finally some action. After the old bat died. Not much yet. Not enough for Shay to understand. But she would figure it out. And the police would, too. Eventually. But by then they wouldn't be able to do anything about it.

And damn, if Shay didn't look to have another hunk at her heels. At least the type of man she favored — he'd hovered by her side at the Foundation reception. Roman Chandler. Wealthy businessman and budding artist. The Chandlers are a well-known family.

He looked good too. Damn good. In many ways, the two suited each other. And Roman Chandler had walls, too. Getting around them was possible, but it would take time — time that wasn't available.

There was a deadline to meet. A death to honor. Justice to be served. It was long past due. But it will be done... Then I can move on.

Chapter 5

Monday mid-morning...

After Roman left the office, Shay pulled in her scattered thoughts and hit the first speed dial number on her phone, trying for a second time to make this call. She leaned back in her comfortable chair, hoping Roman's brother was available. She couldn't ignore the niggling unease in her belly. Something wasn't right.

Ronin must have recognized her on caller ID. "Hi Shay. How are you doing?"

The calm, warm voice on the other end made her smile. How anyone could do the job Ronin did and still have such a lighthearted personality amazed her. Though she didn't know Roman's brother all that well, Ronin'd been there for her every time she needed him. He was a good man to have on her side. As he'd proved when Darren died. She could only hope his brother was a good man, too.

She laughed lightly. "I'm fine. As always."

"Not if you're calling me, you aren't." He paused. "I heard about Bernice. I am sorry." His tone turned serious. "So what's the problem?"

And that was the best part about dealing with the same people over time, the relationship was already in place, and you could go directly to the heart of the matter without the small talk. She passed over Bernice's death and got to the point.

"Dr. David Cummings, the man behind the Westside Dental Center, has passed away. Our foundation funds the center. I'm wondering if you have any details, and if this is something I need to be concerned about."

"I haven't heard anything about this." His tone was brusque. "Is there a lot of money being funneled into that project?"

She heard the tapping on his keyboard as he searched for information.

"Over a million at this point. It's a dental practice for kids in need. It's constantly busy. I think there are four dentists working full time and all the support staff. It's totally charity funded."

"Hmmm. From your end, is there any reason to suspect that there's a problem?"

"Not sure. The application had been received as per the annual deadline, but there were a couple of issues that were flagged so it was brought to my attention. They aren't big. It was more like someone else filled out the paperwork this time instead of the regular person. Someone who didn't know the ins and outs of the Center's paperwork."

"Hmm." Ronin's voice was thoughtful, distant. His keyboard clicked a few more times. "David Cummings keeled over at his home, apparently while talking to a neighbor. According to the eyewitness, he'd been alone for maybe a half hour before he died. Apparent heart attack. No signs of a fight.

"Because he had no history of a heart condition and was only fifty-two, it raises some questions, so an autopsy..." His voice trailed off as he clicked through a few more screens. "It's scheduled for later tomorrow. Depending on case load."

"Understood." This gave her nothing new to go by. "If you hear of anything odd, let me know, and if anything pops up on my end, I'll give you a ring."

"Thanks. And hey, go easy on my brother. He's been waiting to meet you since forever."

Ronin rang off, leaving Shay spluttering, staring down at the phone in her hand, her mind full of Roman – again. *Damn.* She tried to refocus on the problem at hand.

She couldn't run any scans on David's body, as he was already gone, but every action and reaction required energy. And the first law of the conservation of energy said that energy cannot be created nor destroyed. It can only change form. Therefore, the energy involved in this business had either left behind a trail, transformed that trail to something else, or hadn't existed in the first place.

Meaning he'd died by natural causes.

That happened.

The energy from a paranormal being could have physically touched him in such a way as to cause a heart attack. If that were the case, in theory, then its energy would still be on David's body, but it would be dissipating rapidly. It would be difficult for that energy to change form on a corpse. Not an easy medium to work with.

Not that it wasn't possible. The more she understood, the more she realized she didn't understand anything...

There were assholes out there; some were psychics who had skills far beyond anything she'd ever been able to imagine. And it was so not easy to catch up to them.

Stefan might know who and how, though.

She tuned in and sent him a message. It bounced off the door to his mind. She sighed. He was likely painting.

He'd get the message when he stopped and opened his psyche up to the rest of the world again. In the meantime, was there anything she could find out on her own?

She pondered that. Shay knew Dr. Maddy could scan a body remotely. Shay hadn't had much luck with distance scanning.

But there was a technique whereby Shay could retrace her path to take another look at places, people and events that she'd already experienced. In rare cases, she could go back to certain situations that loved ones had experienced by hitching a ride on their memories.

It was great for remembering details. Not great for determining murder or murderers. Still, she couldn't quite let it go. It would at least tell her if anyone in the office held any serious animosity toward David – something worthy of a second look.

So should she try at home, or from here?

Making a sudden decision, Shay stood up, walked out into the main office and saw that both of her office staff had left to take their lunch breaks. *Good.* She returned to her office and locked the door. Setting the phones so incoming calls all went straight to voicemail, she settled into her chair.

She closed her eyes and pictured the center where David Cummings had worked, as it was on her last visit. That's how her skills worked. Because she'd been to a place once, she could visualize it and access it from her mind.

The front door of the center loomed and she pushed it open mentally and walked in. Shay smiled at the office staff, busy on the phone and talking to customers. Just as it had been last time. She hooked into her energy's memory and retraced her steps through the last visit.

David, looking happy, saw her and smiled. He excused himself from the discussion with the office manager and walked over, hand out to greet her – as he had that day.

"Nice to see you."

Her body reached out to shake his hand while Shay's astral body watched the interaction from outside the physical plane. Separated from the physical reality, Shay was free to observe the interactions involving others around her.

Moving forward, David led her to his office.

Shay studied the room and the energy trails of the people who'd entered and left – their energy, wispy and dispersing. Nothing seemed out of the ordinary.

But if there'd been anything obvious, she'd have noticed it on the day she'd actually been there. At least she hoped she would have.

Now that she wasn't grounded in the physical experience, she could take the necessary time to look around. See what else might be going on. She couldn't separate from the memory to wander on her own, but she could turn around and see the main office, the dashes and flares of energy as people communicated with one another.

Every word spoken required energy. Every facial expression required energy and as it manifested, it gave off energy that went to the other person in the exchange. She could see the exchanges. The energy also blended and blurred, shared and moved through the room as people said one thing and meant another. Or if someone spoke to one person but wanted to speak with another. The first person would receive the energy as it was directed to them, but some energy snuck around that person and snaked over to the person that they really wanted to speak with.

Trails and lingering blankets of energy spoke of lots of interactions at many levels.

The staff had their interactions with each other, with the customers and with their bosses, and then there were messages, spoken and unspoken, about their private lives – the stuff people shared with each other and the stuff they kept hidden. And then there were the lies. She hated seeing the details of some people's personal lives.

Some of it was incredibly private and she tried to move on quickly.

And for every action there was always an equal reaction. The energy pushing the message was going to be buffered by the person perceiving or receiving the message. The bottom line was this: everyone left vestiges of themselves behind, and connected to others, and only a few special people understood that some people could see it all.

Some people – like her.

At least when she dropped her walls she could see it all – unless the person protected themselves like Darren had. She refused to drop her walls in public because she'd be inundated with the onslaught. Right now, having stepped back into a memory as she had, it was easier to deal with others' energy than if she were in real time. Like watching a movie instead of participating in a play. She could also apply a filter of sorts and focus acutely on what caught her attention.

What people didn't realize was that energy didn't tell lies, whereas words could. But the energy behind lies was obvious – to her.

One woman was speaking about her coworker's new hairstyle. Shay could hear the disembodied words when she spoke. "I love it. It makes you look so much younger." Those were the words. Nicely delivered. Just the right tone of warm appreciation. Yet the energy, on which the words were delivered, was ragged, shaky, vibrating with something else. Jealousy, maybe even anger. The energy that moved from the first woman to the second was spiteful, and the sentiment was reflected in sickening gray to black energy waves.

The first woman hated the second. But the work environment demanded that they get along in a manner that was acceptable to all. But did any of this have anything to do with David's death? She searched the colors, the smoky clouds and the heavier and lighter energy to sort through recent layers then moved down to the older ones.

To sort through the nastiness to find truly authentic emotions, she had to look deeper.

Not an easy thing to do. She spun away from the multiple people working in the busy office and focused on David. His aura resonated with goodwill and a pleaser personality. A definite media type. But what was underneath it?

Shay moved around him and studied David from the different angles. He couldn't be this happy and friendly all the time. No one was. He stood up to get a file from the table across the room and she saw it.

There was a black circle, small and almost hidden under his good cheer. It wasn't at the heart chakra; it was centered on his third chakra. She studied it, a frown coming to her face. It could portend a health issue, but, it was almost too perfect. Too round.

She had no doubt the circle was man-made.

Planted. It was a marker. Someone who understood energy work had planted it there.

Shit. And once she understood that, her mind spun endlessly. *Why? Who? How?*

"Shay?"

A pounding on her own office door broke her altered state of consciousness, snagging her attention away from the scene playing out before her.

Damn. Rotten timing.

"Shay, are you in there? Your light is on but I can't get through on your phones." After a moment, Jordan's voice came again, higher and louder. "Shay, you're scaring me."

Time to return to her normal reality.

Shay closed her eyes and forcibly disconnected from the memory. Her consciousness slammed back to her office chair, with bile climbing the back of her throat. *Shit.* She hated coming back from a trip so suddenly. The hard landings always made her stomach revolt.

"I'm here," she croaked. She cleared her throat several times, and then managed to get up off her chair. She let the changing energy ripple through her, letting it settle and ground her.

Making her way slowly to the door, she struggled with fingers still not feeling quite normal, to unlock and open it. For Jordan's sake, she put on a sleepy smile and rubbed her eyes. "Sorry. I locked the door to have a nap."

"You scared me shitless. At least leave me a note." Jordan stormed into her office, turned around as if to satisfy herself that all was well, and then came to stand in front of Shay. Her gaze narrowed. "You need coffee."

Shay rubbed her eyes. "Thanks. I could really use a cup."

"So could I. This time, I'm going to lace it with something much stronger."

Shay had to smile. "Feel free. I'll take mine black, thanks." She watched Jordan walk over the side counter and set up a fresh pot of coffee. The whole time the young woman muttered under her breath.

But her energy only showed relief and concern. Caring. That made all the difference in the world. And because they were friends, and Jordan had been scared, Shay said, "I'm sorry. I'll leave a note on your desk next time I decide to have a nap at work."

"Do that."

Shay returned to her desk and sat down. She dropped the smile.

She'd love to take a return trip to David's office for a closer look. But every time she returned to the same place, the energy would have dissipated a little more. And it took a lot of her energy to make these trips happen. She needed to recharge as it were.

Instead, she could only guess at what really happened. And what the black marker meant. And that didn't make her happy.

***

Roman left the office early. He needed to be in his own space for a bit. Even if he was only going to his studio for an extended lunch – it all helped.

He shut the door and strode across the expanse of studio floor to the windows on the far side. Unbuckling the latches, he propped the large glass window wide, giving thanks that he had a place to breathe so deeply. Creativity required space, and as a messy painter, he needed more space than most. Still, he cleaned his studio himself, not trusting his housecleaning service to do it properly in this room.

He rolled up his sleeves as he surveyed the gray Portland sky around him. He had just enough time to pack up a couple paintings for the new show and see if Roger, the gallery owner, had a preference in style. Normally Roman was very private about his art, and this showing was going to push him out of his comfort zone like nothing else. He handled big business and employees easily, but his painting was...private, personal. He didn't have the same hard edge for that part of his life that he did for business.

In the beginning, he'd never signed his creations. Then, after gaining some experience, he started using a different name. Now, after some modest success, he signed the pieces with his own name. Progress came with appreciation. Only no one here on the West Coast really knew about him – except his family. Back East his art was better known.

He knew that would change soon. Not that he expected to be an overnight success. He just hoped his show didn't bomb.

And he hoped to hell that no one recognized his model.

Still, he couldn't help but wonder what Shay would think of his latest works. He hadn't planned on this collection, but after Bernice had sent those headshots of Shay, he hadn't been able to help himself. He called the collection, *Complicated.*

Like she was.

And she'd been the inspiration that fired up his imagination.

Thankfully he'd not painted her face on the nudes.

But he'd used her body.

***

"Stefan. I could use some help."

"Always. What's up?" For all the willingness in his voice, Shay could never really forget that Stefan pushed himself too hard and for too long, too often. Whether it was helping someone, offering his services to someone in law enforcement, or creating his artwork. And right now, it was obvious that fatigue held his voice up, giving his words form.

"You need a keeper," she said abruptly.

That surprised a laugh out of him.

"I'm serious." And she was. But that had nothing to do with what she wanted to talk to him about.

"Are you volunteering for the job?" Amusement slid through the phone. "Although Alex's ghostly sister, Lissa, hangs around enough, certainly filling in that position."

"Good. Someone needs to. Especially if your so-called future partner has any of your abilities and knows about them.

She's liable to kick my ass down the road for not doing a better job."

This time he laughed aloud. "I'm glad you called, Shay. I needed the laugh. My particular future partner doesn't have any idea about me, and that's probably a good thing."

"I don't know. It's going to take time for a woman to figure you out. Then there's that whole needing-to-accept-you stage," she admonished. "You're not an easy person to get along with."

"Really?" He added in a slow thoughtful tone, "And here, I thought I was a model friend."

"You are, but..." She bit her lip, then sighed heavily. "Actually I'm wondering if you can tell me something." She explained about David's death. "There aren't any signs of foul play. An autopsy is scheduled, but should the results come back with nothing definitive, the police aren't going to think it was anything but a simple heart attack."

"But you're not sure?"

"Right. There was this one black spot on one chakra. It was abnormal – perfectly round. It felt like a marker planted there for some purpose." She sighed. "The thing is, I don't know what that means."

"Or if it means anything. Could be just his wife's subconscious way of checking on her husband's health."

She frowned. "I hadn't thought of that."

"Sometimes appearances can be deceptive," Stefan reminded her. "What else did you see?"

"Not much," she admitted. "The energy in the building is extensive, as the place swarms with customers all day long. There are kids, parents, staff – and that's just for starters. You know how confusing it gets when these people add in all their stuff."

"Love how you use that term – stuff."

"It's true. You know that. Everyone has garbage they haul around with them throughout their day. For me to work through all of that is distracting and tiring."

"And you care about this, why?"

She sighed. "That's the crux of the matter. I just want to make sure this incident has nothing to do with the money we've funneled into the Center. Another payment is due to go out next week. If there's any sign of this being more than a heart attack, I don't want to send the check. And..." She paused, then continued painfully. "I want to make sure that I didn't miss something."

"Ah." He left that last bit alone for the moment. "How big a payment?"

"It's big." Happy to focus on the business aspect, she added, "They're planning to purchase a building and renovate it to make a larger facility so they can do more. The purchase price is the bulk of the payout."

"Hmmm. So if this person did die of natural causes, what would happen to the plans and the payout?"

"If they have a chain of command in place, and the business manager continues following the same proposal and building purchase plan, then we'd send the funds. However, if they change things, there would be a hold on the money until we were sure the Center, under new administration, is managed properly."

"So killing this person would actually hurt the Center. It could cause the Center to close. Is that what you're saying?" Stefan's voice sharpened. "I'm looking for motivation to help me figure out if foul play is involved."

"Money? Maybe? It's a large check I'm cutting for them. Someone might want to step up and take control of receiving the funds and the project to have access to the money for another purpose – or to steal them. Or someone within the Center could have a personal grudge against the Center and want to close it." Shay knew there were other possibilities – if David had been murdered – but at this point those possibilities were all moot. No one had declared it a murder.

"Hmmm. We've seen murders done for a lot less." His voice cooled. "And you didn't see any other pathways, darkness, anything in the auras of the other people?"

"No."

"And did you look?"

She winced. "I tried to. Look, I know I'm having trust issues that come into play when I interpret people's energy. But if something had popped, I like to think I'd have taken a second look."

"Yes, you would have. You just need to regain your self-confidence. Don't let Darren's deception make you doubt everything..." His voice trailed off.

"If I can't see the truth, then what's the point of looking? I'm just afraid I'll make the same mistake again." She wanted to hit her head in frustration. After the death of her fiancé, and the doubts about all she'd thought they were to each other, this questioning of herself and her abilities to recognize good and evil had been a familiar feeling. The doubts about her abilities, and what she'd missed had overwhelmed her.

"And I tell you again, Darren was one in a million. The chances of there being a second one are almost nonexistent."

"And yet it feels like..." She hesitated.

"What?" he prompted.

"What if Darren had family I didn't know about?" She bit her bottom lip gently. "What if other family members could also do what he did?"

Stefan's voice sharpened. "I thought you said he was alone in the world?"

"Sure, but what if that's just what he wanted me to think?" She groaned. "Nothing else he said was true, so why would I believe the stuff he told me about his family?"

"Shay, this guy was a man. Not a god. Not some kind of magician. You didn't fail in not seeing him for who he was. He was powerful and carefully kept things hidden from you."

"So why does it feel like I failed?" Not giving Stefan a chance to argue, she hung up the phone.

If a lasting impression of a frowning Stefan lingered in her mind, she ignored it.

Still, his voice whispered through her consciousness. *You might ignore me, but running away isn't the answer.*

***

In spite of the constant headache from the ongoing renovations at Chadworth School, Headmaster Robert Dander couldn't stop smiling – and not because of the school's impressive trophies he was staring at in the school's front entrance. In three weeks, he'd lost twenty-one pounds. Lisa had lost seventeen. They'd even gone dancing over the weekend, something they hadn't done for a long time. Shaking their still substantial booties and enjoying every moment.

Life was good.

The door opened behind him, and he turned to see the UPS driver hurrying in with a parcel. Robert stepped toward him.

"Do you need a signature?" Robert glanced down at the return address on the label. Another order of books. Good. The school needed them – and so much more.

"Not today." The deliveryman touched his hand to his cap and said, "Have a good day."

Robert glanced up at him. The deliveryman's eyes had darkened to a midnight black. Robert frowned. "Hey, are you all right?"

"I'm fine." Only the man's eyes had gone completely black as in no white showed…at all.

While Robert stood in shock, trying to understand, the deliveryman turned to leave. Friendly. Normal.

Except something flashed from the man's body and stabbed into Robert. He gasped and fell back a step, his hand's slamming to his chest.

Oh no, oh no, oh no. Not now. Not when he was getting better and taking care of himself. Not when he was starting to live again.

The pain sharpened, and he opened his mouth to cry for help, and the pain intensified. It felt like his heart was being ripped out of his chest. He tried to speak again and a nasty, hushed groan of pain and terror came out. A gurgle.

The deliveryman turned, frowned and took a step forward. "Sir, are you all right?"

Robert tried to answer and held out his hand. The parcel fell from his numb fingers, hitting the floor with a loud bang. Robert fell to his knees, dimly aware of Bill calling for help.

Footsteps raced down the hallway toward them.

Robert tried to speak, tried to tell them to call 911. Then the beautiful old tile of the entranceway rushed up to meet him.

A harsh whisper sounded close by, almost inside his head. But his own thoughts drowned it out. *Please not a heart attack! I'm not ready to die.*

Chapter 6

Monday afternoon…

The afternoon sped by. There'd been too much damn paperwork to allow Shay to leave work early – not to mention the scheduled meetings with other staff.

She'd hoped to slip down to the Children's Hospital, one of the Foundation projects, and see how the new wing was coming along. She'd heard it was almost done. In fact, several children had already been moved in. Those kids were part of the reason she wanted to visit this afternoon. They tugged at her heartstrings, made her grateful to be able to help in some small way. Only, her schedule wasn't looking good at the moment. Maybe in an hour. She'd see.

Her phone rang. It was her favorite detective – Ronin. "Hey, surprised to hear from you so fast."

"It's not necessarily a good thing, either," he said, his voice serious.

"True enough." She waited for him to continue. When he took his time, she had an inkling she wasn't going to like what he would say next. She struggled to hide the sinking feeling in her stomach, so it didn't show in her voice. "What's up?"

"Do you have anything to do with the school on Bernard Street?"

She frowned. "Chadworth School? Yes, it's one of ours. Why?"

"The headmaster, Robert Dander, collapsed by the front door a couple hours ago. He's dead."

She gasped, her stomach bottoming out and filling with dread. "I don't understand. The headmaster is a great guy. He couldn't be more than sixty, maybe sixty-two, years old."

"He's sixty-one."

"Is it on the news?" she asked. "Normally I'd be notified of something like this." Like she had been about Westside Dental Center.

"The police are still on site. No details have been released at this time. It's the school's connection to the Foundation that has me calling. I thought it was one of your projects."

"The old building needed upgrades to bring it up to code," she confirmed, bringing up the file on the computer. "They're due to get their second payment next week."

"And would a death like this stop the payment of that check?"

She leaned back and thought about that. "Normally not. At least not for long. We don't give the person the money; we give the project the funding. There is, of course, due diligence before we send out the money so we know how the money is going to be handled. We've been helping this school for years now. Robert wasn't the only person we've dealt with there. And they wouldn't get all the money in one lump sum anyway. It's handed out in stages."

She thought about what Ronin had said and what he hadn't said. "Was Robert murdered?" she asked, and couldn't stop her voice from showing her dismay.

"There are no signs of foul play. There were witnesses, but apparently he just keeled over where he stood. An autopsy will be performed. I'll let you know if there is anything odd."

"Okay, thanks for letting me know."

Shay hung up the phone and stared blindly at the computer monitor. She wasn't a big believer in coincidence, but what was the chance that two of the people running projects her foundation worked with, who were each set to manage a large chunk of Foundation money, would both die of heart attacks within twenty-four hours of each other?

She tried to remember the last time she'd been at the school. It had been several weeks ago. Shay took time, at least once a month, to visit each of the Foundation's pet projects.

Other people could perform the checks, but she preferred to do them herself, knowing she would see more than other people might.

The last time she'd visited, the old structure had pleased her greatly. She loved knowing that the school would be able to stay open and that the graceful old lady of a building would continue to stand. Once she'd made that decision, she had no trouble convincing the others on the board about the importance of keeping the school open.

Also, as she thought back on the project and how her foundation came to be involved, she thought Bernice might have had a hand in that project coming to Shay.

Normally she would have picked up the phone and called Bernice to ask her about the school and Robert. Only now Bernice was in the morgue, ready to be buried.

Cold brushed up against her shoulders. She wrapped her arms around her chest.

Too many people connected to her were dying.

Why?

***

The next day, Shay walked up the steps to Chadworth School and opened the door. The school was busy – full of life, full of kids. The way a school should be.

Being there reassured her. That life continued. Kids still attended the school. It was still open and operating. Then again, why wouldn't it be? The death of the headmaster from natural causes was heartbreaking but not something that should stop the day-to-day operations of a project this size.

According to Ronin, nothing suspicious had been found on site. The autopsy should be done by now, but she hadn't heard the results. She'd made the trip to gauge the energy of the school.

She knew everything had energy, including the old building. Part of the reason she'd been willing to help fund the renovations was that this old building, with its tired energy, had been through so much already. She stood here and felt the contradictions you'd find in any building like this: the years of good living, the abuse and neglect, the kids' screams of joy and the fights and rage that had flared up through the decades. Still the old girl had withstood it with a grace and serenity that muted the storms going on around and through her.

With many good years early on, the energy of the building had warmed, grown and balanced itself with every additional successful year.

With time, the energy of the building had shifted slightly. The attitude of each generation of kids had affected the balance; the fight for funding affected the teachers; and the desperation of the parents added yet another element.

The building had maintained a healthy, measured calm. Shay knew its early years had to have been impressive indeed to withstand the ongoing negativity from this least decade. She saw these next years as promising a boon of new, happier and healthier energy as the renovations happened, as teachers, kids and parents realized the school was going to stay open and that children would continue to go there.

She'd come specifically to see how the death of the headmaster affected that balance. And to find out if there was some underlying negativity she had missed before.

That's what really bothered her. One death related to one of her many projects was sad...but that could be considered normal. Two deaths among her project leaders could be very sad but still be thought of as normal, considering how many people and projects she dealt with. Everyone knew, life happened. So did death.

As long as there was nothing ugly floating under the surface at either location where the deaths had occurred.

She walked into the office. The secretary was on the phone. Another worked at a computer in the back. The door to the headmaster's room was closed. Lights out.

The vice principal's door was open. Lights on.

With a smile to the busy secretary, Shay walked toward the vice principal. The Stephen Mortimer nameplate on the door matched her files. She presumed he'd be the one to step into the headmaster's shoes, but she couldn't be sure. A charity like this one had board members to satisfy.

She knocked on the open door. Stephen looked up and frowned. *Interesting.*

"Can I help you?"

"Yes, I'm Shay Lassiter of the Lassiter Foundation. I'd like to speak with you for a few moments."

Awareness shot into his gaze, but so did something else. Wariness? Fear? Or maybe just a hint of insecurity? He rose, stretched and walked around his desk to shake her hand. "Please, have a seat. I'm sorry I didn't recognize you."

"No reason why you would. Normally, I met with Robert."

"Yes." He ran his fingers through his hair, leaving it more than a little rumpled. "It's been a difficult few days. We closed the school on the day of his death, but reopened it the next, knowing that's what he'd have wanted."

"Good. I came to see how everyone is coping."

He smiled. "I think we're doing fine. Robert was a good man...but he was intense. That must have affected his health. I can't tell you how many times we warned him to relax a little and ease up on the stress in his life."

Shay nodded sympathetically. "Funny, we're all told to do that, but hearing it and then acting upon the advice, well—"

"Exactly." He added, "Robert was also extremely overweight. He had a heart condition already, so although his death is a great loss, it's not a great surprise."

Anyone overweight would be prone to such health conditions. And Robert had been obese. "Have funeral arrangements been made? I'd like to attend."

He busied himself with a stack of notes on his desk. "I spoke with his wife this morning. I believe his funeral is scheduled for next Wednesday." He quickly wrote down the name and number of Robert's wife and handed her the note. "Here is her name and number should you want to call her. I can also send you the detailed information when I get it myself." He brought up his calendar and jotted down another note.

An obvious list maker. Shay watched him keep himself organized. His actions appeared normal, assured. No nervousness or strain evident.

She opened her inner vision and checked out his aura. Agitated. Nervous at her surprise visit. Disturbed at the unexpected workload now on his shoulders and a little angry at Robert for dying and even a bit angry at himself for feeling that way.

All normal. And this reassured her.

Finished, he looked over at her, "Do you want to see the progress on the renovations?"

She smiled. "That was going to be my next request."

The next hour was spent going over the plans, highlighting the progress and difficulties with upgrading the old school. By the time she took her leave, the kids were close to exiting their classrooms for the day. She picked up the pace. The place would be overrun with kids soon.

The dismissal bell rang as she reached her car.

While Shay drove home her mind was on the school. Everything had looked great, on the surface and beneath – not that she'd expected anything different. She didn't want to find something wrong. But so often, where money was involved, people's motivations became a little muddy.

However, so far, she'd found nothing suspicious. The headmaster's death appeared to be unrelated to the project – for that she was grateful.

She needed to check in with Stefan.

An hour later, she got him on the phone. "Now two people, both spearheading two charities that my foundation is heavily involved in, have died. Apparently of heart attacks. Both dropped dead, one at home and one at work. No signs of a

DALE MAYER

struggle. No damage at the office. Nothing missing. No foul play suspected."

"But...?" he prodded.

She shrugged and shifted her cell phone to the other ear. "I don't know. I just can't quite feel comfortable about these deaths. Yet I have no reason for this uneasiness." She sighed and stared out at the water outside her window. It was a strikingly beautiful summer day with blue sky and a warm breeze off the ocean. "There is a lot of money involved, but the money has been parceled out for big renovations, salaries, upgrades. It's not like anyone is going to be able to steal the money and walk away without someone knowing. And if money isn't the motivator, what could be?"

"You're presuming foul play in both cases?" he asked.

"Maybe and maybe not. I'd feel better if I could rule it out."

"And how would you do that?" Stefan said. "You're not the police and don't have access to the their personal financial records or know the status of their health or marital situations."

She frowned. "No, but I can ask Ronin to rule those out, I suppose."

"If it's bothering you to that extent, I think you should. Ronin understands. Not everything, but he's been a big help to me over the years. Remember to listen to your instincts though. If something feels wrong, then chances are it is wrong – somehow." He coughed slightly then cleared his throat. "Energy doesn't lie; people can only deceive until you look deeper and see the truth of the energy currents. Don't go in to confirm your expectations, go in looking to find what isn't fitting together."

"Right. I know that." So what was the matter? "I think what's underlying this is the series of odd and seemingly unrelated issues. Like what I saw in Bernice's eyes at the end." Shay paused to take stock. "The black circle on David. The deaths of not one, but two prominent people involved in two of my projects."

Stefan listened and then said, "Speaking of Bernice. Dr. Maddy contacted me this morning. I'd asked her to take a look at Bernice after I spoke to you. Remember I said there was something I couldn't figure out? Anyway, she found something odd in Bernice's energy.

"Odd?" Shay said sharply? "How odd. And did she know Bernice?" Then again Bernice, and Dr. Maddy knew many people so it wasn't surprising to hear.

"A friend expressed concern about Bernice's death so she took a quick look." His voice deepened. "According to her, there was a new hook into her root chakra and the energy drained very quickly. Maddy felt it was deliberate but didn't go so far as to say Bernice was murdered."

Shay gasped in shock. "Oh no."

"She also believes the person visited Bernice in the hospital, either in astral form or by hitchhiking on another person's energy."

Silence. Shay in the process of standing up, collapsed back down on her couch. "That is so not good."

"But we can't rush to the wrong conclusion. First Bernice. Then Cummings. Now the headmaster… One of those events would be fine, two maybe, but because there are too many unusual occurrences, you're afraid they're connected and that they signal a big negative. Not everything that is 'wrong' has to be very wrong. Maybe the victim took too much of his heart medication. An accident. Maybe your personal perspective was skewed by the loss of Bernice and that affected the vision you had. If you can explain away one or two of the occurrences then the others pale in significance."

His voice changed, detaching as if called away. "I need to go. How about we meet for dinner on Saturday, and we can discuss it further?"

She smiled wryly. "Except I actually have a date."

Silence. Then Stefan's amusement rippled through his warm voice as he said, "Wow. I'm delighted to hear it. May I…?"

"You probably already knew. It's Roman, Gerard's grandson and Ronin's brother. We've emailed off and on for years, but now... He just moved here from the East Coast to take over Gerard's business until the board gets through its big power struggle."

"Oh, yes." His voice lightened, warmed. "I do remember him." An odd silence filtered through the phone.

Shay sighed. "What do you know that I don't?"

"Uhm. Maybe you should take a closer look yourself."

She leaned forward. "I did, and came up against a huge wall. So I stopped." She wrinkled her nose and sighed. "Okay, give. What did I miss?"

This time there was no mistaking the laughter in Stefan's voice when he said, "He's safe, but I think you'd better take a closer look. He certainly is."

And Stefan rang off.

***

Knock, knock…

It's me again Shay. Too bad you didn't see how easy my last trick was. That was like pulling wings off a fly. An activity that had lost its appeal a long time ago. Time for change.

It was quite possible that the police would never connect the deaths to Shay. Maybe an anonymous phone call would tip them off? Send them in the right direction. Sad that they might need that.

Still, the three deaths all related to Lassiter Foundation. They should be able to make that much of a connection. To finger Shay, as a suspect, would only be a short hop away after that.

Experts said that revenge was often best served cold, but for her…after having waited a year…a little fire added to the flames would be even better.

Time to move up the agenda.

Chapter 7

Friday morning...

Shay stood at Bernice's gravesite, Pappy at her side. He held her arm tightly against him. Dressed in black to satisfy her grandfather's sense of proprietary, she kept her focus on him and his needs. He looked so frail, so broken.

Gerard didn't look much better. Roman stood at his side.

It was early yet, but already hundreds had arrived for the ceremony.

Long limousines and fancy cars lined the roadway, bringing even more people. The weather had cooperated, ushering sunshine and blue sky to the ceremony. Shay shifted the roses to the other hand.

Bernice had loved gold roses. The area was festooned with them, and a single gold rose lay on the ornate casket. Bernice, being who she was, had picked out her favorite funeral details long before her death. She'd also chosen to be buried in a gown that matched the roses.

The minister, another old friend of Bernice's, brought tears to everyone's eyes as he spoke of the blessing of having known her. She'd been such a major presence, a force, that no one could ignore her. No one wanted to. She'd been a light for them all.

For all her best intentions, Shay felt tears well up in her eyes. She was going to miss the old lady.

Pappy squeezed her arm. She smiled mistily at him and said, "It's a beautiful day for her."

He smiled gently and whispered, "Yes. She'd have loved it."

I am loving it, said Bernice irritably.

Shay started, her gaze widening in shock. She looked over at the familiar shimmering energy of her old friend. Bernice stood between the two old men, clear and crisp as if she were there in person – except she was present only in astral form.

You can see me, can't you? Bernice stared at Shay in delight. *How come you can, but no one else can?*

Shay rolled her eyes. Like she was going to be able to answer that question. She shrugged, motioning to the side. Then, slipping her arm free from Pappy, she excused herself for a moment as if to go and speak with someone else. And she was going to do just that, but her grandfather wouldn't understand how she'd converse with Bernice.

She walked behind the crowd and off to the side. Turning around, she came face to face with Bernice. "Oh!" Shay jumped back a step.

How come no one else can see me? Bernice complained. *I wanted to talk with Charles and Gerard again.*

"They can't see you," Shay murmured.

Obviously, Bernice snapped. *Why not though? I want them to see me, too.*

"How would I know? I doubt many people can." She hesitated, and then whispered, "Why are you here?"

I don't know. Bernice looked around. *I don't think I want to be here. But there's something...*

Shay waited for her to finish the sentence. When no more was forthcoming, she prompted, "But there's something...?"

Bernice looked worried – the edges of her form wavered, thinned, *I don't know. There's something that has to be done. But I don't know what. But something has to be stopped...*

"Something you need to say to someone, or something that you meant to do? Something you started and wanted to see finished?" Shay tried to prompt the other woman's memory.

Doubt and a tinge of fear crossed the older woman's features. *I don't remember. But there is a reason I came here. But what?*

"If we can figure out what that is and see it done, then you can leave."

Leaving would be good. I don't like this, she cried out. And disappeared.

"Wait—"

Shit. Bernice was gone.

Shay looked up to find Roman staring at her from only ten feet way.

Double shit.

***

Roman watched Shay as she stood off to the side. Though she was wearing all black, she was too dynamic to fade into the crowd. He had no idea why she'd separated herself from the group and he couldn't stop himself from checking out what she was doing.

Shay appeared to be talking to someone. Except she was alone.

Giving an excuse to his grandfather, he moved out of the crowd and slipped to the back. Shay was still several feet off to one side. He thought he heard her say something like 'wait!' but when he looked around, she was alone.

Had she been alone?

The crowd was huge. Perhaps what he heard was her talking to someone on her cell phone. That would explain the one-sided conversation. Was her cell phone in her hand?

Or was this something else altogether?

***

Shay managed a wry smile as Roman approached. Of course it *would* be him. *Had he heard her talking to Bernice?* Wouldn't that be perfect? First guy in a long time that interested her – okay more than interested her – and now he'd think she was nuts. Hell, she probably was. "Hi. How is Gerard doing?" she asked as he drew closer.

Roman glanced back at his grandfather who sat with his head resting on his hand. "It's a tough day for them."

"Yes. Pappy is heartbroken. He'd love to join Bernice, I think."

Roman smiled at her, the obvious warmth and the caring doing crazy things to her insides. "I'm sure grandfather has similar thoughts right now. Funerals are for the living to say good-bye. In this case, neither of the men want to do that. They'd rather have gone with her."

"What a trio."

"I have dinner reservations for Saturday." He tilted his head and studied her face. "I'll pick you up at 7:30 pm. If that works for you?"

She nodded, trying to keep her face neutral, masking the surprise and pleasure that lit her up from inside. She hadn't forgotten, but she had wondered if he might. She'd even thought he might want her to forget about it so he didn't have to follow through. *Apparently not.*

"That's perfect. Thank you. You know where I live, right?" And it was perfect when he nodded. Delight unfurled inside only to become tinged with nervousness about taking this step with this man of secrets. And the apprehension she felt should be enough to stop her from moving forward with Roman. If she'd learned her lesson, it would have. But...

"Shay! Roman!"

A call came from the center of the crowd. Gerard was waving at them to come closer. "It's Charles."

"Uh oh." Shay raced over to find Pappy, pale and shaky, leaning on Gerard's shoulder. He looked so frail right now. Her heart squeezed with fear. "Come on Pappy, time to go home."

"There's a reception at the Foundation Center, though," her grandfather protested.

"That's nice. After you've had a rest, we'll see about stopping in. But first, home," she added, firmly.

Grumbling the whole way, Pappy allowed Shay to lead him to her Audi. They said a quick good-bye to the other two men, then Shay drove her grandfather home.

Back at Pappy's high-end apartment, she helped him sit down on the dark brown leather couch before putting on a pot of tea. He needed a few minutes to collect himself and come to terms with Bernice's burial – and *that* she could allow him. She returned to the living room after the tea had steeped. She'd found some cookies in a cupboard and put a small tray together for him.

"How are you feeling now?" She placed the tray on the coffee table. Then poured him a cup of tea.

He took it from her and settled back into the cushions, sighing heavily. "Fine. I'm fine. It's just so hard to say good-bye."

"Isn't that the truth?" she muttered as she sat down beside him and gently patted his hand.

"You know, for a moment there..." He hesitated, then forced himself to say, "For a moment, I thought I saw her. Actually saw her standing off to the side, watching us all mourn her passing." He smiled in a self-deprecating way. "Silly, wasn't it?"

He took a sip of tea.

Shay stared at him. *How interesting.* And how wonderful. She'd have to remember to tell Bernice. She'd enjoy that.

"Bernice would have enjoyed her funeral," she said warmly. It was a lie but it's what Pappy needed to hear. "It was beautiful."

"She'd have enjoyed watching us all honor her," he said with a knowing smile. "For all her faults, I loved her."

"And the loving doesn't stop with death," Shay murmured. How many times had she seen love continue beyond? It made her feel good and it broke her heart at the same time. How hard for the person left behind... Sometimes they never loved again.

How horrible that would be. *Or would it?* This way at least they'd experienced love.

"No. Love doesn't just fade away. I wish she'd been there, today."

Not knowing the best thing to say, she murmured gently, "And maybe she was. She loved you. It makes sense she'd come back to say good-bye, if she could have."

Her grandfather peered at her hopefully. His rheumy eyes filled with tears. "Do you think so?"

She put her arms around his frail body and hugged him. Pappy's heart was huge. He'd been blessed to have loved twice. First he loved her grandmother, who passed on early when his two sons were still young, and then Bernice. Losing Bernice now had to be tough. And would have triggered the memories of his first loss, and the loss of both of his sons since then. There was only his grandchildren, her brother and herself, left. And her brother had lived in Europe for last few years.

Pappy had always been a mainstay in her life. But who'd been there for him?

Bernice.

And he was such a dear man. If he needed reassurance now, she could give him that.

She knew exactly what to say. With her voice full of love for this special, hurting man, she said, "Yes. I *know* she was."

Saturday morning

Roman leaned back from his laptop and rubbed his temple. "Grandfather, this is the third time you've mentioned my date with Shay tonight. Don't worry. I have reservations at the new seafood restaurant downtown for 8:00 pm. So everything is taken care of." The old man was driving him nuts. He'd called a dozen times since Roman drove him home from Bernice's funeral.

He understood it. Putting Bernice to rest had been a big step. Finding closure was important. Grieving would take longer. The need to connect with the living, the reaffirming of life, and the acceptance that his own death was right around the corner made his grandfather a mess right now. He'd seen it many times with victims of crime, back in his old life.

Not for first time, he rubbed the scar on his side.

"Good. Good. When is the reading of the will?" his grandfather asked.

Roman frowned, his hand stilling. "I'm not sure. Why?"

"It's just that Bernice was always very particular about her stuff. I want to make sure her estate is handled correctly."

Not their issue. Thankfully. Bernice had enough money to make even the most honorable consider ways and means of getting a piece of the pot. "That's out of our hands. The lawyers will be handling Bernice's fortune. I'm sure they have everything in order."

The grumbling on the other end of the phone made Roman smile. "Why don't you call Charles and meet him for lunch? He might know more."

Roman could almost see his grandfather perking up. "Do you think he's awake yet?"

Glancing at the clock, Roman grinned. It was almost 4:00 pm. "He was probably up from his nap an hour ago."

His grandfather hurriedly rang off.

Roman leaned back against his couch and stared across the room. He'd painted for hours last night, losing himself in his art. He'd finally put everything away around 4:00 am. No wonder he was tired. Then that's the way his art went these days. Nothing for days, then going into a painting so deeply he lost track of time.

He'd only gotten a few hours rest these last couple of nights. Add in the funeral... Dealing with Grandfather had been the hardest. Ronin would have been there, but he'd been called away on some big case.

That was life in law enforcement, the work tended to take the front seat. As Roman well knew. And of course the other issue frustrating him was about the subject matter of his painting.

His model. *Shay.*

He stood up and strode to his studio. His latest was a charcoal sketch with pastel highlights. A new look. A new technique. *Did it work?* Yeah, he actually thought it did. The charcoal played with the shadows and shapes. The paint highlighted the swells and curves.

He knew this body almost as well as his own. He needed to know Shay, the beautiful soul that called to his soul, just as well.

And damn, he wanted to check out her curves in person.

Chapter 8

Saturday evening...

The doorbell rang like five minutes too soon. Shay's hand slipped with the mascara wand, giving her a nice black streak across her cheek. *Shit.*

Why couldn't he be late tonight? She scrubbed her cheek clean and tried again. With that last bit in place, she stroked on her favorite lipstick and raced to the door. She'd been looking forward to tonight all week, even though she knew she shouldn't. But in this instance, logic and emotion didn't match. And right now, her heart was pounding with nervous excitement.

"Hi. Come on in. I'll be just a minute." Not giving him a chance to answer, she bolted back to her room and slipped on her heels and put in her long emerald earrings to match the skin-tight jade dress she'd bought on impulse, and had yet to wear. Feeling a little better, she did one quick turn in the mirror then walked back out to her living room.

Roman stood with casual grace in the middle of her living room, studying the painting on the wall. Her Stefan Kronos masterpiece. *Of course.* That painting never failed to attract attention.

"Do you like it?"

His gaze switched from the painting, locking on to her so suddenly it left her momentarily stunned. And feeling like an idiot.

Wearing a rueful smile, she apologized, "Sorry, I've been running behind all day.

"It's beautiful." His gaze shifted, a long, slow sweep down and then back up. So hot so sensual she could feel his gaze as a physical stroke. Viscerally. She swallowed and wondered at the intense look on his face. "Roman, are you all right?"

His gaze deepened and he smiled. *Oh God.* That heart-stoppingly slow movement had her gaze locking onto that mouth as the corners quirked. She swallowed.

"I'm more than all right." His head tilted to the side. "You look divine."

She flushed at the blatant appreciation in those dark blue eyes, as well as his words. "Thanks, but I meant the painting."

His smile deepened. "I know. It's a Stefan Kronos piece, isn't it?"

Interesting. Not many people recognized Stefan's work. "It is. I'm surprised you know it," she said lightly, snagging her shawl from the back of the couch. She threw it around her shoulders and smiled at him. Happy to be back into her coolly professional space, she said, "Shall we?"

He opened the door for Shay and waited in the hallway while she locked it behind her. "I own one of his works and have seen several of his paintings at a friend's house," he said.

She gazed at him in surprise. "Really?"

"He's incredibly talented."

"That he is," she murmured. He held the elevator door for her and pushed the button to descend to the lobby. She watched him. Everything she'd seen of him spoke of grace and strength and done with an economy of movement. He didn't fidget, glance around or hesitate. He seemed so centered. When he turned that gaze on her, like he often did without warning, it was to pin her. As if she had his focus, every tiny speck of it, during the time he stared at her. That was as unnerving as it was delightful.

In today's world, how often did one have someone's total attention? Usually cell phones went off, other people interrupted, or distractions continually interfered. She had no way to evade his gaze, and she had no wish to.

Another novel experience.

The new restaurant was a pleasant surprise. She'd planned to take Pappy for a special meal there when it opened. She gazed around, wondering at the sleight of hand that placed them at a private table for two on the rooftop under the stars. The setting was delightful.

"I assume from your expression that this is fine," he said, warm amusement lacing his voice. He held out the chair for her. Waited for her to take her seat.

"Absolutely." She smiled at him, appreciating the way that the material of his suit snugged up against his shoulders as he took his seat.

Damn. If she were in the market for an affair, this guy would definitely get top billing. Right now, though, she was guy shy, and that was enough to keep her hormones in check...

Liar. Her hormones were anything but in check. And this guy was anything but safe. Danger rippled behind those eyes. And promise. So much damn promise.

The wine steward approached, breaking her gaze. She was grateful for the distraction and stared down at the city laid out below her.

When they were alone again, she asked the one question that had kept her guessing all week. "What did Bernice say to you about me?"

He smiled. But this time it was polished, the cool, businesslike smile of a pro. She eyed him suspiciously. "She said you were perfect for me. And that you managed the Lassiter Foundation almost as well as she managed the Folgrent Foundation."

Shay gasped, then laughed. "*Almost?* How typical of Bernice."

He narrowed his gaze at her. "You didn't like her?"

"You've already asked me that." She settled back into her seat, crossing her arms over her chest. "My answer is the same. I really respected her. I even loved her, as one loves an old family friend, but I didn't appreciate how she kept Pappy on a string."

"But you understand it?"

She gave a half laugh. "I didn't say that."

"No, but it's there, hidden in your words."

"After having asked her why she'd never made a decision between the two, then yes, I guess I do. That doesn't mean I have to like it."

He winced. "I do feel for Grandfather. At the same time, he made the choice to stay on the string."

Amusement rippled through her. This man would never let himself be strung along like their respective grandparents. "Bernice said she loved them both too much to hurt the other by picking one."

His gaze widened. Then he gave a short laugh. "If that isn't Bernice all over."

***

Knock, knock…

It's me again, Shay. Damn I wish you could hear me. I could tell you how foolish you are. You think you can close your doors and lock yourself deep inside. That's definitely not going to happen. I don't need open locks to give me access.

I'm like you – talented.

And you'd hate it if you knew.

I know. You'll see. I know all about what you did.

It wasn't fair.

But then you crossed the line.

That's all right. I've crossed that same line many times. In fact, I've crossed bigger and more dangerous lines. But after a few times, it doesn't matter anymore. There's no remorse. No sadness. Nothing. Just an empty space that you can fill however you'd like to fill it. It's exciting in its own way. It's different. Being alone in this vast space with the power to see inside people. To see their real motivations. That's what you pride yourself on, isn't it?

You're happy to sit inside your ivory tower and feel safe. But you're not safe. See, there's more than one type of danger.

And you'll never be safe.

Not from me.

***

Late Saturday night...

Shay walked to her apartment building, aware of the strong man at her side. "I really enjoyed dinner," she murmured, opening the conversation. She didn't want him to come inside. Didn't want to have to invite him in for a nightcap. But knew she would anyway. She couldn't help it. He did things to her insides, lovely hot things. Things she wasn't ready for intellectually. Things she didn't want to face. Not tonight. Maybe not this year. Or this lifetime.

Despite all that, she wanted to be with this man. And she had wanted that for a long time.

The doorman stepped out to open the glass door for her.

"Good evening, Thomas. I hope you're having a quiet evening."

He beamed as he always did when she spoke to him. "I'm having a wonderfully peaceful evening. Thank you for asking."

"Good." Roman walked to the elevator and hit the up button. Shay raised an eyebrow at Roman.

"I'll see you to your door."

She nodded gracefully. "Good night, Thomas."

"Have a good one, Miss."

She didn't need to look around to know Thomas watched their progress with a curious eye. She hadn't brought home a date in a long time.

Once inside the elevator she said, "You didn't need to see me to my door. Thomas has always looked out for me."

"I don't take a lady out for an evening and not return her home."

Simple, clean, and yet his words seemed...a bit cool. Was he upset? She peeked through her lashes at him.

Their relaxed relationship had definitely tightened, changed in the last few seconds. It had been way too long since her last date. This was awkward. She hated awkward.

"Good to know."

The elevator slowed to a stop. He held the door open for her. She walked to her apartment, searching in her bag for her keys.

Finally. She pulled them out and went to slip the key into the lock. That was when she realized the door was ajar. And froze.

"What's the matter?"

She took a deep breath. "My door is already unlocked."

***

Roman hated Shay's nervous fumbling, and especially hated that her nervousness intensified the higher the elevator rose. He didn't think she was aware of it. She'd relaxed over dinner, her wariness easing before finally disappearing altogether. He'd loved watching her settle and open up.

So what made her so nervous? He'd thought they'd enjoyed dinner and that they were past the initial nervous stage. Bernice had shared a lot about her favorite goddaughter, as she called Shay. She'd told him, 'She's been hurt. Badly. Now she is wary. You'll have to work hard. But she's worth it.'

At the time, he hadn't been too worried. He'd been communicating with Shay daily and knew her, but that was before he moved back to Portland. From the instant he'd seen the first series of 'Shay' photos, he'd been interested. Time and online dialogue and painting had strengthened the bond. Whether she knew it or not. But at this moment in time they were barely friends – certainly not looking like lovers.

Roman knew he really wanted to be lovers. And so much more.

She'd been a delight all evening, full of laughter and great conversation and passion that simmered under the surface – until they got out of the car and she realized he wasn't just going to give her a casual 'good night' and walk away.

Hell, he didn't want to walk away at all.

Now, as she pulled her keys out of her purse and fitted them to the door, he realized her composure was firmly back in place – like a protective coating, keeping the world at a safe distance.

Shay's composure disappeared as she stared at her front door.

"What do you mean?" he questioned cautiously. "Did you leave it unlocked?"

Her beautiful chocolate eyes stared up at him, confusion clouding them. "I locked it before we left, didn't I?"

He had to stop and think. "You went to lock it."

"But did I?" She sighed. "Just another glitch… Goes along with my day. Sorry. I'm trying to avoid being paranoid these days."

Something about her tone of voice had him gazing at her intently. "Do you have a reason to be paranoid?"

Something moved in the back of her gaze. His senses sharpened. He narrowed his eyes at her. "Shay?"

"No, of course not." She laughed, but it sounded forced. "Nothing more than being a single female who lives alone." She pushed her door open and walked inside.

He followed her and reached out to flick on the lights. Bright light filled the living room and entranceway as she strode further into the room, her back stiff, her head turning from side to side. "Everything appears normal."

"I'll search the place to make sure."

She gave a sigh of relief. "Thank you."

If there was a little too much nervousness in her voice, he ignored it. She did live alone, and if someone had broken in, that was nothing to fool around with. He closed the front door and opened the hall closet. He searched through the long coats.

"Nothing here." Systematically, he moved through the classy apartment and checked cupboards and corners. He couldn't help but admire the queen-sized bed and its thick duvet dressed in chocolate and gold. There was something especially compelling about the colors and the intimate setting. And he approved, imagined her bedding as a perfect contrast to her chestnut hair and smooth creamy skin.

Ignoring his clamoring body and the visions in his head, he checked under the bed and opened up the double closets. *Nothing.* He closed the last closet and turned to face her. "The apartment is empty."

She nodded. "Thank you."

He looked at her closer. "Shay, are you going to be okay?"

She collected herself and smiled up at him. "I am. Sorry. Thank you so much for checking. I'm sure it's nothing." Crossing her arms she walked to the front door and opened it for him.

No goodnight kiss or hug. Nothing.

An unmistakable message.

Having made sure the place was safe, he walked over and smiled. "Sleep well."

He walked out of her apartment and into the night.

Downstairs, he stopped beside Thomas. "Did Shay have any visitors tonight? When we got to her door, she found it unlocked."

Thomas's eyebrows shot up. "Oh dear. There's been no one in or out that doesn't belong."

"We'll assume then that she forgot to lock up on our way out. Thanks."

Roman walked to his car, deep in thought. He hated leaving her alone. Especially after finding the door unlocked. He'd wanted to stay and watch over her. But she wouldn't have welcomed his presence. Though he'd done a thorough search of her place, and was confident no one lurked in there, something had unnerved him. Something *had* felt off.

But what?

✳✳✳

Shay closed her door behind Roman and locked it. She turned back and leaned against the closed door and studied her living room. It *looked* normal.

It didn't *feel* normal.

Then she dropped her barriers to look more closely. Energy filled the room. Hers. Roman's. Yes, even Stefan's soothing energy hovered. He'd obviously checked in on her earlier.

And so had someone else…

She blinked. And checked again. Definitely traces of another presence.

Then she identified it.

Recognized something so familiar it scared the crap out of her.

Her breath caught in the back of her throat, choking off the cry ready to spring forth. *Oh God. No.* That wasn't possible. There's no way this energy could be here. Absolutely, no way. *He* was dead.

Shivers raced down her spine and her teeth started chattering. She crossed her arms across her chest. Nothing helped. Stepping forward, she snatched up her shawl from where she'd dropped it on the couch and wrapped it tightly around her.

This is not possible. Stefan, please tell me this isn't happening, she whispered. There was no comforting answer in her mind. Stefan wasn't responding.

Stefan!

Jesus. What? Can't a guy get any sleep around her, he grumbled. *What the hell is wrong?*

Because it would save time and explanation, she opened her mind so he could see her thoughts, feelings and impressions through their telepathic link.

Tell me this isn't his energy. Tell me he's dead and forever gone. Please.

Him? Stefan's voice shifted as he shook off the sleep from his mind. *No, it's not possible. It can't be Darren.*

Are you sure? My door was unlocked when I came home tonight. And it shouldn't have been.

That doesn't mean it was him.

No, but the energy was so similar to his – as if he's changed form slightly. She gave a strangled laugh, tears starting to course down her cheeks. *And yes, I know how unbelievable that sounds. Please tell me that he's dead and gone.*

Shay, he's dead. I killed him. You killed him. He can't ever hurt you again.

She sniffled. *Are you sure?*

Positive.

Chapter 9

Sunday morning...

When Shay opened her eyes the next morning, recognized her bedroom and breathed in the soothing morning light, a sense of relief washed through her. It was finally morning. And her apartment felt...normal.

It had taken an hour last night, with Stefan`s help, to cleanse and secure her apartment. She still had no idea what had gone on or who her intruder was. But she'd know that energy again if she ever saw it. The cleansing process had her simply walking around and ushering out the old energy – and refilling the space with warm, loving, protective energy.

And it appeared to have worked. She had slept.

Dragging her sorry ass out of bed, Shay made her way to a hot shower. Something needed to energize her. It felt like sandpaper had been rubbed over her insides, leaving her raw – edgy. She had a crappy day ahead to go along with the night.

Another funeral. And burial at the same cemetery. This time for David Cummings. She didn't have to go, but knew she should. Besides, her consciousness prodded at her to check it out. To make sure all was well.

She stumbled through getting dressed and ate a muffin for her breakfast then headed out the door with a few minutes to spare. For a Sunday morning, there was a surprising amount of traffic. She drove up the winding road to the cemetery and parked. Walking swiftly, her head bowed against the gray skies, she joined the small, private group for the ceremony at the gravesite. David's preference as she understood it.

Staying unobtrusively in the background, she tried to look around at the other mourners. She only recognized one or two of the people, David's office staff. That wasn't unexpected. His family was at the left and a row of strangers mingled. Several appeared to be crying – also not unexpected. She looked at their energy as they stood in their own quiet spaces. Most were contained and solemn. Holding tight, their energy snug against their bodies. She'd expect that in this setting. She took a casual look to the others at her side. Again, the energies were calm, slow and contained.

No surprises here.

Several other people had joined the throng, coming up behind her. She'd stepped around, letting them come closer to the gravesite and taking her place behind them. Standing behind them gave her a better view of all assembled. Still nothing explained her intuition's insistence that had compelled her to come here or the overwhelming need to check out the energy of those around her. A thin layer of energy on the coffin remained, most likely from the workers who'd handled it.

She shifted her position for a different angle. And still nothing. Shrugging inside, she waited until the eulogy was over before slowly approaching the widow.

"I'm so sorry for your loss," she murmured gently to the weeping woman. "I worked with David for several years. He was a good man."

The widow smiled through her tears. "Thank you. I will miss him."

As Shay walked back to her car, she pondered the issue. There'd been a definite sense of loss and grief from the widow and the sister-in-law. There'd been an odd melding of their energies, but that wasn't necessarily anything important, just strange. But it had a caring to it. She hadn't seen anything that spoke of hatred, relief, or that proclaimed any ill intention – and that had been good. If there'd been foul play suggested in their energies she'd have to say something to Ronin....

Still, there'd been nothing there.

Back at her car she gave all the people a final examination as they walked slowly away from the service. Now that it was over, there was no reason for the individuals to keep quiet. At least not verbally. Their energies eased outward. One mentally sniped at another attendee's lack of decorum, thinking she was wearing a low-cut dress more appropriate for a night on the town than a funeral. Another was worried about the time away from his job and resenting that he'd have to stay later that day to make up for lost time. Another marveled at the beauty and simplicity of the grounds thinking it a beautiful spot to rest for all eternity. Shay smiled to herself – the human spirit revitalized itself very quickly. Once the sense of propriety was observed, everyone loosened up. And became their so-normal selves.

Another woman fretted about the traffic and still another was on her way to meet a secret lover, hoping her husband at her side would pick up the dry cleaning on his way to coach soccer. Only, the husband was meeting someone himself.

Shay turned back to her car and got in. So much humanity at the surface in a single gathering. For all their private lives and secretive thoughts, no one appeared to harbor any visible ill will toward the deceased.

She got in her car to head home.

✳✳✳

Roman put the phone back in his pocket for at least the dozenth time that morning. Only now he stood outside her apartment. "Where the hell are you, Shay?"

He'd tried both her cell phone and her home phone. No answer.

He should never have left her alone last night. Not after the unlocked door. All sorts of horrible images had filled his mind since. He'd long given up and had raced to her apartment to check it out for himself. And got no answer. There was a different doorman at the front entrance this time, and he hadn't been able to confirm if Shay had left.

All Roman could do was keep trying. He pulled out his phone and watched the time tick off. Then he hit redial.

"Hello?"

Frustrated relief washed through him, followed by quick, sharp anger. "Damn it, where the hell are you?"

There was a surprised silence at the other end.

Shit. He groaned. "Sorry. I didn't mean that quite the way it sounded, but I've been trying to get a hold of you for several hours now. After last night, when you didn't answer, I started to get very worried."

"I'm fine," she said coolly. "I was at another funeral. One of the people my foundation works with had a heart attack last week."

He ran his fingers through his hair. "Sorry again. That's a tough one. Two funerals in three days isn't fun."

"No, it isn't." She sighed. "And I have another one next week. Same thing."

"Same thing?" His voice sharpened unintentionally. "That's not good."

Her voice trembled as it crept through the phone. "No, it isn't."

"Does all this have anything to do with your apartment being unlocked last night?" An odd silence raised the hairs on the back of his neck. "Shay? Are you in danger?"

"No. No, not at all," she said quickly. "Two men had heart attacks. They ran projects my foundation funded. They were associates. There's no danger."

"Good." Relief was slow to come but when it did, it washed through him in a rush. He'd been so worried. "Good to know. You scared me."

"Sorry. I just turned on my phone. I haven't had a chance to check my messages yet."

"Well most of them will be from me."

"Then I won't need to listen to them, will I?" Her voice turned brusque, professional.

He hated that. As if she was trying to push him back. "Unless you had something specific you were calling about...?"

"I initially called to make sure you were okay after last night. Then when I couldn't get a hold of you, I started to panic. I've actually been standing outside your apartment, wondering if I should break in or not." He laughed, a short sound that made him wince as he heard it. "I was sure you'd been hurt. I've been kicking myself for not staying last night." He ran his fingers through his hair. "I guess I overreacted."

"It's all right. I'm glad you called to check on me." She paused, adding humorously, "At least if I do get murdered, it's nice to know that my body would eventually be found."

"That's not funny."

"I wasn't joking," she said, a bitter tone to her words.

He didn't know what to say to that. He didn't like her words or her tone. But how much was she not telling him? "Where are you?"

"Sitting in my car at the cemetery about to go home to rest."

"You didn't sleep last night?" He relaxed, knowing she was okay now, and happy to be talking to her. He wanted to see her. Take her out of her odd mood. Maybe coax her to share a little more. "Let's go to lunch."

Silence.

"Is that a yes?" he asked carefully. "I thought maybe the Palace Restaurant. They have a beautiful coffee bar and lunch buffet. Are you sure I can't tempt you with some food?"

"I'm tired," she said. "I wouldn't be good company."

"I'm not looking for good company." And he wasn't. He was only just beginning to realize what he was looking for. "I'm looking to spend an hour, stress free, with you. Like we did last night before we reached your place," he coaxed. "We had a wonderful evening, didn't we?"

She went quiet.

***

Should she go? Hell, no. *But did she want to?* Hell, yes.

"I'd like to meet with you again," he said promptly. "Lunch. In twenty minutes at the Palace."

And he hung up.

Shay stared down at the phone in her hand. *What the hell. What if I don't want to meet you, Roman?* Then it was too late to decline, because she'd let herself get caught up in the idea. She should have turned him down right at the beginning. Instead she'd let him assume she'd be there.

She wanted to be there. But it wasn't like she was put together for a luncheon date. She looked down at her black slacks and matching black cotton sweater. To hell with it. If he was so hot to meet her, then he could meet her as she was.

She turned on the engine and pulled out of the parking lot.

Shay?

Damn. Shay was forced to pull onto the shoulder of the road. *Stefan? What's up?*

I was going to ask you that. There's been a lot of odd energy coming off you for the last ten minutes.

She groaned. *That's one way to put it.* Quickly she explained her morning. *So I'm heading over there for lunch.*

Good. It will be good for you.

Says you.

Yes, says me. It's your time for love.

And he left, leaving her mind empty and gasping. Speaking aloud to the empty car, she said, "Damn it, Stefan. That's not fair. If you know something, tell me."

Warm laughter filled her mind.

But he stayed silent.

Irritated, yet feeling better for some odd reason, she pulled back into traffic and headed to the restaurant. *Was Stefan right? Was Roman her life partner? If so, wouldn't she know?* Of course not, not with that damn wall of his...and her luck.

Roman was standing outside the restaurant, talking on the phone, when she pulled up. He finished his call and put his phone away once he caught sight of her.

"I was afraid you weren't coming."

"A friend called. I needed to speak with him for a few minutes."

Roman smiled. "Good. Glad you're here. I have a table waiting for us in the conservatory."

She rolled her eyes at him – of course he got one of the nicest tables in the place. "Who did you have to bribe to get that table?"

He laughed. "No one. A couple was getting ready to leave when I walked in."

She didn't believe him but, what the hell, she'd enjoy a quiet lunch.

As they walked toward the door of the restaurant, Roman asked, "How was the funeral?"

She winced. "Personally, I hate funerals. Don't intend to have one after I'm gone and don't like attending them when friends and family die."

"Many people don't like them, but usually it's because of their sense of loss." He opened the front door of the restaurant for her. "Helps them to find closure."

"Not in my case," she said shortly. "I don't need them, like them, or want them."

"And you see too many people who do?"

She shot him a narrow look under her lashes. *How did he mean that?* It seemed like she was always looking for hidden meanings in everything he said. She hated that. But with her abilities, she found it instinctive to be self-protecting now.

"I've seen too many people put into the ground to find any solace in a funeral," Shay said.

The hostess motioned for them to follow.

He placed his hand on the small of her back and nudged her forward. He tilted his head toward her. "Interesting perception."

She laughed. "Not really. What about you? Are you a fan of funerals?"

He shrugged. "I see them as a necessary stage for the living and the dead."

She repeated his words. "Interesting. And what is your opinion of life after death?"

He looked startled. After studying her for a moment to make sure she was serious, he said, "I don't know that I have one. I guess I believe there is more out there than we know, but as I have no personal experience either way, I'm neutral on the issue."

It could be worse. At least he hadn't jumped down her throat or interrogated her for hours. That was good. They took their seats and ordered coffee.

"You do have an opinion, I presume?" He quirked a brow and studied her.

The curiosity in his voice made her smile. "Maybe. But you'll think I'm crazy."

"Not at all, but now I am curious."

"I thought I saw Bernice in her room that day she died. Then again at her funeral." She hadn't meant to say anything about that.

He sat back, one eyebrow raised. "Interesting."

She leaned back and stared at him. "You say that a lot?"

A lopsided grin slid out. And damn if that smile didn't just burrow a little deeper into her psyche and make itself at home. Funny how attractive acceptance was.

And how unexpected.

"Do you see ghosts often?" His question, so casual and so calm, made her study him over her coffee mug.

She leaned forward and whispered, "You do realize how ridiculous that question is?"

"Is it? Bernice mentioned that she thought you had some weird things going on along that line."

"Bernice did? *Really?*"

He nodded.

Shay laughed. "That old sneak. Maybe she was trying to warn you away from me. Make me out to be a nutcase."

He chuckled warmly. "No, not Bernice. She loved you."

"Yes, she did." Shay's eyes got a little misty. "I miss her."

"Does that mean she won't be staying around and haunting you?"

"I wish. But that would mean she hasn't crossed over the way she should have. I wouldn't wish that fate on her."

There was an odd silence. She glanced up from her plate to find him studying her. "You're serious, aren't you?" His smile deepened. "Of course I shouldn't be too surprised. Ronin has also dropped a few tidbits about you over the last year or two."

Shay put her cup down to give him her full attention.

"And he's worked with Stefan several times." Roman watched for a response.

"Stefan is a wonderful artist." Shay smirked.

"And a skilled psychic." Roman sat back slightly as if to put some distance between them. "Apparently."

She snorted. "You said you were open to it."

"Not quite," he corrected. "I said I had no opinion either way."

She waved her fork in the air. "Splitting hairs."

"I'm open-minded about many things I'd never consider a few years back. I have a friend who is a highly acclaimed healer." He sounded like he wanted to believe her.

"Healing is good." And it was. If Roman could be open on that score, maybe he could be open to more? "Who is it?"

"Her name is Dr. Maddy from The Haven," he said.

Shay laughed in delight. "I know Dr. Maddy. She's a good friend of Stefan's. I'd like to know her better, but we're all so busy."

"If it makes you feel any better, after seeing what Dr. Maddy can do, I've had to re-examine a lot of the things I thought I knew. Am I clear on them? No. Am I open? Yes." He sighed. "How well do you know Stefan?" His deep gaze pinned her in place.

A little more at ease, she said, "Well. He's a good friend. Why?"

He shrugged, dropping his gaze. "No reason. I've heard a lot about him from Dr. Maddy."

"Ah." Shay smiled. "They are good friends. And I know Stefan helps her with her special project. She's an incredibly strong psychic."

"*Psychic?*" He looked uncomfortable again.

"That word bugs you, doesn't it?"

With a sheepish grin he admitted, "I prefer to think of Dr. Maddy as a healer."

"She is, but she's also an incredibly powerful psychic and that helps with her healing work."

***

Tabitha Stoddard stacked up the files and carried them into her office at the animal sanctuary. She had a lot of catching up to do. There was never enough time to take care of things around here. She needed another assistant to just clear off the backlog. As she stared around at her small, overstuffed office, she realized she could really use a full time secretary too. Still, all was good. The new anesthesiology table had been ordered, and the plans approved on the new cat enclosure. Given the trouble they'd had getting this far, she should be delighted.

And she was. Now if only the rest of this work would clear up easily, she could get back on track.

"Tabitha!"

She looked out the window to Sue, one of the younger staff members who waved to get her attention. She opened the window. "What's up?"

"We need a signature." Sue motioned toward a large flat-deck truck backing up to the shed with a load of pet food. "Can you come?"

Right. She'd forgotten about that delivery.

If it wasn't one thing, it was twenty.

She skirted her desk and walked outside into the morning sunshine. She smiled at the gorgeous day. They really did live in God's country.

Sue walked over, a big smile on her face.

Tabitha matched it, opened her mouth to speak, and stopped.

A blast of energy shot from Sue's body at the same time something clamped down on Tabitha's heart and squeezed tight. She groaned. Then gasped. For air, for relief, for breath.

Something was terribly wrong. She'd heard about the couple of deaths connected to Shay's foundation projects, but she hadn't thought that she was in danger. And not from Sue, surely? She'd known her forever. No, the energy felt different than Sue's. Similar but not...quite...the same – and was oh so painful.

Stupid.

"Tabitha? Are you all right? *Tabitha?*"

"Shay. Contact Shay," Tabitha whispered. She had a good idea what this was. But she didn't know how or who caused it. She did the only thing she could think of doing. She sent out a psychic call for help, and she shut down, locking herself inside.

111

Chapter 10

Sunday afternoon...

Shay waited for Roman to pay the check. She walked out into the sunshine, wanting nothing more than to go home and think about the mess her life was in. *Sigh.*

Shay?

Stefan, what's up? Instinctively she looked around but knew Stefan couldn't be beside her.

It's Tabitha.

What? Shay stepped to the side of the sidewalk beside a large flower garden. *What happened?*

She's been attacked. Psychically. She's alive. She shut her system down. I'm at the hospital now.

Shit.

Don't come. You can't help. But you need to find out how these people are being targeted. If Tabitha wakes up, she might be able to shed some light on what's happening. I've called Ronin. He needs information from you.

"On it."

"On what?" Roman stood at her side, looking at her curiously. "What's going on?"

She ran her fingers through her hair, answering even as her cell phone rang. "A friend, someone associated with my foundation has been attacked."

"What?" Roman stared at her in shock.

She held up her ringing phone. Then spoke into it. "Hello, Ronin. I guess you never get a day off, huh?"

His businesslike voice was sharp and rushed. "There is no day off for crime fighters."

Her stomach revolted as she realized why he was calling. "Stefan told me."

"About Tabitha Stoddard at Exotic Landscape?"

"Yes." Shay groaned. "She's a friend. A good one. I just saw her the other day. We were discussing the arrival of several new animals from a Canadian zoo. She applied to the Foundation for funding because she needed to build new enclosures and was hoping to expand the hospital facilities, including the purchase of a larger anesthetic table."

"How was she when you spoke to her?"

"Wonderful as always." Shay smiled through the tears gathering in the corner of her eyes. She felt overwhelmed, and appreciated the warmth of Roman's comforting arm as it slid around her shoulder. "Tabitha is...a very caring person. I know she always had the animals foremost in her mind when she made every request."

"And did you approve the money?"

"Yes. Definitely. And yes, she knew I'd approve the money. We had a great working relationship."

"This case is yet another connection to you and your foundation."

Her stomach roiled at the thought of these three people coming to an early end because of her. That Bernice could be another victim didn't bear thinking about. At least Tabatha was alive. She cleared her throat as the tears clogged her voice. "I didn't hurt them, if that's what you're suggesting. I called you about David Cumming's case because I just didn't feel good about sending the money if someone was killing to get it."

She stared blindly up at Roman. He shook his head and tightened his arm around her shoulders, tucking her up close. "Shh," he whispered against her hair.

"No. I'm not suggesting that at all," Ronin rushed to say, his voice booming above his brother's caring whisper. "Have you sent the money yet?"

"No. And I don't plan to until this is all settled." There's no way she could. "I don't want the media to connect the dots between these deaths and my projects. It would be a feeding frenzy if they were to find out."

"Yet, they are likely to anyway." His voice turned crisp. "I need access to your files for these cases."

Of course he would. "No problem. Can you come to the office on Monday, or do you want to meet me this afternoon?"

"Given that we have two deaths already and another person close to it, now would be best."

She sighed. Ronin was right. They couldn't afford to waste any more time. "I'll meet you at my office in say...half an hour?" Roman slid his hand down her back, stroking away some of the tension. She glanced up at him. He nodded and she felt better already. Not so alone.

"Sounds good."

Not to her it didn't. But she had no choice.

Someone was killing people she knew. *Because of her?* Were they targeting her, in a way?

She couldn't help wonder how many more people would die before this asshole was caught.

✳✳✳

The office was empty and cold when she walked in with Roman at her side. And it felt even colder as she realized something really wrong could be happening. The dark wooden furniture and rich burgundy carpet now looked cold and austere instead of warm and welcoming. Her family's offices were two floors up and housed the various family holdings, although her brother resided in Europe and ran the business mostly from there with Pappy heading up the North American holdings. She had the only family office on this floor.

She kind of liked the independent feel of that. Walking to the side counter, she put on a small pot of coffee. Turning, she stared around the room with new eyes. She'd always viewed this office as a sanctuary. A business sanctuary.

She'd inherited business responsibilities almost ten years ago, when she turned twenty-one, in fact. Pappy had taken her out for dinner and had presented her with the papers as a gift.

Not necessarily a welcome gift, but he'd felt she was the right person to handle this aspect of the family money. The Foundation's money.

She hadn't been so sure. She'd worried about her ability to do the right thing. She'd made a lot of mistakes at the outset. Bernice had helped her and become Shay's mentor. A friend.

Her brother, ten years her senior had been a big help, but too busy for the day-to-day problems she encountered.

She enjoyed her job and all her responsibilities but especially receiving and dealing with the applications for financial help. The process gave her a clearer understanding of what all kinds of people were trying to do and why. Even better, she loved handing out money to those that fit the parameters of the Foundation's funding program.

It had been a joy to see the money go to so many good causes and playing a part to make that happen helped her feel closer to her deceased parents in some way. She hoped they would approve of her choices. There were so many other projects as well, and they were all close to her heart. She stayed in contact with the people and monitored the projects. Often knew what was to come next for them before they understood it themselves.

"We beat my brother here." Roman grinned as if he competed regularly with his brother.

She smiled at the quiet man at her side. She'd never seen the two men in the same room. Should be interesting. "Looks like it." She walked over to unlock the wall of files behind Jordan's desk.

"Good. I want to see your system. I can run some diagnostics and see if someone has hacked into your computer system. If they haven't, and the firewalls are secure, that would narrow the pool of suspects down to only a few people that would know about your projects."

She paused and turned to face him, hope firing inside. "Can you do that?"

"It's what I do." He nodded in the direction of her office. "Let me see."

Perfect. She couldn't get to her computer fast enough. He was an Internet security specialist, and an ex-cop, and damn she was glad to have his help. The Foundation's files should be secure, but she didn't know if their security had been updated regularly to combat today's hackers. In theory, if someone wanted in, it probably wouldn't be that hard to get there. "If someone did hack in, can you find out who?"

"Maybe." He sat down and started clicking away. A look of total concentration took over his hard features. For a moment there, she could see the internal focus, the cop inside the man, the hunter pursuing his prey. Grateful not to be his target, she headed back to the main office. At the doorway, she paused and looked back. "There are two other computers out here, if that makes a difference."

His nod acknowledged her words but nothing more. Shrugging, she turned back to the outer office.

As she'd noticed when they entered, the office had a different look. A colder look. No longer bright and open but rather shadowy and dark. Could someone have been trying to get the Foundation's money? Surely there was an easier way. Like sending in an application. Her gaze went to the large filing cabinet behind Jordan's desk. She didn't keep the unaccepted applications in this office but she knew they were kept for a few years, and then discarded. The ones that were accepted went into the system and were followed up on a regular basis. These files were now mostly electronic.

From Bernice, she'd learned to keep her finger on the pulse of the Foundation's money. As she thought about it, she saw that Bernice had had a bigger influence on her life than she'd realized.

Bernice had mentored Shay and spent time reassuring her until Shay had grown into the job.

They'd often shared stories about the applications. They'd discussed the duplicates – the ones that applied to both foundations for help and the ones that didn't fit one organization but deserved consideration from the other. In fact, they had often sent files back and forth before decisions were made about funding. As Shay stared around the empty room, she wondered if there was another connection between the two foundations, one she hadn't recognized.

Had Bernice died because of that connection? God, she hoped not.

It was much easier to think that Bernice had been an old lady who'd enjoyed life to the max and had died of natural causes.

But after the black energy Dr. Maddy had seen on Bernice, Shay was no longer sure. And then she remembered Bernice's strange words at her funeral...

Could this perp be someone who'd been refused money? Someone angry enough to do something about it? That almost made sense.

A voice startled her.

"Can I come in?" Ronin stood in the doorway she'd forgotten to close. She started. The resemblance to his twin was uncanny. They weren't identical, but they were dynamite males. And very different in some essential way too.

Ronin was just as good looking, but only Roman made her heart beat faster.

"Sorry, please come in." She motioned to the coffee behind her. "Can I offer you a cup?"

"Sure." He loosened his tie and accepted the cup from her. "Are your files digital?"

"Both digital and print. We keep digital backups of most things, but all the applications arrive in paper for reviewing." She motioned to the wall behind him. "Those are all the active projects."

He sighed. "So if someone is targeting your projects, they have a lot of choices."

Ronin frowned. "I'll need all the personnel files for anyone who has access to these files – digital and paper. Then again, unless you've set up a foolproof system, any decent hacker would be able to get into your into your files without too much trouble. I'll talk to Roman about that."

She laughed. "He's in my office, on my computer, as we speak."

"So big brother finally made his move, huh?" Ronin grinned mischievously as he disappeared into her office.

"I heard that." Roman's deep voice rumbled toward Shay.

Heat rolled up her neck like a tsunami on an unsuspecting shore. She took a moment to breathe deeply and shoved the embarrassment down again before joining them. She leaned against the doorway and watched the two dynamos. Both tall and lean, both dark haired with a slight curl. Both had seen a lot of the world's unpleasantness and it showed in their lean, hard jaws.

As she watched them, something else hit her. "I think it's possible that Bernice's death could be related to the other three."

Both men locked gazes on her. She took a deep breath and explained what she knew about the emails. She didn't dare go into what Dr. Maddy had found. Ronin should be told, but not with Roman here.

Roman stayed quiet while she explained, then added, "There's no way to catch her killer if indeed she was murdered."

Ronin pulled out a notepad and wrote something down. "And maybe she wasn't."

Shay shrugged. "I know, but I'd hate to think that anyone shortened her life and got away with it." She winced. "She often received threatening emails and letters. It's just these last few weeks she mentioned there were some more distressing than the others."

Ronin straightened. "You never mentioned them before."

"I hadn't considered her death as anything but natural. However, now—"

"Right. Who do I contact to get a copy of this correspondence?"

Shay quickly gave him Susan Checkers' name from Folgrent Foundation. "She's Bernice's right hand. Was...Bernice's right hand." Sadness swept through her. "Normally emails and letters like these didn't bother Bernice, but something about these ones did."

"I'll follow up on those next." He made a note in his cell phone while the other two watched. "If her death is related to these others, then her death would have been the first," Roman suggested. "That's very important."

That wasn't something she wanted to think about. Because it reminded her of Bernice's last words about making a deal with the devil. A faint tremor rippled down her spine.

And she was starting to wonder if the devil wasn't their murderer.

Ronin moved toward Shay. "Let's get started. The sooner we find this asshole the better."

Turning on Jordan's computer, she pulled up the files Ronin wanted to see. Together they read over the information and compared the three cases. She printed off the material he requested, and by the time they finished, he had a thick stack to take with him. They'd even opened one of the folders containing applications she'd turned down. As there were thousands, they started with the most recent of those.

"Thank you," he said, holding up the folder. "I appreciate the cooperation."

"Thank *you*," she responded. "Please find out who's killing my friends."

With a grim smile, he nodded. "I'm going to."

But likely not in time to save the next one. She pushed that thought away.

She needed Stefan's help. They had to find this guy before he killed again.

Sunday late afternoon...

Hours later, from the safety and comfort of her own home, she checked in on Stefan.

Stefan?

She tested the door in his mind. It was closed. *Shit.* That usually meant he was painting or enjoying some private time. He didn't have a current partner, as far as she knew, but that didn't mean much. She wasn't privy to everything in his life. She generally had free access to him when she wanted. He said she was spoiled.

You are spoiled. Stefan's voice responded to her thought and rippled through her mind along with his laughter.

She laughed lightly, relieved when the connection strengthened. *So what if I am? You love me anyway, right?*

I do. Now what's the problem?

Why does there have to be a problem? Maybe I'm checking in to see how you are?

Maybe. But not this time. So...? And Tabitha is holding her own by the way.

Shay brightened. *That's good to know. I wonder if she should have security to make sure the attacker doesn't try again?*

Already done. I set up an energy field around her body and room. If anyone trips it, both Dr. Maddy and myself will know. It's better to be safe than have another murder.

She winced. *Except it's too early to say that they were murdered.*

Maybe. But three – no four – heart attacks around you in what...a week? That's not a coincidence. That's called a pattern.

I know. But who could do such a thing. And why?

Any kind of people could be responsible, as we know. And considering you control a lot of money... Stefan sighed, the sound a bare whisper breezing through her mind. She smiled.

But I okayed all the money for these places. It's not like I was being blackmailed or pressured to do that. I did it because these centers need the money to keep going. The money went where it was intended to go. If the money had been embezzled or stolen, then maybe I'd understand it, Shay clarified.

So maybe the killer is upset that you're giving the money to the center. Maybe they are trying to discredit you? The Foundation? Stefan's voice strengthened. *No, Shay. These deaths don't show you in a bad light.*

I was wondering if it was someone I'd turned down. Someone angry because they didn't get funding. And her mind had spun endlessly on the names. *I showed Ronin those files as well.*

That would make sense. As much sense as any of this does. It still doesn't put this guy's hand on *the money. Neither can I see how killing these people put money in anyone's pocket.*

I know, she cried out in frustration. *That's what is wrong with the money-as-motivation theory.*

What if someone doesn't like what the centers stand for? Maybe they don't think they should be charities. Or receive handouts, Stefan suggested.

There are too many possibilities. I could speculate endlessly here.

Is there another payout due soon? To a similar type of charity? Each of these centers was set to receive a payment.

Maybe. I'll have to check. I was at the office for most of the afternoon. Ronin left with information on the three charities. He's looking for anything that ties them together. She sighed. *I also told him about the nasty emails Bernice got the last couple of weeks. Ronin said he'll look into that. He needs to know about what Dr. Maddy found too. And Roman did something on my computer system. Set up better security, I think.*

Speaking of Roman...?

She didn't know what to say.

You have to let go of the fear. You can't keep refusing to test the relationship waters just because you got burnt once.

It was more than getting burnt. It was life scarring, thank you, she said lightly.

And I'm not knocking that. But Roman cares. And he's willing to go the distance.

How do you know? She almost winced as she asked the question. Stefan had ways of knowing, and she knew it. But Stefan was already speaking again.

Roman's an artist, apparently.

She remembered Roman's skill with her computer. He'd been totally focused and understood the technology like she couldn't begin to. *Roman an artist?* Interesting to think he might channel that intensity into artistic expression. She had the feeling he didn't go into anything without excelling. Eventually.

Oh, so he's an artist? That makes him all right, does it? Being an artist is on your approved list of occupations, I suppose? And how does that guarantee he's willing to go the distance?

There are other reasons. Some are better for you to find out on your own. But you do need to ask to see his studio. Look at his sketches – if only to help you understand him.

He paused. *Speaking of paintings, there is a unique art show at one of my favorite galleries. Tonight. I'd love to take you. It will be good for you. Help you escape today's problems…your sorrows.* He hesitated. *In fact, I'll pick you up at 7:00.*

Another artist, huh? She had seen artistic strength in those long fingers of Roman's as they tapped her keyboard with precise strokes. If he could turn that same dedication and focus to a canvas, she could just imagine the masterpieces he'd create.

He'd never mentioned his hobby to her, though. She'd love to get a glimpse at that intimate side of his life. What would it take to see his artwork?

Chapter 11

Sunday evening...

The art gallery was decked out with soft, glowing orbs hanging from the ceiling and candle sconces mounted on the walls. Hundreds of people mingled with tall fluted glasses in their hands.

A hushed appreciation – maybe awe – permeated the room.

A quartet played soft music that floated gently under the hubbub of quiet conversation. Shay loved the ambience. The atmosphere of the old stone building, the huge paned windows, and the soaring vaulted ceilings gave the impression of a long-lost era. With the women in gorgeous cocktail gowns and the men in suits or tuxedos, it made an elegant picture. She smiled.

"Are you okay?" Stefan murmured at her side. Resplendent in a classic jet-black tuxedo, he stood out in the crowd. His face wasn't as well known as some people assumed, and that was mostly due to his phobia of all media events – but he stopped women in their tracks regardless.

Shay had been surprised by his insistence that she come to this art showing, but she realized within minutes he was curious about her reaction to something. The artist in him wanted her to see this showing. To show *her* this art.

She shrugged and smiled at him. Swathed in a teal, skin-tight cocktail dress, her hair ina demure twist, she was just happy to feel glamorous and to have something other than the murders to think about.

"That's why we're here. Something to take your mind off all the problems." Stefan's pure velvet voice deepened as he stared around.

A waiter approached and held out his tray in a quiet, unobtrusive manner. The glasses glistened with golden liquid.

Shay smiled. "Thank you." She took one flute. Stefan took another. They moved off toward the first wall.

"What do you know about the artist?" she whispered.

"Not much." He stopped in front of a life-sized nude. "Except he's good."

Shay stared at the massive charcoal sketch that had been overlaid and blended with luminescent paints in jewel hues. "Wow."

"Indeed." Stefan stared at the painting.

The energy in his mind caught her attention. She studied the look on his face, her gaze going from the painting to Stefan and back again. He saw something in this artwork. Something special. She studied the painting for several long moments. The technique was stunning. The use of color as a highlight for this mix of charcoal and paint was unusual, yet it worked. It defined the artist.

There was a compelling need to stare at the painting – to get lost in the art.

"Let's keep walking." Stefan, tucked her hand against his arm, then walked to the next painting, stopping for a long look before he moved on. Shay studied the paintings. Each was more compelling than the last. All were of the same woman. Though all were nudes, all paintings of the woman were tastefully covered – in the right places. Yet the hint of what was underneath, the promise of more hidden beauty, was there. The paintings were innocent yet alluring, sexual yet classy. Blue highlights decorated all of them, adding an interesting creative touch.

"He's exceptional."

"He?" Stefan glanced at her, amusement in his gaze. "Isn't that a big assumption?"

"Is it?" She motioned to the compelling series of nine pictures, each a portion of a painting, that when fitted together showed the whole picture. "All of these are of one woman. The same model was the muse for this series. You can tell she's so much more than a model. She's the artist's passion. The other half of his soul."

Stefan stared at her, an intuitive, almost secretive knowing evident in his gaze.

"What?" she smiled. "Oh, I'm assuming that it's a he because he loves this woman. Whereas it could just as easily be a female artist who loves this woman." She shrugged. "Guilty." She stared at the bold brush depicting the well-painted form...and the undecipherable signature. "I can't explain it, but there's a male energy evident in the work."

"Energy you are seeing?"

"No. I'm not seeing. I'm not looking. I'm enjoying the show."

"Good. And in this case, you are right. It is a male artist."

She laughed. "Is there a difference between the sexes in the way an artist draws?"

"Definitely, but that doesn't mean that we can't be fooled."

They continued to stroll through the area, discussing the various poses, strokes, looks. Several times they exchanged their empty glasses for full. It occurred to Shay that this was the first calm, enjoyable evening in weeks, other than her time with Roman. "Thank you, Stefan. I'm so happy you dragged me here."

"Good." He patted her hand. "Shall we meet the artist?"

"Sure." Shay looked around. "Who is it?"

"You know him. That's one of the reasons I wanted to bring you here."

She turned to face him, surprise making her smile bright. "Really. Who is it?"

"Hello, Shay." The deep voice interrupted their conversation.

Shay looked up to see Roman standing at their side, a fluted glass in his hand. Her smile flashed. Damn, he looked good. She responded, "Hi. I'm surprised to see you here."

He laughed, a hint of mockery in his voice. "Why, don't I look like the artsy type?"

His tone of voice had her backing up slightly. "Not at all. I just didn't expect to turn around and see you standing there."

His smile turned rueful as he nodded toward Stefan. "Sorry. Introduce me to your friend."

Shay made the introductions, her gaze on Roman as she said Stefan's name. His eyes widened. His eyebrows shot up.

"Are you enjoying the show, Shay?" he asked.

She smiled warmly. "Absolutely. It's stunning work."

She smiled at him and then looked over at Stefan. It was Stefan's smile that made her wary. And that hidden laughter in his gaze. She eyed him suspiciously. *What?*

He stayed quiet, but his laughter was almost to the point of spilling over.

She glanced over at Roman.

Roman smiled at her. "Thank you. These are some of my favorite pieces. I've done several more but I believe these are my best."

Oh crap. Her gaze widened and her mouth dropped open. From the grin on Roman's face, he was enjoying her shock.

Damn Stefan for not warning her this was an art show of Roman's work.

On cue, Stefan's chuckles rolled through her mind. She shot him a dirty look and turned her attention to Roman.

"At least you know I was being honest, because I had no idea," she said, chagrin in her voice.

"I do appreciate the honesty. Not everyone is the same."

She turned to study his paintings, her mind now connecting the passion she'd seen from the artist to the model. The artist being Roman.

Oh shit. He had loved his model. Did he still care about the woman or was he over her? Could it be his ex-wife? He'd mention a divorce, in passing, a long time ago. Surely he didn't still carry the torch for her. Shay's mind twisted over the implications of her relationship with him. She could hardly ask him, especially here and now.

But the one thing that played over and over again... Roman, the painter, loved this woman.

So who was she? And was she still in the picture? Figuratively speaking.

***

Roman had been deep in conversation with several clients when he glanced up and saw Shay enter the gallery. With a man. And damn if jealousy hadn't taken over. Her distinguished looking partner stayed close and was attentive the whole time. With their heads bent together, they walked the gallery, discussing his paintings.

Then he'd realized the danger. *Would she know? Did she see herself as he saw her?* In his paintings?

Having her here was incredibly personal, and invasive to his peace of mind. And it had the potential to be incredibly embarrassing, even catastrophic, if she recognized herself as his inspiration.

He hated the nervous energy that filled him. He kept up an ongoing conversation with many people as he kept a quiet watch on Shay's progress and body language. Finally, he couldn't stand it anymore. She'd tortured him enough. He had to find out.

He walked over and found out who her companion was.

Stefan. Jesus. He'd heard so much about this man. Talented artist, tortured psychic. Shay's friend. Dr. Maddy's friend. But not until now had he understood just how good a friend he was to Shay. He studied the two of them, reading the caring, friendliness, even the loving, but...not – and he breathed a quiet sigh of relief – he somehow knew Stefan was not her lover.

Just then Roman caught Stefan's gaze. Heat rose on his neck. Damn it felt like Stefan knew what he was thinking. Amusement simmered deep in Stefan's gaze and he just sat back as the scene played out. Roman shifted his gaze from the painting in front of him to the woman with the same jaw line. The same curve to her shoulder.

How could she not know?

He shifted his gaze quickly to Stefan.

And there it was. It was in the knowing look in his eyes, the knowing curve of his lips. Damn. There was no fooling the man.

Stefan knew.

***

When they'd seen enough, she took a moment to say good-bye to the gallery hosts. Then, with Stefan at her side, she slowly did one more stroll past the paintings. Roman had returned to speak with his other guests and she was left alone to dwell on this sudden shift in her world.

A nice shift, though.

She'd gotten over the shock of discovering Roman was the artist. If she understood one thing, it was that seeing this amazing work made Roman even more attractive.

How did that work? Was it that she appreciated the man's talents? That he had a softer side? That there was an honesty to his work, to him? She already knew that from their years of correspondence. Could it be that he reminded her of Stefan? She adored Stefan. They had a bond unlike anything else she'd experienced. But the bond with Stefan wasn't a lover-like connection.

"Are you ready to go home?" Stefan asked gently.

She smiled. "Yes. Thank you for bringing me. I don't know how long it would have taken before I found out about his art another way."

"I thought this might be good for you." He nudged her toward the last painting and the large glass window. Shay stopped for one last look at the stunning woman.

"She's very beautiful."

"Yes, she is."

"There's no way he could create these...gorgeous paintings, if he didn't love her," she murmured, casting a final long look at the picture.

"No. Not likely."

"I wonder if he knows," she mused.

"I wonder." Stefan's voice was noncommittal, as if the answer was of no interest to him. And true enough, it probably wasn't.

"Maybe a better question is this: Does *she* know how he feels? It would be terrible to love someone to that extent but for them to be oblivious."

"True."

At the large window, she stopped. She could see the huge painting behind her in the reflection.

There was something familiar about the line of the woman's jaw, her neck. Shay couldn't place her. Recognition sat just outside her consciousness. Inside, she understood one thing – the woman was someone she'd met.

Somewhere.

But who?

"Ready?"

Turning back to Stefan, she smiled and nodded. On his arm, she walked out of the gallery without a backward glance.

***

Shay crawled into bed that night in a smooth, happy state. She'd enjoyed the evening. Any time spent with Stefan was special and this had been no exception.

Not to mention that their energies, when combined, always went to new heights. She'd often wondered what it would be like to have a lover that had psychic abilities like his, even if he only understood the way energy worked. And how combined energies changed, grew and melded.

It could be incredibly special.

And something she really wanted to experience in her life.

And that was not likely to happen. Not with her trust issues preventing any real connection with someone.

She pulled the bedding up to her chin and turned off the light. Peaceful, she dropped into a sound sleep.

And woke up some time later, her heart pounding, her breath rasping as it fought its way up her throat.

Shit. *Something is wrong.*

What? She hopped out of her bed and ran to her living room and felt like she was once again caught in the panic she'd felt that night, a year ago, when Darren had broken into her place.

The living room was empty. She ran to the front door. It was still locked. The bolt in place. She spun around and leaned back against the door, her body shaking with emotion.

It was just a nightmare.

Just a nightmare.

Please, let this be just a nightmare.

With a semblance of calm restored, she walked the apartment and searched, unconsciously imitating Roman's movements from the other night. As she finished, she realized what she'd done. She'd taken almost the same route that he had. Laying down another path of energy over his.

And why was that significant?

She didn't know, but patterns were just as significant in energy work as mathematics. She took a deep breath as she walked into the kitchen. A cup of tea. She needed a cup of tea. And some time to think this through. And as she walked from the kitchen to the living room and back to her bedroom, she saw the different energy field.

She came to a dead stop. And crouched low.

The energy was thin and low. Older. And covered in a soft black. Hidden in the shadows of her dark room. It was the oozing blackness of it that made her skin crawl. The only time she'd seen that same black was with Darren's energy. True, she'd seen a few things that came close – after all black was a common enough color in energy, but never did anything else have the same oozing blackness. Not before Darren, and never since.

Thank God.

She studied the pattern of the dark energy in her apartment. It centered in her living room. She twisted and bent up and down, trying to see the path, to find the person behind it. But that was impossible. There were just wisps of something there. Not enough to read. Just enough to make her nervous... *Very* nervous.

From all of this she knew one thing. Someone had been in her apartment. *Again.*

And that someone had the same energy signature as her last intruder. How? Tonight. They'd probably entered as soon as she'd left... Yet the door had been locked when she came home. And there'd been no sign of any disturbance.

Surely that meant her visitor had come in astral form. She knew she could walk through the memory of her apartment, in the time before she left for the evening and check.

Moving back to her bed, she sat down, her tea long forgotten. Closing her eyes, she turned back the clock in her head and stepped out of her body – and into the vision.

Giving herself a moment to adjust, she followed herself as she went through the preparations of getting ready for the evening. The room looked normal.

This was her space. She knew this energy. Everything was as it should be. She went through the same clothes change and then watered the plants, picked up of her purse and phone, turning her head as the doorbell rang. She walked to the door. She watched herself greet Stefan and Stefan greet her. Normal.

Everything was the way it was supposed to be. So now she was sure the visitor had come in after she'd left for the gallery.

She stepped out of the vision and back into her own time in her own bedroom. She knew what she had to do, but could she do it? Now that was something else. She walked into the living room and stood over the energy wisps that littered the room.

Then she picked one and jumped inside.

Chapter 12

Immediately, Shay was tossed into the turbulent emotional storm. Anger was the dominant sentiment. Whoever this person was, revenge powered all his actions. There were even threads of hate spinning through the wisps.

For her.

She shuddered at the completely unexpected emotional maelstrom.

She hadn't thought this trip would bring any results at the beginning. Instead she'd been sucked in and washed away in the emotions left behind. Since it was energy, she could see the approximate time it arrived and anything that happened while the energy was active. But it didn't allow her to see the person. She could see and feel some of what the person felt, but since she was inside the energy, she saw nothing to identify the person.

Neither could she read the person's thoughts. But the emotions stormed right through her.

What could this person want? They'd come to Shay's personal space. *Why?*

She followed the energy as it walked through her apartment. It stayed to the main areas. It never ventured into the bedroom. Odd. A psychic burglar would have gone after jewelry, money, something that was easily pawned, then plan a physical trip to take advantage of the loot they'd seen.

This energy didn't travel around. It sat, as if festering. There was a faint throb to the energy. Even though it was cold and had almost dissipated, the throb was strong enough to be felt. *Double odd.* Shay looked around her apartment, hoping for something, anything to clarify the identity of her intruder.

Another odd twist. Normally she could see the energy left behind by people...for a day at least, sometimes days. If the person experienced strong emotions, it should be even longer.

This person *had* been driven by strong emotions, but the force of their feelings didn't keep this particular energy warm and heavy, allowing it to stay. Instead, it was as if this person had burned up all their emotional energy, leaving little trace behind.

And what was with the cloaking layer of black energy? She'd seen something similar with Darren. She had to watch to make sure that fear didn't have her judging the energy and assume it would have the same behavior as Darren. Or having her afraid that it *was* Darren and that he'd somehow found a way back to taunt her.

No. She knew Darren was dead. It was a fact.

She'd heard horror stories from Stefan about various non-dead entities making last grabs for life through the living. If those stories didn't make one scared, then nothing would.

She didn't think that trick was within Darren's capabilities, but she didn't know for sure. Thoughts that he might return haunted her sleep and kept her nightmares alive.

Still, for all the similarities to this energy, it didn't *feel* the same as Darren's. Close. But it wasn't him. So how were they alike? She just couldn't say.

She also wasn't prepared to have entities, living or dead, walking through her apartment at will.

Tired, and knowing she'd need to rest, she added another layer of protective energy around her apartment.

Returning to reality, she recognized that her body needed to be horizontal as soon as possible. In the morning, she'd call on Stefan's expertise yet again. Something was up. If he could help her guard her space then she needed him to do that for her.

Whatever it was she needed protection from...

The two of them had put a clean, soothing protective energy around last time. She believed it would be enough.

She'd been wrong.

Monday morning...

The next morning Shay walked down the hallway toward her office and heard Jordan bitching to Rose about the state of her files. Shay winced. She'd left the files she'd pulled for Ronin on Jordan's desk. And Shay knew that for all her multi-colored hair and free-spirit clothing, Jordan was a neat freak. On the other hand, Ronin had needed the material, and Roman had set up some new security on her system.

The good outweighed the bad.

She opened the door with a bright smile. And kept it in place, while she pointed to the files in front of Jordan. "I'm sorry." She walked over to Jordan. "I had to pull the files at the request of the police. They didn't want to wait for Monday, and I figured that if I put them back in the wrong place you'd be even more upset, so I left them for you to file away."

Jordan glared and then blew a strand of turquoise hair out of her eyes. "I hate people going into the files. Almost as much as I hate people touching my computer." She flung her multi-colored scarf over her shoulder and sat down with a thunk.

"I know." Shay said meekly. "I'd have just given them a copy of the digital files, but they wanted to see the hardcopy stuff as well." She shrugged. "You know the paper files are more complete."

"And now messier," groused Jordan as she reorganized the contents of the top file. "Did you have to mess up the order too? They *were* chronological..."

Shay smiled at Rose, who gave a small eye roll, as Jordan slapped the file closed and then placed it in its proper spot in the huge filing system behind her.

"Glad you can keep it all straight for me." Shay walked into her office to hang up her coat, relieved that moment was over. Jordan was incredibly efficient, and normally she was even-tempered. But disturbing the files was one thing guaranteed to piss her off. Shay sat down on her big chair and put her purse away in the bottom drawer of her desk. She turned on her computer and called out, "Are there appointments this morning?"

"One." Jordan called back. "At eleven. Your ten o'clock cancelled."

Good. But she didn't say that out loud. The less pulling on her today, the better. She needed a nap already. And she also hoped to stop at the hospital and see Tabitha today.

No. Stay away from her.

Stefan? Why?

Keep her under the radar. As far as the world knows, she's in a coma. If you visit her, you'll be alerting her attacker. Because Tabatha's alive, he might see her as a loose end.

Damn. He was right but she was desperate to see for herself that Tabitha was okay.

She is, but she's staying in the ethers. Don't contact her that way either. This person understands energy. Let's not give him a reason to go after Tabitha again. I've told her what happened and that she's still in danger. Ronin also knows. She did say that a force came from Sue, her assistant at the time of the attack. She also says she's known Sue for years and it wasn't her energy that did this.

Damn. Shay knew Sue as well. She couldn't see her being involved. *So someone else is hitching a ride with people in order to attack other people?*

Possibly. They'd have to stalk the victim enough to know who and what they'd be doing and with whom, in order to pick the right opportunity.

Shay thought about that as a glimmer of something, perhaps understanding stirred in the back of her mind. She tugged it forward. *Not if this person already had anchors in the victim. And that's easily done. They just have to be able to see the person and access their chakras. If they already had those, they could just use the anchors when they wanted, and pop in and view the world from the new perspective.*

Oh shit. Realization hit her in the heart. *Like the extra eyes she'd seen in Bernice's gaze.*

Silence, while Stefan pondered that. *It would take a lot of skill.*

Would it though, Shay agreed dryly. *Think about it. Early on, they could have put hooks in to make their takeover of the unknowing individuals easier to do their will, yet again. Even better. They could even have already created a hook from the victim to the innocent bystander. Then used that as the highway for the energy to attack the victim. Even better it would look like a heart attack or rather it wouldn't look like anything hard science could figure out – and therefore investigators, medical and otherwise, would find nothing suspicious. They'd believe the person just dropped dead.*

Scary thought, Stefan murmured. *But all too possible given we have no idea the limits of energy work – for good or evil. I guess I'll need to speak with Tabitha again. In the meantime, we're all working on this case. Stay safe.*

"Here's the file on the eleven o'clock appointment." Jordan came in holding a thick folder in her right hand. In her left she had a stack of papers. "And these are the new applications for you to go over."

Shay shifted mentally. Stefan had left, and she needed to focus on today. "Good. Anything interesting?"

"A few. Then again, I always think they are all worthy, whereas you go through and see the stuff I don't." Jordan smiled, back into her normal mood now that the filing was taken care of.

"That's because you don't have to make the decisions as to who benefits the most from these grants. There's only so much money and making it stretch is a feat – and not an easy one."

"But you do it so well." Jordan laughed lightly. "So did Bernice, didn't she?"

"Yes." Shay sat back and looked over at the young, bright girl who'd quickly become a friend. Rose had too, but not with the same connection as Jordan and Shay had created. "Bernice had a talent for both sides of the business. Men handed money over without a whimper and she found worthy causes for all of it."

"Yes. That's her. I'd like to have her money to hand over."

Thinking of the grande dame, Shay nodded. "She had men eating out of her hand all her life. I don't know that she was ever caught by the same love bug as the men were, though."

Jordan raised an eyebrow. "Really? She never married?"

"She liked playing the field too much. And no, she never had any children either."

Jordan's second eyebrow shot up, to disappear under the bright strands of her hair. "Wow. Who's going to get all her money?"

Shay frowned, staring out the window. What a good question. "You know, I'm not sure. I guess that will be taken care of this week. It doesn't involve me, thank heavens."

"You have enough of your own already." Jordan walked back out. "But if they are looking for people to give it to, there is always me."

"Chances are good that all her money will go into her foundation and the board will have more to hand out. They'll need to hire someone to take over her position. That might already be in place. I've been out of the loop the last few days."

"I'm sure you have enough on your plate to deal with."

Familiar noises in the other room made Shay smile.

"I made coffee. Will you have one?" Jordan called.

"Always."

Happy to have the office back to normal and a good brew coming, Shay pulled the file toward her for her appointment that morning.

Right.

This was a soup kitchen that requested funds for two delivery vehicles and a salaried driver to deliver food to seniors and other people who couldn't make the trip on their own. Shay remembered this project, but could not remember the details. She glanced at her clock. She had an hour to get caught up.

Jordan walked in with a cup of espresso in her hand. "Are you approving this request?"

"Yes. We'll need to keep on top of their accounting to see if it's worth continuing after a year, but this isn't exactly a service many people provide. If it helps the community, I'm all for it.

"Let's hope the organizer of this charity doesn't have a heart attack like the others." Jordan returned to her desk in the outer office.

Shay swallowed. Hard. Now that wasn't a thought she wanted to dwell on. But it's not like she had a way to stop it.

Or did she?

***

Stefan opened his eyes. The skylight stared back at him. Out of habit, he reached, and pinched himself. And winced. His experiences when he shifted realities were sometimes so strong and clear that occasionally he'd get lost inside them. Sometimes he couldn't tell if he was caught in a vision or had returned to reality – a sad state of affairs. Some said he was psychic; others called him a charlatan. And many labeled him just plain crazy.

He was probably a bit of each.

Stefan closed his eyes, his mind suffused with difficult memories. He always helped those that ended up on his doorstep. More often than not, they were brought there by an officer of the law. He'd worked enough with law enforcement agencies over the years to build a large network of people who called on him.

So far Shay had kept herself apart from the others and from formally working with law enforcement. She didn't think her abilities offered anything to the other psychics. She couldn't be more wrong. She could do stuff with energy he'd never dreamed possible. But she also talked about his cases as if they were only his – showing a distinct separation in her mind. Yet, if she chose, she could be an immense help to his work and the work of others.

The phone rang on cue. He rolled over and looked at it. Did he want to talk to Detective Chandler? He wracked his mind for the connection. The phone rang again. Right. Ronin.

"Hello, Detective Chandler... Ronin."

"You do realize that more people would view you in a kinder light if you didn't do that."

Stefan smiled. "Do what? And what's going on with Shay's projects?"

"See, things like that. How do you know anything is wrong?"

"Because you wouldn't have called me otherwise."

The detective laughed. "True enough. Have you spoken with her about the Foundation deaths?"

Stefan frowned. Right. *Death. Heart attacks. Charities. Tabitha.* "Yes. Almost every day."

"Good, it helps to know we're all on the same page." The detective chuckled then let his laughter die out. He cleared his throat. "I know that there isn't likely to be a connection between these deaths and what happened with Darren a year ago, but as that was my first entry into the psychic forces and the damage they can do, and now there is another weird scenario happening with Shay again - almost a year later, to the exact day…well it would be nice to know for sure there was no connection. Can you see anything linking Darren and the current cases?"

Stefan had already considered that. "Darren is dead," he said simply.

"Right." Relief washed through Ronin's voice. "I guess I just wanted to make sure. I was hearing some weird stuff with the police gossip recently. Something about dead not really being dead?"

Stefan sighed as he realized that Ronin must have heard about some of his weirder cases if he'd heard talk about dealing with the undead.

"Darren was motivated by money. People that try for the un-dead state are looking to extend their human existence," Stefan said, thoughtfully. "Usually it has nothing to do with money."

"Good. Then I can forget about Darren being involved?" Ronin asked cautiously.

"Yes. I believe so." And Stefan did believe that. He'd gotten Shay's slightly garbled message about recognizing the same energy as Darren's in her apartment, but he didn't believe she'd read it right. That asshole had been dead a long time. "Except..."

Dread filled Ronin's voice. "Except what?"

"Shay believed Darren was an orphan. I don't know if that's true."

"And if he wasn't, how does that change anything?"

"Genetically, he could have family with similar abilities."

"Right."

Stefan could hear the click of keys as Ronin worked at his keyboard. "I'm going to work that angle in my spare time. Let's not leave anything out. I've spent hours going through the files Shay gave me." He gave a short laugh. "And the nasty emails Bernice had recently received."

"Find anything?"

"Not enough. Someone was trying to blackmail Bernice, but apparently she died before she made any payments." Frustration marred his voice. "So far, there's no visible connection between the victims, outside of them being involved with projects from Shay's foundation."

"Shay's foundation. So not from Shay herself?"

There was a slight pause. "There is a difference, isn't there? I was looking at the Foundation being the connection, but it could just as easily be Shay."

"There is a lot of money involved in both scenarios."

"I wonder if someone is looking to take out the competition for the Foundation money." He gave a short laugh. "Listen to me. We don't even know for sure if these deaths are suspicious."

"Not true," Stefan corrected quietly. "They are definitely suspicious. What we don't know for sure is if foul play is involved...but at this point we have reason to believe it is." He caught Ronin up on Tabitha's message about a force coming from the delivery person but not appearing to be that person's energy, and he also shared what Dr. Maddy had seen and Shay's insights.

Just as he was finishing, his focus changed, wavered.

He hung up quickly. His sunroom disappeared into a dark clouded sky. From sunlight to darkness in an instant.

As if a storm was building.

He could only hope he'd get some warning before it broke.

***

Roman walking into the gallery for the first time since the opening night of the show. As he stared at his paintings, Shay's face as Stefan had escorted her out of the gallery flashed in his mind. Inside, his stomach had clenched in fear. *Had she figured it out?* Stefan had absolutely recognized the model in his paintings. How he'd known for sure it was Shay, was something that Roman didn't want to think about. What really bothered him was fear that Stefan might have told her.

That look in Shay's eyes... As if she'd almost recognized herself. That wasn't something he was prepared to deal with right now.

He couldn't. He didn't have the right answers for himself.

But should he tell her – before someone else did?

Why had he thought it would never come out? He might fool most of the public, but the model herself? And Stefan...

His phone rang. He glanced down and frowned. He didn't recognize the number.

"Hello?"

"She didn't recognize herself. But I did. I sure hope you have an explanation for her when she finds out."

Oh shit. Stefan.

"Not a good one, I'm afraid," Roman admitted, quietly. "I saw her confused expression as she walked out last night. As if she were on the verge of seeing the truth. I had to admit I didn't sleep well afterward."

"She hasn't put two and two together, but she will," Stefan said. "She's very astute. Right now she has something very

142

troubling on her mind or I'm sure she would have made the connection herself."

"For some reason, I never anticipated the day she'd find out."

"It's already here. More than that, her astuteness let her see something I'm not sure that *you* see yet."

Still holding the phone to his ear, Roman looked around, glad to see he was still alone in the gallery. He walked over to the one painting that showed the line of Shay's neck and chin. "What's that?"

"The relationship between the painter and his model."

Roman frowned. "Sorry? Shay's the model. That's all."

Stefan's warm, knowing laughter filled the line. "No. It's not all. She's a lot more than a model. And I believe Shay was correct in her interpretation. Interesting times ahead."

"Whoa. I don't know what you mean." Roman walked around the room, studied the paintings, keeping a lid on his emotions. Cautiously, he protested, "True, she's been my inspiration for the last couple of years..."

"Exactly," said Stefan, "and you need to reflect on what that means." He paused as a weird sound filled the air. "Ah, I see what you aren't ready to admit." He laughed. "Shay may not see herself in those paintings yet, but she sees you very clearly as you relate to the model."

Roman stared. "What do you see? I don't understand."

"I know. But you will. I suspect Shay will have fun telling you, if you ask her." And he rang off.

"As if." There's no way he could bring the subject up with Shay. And Stefan knew that.

Damn. What had Shay seen that he hadn't?

Chapter 13

Late Monday morning…

Shay studied the nervous man in front of her. It was that personality issue that caused her concern. She was used to people sitting in her office and being nervous because they wanted her support. But this guy seemed really nervous. As if something else bothered him.

But what?

She sighed. She opened the file in front of her. "Wilson, tell me about your project." And she looked him directly.

Wilson froze like a deer caught in the headlights. He opened his mouth to talk, but no words came out. He ran his fingers through his hair and then tugged at his tie. He stopped fidgeting, and his whole structure slumped. "I'm sorry. I'm just so nervous."

Using her inner eye, she studied his chakras looking for deception. Lies. Deceit.

She watched the energy circulate in his first chakra. Fear. Nervousness. Not quite panic, but a definite wish to rush away. A need to get out. The longer she watched him, the more the energy swirled, becoming a frantic vortex. So *not* healthy. She gave the rest of his chakras a glance. He was definitely centered in the heart and came from a sense of needing to be of service. A need to redeem himself.

She dropped her gaze. That part bothered her.

Redeem himself, from what? What had he done so wrong that he needed to help others in this way?

She decided to ask him. "Wilson. How did you choose this to be your calling? Or did it choose you?"

He got that deer in the headlights look again. "I...I don't know."

"You run a soup kitchen. Were you ever homeless? Were you raised in hardship?" She smiled gently at him. "I'm trying to understand why you are doing what you are doing. To see if you are going to be there in a week or a year or whether this is a fly-by-night type of thing and you'll be gone the day after I give you money."

He blinked. "You're thinking of giving me money?"

She laughed. "I think that's why you came here, isn't it?"

"Yes." He straightened, brightened. "Yes. I need money for a delivery service. There are so many people who can't come to us. We need a way to take meals to them." He leaned forward and there was the animation, the passion she'd been looking for.

Good. "Then tell me what you are looking for? A mobile kitchen or a delivery van. One with customized interiors. What?"

After that he opened up and poured the information out. She had to redirect him a couple times to make sure he answered the specific questions she needed. At the same time, she managed to satisfy her own mind that he was indeed passionate about his calling. There'd been no explanation for the issues she could see in his first chakra but she suspected it had something to do with his family life growing up.

"What about your family?" she asked gently. "Are they supportive of what you do?"

He stopped, a sadness leaching the animation from his face. "My mother passed away a couple of years ago. A system like this would have made her life much easier." He stared out the window. His first chakra oozed energy in the direction of his past. His memories. "She was bedridden for the last year. I did everything I could, but it seemed like she had deteriorated more every time I stopped by."

This was the source of the passion. Guilt and redemption – two of the biggest driving forces behind do-gooders.

But it made her feel better to know he had that type of motivation.

He'd be her next project.

She spoke with him for another hour while she finished filling out her forms. After they were done and he'd left, she sat back and smiled when Jordan asked how it went.

"It's great. He's a perfect candidate. We should be able to help him out. I'll do up the paperwork, send it out to the board, and we should be able to put this through within a week or two."

Jordan's eyebrows – was that a new ring in her eyebrow – flew up to her hairline. "Wow, that fast? You normally take weeks to months."

"But this one needs to happen sooner with the fall weather coming. He's got to get the vehicles outfitted, drivers hired and trained, and find the necessary customers – the word needs to go out soon. Once the cold weather hits, and people can't get out and about easily, they might need to double the vehicles or at least run on rotation."

"Still, this one must mean a lot to you for you to give it this kind of attention." Jordan stared at her speculatively. "Unless there's something going on here I don't know about."

Shay laughed. "Not at all. He's got good timing, that's all."

Jordan sent her a doubtful look. "Okay, if you say so." She returned to her desk, and Shay returned to hers, just as her cell phone rang.

Pappy.

"Shay, did you not get the letter?"

She frowned. "What letter?"

"About Bernice's will. They are reading it in about ten minutes, and you're supposed to be here."

"What?" She glanced at her watch. "Where's the meeting? I can leave now, but I can't get very far in ten minutes."

"We're in your building. Lawyers McIntosh, McWilliams and Malory…on the seventh floor." He sounded anxious as he added, "Can you come?"

"I'm on my way." She closed her phone, logged off her computer, snagged her purse and ran out of the door. "Rose, take my calls, please. Back in an hour or so."

She hoped.

***

Knock, knock...

Can you hear me, Shay?

No, I guess not.

Too bad. I just wanted to let you know who is standing at the elevators. Your grandfather. Charles Lassiter. Standing lost and worried in the middle of the hallway.

Waiting for you, his precious granddaughter, most likely.

Not that he's going to find you. This is too good an opportunity to waste.

You'll worry, Shay...

But there's no real need, I'll take good care of him.

This time...

***

Roman didn't know what he was doing here in the Bernice's lawyers' office, except that as a support system for Grandfather.

He wasn't mentioned in Bernice's will. He knew that because Bernice had made it clear. Thankfully. Bernice had loads of family, even if none were close.

Still, millions of available cash brought out relatives that only dreamed of a blood connection. And the room was filling up.

He frowned. It was unusual to see so many attending this type of meeting.

"See. I said the rats would be coming to the party." Grandfather shuffled closer. "Bernice wanted everyone here so they'd know where they stood."

"Typical her." He motioned to a chair at the back row and led his grandfather to it. "We'll stay in the back."

147

"Good choice." Grandfather sat down. Roman stood slightly behind him and watched the proceedings.

Just when he thought everyone who was coming had arrived, Shay raced in. She stopped at the doorway, her chest heaving, her eyes surveying the crowded room. Her gaze landed on Roman, bounced off, and then zipped back. She walked toward them.

"Have you seen Pappy?" she asked in a low voice.

Roman frowned and searched the room. "No. Actually I haven't. Grandfather?"

"He was here. Saw him downstairs." A querulous tone entered his voice. "Where could he have gotten to?"

Roman leaned down. "I'll go check the men's room."

His Grandfather's face lit up. "Yes, that must be where he is."

Just then, the lawyer entered from the side door. Roman caught the look on his face as he noted the size of the group seated in front of him. He pressed a couple of buttons on his desk. Instantly a second man, dressed in a suit, but looking more like a henchman, entered and stood slightly behind the lawyer.

Interesting. They were prepared for trouble.

Shay immediately sat down beside Gerard.

Roman slipped out the back quickly and walked to the men's room. There was no sign of Pappy on the way. He pushed open the door to the men's room and walked inside.

"Charles? Are you in here?"

No answer.

Bending down, he checked the floor under the doors. No one. The room was empty. Given Pappy's and Grandfather's ages, anything could have happened.

He couldn't help but walk to the other end of the hallway and enter the stairwell and look over the railing. The stairwell was empty. No collapsed older man on the stairs. He'd take that as a good sign.

He retraced his steps to the meeting. As he entered, the group turned to look at him. He calmly took a seat beside Grandfather and, feeling the worried glances from Shay and Grandfather, he shook his head.

The lawyer continued to read from the will, his voice droning on and on.

There was rustling as several people shifted position. The audience waited, their impatience barely veiled.

Roman smiled inside.

The lawyer stopped speaking. He raised his head, took a drink of water and said, "And now I come to the bequests. To my long-time companion Grace, I leave five hundred thousand dollars."

A gasp sounded from the audience, followed by weeping from an older woman in the front row. Roman thought she might be Grace. He'd only ever seen her once. The lawyer went on to mention several other similar bequests. Then he stopped and laid the papers down on his desk and stared out at the audience.

He cleared his throat, took a deep breath, and said, "I, Bernice Folgrent, leave the rest of my estate, in its entirety, to my goddaughter, Shay Lassiter, in the hopes that she will find a good use for my life's work."

Silence.

Then outrage.

Several people jumped up and yelled. Several people burst into tears, and the lawyer was instantly besieged by nasty comments.

"This is wrong."

"There has to be a mistake."

"We'll see about that."

Grandfather gripped his hands tightly together and whispered softly, "Oh dear."

But all Roman's attention was on Shay. She slid down slightly on her seat and dropped her head back to look up at the ceiling and then she groaned.

He heard her whisper, "Oh shit."

Chapter 14

"Bernice, how could you do this to me?" Shay whispered into the chaos going on around her. She sank lower in her chair, wishing she could hide. The entire room had worked itself into a frenzy.

Slowly she became aware of a gentle stroking on her hand. She let her head drop to the side and looked into Gerard's concerned gaze. Above his head, Roman gazed down at her, a half-humorous and half-worried look in his eyes.

Gerard leaned closer and whispered, "She did love you."

Shay looked deep into those warm caring eyes and understood a smidgeon of what Bernice felt when she'd looked into them. Gerard had a huge capacity for loving.

"If she did, why would she land me with the responsibility of her money?"

"Because she trusted you. She knew you would do the best you could."

Shay closed her eyes briefly. The noise still went on around her. One group had braced the lawyer around the desk, leaning over to intimidate him while they shouted their displeasure. Shay watched as the security guard struggled to keep the group back.

"Things are going to get even uglier soon. Can we slip away?"

"Absolutely." Roman stood up and helped Gerard to his feet. "Let's go before anyone figures out who you are."

"Oh Lord." Shay snagged her purse and stood up. Without a backward glance she walked to the door and slipped into the hallway. The din from inside instantly eased as the door swung shut behind her. Still shell shocked from the bomb the lawyer had dropped, Shay kept walking to the stairwell. There were a few people around, but not many. Behind her she heard Roman talking to Gerard.

"Stairs or elevators?" Roman asked.

"Elevator. At least, I will. I think you should walk down with Shay. I don't think she should be alone right now."

Shay frowned at that whispered comment. She turned around and looked at them both. "I'm all right, Gerard. A little confused. Definitely not happy, but I'll be fine."

Gerard took several small steps toward her. "I don't think you have fully thought this through. Until you have the papers signed and your own will sorted, if anything should happen to you...then any one of those people in that room could possibly inherit instead."

Shay groaned. "Seriously? I don't even get a chance to consider my way through this, and now I have consider that one of those people might try to eliminate me? Really?"

Roman took several steps forward. He pushed the button for the elevator. The door opened immediately. He motioned Shay inside. "Let's stay together. We can go to your office if you prefer, or we can go out for lunch. Somewhere private where we can sort this out."

"Lunch?" Shay spun around. "Where's Pappy? I thought he'd be here by now. We'd spoken about having lunch together earlier. Then this mess came up and I forgot about it."

"I don't know. I assumed he'd changed his mind about attending the meeting," said Gerard.

She frowned. Pulling out her cell phone, she checked for messages. None. She quickly called Pappy. No answer. "He's not answering." She gazed worriedly at the other two. "That's not like him."

Gerard pulled his cell phone out and checked. "He hasn't called me."

"He wouldn't have gone anywhere. He called me and told me to show up for the reading of the will. That's why I was running when I arrived. Before that, I hadn't even known about the meeting today."

"Maybe he's sitting in your office, waiting for you," Roman suggested. "Especially if he couldn't stand to be part of the business of Bernice's estate."

That actually made good sense. Shay punched the button for the seventh floor. The elevator came to a stop a few moments later.

"Let's go and see."

Her office was locked when she reached the main door. "Pappy wouldn't be here alone and Jordan has obviously gone for lunch." She pulled out her keys and unlocked the door. The lights were off. The main office, empty.

She walked into her inner office. "He's not here either." She spun around. The place looked normal. The energy normal. Hers, Rose's, Jordan's and that of the client who'd been here this morning. Nothing else. "Pappy hasn't been here at all today."

"So where is he?"

"Maybe he went home. To deal with his grief in private," Gerard offered.

Both Roman and Shay looked at Gerard. He shrugged and opened his hands. "Just an idea."

Shay noticed the blinking red light on her phone. She hit the voice mail button and listened to the three messages. None from Pappy. She quickly called his home number, wondering why she hadn't thought of that earlier. Nothing.

"I wonder if he's lying down..." She looked at Gerard in consideration. "I think I'll go see."

"We'll all go," Roman said. "He's normally in close contact with us. It's unusual for him not to have been at the meeting. Regardless of his personal feelings, this was another connection to Bernice. He would have wanted to have experienced that defining moment with her."

Shay closed her eyes briefly. "That is so true." She ran her fingers through her long hair. "I'm not thinking straight." She pursed her lips, hating the nerves that squeezed her gut. "Then where is he? I feel like something bad might have happened to him."

As she spoke the words, her inner sense of conviction grew stronger. "Something is wrong." She glanced at the doorway. She knew what she had to do. And what she should have done first.

"I have to go upstairs." She turned and called over her shoulder, "I'll be right back."

"I'm coming with you." Roman said at her shoulder. "Grandfather, stay here. We'll be right back."

Gerard settled into the closest chair at the reception desk. "I'll keep trying to reach him."

Shay raced out of the office with Roman close behind her. She closed the door behind her, hesitated, and then locked it. "Let's make sure we don't lose Gerard."

Roman was already at the stairwell door. "Stairs?"

"Yes." They raced up the stairs. "Pappy often takes the stairs, but I wouldn't have thought so today. He was pretty stressed."

"About the reading of the will?" Roman questioned.

"About wanting me to be there."

"So he knew? He knew what Bernice had planned?"

She paused in the act of stepping up another stair. She completed the step thoughtfully, remembering Pappy's tone of voice. "You know. He just might have. He was pretty insistent I get there."

"Would Bernice have used him to witness her will, perhaps? Or told him about what she'd done?"

"Could be either. He loved her. With no limits." She sighed heavily. *What would that be like?*

"It sounds like you don't approve."

She looked up at him in surprise. "Oh, I didn't mean that."

"No?" He didn't sound convinced.

She was quiet for a long moment. "I was wondering what it was like to be loved like that. By two guys, no less."

"Don't you already have a long string of admirers?"

She laughed. And shook her head. "So not. I'm not that femme fatale type."

With a yank, she pulled open the door to the proper floor and walked through. Behind her, she thought she heard Roman mutter, "Good."

She turned to look at him, but his face was neutral. Unreadable. A poker face.

Raised voices told her that the lawyer's office hadn't emptied yet. *Poor lawyer.* She shifted her vision to use what she called her inner eye. Energy flowed in a kaleidoscope of colors. Power fused through and around the colors, infusing the mess with an anger that was unmistakable. People were beyond angry. Some of the individual energies twisted and turned as if searching for an outlet. As if looking for a target.

She didn't dare draw attention to herself. This energy had power. Passion was like that. Anger kept senses sharp and aware. Aware in another way too, like a predator looking for its prey. That same energy allowed people to be super tuned to the whereabouts of the person they were angry with.

In this case, she was that person – the indirect object of their anger. Once they recognized who she was, she'd become the direct object of their wrath. She so didn't want that to happen.

She searched the chaos, looking for her grandfather's energy. She'd be able to identify it anywhere, but right now she was having trouble finding it in the angry crowd.

"What are you doing?"

She paused, turning to look up at Roman, and realized she'd crouched down low to search for low-hanging energy. She probably looked like an idiot.

With a slight groan, she straightened, her mind searching for a plausible answer.

Roman waited. When she didn't answer, he quirked an eyebrow at her.

She shrugged. "Just looking. For anything that might tell me where Pappy went."

"And checking out the carpet is going to do that, how?"

His tone sounded neutral, too neutral. She searched his face. Did he suspect what she'd been doing? She hoped not.

She shook her head to clear her thoughts. Then she spun around and headed into the lawyer's office. Security was assisting the last of the group out of the door, the ones that were still arguing. Shay slipped around behind them and squeezed behind the security officer to enter the room.

The lawyer was standing, staring outside, to beyond the window.

"Mr. McIntosh?"

He started. Then slowly turned around. "You're Shay Lassiter. I'm pleased to meet you." He stepped forward, his hand extended.

Shay grimaced. He looked like he'd walked through a war. "Even after today?"

He laughed. "Of course. I spent a lot of time with Bernice. She spoke highly of you."

"She was a beautiful woman." Shay felt her throat choke and tears welled up in the corner of her eyes. "And I loved her." She sniffled.

He nodded to the room behind them. "I'd hoped for a private reading, but Bernice wanted them all here, hoping that if they all heard the news up front, they'd stop hoping and pestering for something they would never get – and leave you alone."

"She would do that." Shay had to smile. "Speaking of terrible things, have you seen my grandfather, Charles Lassiter?" She studied the lawyer's face anxiously. "He called me from somewhere in the building before the reading, but when I got here, there was no sign of him." She motioned to Roman. "We've been searching for him, calling his home and cell phone, but there's no sign of him."

"Oh dear. He *was* here. I spoke to him earlier."

"When?" Roman's voice cut across sharply.

"I don't know. Maybe twenty minutes before the reading of the will." The lawyer looked down at his planner. "He was worried about you, Shay. I know he planned to call you if you were late."

"And he did. I just don't know where he went after that." She walked the room casually. There was no sign of Pappy's energy anywhere. Inside, a cold nugget of suspicion started to form. He'd been here. At least according to the lawyer...

Or had he? She turned back to face the lawyer. "Did you see Pappy in this room?"

He looked surprised at the question but answered smoothly. "No. In my office." He motioned to the door on the right. "It's through here."

Roman walked around the small austere room.

She asked, "Did he sit down?"

"Yes, he was there in the visitor's chair." The lawyer motioned to a heavy, maroon chair.

Shay moved toward the chair, then stopped and looked at the lawyer, a question on her face.

"Sure, take a look. Maybe he left something behind? Maybe his cell phone? It would explain why you haven't been able to reach him." He shrugged. "I wouldn't have heard it ringing with all the commotion going on in the other room."

Shay took out her cell and tried her grandfather's number again. Nothing.

"Maybe his cell phone battery is dead," Roman suggested.

"Good point." She gave the chair a good going over. "Nothing here." She used the opportunity to look for Pappy's energy signature. There it was. Strong and clear. Weird. It went out the other door – probably the main doorway to the office. She needed to go out there and follow his trail. With a smile directed at the lawyer, she thanked him, adding, "I'll go and check my office. He might have shown up there by now."

Roman spoke up. "Are there provisions in the will in case Shay dies before the assets are transferred?"

The lawyer raised his eyebrows so they were almost hidden under his hair. "Bernice insisted I put in a clause so the assets would go to five different charities if that were to happen."

"Good." Shay moved away from the chair and looked under it. "Make sure I know the list of charities. I'll take a look at their needs to determine the amount of money they require on an annual basis to keep them flush."

The lawyer smiled. "And that's what Bernice would have wanted."

She walked to the doorway Pappy had left by. Roman fell into step behind her. In the main reception, Shay followed the energy instinctively, taking the same route her grandfather had.

"Shay?"

Roman's voice stopped her. She turned to look at him. "What?"

"Where are you going?"

She blinked. And turned around. Pappy's energy went to the left. The main exit was on the right. Turning toward the receptionist, who was busy on the computer, she asked, "Excuse me, what's in that direction?"

The receptionist smiled. "That's McElroy's office. Did you need to make an appointment to see him?"

"I'm actually looking for Charles Lassiter. He was here close to an hour, maybe an hour and a half ago. He's gone missing and given his age..." She gave the woman a small concerned smile. "I'm worried."

"Charles was here. He saw both lawyers. But he left before the reading."

"Oh? Do you know where he went?" She held out her own cell phone, habitually checking for messages once again. "I haven't been able to locate him."

"He didn't say." She smiled. "He did say he was planning to meet a special lady for lunch."

Shay felt something go still inside of her. Surely that was *her*. Had he made other plans and forgotten to tell her? "Do you know who he was meeting?"

"No. He didn't say."

Shay didn't know what to say. Talk about being sidelined by the unexpected. Roman came up behind her. His hand landed on her shoulder and he squeezed gently. "Maybe Charles had other plans for the afternoon?"

Shay couldn't see it, but...what did she know of his private life. He'd loved Bernice...but Bernice hadn't been available... Did he have another lady friend? She'd never looked into the energy in his private life. That was...private. And came under the heading of something she'd never do to him.

"Come on. Let's go collect Grandfather. We could all use some lunch."

He led her toward the hallway and the elevator.

She was still surprised. "I'd planned to have lunch with him myself. Surely he was talking about me? I can't see him having a date."

"Why not?" Roman laughed. "And all the power to him."

"No, you don't understand. He *loved* Bernice. This is a traumatic time for him."

"And maybe he's not on a date, but enjoying the comfort of an old friend. It's *not* you obviously so let's give him some space. We'll give him another shout after lunch."

With that, she Roman led her back toward her office.

Now if only she could find some sign of her Pappy on the way back.

***

They'd barely left the lawyer's office when Roman once again found himself wondering if Shay had psychic abilities of her own. He hadn't connected the dots until he'd seen her studying the carpet. And considered her connection to Stefan – whatever they called it. He choked on the term psychic but knew Dr. Maddy and understood some of what she did. Stefan's reputation preceded him. His skills were proven in the field.

What about Shay? Did she have similar abilities? And if so, what could she do? He'd been wracking his brain looking for a reason for her odd behavior. Even in the lawyer's office she'd gone around the room, as if following something no one else could see. But now...

"What's going on, Shay?" He turned to look at her, but she was back to studying the floor.

Roman shook his head. What would it take to have her trust him? He was a fine one to talk. And he probably should fix that. But if he confided to her it could bring up questions he had no answers for.

"Shay?"

Startled, she spun around to look at him, concern pleating her forehead. "I'm trying to figure out if Pappy came this way."

"I understand that, what I don't get is *how?* What could studying the floor tell you?" He dropped to crouch down beside her. He studied the different expressions as they crossed her face. Consternation. Dismay even. Confusion. "You can tell me, you know."

She hesitated, studying him intently. *What did she see? How deep did her insights go?* It bothered him that there was something she saw in him and his work that he hadn't seen himself. And Stefan... He'd figured it all out. Knew Shay was the model and he also had heard and understood Shay's insights into the artist's character and motivation. And until Roman had those same insights...well, he wasn't looking to share his most intimate thoughts.

Her lips quirked. "Can I?" She cast a last look on the floor then straightened in a smooth graceful movement that made him realize the superb muscle tone of her thighs. His artist's eye immediately filled in the dense quad muscle stroking up the length of her leg, the lean hollow hips, and the long, smooth expanse of skin in between. Damn. He closed his eyes.

He wanted her.

But if that wish came to fruition before he could explain his art to her and she found out...yeah, that would be a bad deal all around.

A little *too* much too explain, and a whole lot *too* late.

***

Shay didn't know what to say. Casting another fruitless look around, she realized she was on the verge of telling him about how she could see the energy people left behind. And how she was reading that energy to try and track her grandfather, but something held her back. There was the whole trust issue again. "I don't think I can share that with you." She stared at him directly.

His brows met on the bridge of his nose. His gaze narrowed. "And why is that?"

"I don't want to deal with any criticism you might have. Especially right now. I have to stay positive – in the light." She hit the button for the elevator. She couldn't figure out why she couldn't see Pappy's energy. According to the receptionist, and Shay had no reason not to believe her, Pappy had left with the intention of meeting a special woman for lunch. If so, then his energy had to be here. And it wasn't.

She just couldn't see it. *And why was that?*

She also realized that Roman was unnaturally silent at her side. The elevator opened. She walked in. Roman followed her and stood slightly behind her. She sent the elevator down to her floor. Roman never said a word.

161

As the door opened, Roman spoke quietly behind her. "I'm not sure what that means, but I'm not critical, you know. I try hard to be very open minded."

She cast a surprised glance behind her. "Are you?" At his nod, she muttered lightly. "Good thing."

At her office, she unlocked the door once again.

"Finally. I was about to come and get you." Gerard sat up from his slouched position on the couch in the waiting room. "Did you find him?"

Roman said, "No. But apparently he left the lawyer's office heading for a luncheon with a special lady friend?"

Surprise lit Gerard's gaze. He was still for a moment and then he laughed and laughed. "Good for him. Sly old dog."

"That's it? That's all you can say?" Shay shook her head and motioned toward the main door. "Let's go now that *I'm* not having lunch with Pappy. I could use something to eat before my assistants bury me in work."

With Roman and Gerard discussing Pappy's life choices, she led the way to the street level. Outside, she took a deep breath and smiled as the sunshine brought out the optimist in her. The sun always seemed to keep the worries away. Still, she had no explanation for why she couldn't see Pappy's energy upstairs in the hallway or leaving the lawyer's office. She should have been able to trace him in this amount of time. Pappy was older, but his vitality was strong. His energy was normally a strong, pulsing wave.

Unbidden, Tabitha came to mind. Then Pappy's strange disappearance... Could her attacker be after Pappy? She hoped not. But was Shay missing something simple?

Such as Pappy having an innocent lunch with a lady friend? If Shay was wrong about that, was he in danger? As they didn't know who the friend was, there was no way to know. If he were in danger, Shay should have seen an indicator, something that would reveal a negative energy at work. Feel something.

Unless the negative energy was hidden...

Or an energy was hiding her Pappy?

***

Knock, knock...

Hey, Shay, once again, this job has proven to be too easy. I had hoped for a bigger challenge. Honestly, is this the best you can do?

Since I began this vendetta, I've watched you work. I've watched you play. And boy, you don't play much.

Do you know what I could do with all that money?

A hell of a lot more than you.

I know how to live. How to have fun.

You sit in your ivory tower and dream of better days, but you don't DO anything.

Like how pathetic is that?

Chapter 15

Monday, early afternoon...

Shay walked back to her office on her own. Lunch had been a simple affair. She'd barely spoken, and Roman and Gerard had kept to general topics. She'd ignored Roman's worried looks directed her way.

Her mind was too full. She called her grandfather as she entered the elevator again. She probably should have walked up the seven flights of stairs, but she hadn't been able to stop the feeling that she'd missed something. That she should have been at the office before this. *Available for Pappy to find her.*

But he could have called her any time. In fact, she'd called him a dozen times. And still no answer. Maybe she should go to his apartment. See if he was sleeping.

At her office, Jordan bustled around, filing away documents. Rose was busy on the phone. As always, Jordan's cheerful personality made Shay feel better. Just being around the two women brightened her mood. "Any messages, Jordan?"

"The lawyers handling Bernice's estate called to set up an appointment for tomorrow for you to go over some paperwork regarding Bernice's bequest to you in the will."

"Right. I should have done that when I was there." Shay walked through to her inner office and sat down. Jordan trailed behind her.

"Should have, but they caught up with me instead, so no worries. Although..." She turned and gave Shay a curious look from the doorway. "I guess you're even wealthier now?" With a casual shrug, she called out as she walked back to her desk. "Lucky girl."

"So not," Shay muttered. She heard the other two women talking.

"You shouldn't bring stuff like that up," Rose said disapprovingly."

"Why? I'm just curious." Jordan sat down so hard, Shay could hear her chair squeak. "I didn't mean any harm."

"It's her personal life. Not office stuff."

"Whatever," Jordan said casually. "She doesn't care."

And that was that. Shay almost laughed. If only the bequest could be handled so simply. She checked her emails. Nothing important. Good enough. She walked back out. "Ladies, I'll be out of the office for the rest of the afternoon. I'll take some of these applications home tonight. Hopefully, I'll have time to go over them this evening."

"If not, then not." Rose gave her a comforting look. "You don't need to work so hard."

Jordan shook her hair, and turquoise braids flipped around her head. "You don't need to work at all. You haven't even had time to grieve for the loss of your old friend yet."

"I know. And I'm not likely to have more time anytime soon."

"All these funerals make one think, don't they?" Rose sighed and stared out the window.

Rose's statement hit Shay as she was reaching for the door. "In what way, Rose?"

Her receptionist looked up in surprise. "Oh, just about life and our lives. The parts we waste and the parts we do well with. It's like our time here is so short, and we don't understand it until it's too late."

"Now if only we could learn that lesson early in life."

With that, Shay walked out, her arms full of new applications. At the parkade level, she walked through the empty basement to her car. Unlocking the vehicle, she dumped the work in the passenger seat and hopped in.

It was just a few minutes to drive to Pappy's place...only his car wasn't parked in his spot in the parkade. She had wanted him to give up driving last year after he'd had a fender bender. It wasn't the accident so much as the stress he went through afterward. It had been days before he'd been able to drive again. Shay had suggested that it might be a good idea to give up driving, but that had made him all the more determined to get back behind the wheel. He was a good driver. But he was eighty, and his reflexes had slowed.

Regardless, Pappy hadn't appreciated the suggestion.

She hadn't repeated it.

Where could he be? He was never out of touch like this. Not this long. Unable to leave without checking his apartment, she parked in his spot and walked to his condo. On the ground floor, she let herself in with her key.

"Pappy. Pappy? Are you here?" The apartment appeared empty. She walked through, checking out the small space. Pappy definitely wasn't there. She pulled her cell phone out of her pocket and called Pappy's number. There was no answering ring in the apartment. So he hadn't left his cell at home. Unless his damn battery had died. She checked his bedroom again, but there wasn't any sign that he'd come home and laid down either. The room was spotless, as always.

She opened her inner vision and searched for any lingering energy to show he'd had a visitor.

There was nothing new. Pappy's energy hovered from early this morning, but there didn't appear to be a second energy. So he hadn't returned here with his lady friend. She locked up and walked out. At her car, she turned around and studied the area. He wasn't out walking. That didn't mean his car wasn't broken down on the side of the road or that he wasn't visiting friends.

His absence *could* be nothing.

But it didn't feel like it.

It felt like everything.

"What is going on between you and Shay?" Gerard walked from the building out into the sunshine ahead of Roman. He dodged around a large group that streamed passed. A horn blared and a taxi sounded its horn in response. Another typical business day in the city.

Roman laughed. "Nothing." And under his breath, he muttered, "Apparently."

"No, there is definitely something there." A teasing lilt in Gerard's tone made Roman groan.

"See, I know." His grandfather shook his finger at him. "A man knows about another man."

"And what do you know?" Roman glanced down in amusement at his grandfather. Word had it that he'd been a hell raiser in his day.

"I know you have a thing for her."

Roman shook his head. The last thing he wanted was to be grilled by his grandfather. In an effort to ward him off, he asked, "Any idea where Charles could be?"

Grandfather took the bait. "Not unless he's holed up in a hotel with that young thing he'd planned to meet for lunch?"

And was that possible? Roman would love to think by the time he hit Charles's age, he was still capable of enjoying an afternoon pleasuring a new lady. But it was hard to believe in this case. Charles had been worried about Shay. And he had a connection to Bernice and planned to attend the reading of her will; *that* he wouldn't have missed. No, it didn't make sense that he'd take off like this.

"And if he isn't with this young lady, do you have a second idea?"

Gerard shook his head and motioned around the streets. "He could be anywhere. Shopping. Resting. Doctor's appointment." Gerard shrugged. "Anywhere."

"Does he have any medical issues? Does he take any medication?"

"No, not at all. He's very healthy. I don't think he's on any medications except for his cholesterol, maybe." Gerard walked beside Roman as they returned to their vehicles at the office building where Shay worked. "I think he's healthier than I am."

"Good. As long as we don't have to be concerned with that aspect." He held the sleek Audi's door open for his grandfather.

"Not that I know of. Then again, given our age, we don't often find out what's wrong until it's too late."

Roman looked around at the busy street. What could he say to that? His grandfather was right.

As the older man buckled up his seat belt, he said to Roman, "And now that you know there's something between you and Shay, do you really want to miss out on the opportunity? I gotta tell you that even if it only lasts for a short time, it could be the romance of a lifetime." He smiled reminiscently. "And I for one, have no regrets answering that call."

With that he drove off, leaving Roman standing and staring behind him.

He didn't want to have any regrets at that age either. But he still wasn't any closer to getting to know Shay better, spending time with her, finding out what made her tick and getting her into his bed. He was even further from having her in his life on a long-term basis.

And if he failed in that endeavor, then he was afraid that he *would* have regrets.

And he didn't want that.

Shay had to stay safe. And he'd done what he could to help that along. He'd made inquiries about a new security system for her. She'd okay the installation. He'd set up his program on her computer and let it run. If there'd been any signs of a hacker, he'd find it. In the meantime, he'd ensure the security on her system was operating at peak performance to make sure no one else got in.

Damned if he was going to lose her when he'd finally found her.

✳✳✳

Monday afternoon…

Shay walked into her apartment several hours later, feeling disoriented and out of touch. Tension ran through her muscles. She'd checked every one of Pappy's frequent haunts. She'd returned to his place to see if he'd come home, and she had been on the phone incessantly looking for him. She'd called everyone she knew in his circle of friends. She couldn't leave it alone.

It was as if he'd just vanished.

Something had to have happened to him. And as much as she hated the thought, someone was likely to have 'happened' to cause that. He was eighty years old and that just added to the problem and her fears. His car was also missing. And that led to her next step.

She picked up her phone and called her favorite detective.

"Ronin. I'm glad I could reach you."

"Shay, what's the matter?"

"It's my grandfather." Quickly she explained.

"But it's only been what…? Four or five hours since you last spoke to him?"

She winced. "I know. It's too early to file a report as a missing person, but he's not a young man any longer. For all I know, he's had a heart attack in his car, and is parked somewhere on the street."

"What type of car is he driving?"

Relieved, she gave him the license plate number and the description of the car.

"I'll let everyone know to keep an eye out for the vehicle and I'll also give them a description of your grandfather. Now does he have any health issues? Is he a diabetic and in need of medicine at a particular time?"

Groaning at how little she knew, Shay ran through the information that she did have. "He doesn't get forgetful, at least I haven't noticed that. He's very sharp mentally. He has sustained a personal loss last week, but he's not suicidal. He doesn't have diabetes, but he has a slight heart condition and high cholesterol – nothing too bad and nothing more than anyone else his age. But I can't stress enough how unlike him this is. With evening coming, he should be home safe and sound. He also always has a nap in the afternoon. At the time he usually lies down, he wasn't at home. I know because I was there, and he wasn't."

"But he could have slept in his car. You know, just pulled off to the side of the road and laid his head back."

"It's possible," she said doubtfully, "but that's not like him."

His calm voiced suggested, "Still not out of the line of possibility."

"True. But with all the other coincidences I can't help but wonder if someone hasn't kidnapped him or worse." She hesitated. "I know it's too early to panic, but—"

"But you're worried." His voice turned businesslike. "Good enough, I'll see what I can do."

He hung up, and Shay dialed Stefan. She'd tried him several times since the reading of the will, but so far he hadn't answered telepathically. But then, when he wanted the world to go away, he was good at making that happen.

Maybe he was home now.

She waited while the phone rang and rang. Finally, just when she was about to hang up, she heard his tired voice. "Stefan?"

"Who'd you expect," he grumbled, "Santa Claus?"

She winced. "Sorry. Not a good day, huh."

"No. I'm working with the police on another case in Seattle." He sighed. "People are dropping like flies. For no reason except someone is having a damn killing fest."

"Ouch. Kinda like my life feels right now. Sorry, I know you're busy."

"Sometimes it gets pretty crazy." His tone changed, eased. "What's up, Shay?"

"It's Pappy. He's disappeared and I can't find him." Stated like that, it shook even her.

"What have you done to find him?"

Shay gave him quick description of her afternoon.

"You say he was at the lawyers', but you couldn't find Pappy's energy leaving the rooms? And he wasn't still there?"

"No. Several people said they'd seen him leave."

"Odd."

"That's why I went back up and took another look at the energy. There was nothing to show he'd gone down the elevator or the stairwell. But he wasn't still in either lawyers' offices."

"That you could see."

"True enough." She thought about that. "I don't want to sound paranoid, but is it possible for someone to have hidden Pappy's presence from me there? I can't see any other explanation. I was thinking about Tabitha's attacker, wondering if they could, through hooks, hide their energy? Maybe do the same with Pappy. And if so, why? And that makes me really worried."

"More likely they're extending the energy of the person beside them enough for them to hide behind...maybe? Like grabbing a corner of their aura and tugging it around them, as if wrapping themselves in a blanket. Such a thing would be new...again, but as you know, it's always possible to do the impossible. Of course is they can hide in someone's aura, they might be able to hide a person in their aura as well. And we won't know the extent of a person's capabilities until we see them."

Damn.

"Still," Stefan continued, "What could possibly be the purpose behind hiding their presence in your grandfather's aura? You inherited all that financial headache, he didn't."

She laughed. The first lightness of the day filled her soul. "Thank you for seeing Bernice's actions for what they are. I gather you heard me screaming earlier?"

"I didn't have a choice," he said, humor to his voice. "It's because of that I had to shut you down this afternoon. I needed to stay focused on this other problem."

"Understandable. And sorry for transmitting so loudly."

He sighed. "You want me to go looking for him, don't you?"

She hated to ask yet more of him, but.... "I'm not the tracker you are," she said apologetically. "And as I haven't been able to find him my way...I wondered if you could drop in and see where he is?"

"Okay then, while I take a look, you revisit the scene at the reading of the will. If Pappy has been kidnapped, look to the people who lost out today. Chances are they'd have the biggest reason to do something like this."

Stefan rang off, leaving Shay staring in shock at the phone. He was right.

Why hadn't she thought of that? Because she'd done her damnedest to forget that whole nightmare of being named beneficiary. How could Bernice not even mention that disaster waiting for Shay?

She crossed to her rocking chair and sat down. Now that she'd gotten hold of Stefan and he was off looking for Pappy, relaxation was easier to achieve. She took her mind back to that morning, to her grandfather's call and her dash to the meeting where the lawyers read the will. She popped into her own energy at the doorway where everyone had collected – and stopped to look around.

The room was more full than she remembered. Then again, she'd slipped into the closest vacant seat and hadn't had much chance to look around. There had to be at least two-dozen people. Most of them she didn't know at all. There were five women that she could count, maybe more. All up in the front.

She recognized Grace, Bernice's assistant, and a younger woman at her side – probably Grace's daughter.

The men she hardly recognized. There was Bernice's driver on the right-hand side and a man that Shay had seen around Bernice's big house. He'd handled most of the household and gardening stuff for her. Their presence made sense. The other men...well she wasn't so sure.

With the meeting started, and from her vantage point, she walked as far forward as she could to see their faces. Then she watched as the final, shocking announcement was made. Grace only nodded, as if she'd expected the news. The same for the two men she'd recognized. Bernice might have already told them her plans. They'd been with her a long time. They were trusted friends.

People in the other rows showed shock, dismay. Some seethed with anger. But at the same time, she saw that no one recognized Shay in the back row. No one turned to point a finger at her. To them, Shay had been just a name. Not a recognizable target.

Good thing.

Still, outside of the anger and threats to contest the will in court, and any number of profanities flung at the lawyer in the front and center, she didn't see anything deceptive.

But because Pappy was missing, she looked deeper.

Hating to do it, she checked out Grace first. No subterfuge there. Grace was mourning the loss of a good friend. She was happy with the thought of all the money coming her way, and she would share that with her daughter.

Shay checked out the daughter. She'd come to support her mother. Was touched at actions and was horrified at the actions of those around her. So far...nice and normal.

Nothing untoward or suspicious.

In fact, the daughter had whispered to Grace, "Poor Shay. That's not going to be easy."

Shay checked out the men next. The first one was touched at his inheritance, but damn if he wasn't grieving the loss of a loved one. Bernice had this fifty-year-old man on the lover's string too. The second man appeared to have a longstanding friendship with Bernice, but it was not loverlike. He was also happy with the money. He'd have liked more, but that's because he wanted to go to Vegas and spend most of it.

Sighing, Shay moved to the next row. There, a bitter unfairness permeated the air.

Fucking bitch.

How dare she?

Good thing she's dead, or I'd have killed her myself. This from a distant relative that had hoped to inherit enough to avoid bankruptcy.

All these thoughts circled with the anger and disbelief. So much hatred. But in a way, the emotions were all normal. Many of these people had come expecting, hoping, for so much more. They'd been told to come, after all, so they had a right to their disappointment. And they hadn't even gotten a mention.

Typical Bernice. Do things her own way and to hell with the others.

She switched to studying the dark red, swirling anger on the left. Wow. Now these three were pissed. She studied their faces, hoping to recognize them in the future. She didn't even know them. She studied the energy that bled from their chakras. The majority bled from the first and third chakras.

Those two chakras covered money, survival, and all the basics in life. These people were also afraid. They needed the money. They had debts, big ones, borrowed from unsavory people, and fear wrapped around the hooks into their chakras. Other people's hooks. She winced at the rate of bleeding from that chakra. And the stream pulsed with fear.

How desperate were these people? Enough to come after her? Had they known ahead of time? Could they have snatched Pappy? Were they planning to hold him hostage until she paid a ransom? And she would. In a heartbeat.

She tried to take a breath, but the pain and fear made it difficult. And she knew better.

She closed her eyes and sent a bolt of white energy down her spine and deep into Mother Earth. Then she sent the energy straight up and out of her own crown chakra into the sky. Instantly her world righted itself, balanced itself. Stabilized. Her chest eased, and she could breathe again.

From her new perspective, she could study the streams that twisted and seethed throughout the room.

One man, a little further back, bled from the heart chakra. But it was his anger that caught her attention. He'd had a relationship with Bernice, and he'd felt he deserved something from her death.

Deserved. But he hadn't caused Bernice's death.

Still, it had been a few minutes now, and she didn't see anything new, just had garnered a deeper insight into the greed of mankind. What she hadn't seen, was any sign of Pappy's energy here. She could do one more thing.

She carried on into the lawyer's office where she had seen his energy right after the reading of the will. Standing in her own memory with the wisps of Pappy right in front of her, Shay couldn't resist.

She took a deep breath and jumped into her Pappy's energy. Opening her eyes, she surveyed the location. Pappy was speaking with his lawyer, not Bernice's.

The conversation moved on around her. Dimly, Shay felt the emotion running through Pappy over the discussion he was having with the lawyer. The discussion was intense, but neither man appeared upset. In fact, they seemed to be hammering out the details of something.

Pappy's business. Not hers. Always mindful of personal boundaries and ethics in a position that gave her greater awareness than she would be privy to in any other way, she tuned out of the conversation and studied the energy pouring off the lawyer. He appeared concerned, yet caring. His heart chakra was engaged, so he cared about Pappy and understood what the man wanted to do. *Good.*

She studied his chakras more closely and realized the lawyer had issues in the very root of the first chakra. She sighed as she understood what the problem was. His energy snaked forward and around Pappy, sliding out the doorway toward the receptionist, where it hooked into her first and fourth chakra. The lawyer was having an affair with her. And she was in love with him. As Shay studied the chakras involved, she realized there was no joy to be had there. She was in love, or believed herself to be, and he was only in lust. She saw that he'd had affairs with the last three women who'd sat in her chair.

Damn. And he was married. With kids.

The receptionist's energy wrapped around the lawyer's body, and there was just way too much of it sitting on the desk. It made Shay shudder, and she forcibly tried to put it out of her mind. Yet again, she found herself in a situation where she didn't really want to see this stuff – unfortunately people left traces of every action, including a hump and bump on the desk.

Her opinion of the lawyer dropped several notches. He might care about Pappy's wishes, but he sure as hell didn't take his business sense into his personal life.

Too bad. Now he had an icky look to him. She was afraid she would even have trouble shaking his hand. He wasn't her lawyer, thank heavens. She'd have a hard time if he were. She'd like to think morals and ethics were a personality trait and not a business asset, to only be used in one area of a person's life. Still, he wasn't embezzling funds – *that* she could see. Or attacking vulnerable old men.

She shuddered again and stretched as far away from Pappy's energy as she could for a better view of the rest of the office. She didn't have a very far leash in this case, but she had enough to stand at the doorway and study the other occupants.

On the other side of the room, Bernice's lawyer was on the phone. The energy drifting around the partially open doorway told Shay that he was trying to change an appointment he'd made with his wife. Good enough. All in all, the energy she saw was normal people stuff. Nothing excessive or dangerous.

Nothing more negative than she'd find in any group of normal people.

She watched as Pappy stopped to say hello to the lawyers' office receptionist. Her energy was warm and caring, same as the lawyer's. Interesting. Still Pappy was a loveable soul. Shay hadn't really expected anything else. He walked out to the hallway and pulled out his phone. She heard his phone call to her.

She could hear her own responses in a tinny, distant sort of way. She studied his actions. He appeared slightly worried about her but nothing untoward.

Up ahead, he walked down the hallway to the men's room.

She waited outside as he went in. That too was normal. She had boundaries she didn't cross. Not unless she was forced to. Going into the men's with her grandfather was one boundary she hoped she wouldn't ever be forced to cross.

Except her grandfather didn't come out of the bathroom.

Shay?

Stefan.

***

Knock, knock...

Damn, Shay, there are none as blind as those that think they have perfect sight.

You, my dear, are as blind as a dead man in this case. And a dead man is what your grandfather is going to be soon.

And you won't know what happened.

I couldn't believe it when I found out that you, with all your millions, just received many more. For what? For nothing.

For that added insult, you will pay yet again.

I just have to make sure you understand that when he and all the others die, it will be because of you.

As a general rule, I don't like to kill little old men. But I will.

I have nothing personal against this dear old man. Now little old woman, that's a different story. Bernice deserved what she got. Honest. Your grandfather, however, could live out the rest of his life in peace and quiet, except that he's related to you.

You're lucky because there was something odd about him today. Something different about his energy. I let him go because I know where to find him again. Still, I made you worry, didn't I?

Slowly, unable to stop it, everyone related to you is going to disappear — one by one.

I'd prefer that you knew I was doing this, and I need to figure out how to make you really worry. I want you scared. I want you panicked. I want you to know it's you that I'm hunting. Even if you don't understand why at first…

You will by the time I'm done.

How?

Wait and see.

For now, I'll leave your grandfather alone for a little longer. And pick on someone else.

Your grandfather will still get what's coming to him, but then, so will you.

Eventually.

I'm going for maximum pain. And that means I need this to last a little while longer.

Chapter 16

Shay blinked several times and retuned her consciousness to her apartment.

Stefan, I'm here. With her return to the present, all her worries came flying back. She hoped Stefan had found answers that she hadn't.

What did you find out?

He's alive. But he's unconscious.

Shit. How do you know?

I could track him to his position but not to his mind. I can't see his physical location. I can't tell if he's badly hurt, either. In fact, although I can tell he's alive, I can't tell if he's injured. It's like a fog protecting him. A feminine fog.

What? What do you mean a feminine fog?

Stefan's voice, although tired, had an amused ring to it. *If I had to guess, I'd say a woman was trying to help him. Or hide him,* he added thoughtfully. *Not sure that there couldn't have been two women though. The space he is in is public. Lots of energies. Have you seen Bernice hanging around lately? This sounds like something she'd do.*

Hide him? Do you think someone has hurt him?

I'm not sure. I couldn't see clearly because of this energy. I couldn't even say that it was Bernice there, just that there was a heavy white energy blanket around him.

Would a blanket like that protect him from other people's view?

Hmmm. Maybe. Stefan's voice was slow, thoughtful. *That's possible I suppose. I found him easily enough with your energy markers. You love him and he loves you, and that means there is a strong energy exchange between you. That makes it easier to see markers. What I don't know is why you couldn't see him.*

She winced. Please do not let it be her current insecurity on reading energy. If anything happened to Pappy because of that... Then she remembered Bernice's concern words...

I suppose Bernice could be helping – or maybe hindering would be a better way to say it. She said she had to stay here for some reason. Maybe it was because Pappy was in danger? On the other hand, I don't know how much danger he could be in, so she might be helping him out more by keeping the fog there. Damn. I need to find him.

Yes, you do, Stefan said. *His life force wasn't terribly strong.*

Was he lying down? Sitting? Standing? Could you tell?

Stefan fell silent. *He's lying down, on his side, almost curled into a fetal position.*

Her thoughts turned even darker. *So he could be in any small space, and he might be injured. Did you sense a massive drain in his energy in any way?*

No. His energy is holding. He's not been shot or anything that I could tell.

Well that's good news. But not good enough. Any suggestion as to what to do now?

Slip into my energy. Track him back. His voice changed. *I have to go.*

And just like that Stefan was gone.

Shay didn't waste time thinking through the process, she closed her eyes, picked up Stefan's energy and stood in his warm glow. Damn. There'd been very few times she'd been in here, and each time there'd been a sense of wonder. So much love. So much power.

Move it. Stefan gave her a psychic prod. *Now.*

If she'd had time she'd have laughed. It's as if he were embarrassed. Then she was in his personal space. Had access to so much private information of a very private man. Good thing she held to a strong code. But she was moving swiftly, following his earlier path to her Pappy. As she didn't have to search like he had, the journey was fast.

She landed on a bench in a downtown square. Pappy's car parked in front of her and Pappy curled up on his side beside her, as if homeless and asleep. Her heart broke. He looked so lost. But also healthy and alive.

Confused and more than a little worried, she gave him a quick once over but his energy flowed, his vitals, although weaker than she'd like, were solid. He wasn't hurt. Relief washed through her.

***

There you are, Bernice complained. *Do you know how long I've been sitting here watching over him? Trying to hide him. You know what could happen to him out here like this? What took you so long?*

Shay stared at Bernice's ghost in disbelief. She'd been hiding him? Since when?

As if anticipating her question, Bernice volunteered. *I could feel something was wrong. When I thought about him, I found myself transported here. With him lying like this. Is he going to be okay?*

Shay grinned. He's going to be fine. At least she hoped so. She couldn't be happier that Pappy had Bernice for his guardian angel. *You don't know how he got here, do you?* Shay asked.

Bernice's energy shimmered. *No.*

Figures. Shay studied the area, and realized she could just see the street signs at the intersection through Bernice's 'cloak.' Damn who'd have thought she ever be able to do that?

The sign read: Thurlow and Rasford.

Perfect. She sent that message back to Stefan, asking him to tell Ronin.

Done, came the whispered acknowledgement.

Knowing that help was coming, Shay studied Bernice. *The police are on their way, Bernice. I need you to drop your protective cloak and let him be found.*

But what if someone else finds him first? the older woman fretted. *What is going on Shay? I don't like this.*

Neither do I. But you have to leave him alone so he can get help. Inspiration struck. *Bernice, head to the hospital so you'll be there waiting for him when he comes in.*

Just then a cop car approached slowly.

Bernice shimmered in place for a moment, then she slowly disappeared.

The cop car came to a stop.

Thank heavens. Sure that Pappy was going to get the help he needed, Shay let go. And found herself sucked at sonic speed through the ethers on Stefan's golden energy highway until she was dumped back into her body on her chair.

She groaned as her physical body struggled to adjust and her consciousness took a little longer to recover in the physical confines of reality.

The phone rang as she struggled to reorient herself to the new reality.

She picked up the phone. *Ronin*. With her voice, slow and groggy, she answered, "Hello."

"We found your grandfather. Thanks to you and Stefan."

"Oh that's wonderful," she cried. "Where is he?"

"He was found on city bench just like you said and close to his parked vehicle. He seemed disoriented and confused but in good health. He was able to talk fine, but he couldn't explain how he got where he was or what he was doing there. He's on his way to the hospital."

"Thank you so much." Shay's heart wrenched at the thought of her grandfather all alone and hurting.

"I'm hoping you have a set of keys and can move it his car?"

"I have spares. I'll take care of it." She'd have to call a cab, though that was minor. After effusive thanks, she rang off and called Gerard. His line was busy.

Not wanting to waste time, she called the cab company, grabbed her purse along with Pappy's spare keys, and headed out.

The cab dropped her off at the car. No tickets. Thank heavens for something. She hopped in, was grateful when it started, and drove the car to the hospital. Outside in the lot, she tried to call Gerard one more time. Still nothing. Roman was next.

"Shay?" his growl filled the line, sending shivers down her spine. She so had to deal with that attraction soon. "Do you have any news?"

Quickly she filled him in.

"I'll bring Grandfather."

He wouldn't listen to her assurances that she'd call after speaking with Pappy's doctor, and knowing how close the two old men were, she didn't bother arguing any further. Closing the phone, she strode inside toward the receptionist. Her grandfather was in a cubicle off the emergency room, leaning back on the white bed, staring at the ceiling. Bernice sat quietly at his side as a warm loving energy stroking Pappy's arm. Shay gave her a beaming smile as she entered.

"Oh Pappy!" She ran the last few steps and hugged him. Lying in bed, he seemed so frail and old. She couldn't think about losing him right now.

"Shay, I'm fine." He patted her back. "There, there."

She pulled back to stare down at him mistily. "Are you? What happened to you? I've spent all day searching for you." She tried to keep her voice down and in control, but failed on both accounts. Realizing she was attracting attention and disturbing others in potentially worse situations, she calmed down enough to perch on the side of his bed.

She sniffled back tears. "Are you feeling okay?" She studied his skin color. He looked fine. Maybe tired, but his color was strong. She looked deeper. His energy ran smoothly, the pulsation normal, vibrant.

Did nothing make sense anymore?

He looked embarrassed at her questions. "I don't know," he admitted. "It's like the afternoon is a blank. Just didn't happen."

"Do you remember calling me?" At his nod, she continued, "I came right to the lawyer's office, but you weren't there." Hot tears welled up again. Willing herself to calm down before she burst into tears and upset them both, she repeated helplessly, "I spent all afternoon trying to find you."

"I guess I went outside for a walk to clear my head, apparently drove off, and ended up at City Park. At least that's where the police officer found me sitting. My car was in front of me, but I was sort of napping on the bench – I guess."

"Napping?" she said cautiously, hating that he'd blanked out like that. Could he have been drugged? She'd have to wait to hear back from the doctors on his condition. "You might have been really tired if you didn't have your regular nap. Which I know you didn't have at home, because I went there and checked."

He brightened. "Did you? Well as much as I'm sorry for causing you unnecessary worry, it's nice to know you went to such lengths."

She smiled down at him. "Oh you are, are you? Well don't do it again, please. It's too hard on my heart."

"Bosh. You're a young'un. Your heart is just fine."

"And what about mine, Charles?" Gerard's shaky but surprisingly loud voice cut through the chatter.

Pappy smiled. "You didn't need to make the trip. I'm just fine."

"If you were so fine," Gerard replied testily, "then you'd know how you ended up on that damn park bench. Can't let you out of my sight without you getting into trouble. I even saved you a seat at the zoo of a will reading." Gerard shook his head. "You really missed something. Too bad Bernice couldn't have seen that chaos."

"She'd have loved it." Pappy laughed. "Nothing Bernice liked better than a good scrap. I suppose she left little bones to most people, a couple of meaty bones to a few, and a hind quarter or so to those she cared about, huh?

Gerard grinned. "Exactly. Then she threw the whole carcass at Shay here, along with the responsibility to do right."

Pappy winced. "Typical Bernice. She didn't mention anything to you before her death, Shay?"

A snort escaped her. "So not. I'd have told her what to do with her money."

Pappy grinned. "That's why she didn't. If she'd let you know ahead of time, she'd be leaving the door open to you trying to get out of the inheritance."

"Damn right I would have," Shay muttered.

"Not many people would turn down a fortune." Roman's deep voice interrupted them.

She turned to see him standing at the end of the bed. *When had he arrived?* And damn, he looked good. She blinked and forced her gaze back to Pappy. Unfortunately, Pappy had caught her look and winked at her. Heat washed up her neck, again. She glared at him. She was so not going there with him.

Speaking of such things... "Pappy, the receptionist at the law firm said you were meeting a special lady for lunch. Who was it?"

His face went blank.

Her heart ached. This couldn't be much fun for him. She smiled down at him. "I figured it was me."

"We tried to convince her, Roman and I, that you were entitled to your flings just like any man," Gerard said a little enviously. "I hope you had a dashing afternoon."

Pappy laughed. "Damn, I hope so. Too bad I don't remember a blasted thing."

Gerard grinned. He leaned forward and whispered, "You might have to check your supply of the little blue pills to see how successful you were."

Shay rolled her eyes and caught Roman's big grin and barely hid her own smile. Men were men, no matter what age they were. And if this conversation put a smile on her grandfather's face, then she was all for it.

***

Monday evening...

Due to the lateness of the hour, and the fact that the tests hadn't all come back, Pappy was admitted to the hospital overnight. He started to show signs of exhaustion so Shay waited for him to fall asleep. Bernice disappeared hours ago.

She was pondering the unusual amount of time she'd spent at hospitals lately when a nurse came in and nudged her arm.

Startled, she followed the nurse's movement to see Pappy was sound asleep.

"He should sleep through the night. Go and rest yourself. You look like you've had a tough day."

Standing up, Shay nodded. "I think I will. It has been tough. Tough and long."

"Go. You can't look after him if you aren't strong and healthy yourself."

With a last glance at her grandfather, Shay walked out of the hospital into the cool evening air. She had totally lost track of time. It wasn't just evening, it was pitch black outside, the dark of night. She pulled out her cell phone and realized it was past midnight. No wonder she was tired.

The thought of driving home didn't appeal, but the lure of her own bed was enough to push her forward. The streets were empty.

Her apartment was cool and dark. Not that she cared at this point – she just wanted her bed. She dumped her purse on the couch and kicked her shoes off at the front door. Walking to her bedroom, she started undressing, intent on becoming horizontal as fast as she could.

She only made it three steps inside her room when she felt it.

Something.

Off.

And damn scary. Blackness like she'd never seen before surged up in front of her. She stepped backwards. Then she turned and ran for the door.

But not fast enough.

She collapsed on the living room floor. Out cold.

***

Stefan bolted upright in bed. *Shay?*

He gasped, choked, his hands flailing at his chest and neck. A haze of blackness filled his room, strangling him.

He pounded his chest, trying to get oxygen into his lungs. Only to realize he had no trouble breathing.

With that he understood he was caught in a vision. Someone else's vision.

Shay's vision.

He closed his eyes, took a steadying breath, focused on Shay and jumped into her mind. Her soul stirred.

Stefan?

Yes, it's me. You're unconscious. I don't know why.

Blackness. It came out of nowhere. Surrounded me. Smothered me.

Yes, I felt it. But it's an illusion. Like a cloaking energy again. It's not smoke. It's not fire. You can breathe. You need to wake up.

She groaned. *It's hard to move.*

I'll get help.

Stefan walked throughout Shay's apartment in his astral form. He couldn't see any immediate danger, but...he didn't want to leave her alone either.

He zipped back into his body and shrugged into his skin suit, as he liked to call it. Feeling the normal, yet confining sensation of being reoriented back into the right reality, he opened his eyes. He needed to track that energy back to the source – but first things first.

Stefan opened his phone and called Roman.

"Hello." Roman growled into the phone. "You better have a damn good reason for calling."

"Shay's been attacked. You need to go her apartment. I don't have time to explain." Stefan closed the call and tossed the phone on the bed, and then lay down and jumped free again.

He slipped into predator mode...and went hunting in the ethers.

***

"*Shay's been attacked? What the hell? Stefan. Stefan?*" The dial tone rang endlessly in Roman's ear, and he knew Stefan was gone.

Shay. She was in trouble and Stefan had called Roman to deal with it. A fact that disturbed and delighted Roman. He threw back the covers and quickly dressed. Five minutes later, he was heading for Shay's apartment.

The next problem was security. How was he going to get inside the building and inside her apartment?

Luckily, the doorman recognized him, called up and buzzed him in. So Shay was talking at least. Or someone was with her who'd answered the call. With a casualness he was far from feeling, Roman strode over to the elevators and caught a ride to the twelfth floor. Once outside the right apartment, he pounded on the door. Stefan didn't say if Shay was hurt or unconscious. Roman presumed he'd have called for an ambulance if she couldn't get to the door.

The door opened in front of him.

Shay, still dressed as she'd been at the hospital, rubbing the side of her head and looking dazed, stared up at him. "Roman? What's the matter? Why are you here at this hour? I couldn't believe when the doorman called up to me." Her gaze widened. "Oh my God. Is it Pappy? Has he died?"

She grabbed his shirt with both hands and shook him – or tried to. He had close to a hundred pounds on her. He wrapped his hands around her much smaller ones and gently disentangled them, but he kept them in his grasp. "No. Pappy's fine. Let me in, please."

"Oh." She blinked owlishly at him, and then hurriedly stepped back. "Sorry. Of course. Come in." She closed the door behind him.

He ignored her for the moment, looking around to see what had caused Stefan's worry. The apartment looked as normal as he'd seen it last time. He walked further in. Nothing unusual.

He spun around and studied her. She looked like she'd come dashing out of bed with a pounding headache. Except she was still fully dressed in slacks and blouse. Just a little scattered.

"What's the matter?" she asked, confused. She walked over to her couch and sat down, pulling her knees up to her chin and staring at him. She blinked several times, as if having trouble focusing. "I don't understand what's going on."

"Neither do I." He ran his fingers through his hair and sat down on the closest easy chair. "I can only tell you that Stefan called me fifteen minutes ago and told me to get over here. He said you'd been attacked."

"Attacked?" She gazed at him in shock. "I did wake up a few minutes ago on my living room floor, but why would Stefan call you?"

He glared at her. "I don't know. Ask Stefan." He looked around the apartment. "I can't see anything wrong. So I don't understand... What did Stefan mean?" He spun back. "*You woke up on the living room floor?*"

She looked at him from under her lashes. What was she thinking? Was she trying to hide something? And if so, what? Groaning he leaned forward, placing his forehead on his hands. How could he get her to trust him? Damn it.

"Are you okay?" A warm hand landed softly on his. "I'm sorry Stefan worried you like this. It's late. Go home."

He snorted and glared at her. But his hand ensnared her fingers. "Stefan told me you'd been attacked. I have to trust that he didn't make that up and that means, for whatever reason, either you don't remember the danger, or you don't want me to know. Either way, that pisses me off."

She tugged her hand free. "Stefan shouldn't have called. There's nothing you can do."

"Nothing?" he snapped, jumping to his feet. "I can stop whoever attacked you from coming back and trying again. Surely that's something." His hands clenched and unclenched in frustration. "Good thing that security system is being installed in the next couple of days – it'll be tomorrow if I get my way."

"That won't help."

"Why not?" he roared.

As the last words left his mouth he watched her lower lip tremble, her eyes begin to shimmer with tears. "

"Oh God. I'm so sorry." He sat down beside her and gathered her into his arms. "Why do you fight me so?"

"Because you don't believe in me. In us. Because you have walls and are keeping secrets from me." She whispered the last bit so softly he struggled to hear, even then doubting what she'd said. He leaned back slightly and stared down at her. He didn't get it. Cautiously, he asked, "Believe in you? Of course I do."

"No," she whispered from against his chest. "You don't."

"Then explain it to me, so I *can* believe." He reached down and tilted her chin up. "Make no mistake, whatever other parts you are confused about, know that I believe in you." He paused, waiting until she looked up at him, and added, "And I believe in us."

She studied him, as if trying to peer into his heart.

He let her. Something major was going on, and he needed to know what it was.

She dropped her lashes.

"Don't." He said roughly. "Don't shut me out like that."

Her gaze flew open again, this time she had a dawning realization in her hazel eyes. The colors swirled with mystery. If only he could put that on canvas.

"Are you saying...?" She tilted her head slightly, locking her gaze on his face. "Are you saying that you *care*?"

He opened his mouth to give a trite answer. And her eyes narrowed. As if she knew. He bit back the words and thought about what she'd asked. "Yes, I care."

And he left it at that.

But she wouldn't. She studied him for a little longer. "As a fellow human being, as a friend...or as something more?"

"You already know I want much more."

"Yeah?" she leaned back and stared, pinning him with a deep mysterious gaze. "How much more?"

Shit.

He felt his body freeze. While he understood something momentous was happening, he hadn't been thinking about bleeding out truths himself. Or baring *his* emotions. More like she should be the one telling the truth. Instead he'd been put on the spot. With options. And he hated this type of conversation, so full of hidden land mines.

And what should he say? It was hardly the time to tell her about his paintings. And he doubted she was ready to hear how much he really cared. Not when she'd been playing the nervous avoidance game.

He didn't want to send her running. Not now. Her life was in danger and he needed to be here. He couldn't take the chance.

***

She watched Roman freeze mouselike, as if sensing a predator. She was no predator, but she dealt in truths. Ones he had no idea even existed. She had to know where he stood before she discussed this any further.

She had the option of watching his energy, and that reassured her like nothing else could. It swirled around her, around *them* gently. His, caressing her energy and blending with hers with loving attention. That was one truth she could count on.

That he took time to answer meant he was trying to determine the level of involvement he wanted or was willing to admit. No one had trouble saying 'friends'...unless there was something more... Perhaps neither of them had taken that path mentally.

His energy said his all was in this relationship. If she had to, she could let him off the hook and take it on faith. But – and this was a different problem – if she wanted him to commit, she had to be prepared to say the words as well.

She'd known him as an email friend for months. And he'd intrigued her then but now it was different. He'd come into her life personally with Bernice's death. Her life had been crazy since. But he'd been there every step of the way. She hadn't been exactly open and straightforward with him either.

She sighed. "That you don't answer speaks more than real words."

"Does it?" his strangled voice made her laugh.

"Yes, it does." She grinned. "I'll take it we're somewhere between friends and something more?" She looked directly at him.

"Agreed." He nodded immediately, and she laughed.

"Good. That's on both sides. Where we go from here is our choice. We appear to be at a crossroads. I can't go forward unless you believe in me. And I can't share what happened tonight unless you have an open mind. A *really* open mind." She gazed out the window for a long moment. "Like Stefan has. He is the one person who I trust over anything and everyone."

At the slight twist to his lips, she paused. "And considering that we might be heading toward the more-than-friends side of life..." Was it just yesterday that she said she wasn't going there again? Anyway, she focused on his narrowed gaze and that eerie stillness, and finished with, "Stefan and I are friends. Only friends...we've *never* been lovers. I love him like a brother and trust him with my life."

His lips untwisted into a warm smile. "Thank you for sharing that with me," he said with sincerity in his voice. "You're blessed to have that relationship with him."

She couldn't help it. She chuckled. "It comes with its own set of problems. He can read your thoughts, jump into your mind, see what you're feeling, and that's just for starters."

"So he's really...psychic?" Roman asked.

"Oh he is." She leaned back slightly, losing the hint of humor that had kept the conversation light. "And that's one of the things I need you to believe. Stefan *is*," she stressed, and then continued, "the real thing." She took a deep breath. "And so am I."

Chapter 17

Late Monday evening…

There it was. The answer to that very question he'd been wondering about.

Roman turned his head, his gaze pinning her in place. She looked so normal, beautiful even though exhausted – but she also appeared to be calm. She lounged on the couch so casually after dropping a fairly important bit of information.

And indeed, her claim wasn't exactly a claim everyone would make.

"Oh." Not very intellectual but it's all he could think of to say.

She nodded her head. "Yeah." She shrugged. "It's not a term I think of when I consider my abilities. But that's what the world calls it."

"What *would* you call it?"

"I'd prefer intuitive, maybe energy specialist. I do a lot of different stuff, but most of it…only rarely." She shrugged. "As my abilities defy categorization, I try to avoid doing so myself."

"And can you do all that Stefan can?" He knew some about Stefan's telepathic abilities and mind reading from Dr. Maddy, and he wanted to ask if she could read his mind too, but at the same time, he desperately didn't want to know the answer. The humiliation, if she discovered his secret, would be too much.

"No. Not at all."

Thank heavens for that. He took a deep sigh and released the breath he'd been holding.

She laughed. "I'm not a mind reader, if that's what you're worried about."

"Then what do you *do?*" he asked curiously.

A self-deprecating smile slid off her lips. "I read energy. I can see where people are coming from, see how they use their energy, and see what they use their energy for. If they are the kind to cheat others, their energy will tell me. It they are the type to cheat on their wives, I'll usually be able to see it. And that is just for starters."

"Wow." He didn't know what to say. An interesting concept. He could see why she used the term intuitive, as much of what she saw others would intuit from body language, facial expressions, and even nuances in a voice. And he had to admit it was a relief that she couldn't read his mind.

But what *could* she see of him? He decided to ask, remembering Stefan's words on insights.

"And what do you see...with me?"

She shook her head. "I make it a policy to not delve too deeply with people I know. I use my skills to administer the foundation money as well as I can." She sighed. "It's a problem with friends. Whether it's me being afraid of reading too much into the issue or not being detached enough, I find it difficult to read my friends."

"Good. I think." But it didn't answer what he really wanted to know. And damn it, he really wanted to know. He took the plunge. "Stefan mentioned something about you having interesting insights into my artwork. Is that the type of stuff you can pick up?"

She waved her hand around. "Stefan told you that? Interesting." She shrugged. "It's not much. I just saw how much you related to your model. That she's your muse. Your passion." She hesitated. "That's why I'm surprised you're interested in me. The way I see it, you're madly in love with her."

Madly in love with her.

With his model. With Shay. She could see *that*?

He sat back on his heels. Rocked by the revelation.

His heart sighed at a sad lonely truth. Though he hadn't admitted it, he'd been in love with her for a long time. His mind filled with images he'd poured over to get everything about her, down just right. The curve of her shoulder as he painted it, the long smooth strokes making the skin glow like it was meant to. He'd tried to paint other models, women, children. He'd even tried to get into landscapes. And he hadn't managed any creative energy at all.

Was that why? He was painting the object of an unrequited love. God, that made him sound like a schoolboy. Or worse – a teenager.

"I'm sorry."

He quickly turned his head back to face her.

"I didn't mean to bring up a painful topic. It's not like I was reading energy or anything, it's just that it was obvious to me that you were obsessed with her. In a good way," she added hurriedly.

"Obsessed." *Interesting… Was he?*

Absolutely. What else could he call it? He'd given into the need to paint her two years ago then had worked up the nerve to contact her. Bad timing on his part as her fiancée had just passed away. Still, he'd stayed always there, slowly building the relationship until he could get back to Portland. Hoping she'd be ready for him. That he hadn't been able to paint anything different since that first canvas *might* be viewed as an obsession.

"That she is the other half to your heart." Shay sounded distant, hurt…insecure.

And he got it.

Oh God. And how did *that* work? He had been trying to get Shay to move forward with this relationship, and she'd assumed what, that he'd lost his heart to the model? That she was his second choice? A poor one at that?

He couldn't possibly have seen this coming. Who could?

"So, I don't want to know what happened between the two of you, but I am sorry."

"Sorry?" He felt disconnected. As if he were hearing the conversation from a long distance away.

"She's obviously unavailable to you for some reason."

He blinked. *Say what?*

She flushed. "I'm getting personal, again I'm sorry. Forget I said that."

She went to stand up, and he tugged her back down. "Please, finish what you were going to say."

Troubled, she said, "It's just that I feel like you've always admired, loved this woman from afar. The paintings are stunning. But the woman was distant. As if your love was never recognized. You never had a chance to fully experience that passion. You painted it on the canvas because you couldn't have it, have her in your life – in your heart."

He sat back. Oblivious to everything but the second truth bomb she'd just dropped. How could she possibly know all that? Especially when he hadn't seen it that clearly himself.

And even worse. How could he ever explain that she was the model? She was the one he pined for? That he loved.

And now he was certain – Shay *was* the other half of his heart.

***

Shay studied the shock on his face. He really hadn't known it. How could that be? And if he hadn't known it, then he wasn't ready to move on with another relationship. And maybe that was a good thing. With the mess going on in her world, she didn't need another complication. And Roman was complicated. Even as they spoke, his energy curled up next to her. Twining into her own energy. Wanting to be close. To her.

Wanting to be with her though a part of him was unsure. Was it his own feelings causing that hesitancy or was he uncertain about his welcome?

That lack of clarity made her uneasy.

And the one truth she'd always believed was that energy never lied. But people did.

So, for whatever reason his mind might be stuck on his model, his heart and his energy from his heart, said he was ready for so much more.

Stefan had said it was time. When he'd told her, she didn't agree. She was still unsure. But Stefan trusted Roman. And if she trusted one thing for sure, it was Stefan. His judgment. His ethics. His understanding beyond what she knew. And that knowing she could trust him brought her some relief—she had to trust *someone*.

Besides, Stefan had inner knowledge about her supposed time for a relationship that he hadn't shared. And he wouldn't give her any more information at this point – suggesting free will and all that.

She mentally knocked on Stefan's mind – and found it locked against her. She sighed. Now what was he up to?

"Problems?"

"Stefan isn't answering," she said absently.

"And you know this how?" His extremely neutral tone of voice alerted her.

She turned to look at him. "Remember about that whole belief stuff? Well, I just knocked on Stefan's mind to see if he was home. I planned to ask him why the hell he contacted you when I'm fine."

He opened his mouth as if to speak, then shook his head and said, "Was he so wrong? Weren't you *not* fine a few moments ago? You said you woke up on the living floor. Surely that's not normal."

"He's rarely wrong. But that doesn't mean he's thinking the same way I am." She closed her eyes and mentally reached out for Stefan again. "He's still not there."

"I think, from what I understood, he couldn't be with you because he was going after someone."

"The black smoke. Right I remember now," she whispered as the memory of being smothered in dark nasty energy overwhelmed her. "I wonder if he can get the answers we need."

"Black smoke? If he can *what*?"

She didn't answer.

Roman leaned forward and placed a gentle hand under her chin and tilting it up so he could see her eyes. "Tell me."

Taking a deep breath, she broke the code of silence she'd kept all of her life. And she told him exactly what she knew about tonight.

He sat back and listened quietly. Not judging.

For that she was grateful.

She ventured a glance up at him. He was still studying her quietly. She dropped her gaze and sighed inwardly. What had she expected? Understanding? Acceptance?

She should be grateful his energy hadn't whipped back to wrap tightly around his body. Instead it stayed, shimmering up against her energy.

"You know how farfetched all this sounds?"

It was the thin thread of amusement in his voice that had her head coming up sharply.

"Oh yes," she said softly, a tiny smile playing at her lips. "I do. It must sound totally crazy."

He sat back, crossed his arms. "You mean what you say, but I hope you won't mind if I ask Stefan to confirm this?"

She laughed. "Ask away."

"Well, I'll have to call him."

"Don't bother. He's here now." And sure enough, Stefan's warm laughter flitted through her mind. "Go ahead and ask him. He'll answer."

Roman laughed, disbelieving. "Sure, but you'll be telling me what he said so that won't help any."

Oh boy. She grinned. "Do you really want to know the truth? Deep inside? Do you want to know if any of this woohoo stuff is real?"

"You're talking about proving it to me?"

"Yes." She laughed. "That's what I'm suggesting." She tilted her head. "So yes or no?"

He lifted his shoulders then dropped them. "Sure. Go for it."

Inside she laughed. *Go for it, Stefan. Let's make a believer of him. We could use a few more good guys.*

Her mind was instantly empty, no more Stefan. She sat back to watch.

Roman sat bolt upright, his face went slack, and if the color could be wiped off in a single stroke, that's what it looked like.

Shay laughed delightedly.

His head swiveled in her direction.

His jaw dropped, and when he could, he said, incredulously, "He's in my head?"

"Not really. But he is speaking to you telepathically."

Roman's gaze narrowed. "Stefan? Can't you appear in the living room or do something not so...private?"

Shay laughed. "It's amazing, isn't it?" She looked for Stefan's form to materialize. Her gaze switched from chair to chair, and then she realized that Stefan had sat down beside her. She switched over to look at Roman. He was looking around the room.

"Can you see him, Roman?" she asked curiously. "He's sitting beside me."

Roman studied the couch. "No. I can't."

"Too bad. It would provide the proof you seem to need."

"Or he could tell me something that no one else would know. That could be convincing proof," he challenged.

It was impossible not to chuckle. "Really? Like, do a reading?" She turned to face Stefan.

"Stefan? What about it?"

I feel like a circus show. There was a moment of silence, then Stefan sighed and said, *Sure. What the hell.*

***

Roman settled back in his chair to see what would happen next. He couldn't believe what he'd felt so far. Then he felt that weird inner sense of connectedness again. He straightened.

Stefan's voice floated through his mind, warm and mocking. *This time and this time only I will be nice. I chose this method of providing proof for one reason only – that is to save Shay the embarrassment of finding out what I'm going to tell you. You want to know something personal that no one else would know, as proof I'm not a charlatan?*

"No. Actually I believe in you, but I'm not sure about this whole woowoo business. It's a little tough on the uninitiated."

He could see laughter flit across Shay's face. *Was she tuned in too?* He wanted to ask her a mess of questions but Stefan was speaking again.

No. She isn't 'tuned' in. Although I know why you'd be worried. You don't want Shay to know that she is your model. That you have been drawing her body, in intimate detail, for two years? Or how about this? The real reason you can't paint her face is because you can't face her? You feel that there is something deceitful in your creating her likeness without her permission. I also know why there is blue in your earlier paintings and just a skim of it in your later ones. But that revelation will have to wait a bit.

"Oh shit." Roman leaned back and closed his eyes. Now he was in really deep shit. "I'm sorry. What do I need to do to get out of this with my dignity?"

Apologize? I presume you're convinced by now.

"Yes. Sorry," he muttered. How had he gotten into this shit anyway?

By being you. Shay needs you. You need her. Why am I the only one that sees this?

Roman cast a wary glance at Shay, who appeared to be enjoying this. He wasn't. He didn't want to insult Stefan any more than he had already but…

I'm gone.

And just like that Roman's mind emptied, cooled. Stefan was gone.

Thank God.

But would Stefan keep Roman's secret?

***

Tabitha floated on the peaceful clouds of the ethers. She walked here often, but normally she could return when she wanted to. She didn't understand what the problem was this time.

Something had happened. Something painful.

She wasn't what anyone would call soft or delicate, but even with her abilities, she felt vulnerable out there. She could hide in here. Not something she did well. Or often.

So why was she hiding now?

Danger.

She was in danger. So was someone else. *Who?* She tried to concentrate. To focus on the problem. But that was the problem with the ethers – real life problems weren't tangible parts of this reality. They felt distant. Unreal. Hard to care about.

And with that thought, Tabitha floated off again.

***

Knock, knock…

Ah Shay.

You don't even know that I had your grandfather. That I led him away like a puppy on a leash. Now how wrong is that? I should have left a note in his pocket. Let you know that he'd been targeted.

Or maybe I should have just killed him outright.

But then you wouldn't have spent the day and evening worrying. Maybe I should visit him again in the hospital? No. I think I'll send you a more serious message. One of those other family members maybe.

Or a close friend.

Maybe, if they turn up dead, you'll get the message this time?

I have another targeted charity to take care of too. Isn't that new wing at the children's hospital completed now? I heard how much you love that project. Sounds like my next stop.

'Cause I'd like to up the stakes a little. And hitting the children's hospital sounds like maximum pain. Too bad you don't have any pets left to torture.

I'll have to pick off your friends instead.

And, of course, your family.

Chapter 18

Shay sat back on her plush leather couch and watched the expressions cross Roman's face. He was a strong man and taking a hit like this wouldn't be easy. It's not that Stefan would be harder on him than anyone else, but more than likely Roman had secrets, deep ones, ones he wouldn't appreciate anyone accessing. So far, she'd yet to see anything Stefan couldn't find out within a person's psyche.

Thank God she trusted Stefan implicitly or it would be incredibly unnerving to have him in her head. By asking for proof, Roman had opened himself up to a new reality. A scary one.

And that loss of innocence was tough for everyone...even traumatic for some.

She watched him blink several times.

Stefan? Isn't that enough?

I'm not in there anymore. He has a few new truths to deal with. That's all.

But you trust him? You didn't find anything in there that concerned you? That I should be concerned about?

He cares about you. He's confused about it, but there's no doubt he'd be devastated if something happened to you.

She didn't know what to say. It pretty well matched her impression. *I don't know that I want to fight a ghost.*

A ghost?

Yes, his model. If I'm in a relationship with him, I want him to be passionate about me. How can I know he's thinking about me and not her?

Humor threaded Stefan's voice as he answered, *I don't think that will be a problem. Trust him.*

Says you, she muttered.

He laughed. *I'm going to bed now.*

Wait, what about tonight? What did you find out about my attacker from this evening?

Nothing concrete. I'm going to do some research. Something odd is going on in the ethers. Not sure just what.

With that she had to be satisfied.

"Were you just talking to Stefan?" Roman asked in an odd voice. "Did he say anything to you?"

She understood his wariness and didn't pretend to misunderstand. "No he didn't share your secrets. He wouldn't. Stefan is all about principles and morals."

The relief on Roman's face made her laugh, but inside she didn't find much to laugh about. What concerned him so?

"You don't have to look so relieved," she said. "If he can see it, you can bet someone else can find out your secret."

He frowned. "That's the problem with secrets, isn't it? They can always come to light and hurt people."

Now she really had to wonder what he was hiding.

He sat down beside her. "If there's one thing Stefan's little demonstration showed me, it's that you two have a closeness I can't imagine. I might have dreamed of such a thing a long time ago, but to actually be able to communicate without speaking like you two do, well, that's impressive. And...I'm jealous. I'd love to have something similar," he admitted.

"Yes. It's comforting, reassuring, and also damn irritating at times. See, Stefan doesn't just get to see the stuff I want him to see, but he can see stuff I hadn't considered that anyone would ever know about." She shook her head, and continued, "No, I'm not talking about secrets, although he obviously could know about all those if he cared to look... I'm talking more about casual thoughts." She laughed. "For example I was looking in a store window at some women's clothing and I saw a pair of stilettos that I loved. At the same time I was thinking that they looked like hooker shoes. And I thought that I'd probably come off looking like a tart if I tried to wear them."

Her grin widened. "Stefan immediately laughed and added that he'd have said a high-priced call girl instead."

Roman's gaze widened. "So he's there all the time?"

"Not always, but we often leave the door open between us. I was involved in a bad scenario a while back, and I almost died." She swallowed hard. "Without Stefan, there's no way I'd have survived. Since then, that door between us is rarely closed. I don't always hear his thoughts, but every once in a while I'll hear and answer him the same as he did for me."

Roman grinned. "You are blessed to have him that close. Is this something I could learn?"

She looked surprised. "I imagine. Stefan mentors all kinds of people with various abilities. I don't know if you have any psychic gifts, but I'm sure he'd say you do even if you don't actively use them." And she'd seen for herself the power was there, sleeping.

"I'm not sure I'd want to ask Stefan for very much after tonight."

"Telepathic communication is very personal. But I like it. I never feel alone."

"And you used to?"

She thought about that. "Yes, I guess I did. Even with my fiancé, there was a sense of not being connected the same as I am with Stefan."

Just then her phone rang. She stared at it. Then at her clock. "It's two in the morning."

"I hope it's not Pappy." Then she snatched up the phone.

It wasn't. But it was the hospital. One of her relatives. A cousin, who she hadn't seen in years, had been admitted to the hospital. She'd had a note in her pocket to call Shay if anything happened to her.

Shay, after saying she'd be right down, hung up the phone slowly.

"Shay? What's wrong? Is it your grandfather?"

He had his own phone out, as if ready to call Gerard.

"No." She shook her head. "I don't get it." She explained what the hospital had said. "But I barely know this woman. I've had nothing to do with her for years."

He stood up, held out a hand to her, and said, "Then we'd better go down there and see what we can find out."

We? She eyed the hand he extended to her. It offered her more than help from the chair. The gesture seemed symbolic as it waited for her to respond.

Intrigued, yet wary, she placed her hand in his and let him help her up.

What bond had she just sealed?

Because that's what it felt like.

A bond, an agreement of some kind, that he had a place in her world.

Whether she was ready or not. Whether he loved another...or not.

✳✳✳

Stefan lay in his bed staring up at the ceiling. With Shay heading into a deep relationship, he had to admit to being slightly off-color himself. He had their privacy to respect as well as concerns about how her relationship with Roman, once it moved to the intimate level – and given what he'd seen of Roman's emotions, that wouldn't take long – would change his relationship with Shay.

And Roman was holding a time bomb by holding onto his secret about his paintings. And once Shay made that connection...

There were going to be fireworks.

Only Stefan knew Shay had to work this out herself. With Roman.

Still he'd need to watch her because of other dangers he hadn't identified, though he'd try to keep their connecting door closed more from now on. Shay wasn't out of danger from her attacker. Indeed, with the undercurrents moving on the ethers, she was mixed up with something nasty.

He could only hope her doors were open to *him* when it all went to hell. It was dangerous for her to stay too focused on Roman. Someone could take advantage…She could make a mistake that could cost her life. Yet he understood Shay's lack of focus…

The emptiness he'd felt for so long was disappearing and an expectation was building. He too felt there a special person would be entering his life soon, one he couldn't identify yet and didn't dare think about. As long as nothing sent their universal plan sideways. He'd long ago learned that it could do that in a heartbeat, when he least expected it.

And he didn't dare have something go wrong now. He'd waited too long for this vision to come to fruition.

And he'd waited too long for her.

It's going to happen. Soon.

Stefan groaned. He closed his eyes and just once, for just a quick moment, he reached out mentally and stroked the aura of the woman he loved.

The woman who didn't know he existed.

And then, he, Stefan the esteemed artist and psychic, felt a measure of doubt. Given his shadowy world, how could he ask anyone to share that with him?

Even as he basked in his recent connection to her aura, something dark slid across his consciousness. Something familiar. Something deadly that raised all his psychic hackles.

***

Early Tuesday morning…

The hospital was quiet when they arrived. At least quiet on the outside. Brilliant lights lit the almost empty parking lot but the halls were dimmer than normal. Shay led the way to the emergency room, stopping to speak with the nurse at the desk.

"Good, I'm glad you made it. The police are waiting to speak with you." She smiled and led the way to the bed at the far right. "She's seen the doctor, and he's ordered a bunch of tests. But she's been unconscious since she was brought in."

"Who found her?" Shay asked, but the nurse had already walked away.

"We were going to ask you a few questions about that?" A police officer stood slightly off to one side. "I'm Detective Marsden. You're Shay Lassiter?"

Shay nodded. "That is correct." She walked over to stand at the end of her cousin's bed. She was almost ashamed to admit that she barely recognized her.

The woman who appeared to be in her early forties was tall, slim, with short dark hair and a hint of curl. Nothing about her cousin's appearance was familiar in Shay's mind. Really, she could have been a stranger off the street.

Shay could vaguely remember her, but that was it. How long had it been? Ten years? More? She wasn't even sure she knew the tenuous blood connection that linked them. After they lost their parents, she and her brother had clung to Pappy. Grandmother Isabella had been alive back then and Shay and her brother had grown up feeling loved and cherished.

After her grandmother's death, Shay had become even closer to her grandfather. The cousins had been there in the distance. But as Pappy hadn't been close to Grandmother's family, Shay hadn't become close to them either.

Right. Now she remembered the woman. Marie Short. Marie's grandmother was the older sister of Shay's deceased grandmother.

"You know this woman?" asked the Detective Marsden. He consulted his notebook. "Marie Short?"

She frowned at him. How did one answer that question? She didn't really know her, but she knew of her. Then she realized that Roman stood close to her side, his arm around her shoulder, to offer comfort and support should it be needed. A nice gesture, but not necessary.

"She's a distant cousin."

"Distant? How distant?"

Shay explained the relationship. "In fact, I'm not sure I've seen her in the last decade."

"Have you had any contact with her? Phone calls, emails?"

Shay shook her head. "No. Nothing." She frowned again. "I don't understand what's going on."

"This was clutched in her fist." The detective held out a small plastic bag with a scrap of ivory paper inside.

Shay reached for it and read it aloud. "If anything happens to me, call Shay Lassiter. She'll understand." She turned to stare at the unconscious woman. "I have no idea what this means." She wagged the bag in the air. "I hardly know this woman."

The detective studied her face carefully. Then he took back the evidence. "Well, if you come up with anything to explain this, please let me know."

He'd almost gotten out of sight when it hit her. She spun around and raced after him, Roman on her heels.

"Wait, Detective Marsden."

He turned around. "Did you think of something?"

"I don't know. It's just there's another odd issue going on right now, and I'm afraid that the two odd incidences make a coincidence, and I don't—"

"Believe in those," the detective finished for her. "Neither do I. So tell me what's going on."

Wincing, Shay said, "You're probably better off calling Detective Chandler." She rubbed two fingers against her temple. "But I'll give you a quick rundown." And she did, and then she checked her watch. "So much for sleep tonight."

"I suggest you head home and grab a few hours." He handed her his phone number. "I'll catch up with Detective Chandler, and if you think of anything else, call me."

She watched him walk away, slowly becoming more aware of the ever quiet Roman at her side.

"You didn't tell him about tonight?" he asked in a neutral tone.

She glanced up at him. "How can I?" she asked simply. "Look how much trouble we had convincing you?"

"Good point." Roman glanced back toward the hospital bed. "Do you want to stay with your cousin?"

"Want to? No...but I will, just for a moment." She made her way back through the quiet hall to where her cousin, Marie, slept. Taking a look at her aura, Shay studied the energy flow from the woman's chakras. Dark purple and a deep red swirled in a tempest through several of the chakras. Backing out from the chakras, she studied her cousin's aura, realizing it lay close to her cousin's body, snug, as if unable to loosen up and flow normally. Shay narrowed her eyes and looked for a cause.

It was almost as if her cousin's energy was being restrained...only there was nothing holding her there now. But there could have been earlier. But to hold that kind of grip on the aura and to have it continue long after the restraints were gone... And who or what had constrained her?

She stepped closer, and after a quick look to make sure she was alone with Roman, she reached out with both hands and stroked the surface of her cousin's aura, moving the darkness away and adding in her own, lighter energy. Then she stroked up towards Marie's head, removing the stress that had cramped her aura, easing the stiffness and the tension holding it tightly in place.

Taking her time, Shay eased the other woman's fear, a palpable emotion Shay felt the same way. She didn't know what had scared Marie so much, but something had to have made her retreat so deep inside. As she kept her auric energy in tightly, she'd also gone inside mentally.

To protect herself.

That was it. Her cousin wasn't unconscious. She was in hiding.

Shay needed Stefan's help.

Damn. She called for him. No answer. Given the time, chances were he was asleep and wouldn't appreciate being woken up. Right now, it didn't matter. They needed to bring this woman out of her self-imposed cage and find out who'd done this to her.

She called Stefan again, louder. Stronger.

Stop yelling. I'm here.

Shay explained the situation.

Stefan immediately kicked awake. *Let me take a look. See if I can find her in there.*

Good. Her energy is very low. Dangerously low. I think her consciousness is hiding.

It probably is, Stefan agreed

And he disappeared.

***

Stefan shifted and landed his consciousness beside Shay at the hospital. The disembodied world he walked made it hard for others to detect him. Even those that walked between realities like he did. Shay could see him if she'd looked but she didn't take her eyes off the unconscious woman in bed. *Shay.*

She turned toward him and grinned. "Hey," she said.

He smiled, loving her easy acceptance and lack of questions. Then he jumped into her cousin's mind. Silence enveloped him. Normally, in a quiet mind there was still a distant chatter in the background, but here there was nothing. A muted silence, like something pressing down...putting a buffer between this world and her thoughts. Like cotton wadding plugged in between her and whatever she was hiding from.

Shay had a similar sensation when she'd been attacked by Darren. She'd experienced an odd sense of not caring what happened to her. But this wasn't Darren.

He dug deeper. So odd. It's like there was nothing but emptiness. A blackness devoid of all thought. How could that be?

He wandered around, looking for a weakness, a way through the blackness to something else.

The more he pushed or tried to weasel through, the thicker it became. Cloying and stale, the denseness pressed in on him. How could *nothing* have weight? Then he understood. The black energy wasn't hers.

Someone was in her mind. Except there was no sense of a life force. The energy felt dead…or deadened, maybe. As if there was nothing vital or alive left in it. There was a distancing as if life wasn't prized enough to care about.

He spun around and realized the dark energy had been stuffed into this woman's mind. Filling it, making it seem like it was hers. Leaving no space for Marie. Almost suffocating her.

How interesting. The scientist, the student, in him was fascinated.

He'd been in other people's minds and he'd seen other energies with similar capabilities. And some with their own twisted variations. Still he hadn't quite seen *this* before.

Was this woman's mind still connected to her body or was she brain dead – and not in the sense doctors meant when they said something was dead. In this case, it appeared as if the woman's body was still alive and the brain functioning, but the consciousness had been sucked out. Shay's cousin was alive – but also dead.

He'd laugh if it wasn't so serious. This was stuff from zombie movies. He had to try and save her if he could. If not…then he needed her shell to die before someone else tried to take it over.

With his goal in mind he reached out, calling for her. *Marie?*

No answer. Not that he'd expected any. He searched the space, walking blindly forward, calling out for the woman. For a flicker of life.

Nothing.

How could he find the person who belonged here?

By tracking the person that didn't.

Chapter 19

Shay studied the patterns of Marie's energy as her cousin lay unconscious. There was so little of her energy, it scared her. Not only was her aura snugged up tight, but the chakras appeared sluggish and seemed to be losing their ability to circulate energy – as if she were dying. But what had caused this?

The doctors said her cousin had no physical injuries. None that modern medicine could see, at least.

Psychic attacks chilled her to the bone. Her experience with Darren had been bad enough, but to think there could be others... The psychic conflagration in her apartment that had engulfed her ghost cat, Morris, caused a heartache she still had to deal with. The cat had been dead for a long time, but she'd so enjoyed his spirit. He'd always put a smile on her face. And she missed him dearly.

A disruption at Marie's crown chakra caught her attention. The crown chakra, the connection to the universe, or the connection to what lay beyond, held what some people referred to as a bank account of grace – goodness to draw on in need. It always fascinated her.

In Marie's case, it was empty, running on a deficit.

This was beyond odd.

And the heart chakra had a faint glow, an otherworldliness to it.

Not good.

Shay chewed nervously on her bottom lip. This felt too close to the edge. Shay opened her own heart chakra and poured energy into Marie's first chakra.

Stefan, hurry up. Shay hurried to the bedside. She reached out and caught Marie's hand. "Hold on Marie. Please, hold on."

Stefan! I think she's dying. Hurry.

Shay closed her eyes and sent warm, loving energy into the struggling heart chakra. But the energy swirled helplessly in place.

"Shay? What's the matter?" Roman came up on the other side of her, his arm wrapping around her shoulders. "The nurse said she was going to be okay."

She looked at him, sadness in her voice, "The nurse was wrong. Marie is almost gone. I don't think Stefan can even stop it."

"Stefan." Astonishment laced Roman's voice. "What's he doing here?"

"Helping me. We were trying to figure out what happened to her and how what's happened could be connected to me." She waved a hand at her cousin. "Then this...change, this lack of life presented. I can't explain it," she whispered. "I think it's too late."

***

Stefan focused on the black energy trying to absorb it into his psyche. There was a familiarity to this energy. He looked for the energy signature. But the energy was old, the signature dissipated, or he'd have seen it at the beginning.

And that damned energy still felt wrong. As if it wasn't real energy.

Shit. Stefan spun around in amazement.

It wasn't real energy in here. It was the *illusion* of energy.

With that understanding, the illusion faded from his psyche, and he could see the poor woman's mind.

Even as he watched, he saw the silver cord, barely attached at the body, start to separate.

No!

He jumped forward, frantically wrapping the cord in warm, healing energy. For several moments, he worked, calling out.

Stop. Don't leave. We can help you. It's not too late. He poured energy into her mind, into her aura, into her cord.

And all for naught.

He couldn't hold onto the cord.

It separated in his grasp. Hovered briefly and slipped free.

Stefan stood, shocked, scared, and silent, in the empty shell where Shay's cousin had once lived.

***

She picked up Marie's hand and held it close to her chest.

Stefan's exhausted voice slid into her mind, tinged with frustration and overwhelmed with sadness. *Shay, I lost her.*

I know. Shay looked over at Roman, fat tears running down her cheeks. "She's gone."

He looked at her in surprise, and then moved to the other side of the bed and checked for a pulse.

His gaze, when it met hers, was black and lost.

"How? I don't understand. She doesn't have any sign of injury."

"No," Shay whispered. "She died from a psychic attack." And she knew, even as she said it, that this would be hard for Roman to take in. Hell, she was still struggling with what happened.

"Is this related to the attack on you earlier tonight? That I came racing to your apartment for?" he asked in a hard voice.

She bowed her head. "I don't know, but I'm afraid it could be."

"Does Stefan know?" Anger and fear had him striding toward her. He reached out and shook her shoulders gently. "Ask him."

With a nod, she did as he requested.

I can't be sure because I can't get a handle on the energy signature. But...I think it is.

"Stefan says, quite possibly but there's no way to be certain."

And that scared her shitless.

"Well you won't be alone again until this asshole is caught." His voice hardened. "I'll be bunking at your place for now. I may not be Stefan but at least I can watch over you. Call Stefan if you need help."

She studied him. She wasn't averse to having company until this was over. It's one thing to fight an attacker in the flesh. It was quite another to fight one you couldn't see.

And Roman had no idea how bizarre these attacks could get.

But neither did he know how to fight them either.

***

Once Stefan was back in bed, he opened his eyes to stare at the ceiling. He'd seen a lot of death. He'd seen people before death, after, even during the process. He'd yet to see this sad, lingering, letting go. As if life wasn't precious enough to fight for or to believe in.

Stefan had seen suicidal people who cared more than Marie had. Often a suicidal person changed their mind when it was too late. Marie didn't seem to care either way. He didn't understand it. Had that other energy put thoughts of despair in her head, been so pervasive that Marie felt she had no choice but to let go? As if only darkness remained for her if she stayed.

Shay had experienced something similar a year ago. With Darren. He thought about that. What would be required to do that?

He couldn't fathom the answer. As someone who walked on both sides of the veil between life and death, he'd yet to see this. It bothered him. If they had a new type of predator, he needed to know.

He'd done his best, but sometimes unforeseen things...happened. Like now.

He didn't want to think that an old adversary could have survived, but what if he had?

218

He'd spoken with a psychic friend who'd been locked in the ice palace in her mind. She'd told him the longer she was there the more she wallowed, just didn't care.

But the energy inside this poor woman's mind had such a different feel. Like she had no thoughts whatsoever. And it had all been an illusion that disappeared when that realization took hold.

Stefan let out a sigh of relief. So it didn't sound like Darren after all. Thank heavens for that.

And this energy only seemed to dissipate because it was old. He thought about that difference for a moment longer. It appeared his attacker could mask energy. Their own, and that of others, so they hide their identity within another person. And that person could look normal to everyone, but on the inside, this psychic controlled the other person without the awareness of the other person. Sounds like another asshole who needed to be eliminated.

Oh, if only the ones that died...would stay dead."

***

Knock, knock...

Yup me again. Shay, you still don't get it, do you?

I heard you went to the hospital to see your long-lost cousin. Why though? She didn't even remember you. And I asked her long and hard.

Too bad. All that and still she wasn't much help.

Of course, I'd hoped for a closer connection between the two of you. But it wasn't to be.

I guess I'll have to go back to your grandfather after all. He is all alone in the hospital...

Easy.

Maybe too easy.

I could go after some of your best friends first.

Oh, but maybe you don't have any.

Bernice is dead. That wasn't much fun either. And in no way did it have the intended impact. I wanted you devastated. She was a surrogate mother to you. You should have been hurt by her passing. Instead all you did was gain from it. Maybe you even wanted the old bag to die so you'd get her money.

And your friend Tabitha is dead, but that caused hardly a ripple in your world. Sigh.

I was hoping to toy with you. But this is damn boring.

Isn't there anyone else in your life who you care about?

God you live like a nun.

With all that money, too.

What a waste.

That's all right. I'll see what I can do about relieving you of some of that money.

Then I'll take care of you.

✱✱✱

Tuesday morning…dawn

Shay? Call Ronin. He doesn't want to wake you.

Sleepily, Shay blinked several times, trying to sort out Stefan's whisper through her mind. And adjust to her surroundings. She was home in her own bed. But she'd only been there for a few hours. *Damn.* She glanced beside her. Alone. *Double damn.*

Focus. This is important. It's about Darren. You don't have a problem calling Ronin, do you?

No.

Now she was awake. Talk about a subject guaranteed to keep sweet dreams a long way away.

She reached for her phone. *Stefan, do you know what's going on?*

Yes. But not all of it. I asked Ronin to search out more family members of Darren's. Just in case there is someone else with the ability to do what he did.

And of course family members have the closest chance. She held the phone up to her ear, her heart pounding nervously in her chest. Darren had told her that he had no family. But then he'd lied about everything else, so...

"Shay. Glad you called." Ronin sounded too perky for this time at night.

While Shay listened, trying to shake the sleepy cobwebs from her mind, Ronin gave it to her, short and succinct. There was nothing sweet about it.

"*He had a twin?* A twin brother?" Shay shook her head, slumping back against her headboard. "Not possible."

"Not only possible, but definite, at least according to his foster care history. The brother's name is Danny."

She didn't know what to say. "Wait – did Darren even know him?"

"It's hard to say. We're looking for him right now. But there's no proof to say they'd actually hooked up."

"So it could be that the twin wasn't in contact with Darren or even know that Darren existed?"

"Absolutely. Both were in dozens of foster homes before they hit fourteen. Darren ran away several times and ended back in the system and the inevitable round of homes. His brother Danny ran away at seventeen and dropped out of sight. We're investigating the possibility that the brothers found each other...somehow...but I don't know how."

Their abilities would have drawn them together, Stefan murmured. *They wouldn't have been able to resist the pull of another like themselves.*

"But he's alive?"

"No reason to believe he isn't. Like I said, we're looking for him."

Stefan's thoughts whispered through her mind again. *Make sure he lets you know as soon as he finds out.*

"Thanks Ronin. Please keep me in the loop. Oh, and did you ever go through the personnel files I gave you?"

"First thing. They both check out, so do the staff at Folgrent Foundation. No worries there. And I'll call if I find out anything."

She hung up the phone slowly. "Damn it, Darren. When will you leave me in peace?"

Soon. Stefan murmured comfortingly in her head.

I hope so.

"Darren? Your ex-fiancé? What's going on, Shay?"

Oh shit.

Yeah, that's my call to leave. With a chuckle, Stefan disappeared.

She glanced at her doorway. And gave a start. Roman, bare-chested and looking lethal as hell, slouched against the entrance to her room, his hands shoved into jeans riding dangerous low. She swallowed. Just now realizing how little clothing she had on herself. A white cotton cami and matching boy panties.

She'd forgotten he was sleeping in her spare room.

How had the temperature in the room risen so quickly?

This man was dangerous – in so many ways.

Taking a deep breath, she tried to collect her thoughts and said, "That was Ronin. Apparently Darren had a twin brother."

Those dark eyes burned with a fire inside. "And you are thinking this twin had something to do with these attacks?"

She nodded warily, took a deep breath and explained what Darren had done. "Ronin is trying to find him now."

He'd straightened at her explanation but had let her get it out. He sauntered a few steps closer, his gaze holding hers so tightly she could barely breathe.

The room seemed hotter with his every step closer. She had a dozen reasons why she needed him to leave. Why she needed sleep tonight. Although to be honest, the night was mostly done. But now, all thoughts of sleep fled. And they were replaced with thoughts of being with him in bed.

Even as the dangers registered, her skin warmed, her nipples tightened, and she struggled to take her eyes off him.

She didn't think she was ready for this. But her body was screaming for him. It had been a year. A long, lonely year of sleeping alone, of never being held, hugged or touched with caring. Without love.

Dare she trust Roman? Dare she trust her own emotions? Her own body? She'd been so wrong before. She couldn't stand to be wrong again.

Roman sat down on the bed beside her.

"Does Darren have anything to with *this*?" His voice flowed over her like liquid heat.

She swallowed. *This?* "No, he has nothing to do with anything, including us."

"And he's gone from your heart and mind?"

"Heart, definitely. That happened a long time ago. From my mind?" She'd answer if she could think straight, but his nearness and intensity were doing things to her insides along with that blatant look that said he wanted her any way he could get her.

And damn it if she didn't want him too.

"Yes," she said simply.

"Good."

In a last-ditch effort to find some measure of control, she summoned up the courage to challenge him. "And your model? Is she an issue here?"

Her gaze locked on his lips. He smiled, a slow, long movement that made her heart race. Mentally, she could barely function at all.

"She was never an issue. She's an important part of my life. Then, so are you."

"So you aren't lovers?"

Dark secrets lit the depths of his gaze. Still, for all that she saw and all that she could sense, there wasn't anything malicious in him. Stefan would have warned her if there had been. Roman was entitled to his privacy. God knew she needed hers too.

"No. We've never been lovers."

And his energy wasn't lying. Streaks of gold slid toward her, reached for her. Waited for her. She hesitated, searching to maintain her sanity. Then she realized some of those waves of color were coming from his heart chakra. This wasn't just lust or a need to be slaked. It was obvious this was more. So much more.

He wanted *her*.

Relief blossomed inside. She smiled.

She didn't know how much she wanted him either, but maybe, just maybe, they could give it a try and find out.

***

Roman watched her awareness of him grow, and along with that, the unmistakable bloom of sexual longing in her gaze. He saw the almost imperceptible shiver whispering across her skin as she gazed at him. Good. He'd better not be the only one going crazy in this relationship. Despite the words of caution she wanted him too...yet he felt like he had to move slowly. As if any sudden move could have her changing her mind. And then she'd bolt.

With wide eyes, she stared at him. He glanced over her – enough to realize she wore only a thin cami – make that a transparent cami - and forced himself to look away.

He'd wanted her for such a long time. Too long. He didn't want just one night. He needed more.

He didn't know how much more, but if he could get her to take this step with him, they'd both find out.

Passion shimmered through his body. Lust heated his loins and fired his gaze. He tried to pull back and like a doe trembling in the headlights, she waited for his next move.

He leaned forward and gently stroked her plump lower lip. Her mouth opened, her tongue slipped out and stroked the pad on his finger. He stopped, then leaned forward and gently placed his lips against hers.

She didn't withdraw, nor did she throw her arms around him. She waited, tasting, testing the feel of him against her skin. So honest. So captivating. So sexy.

Just that bit of experimenting, that willingness to give this a try, sent shivers down his spine. God, he wanted her. He deepened the kiss.

She stiffened slightly, and then relaxed.

He withdrew slightly and she whimpered so he tugged her into his arms and kissed her as he'd been wanting to kiss her since forever.

Chapter 20

Shay lost herself in his heat. It warmed her from the inside as he surrounded her with his caring.

She'd forgotten the joy of being in a relationship. For all her time with Darren, she'd never experienced this specialness, this sense of being a part of a private twosome. Or realized how much being held mattered.

Only now. Only with Roman.

Her lips parted under his assault and she couldn't think.

There was something important happening here, but somehow even finding out what that was didn't matter. At the moment, it seemed that nothing else would ever matter again – except that he never let her go.

She closed her eyes and let the tidal wave carry her off. And gave herself over to his care. She wrapped her arms around his neck and sighed sweetly. She wanted this. Wanted him.

He didn't disappoint. Holding her gently, carefully, as if she was delicate china, he deepened the kiss and held her captive in his embrace until she sagged into his arms, unable to think. Only feeling. And that was what she needed. What they both needed. To be together, just the two of them.

He lifted his head and held her close. "I've been waiting for this." He dropped tiny kisses along her cheek to her ear. "I've needed this…" He whispered into her ear, sending shivers down her spine. "For so long."

She turned her head, her hands moving to hold him so she could recapture those wandering lips with her own. She kissed him long and hard.

Pulling back slightly she said, "So have I." She smiled. "So how about a little less talk and a little more action?"

He froze, momentarily. She'd caught him off guard. He'd been gentle and caring and considerate. Worried about her. But as well as that she wanted his passionate heat and to experience his real need, to experience his passion.

And match it with her own.

A glint of lust glowed deep in his blue eyes. "Your wish is my command." And he lowered his head, taking her on a glorious ride of abandonment. Her cami disappeared under his expert actions. Her panties were tossed to one side. Before she really understood what was happening to her, she lay completely naked in front of him.

Instead of feeling embarrassed or uncomfortable, she felt sexy and desired. The blatant appreciation in his eyes raised her temperature even more, but she hated that he still had clothes on.

But she could take care of that.

She scrambled to her knees and moved his fingers away from his belt. With his hands out of the way, she quickly opened his belt and the top button of his jeans, unzipping the fly just enough to thrust her fingers inside.

"Jesus," he roared, grabbing for her hands. "Slowly. We don't want this over with before it's even begun."

She laughed.

He grinned, and raised her arms above her head and pushed her gently backwards. She stretched sinuously up, her breasts stroking against his bare chest. He groaned and lowered his weight to rest gently on her.

Heat raced across her chest as skin burned against skin.

Wanting the freedom to touch him, she twisted beneath him, trying to free her hands.

"Oh, no. Not so fast." He shifted up onto his knees. Holding both of her wrists in one hand, he awkwardly pulled off his remaining clothes.

She laughed. "It would be so much easier if you let me do that."

But he was already done. He released her hands and shifted so he straddled her lower legs, pinning her in place. Then slowly he stroked up her body. She murmured and shifted under his expert touch as he caressed her, feeding the heat building between.

She wanted, no, needed to touch him as he was touching her. She sat up in a smooth movement and wrapped her arms around him. With her face against his neck, their bodies were flush with each other's, his erection captured between them. Slowly, smoothly, she slid to one side, then just as slowly back to the other. Letting her hardened nipples stroke across his chest, she tilted her head and nipped at his chin.

He lowered his face, and she kissed the corner of his mouth, his lips, and then kissed him – hard.

He responded with deep, drugging kisses, and she reacted mindlessly, helplessly. Going where he led and happy to follow. When he pulled her up and reversed positions, she barely noticed. Except for the sheer expanse of male in front of her, available to her.

She straddled his body, her core perfectly positioned to rest on his hips. She reached down to grasp him in her hand. His groans were music to her ears as she caressed and stroked, squeezed and teased – it was his turn to thrash on the bed.

He reached up to pull her down, but she resisted. Changing her position slightly, she rose up high enough to take him inside. Slowly, very slowly, she sank down until he was fully sheathed within. She gasped and stilled, feeling the sensation of fullness. She let her body adjust while he lay shuddering in place.

She leaned over and smoothly lifted off. He opened his eyes and she sank back down. He shuddered.

She did it again, and again, settling into a smooth ride. He grasped her hips, his fingers digging into her soft flesh, and he rose up beneath her. Together they set a slow pace that quickly drove them forward. She cried out, her back arching as the tremors started deep inside and spread throughout her body.

He groaned and bucked desperately beneath her. Then he arched, the cords of his arms taut, as he held her locked in place. She sagged as he collapsed down on the bed.

Then he tugged her forward into his arms, crushing her up against his chest, his heart.

Exactly where she wanted to be.

***

Roman rolled over, tucking her up close against his side. To say she'd rocked his world would be to minimize this experience of a lifetime. He had no idea it could be like that between them.

And though she'd dominated his dreams for years the reality of her, of them like this, was so much better.

He dropped a tender kiss on the tip of her nose. His artistic eye caught, and then memorized, the tiny details. The small bump on the long, patrician nose. The full definition of her lips. Her eyes. How did he paint that stormy brown with gold flecks?

He tightened his grip on her, wishing he could slip her inside his soul and keep her there. Never to be separated.

She murmured softly.

He loosened his grip. "Sorry," he whispered against her temple. "Sleep. You need to catch a few hours."

"Need more than a few," she answered softly. "But I'll take what I can get."

Reaching for the crumpled bedding, Roman tugged it up and over them both. Settling deeper into the center of the bed, he held her close as she drifted off to sleep.

He knew that somehow he had to share his secret. He should have done so before this. But he hadn't quite foreseen their relationship coming to this stage so quickly.

Not that he had any regrets. He'd have to hope she'd understand when the time came.

That she asked about his relationship with his model was both amusing and touching. That she might feel the fool after she found out, could be an issue.

He hoped not because finally one of his dreams had come true.

Now he had to work on making the rest happen.

He knew one thing for sure. Now that he'd gotten her this far, he was never letting her go.

***

Tuesday morning…

Shay woke feeling surprisingly rested, considering the late night. She went to sit up and realized Roman's arm held her in place. She smiled and tried to wiggle out from underneath.

He grumbled, his voice deep, and yet gentle in her ear. She studied his shadowed face, realizing she had nothing in the apartment that he could shave with. Too bad.

Then again, she kinda liked the shadow. Stretching up, she dropped a gentle kiss on the dimple in his chin. As he shifted in his sleep, she slipped out from under his arm and escaped to the bathroom. Once done, she grabbed a silk housecoat from behind her door and, knotting the belt, walked to the kitchen to put on coffee.

She needed a shower. Glancing at the kitchen clock, she realized the memorial service for Robert Dander was in an hour. As much as she'd come to hate funerals, she felt obligated to go. And maybe she could learn something.

Lost in her thoughts, she didn't hear Roman get up.

"Do you mind if I take a shower?"

She spun around. He stood in the doorway, bare except for softly hugging cotton boxers. Mutely, she shook her head.

He grinned, and said, "Join me?" He disappeared from view before she had a chance to answer. But not before she saw his sculpted butt disappear. She sighed. He had a really great ass.

I so didn't need to know that. Stefan's sardonic voice whispered through her mind.

She gasped, and then broke out laughing. *Sorry, Stefan.*

She gently closed the door in her mind and raced after Roman, still grinning. She couldn't get there fast enough. He'd just stepped under the hot spray when she dropped the housecoat and opened the glass door.

"Don't mind if I do," she murmured, holding up a bar of soap.

His happy gaze widened to delight when her bar of soap stroked down his front and over the hard length of him. He groaned as her fingers slipped over his shaft. "Like that, do you?" She smiled, her hand movements sensuous but teasing.

"Witch," he said thickly. In one smooth movement, he turned, lifted her, and pinned her to the wall. With his hard length poised at the heart of her, he said, "Two can play that game."

She laughed and then groaned as he slid deep inside. Hard and fast he pounded into her as the shower water pounded down on them. She cried out. Secured against the wall she couldn't move. She could only hang on as he rode her to the edge, then drove them both over.

She hung suspended against the wall, floating free in mind and spirit. Then she gently floated back to reality.

"Damn, you're good."

He laughed. "Glad you think so. Now I think we both need to finish this shower before we run out of hot water."

***

Tuesday, later that morning...

The funeral for Robert was bigger than David's. That made it easier to blend into the crowd but harder to sort through the energy of all those attending. Robert had been the headmaster of Chadworth School for over three decades. He'd interacted with the parents and students and the children of his students. It was a sign of the impact he'd left on the community to have such a crowd.

With Roman at her side – she'd been surprised at his insistence to attend – Shay tried to get an overall impression of the energy flowing through the crowd. There was a lot of it. Streams twisted and churned from person to person.

The crowd swelled as more and more people arrived.

When the memorial service was over, the crowd broke up and some moved on to the gravesite. The family was seated up close and the rest stood in a surrounding circle. Lisa Dander stood head bowed, shoulders shaking and surrounded by her loving family. And there was much love here.

There was also many other emotions. She could see the family strife, the arguments between siblings, the worry over money, and fear that there wouldn't be any inheritance coming to various members. Astonishing how much of the world revolved around who had what and how they were going to get more of what they wanted. What didn't surprise her after so long was how most of the people spent time wondering how to get what they wanted from other people.

The man on her left wanted a raise from his boss. The woman directly in front of her was hoping for a small inheritance – she wanted more, but figured she might be good to receive a little something. The two kids, forced to attend, were wanting fast food as soon as they were done, and indeed that had been the bargain struck for their good behavior here.

She almost snorted aloud. So typical. Still, nothing that she could see indicated anything untoward. If her attacker was here, she had no way to know who it was, if they were hiding or what they wanted.

Again, all for nothing.

As they retreated back to the parking lot she caught it.

Just a hint.

The same energy she'd come across in Marie's mind. And from David's office. Her apartment.

How? More importantly, who? She stood on tiptoe, searching the wandering group. The energy drifted off to the left. Without a thought, she bolted in that direction.

***

Roman started as Shay bolted. He turned to see her running, not walking fast, but racing as if she were being chased. And no one was chasing her. Or even appeared to notice her. Yet in a world of slow and somber she was a darting oddity.

And hell, she was almost out of sight. He took off after her.

He couldn't see anything that would cause her wild dash. And was especially concerned because she'd taken off without saying anything to him. She was moving fast.

He picked up the pace as she went around a tree. He didn't dare lose sight of her. By the time he reached the spot where she'd disappeared, he realized he'd taken too long. She was nowhere to be found. *Damn it, Shay. Where the hell are you?*

She had to be close. He ran several feet forward, glancing from side to side. Turning around, he kept on the move, searching the way they'd come.

Shit. He stopped. Changed direction and searched again.

"Shay?"

No answer. He kept calling for her.

Damn it. He pulled out his phone and called her. The phone rang and rang. She'd probably muted the ring so as to not disturb anyone at the ceremony. He put the phone away.

Now he was getting worried. With a keen eye to the parking lot, which appeared more empty than full now, his mind raced over possibilities. Could she have gotten into a car with someone? Surely, not without him noticing. And not without telling him. Not willingly at least. And not that fast.

His mind balked at the idea she'd left without him. That wasn't her style. He frowned. She had to be here somewhere.

He retraced his steps slowly. Back at the trees where he first lost sight of her, he stopped and slowly assessed the area. She hadn't had but a minute to move away. The area was treed, but he'd have seen her if she'd still been pursuing something. So she had to be close by, out of sight.

There were only trees for cover. He walked, circling each one to make sure she wasn't lying beneath the boughs.

He didn't want to contemplate why or how she'd be in such a position.

At the next patch, just beside the first, was a low-lying spruce tree with heavy, arching branches. He pulled the branches aside, feeling like an idiot. Unable to stop himself, he searched underneath—

And caught sight of something on the other side. He hurried to the far side, lifted up the branches and found Shay lying underneath. He dropped to his knees.

He placed his fingers against her throat, and felt for a pulse. His breath whooshed out with relief when he felt the slow steady beat of her heart.

She was alive.

But what the hell happened? Anger stirred inside. She might have collapsed for some unknown reason, but she wouldn't have rolled under here on her own. More likely she caught sight of someone, ran after them, was knocked unconscious and then was dumped under the closest cover.

He did a quick check to make sure there were no obvious signs of injury before sitting back on his heels. No blood, no breaks, nothing to show she'd been attacked.

Then again, with what he'd learned from her and Stefan, attacks could happen in other ways. And those could be deadly.

He pulled out his phone and contacted Stefan.

"Stefan, I need help." He explained the situation, finishing with, "I don't know if I should move her. Do I call 911?"

"Don't move her. I'll call you right back."

Roman stared at the dead phone. What was going on? He studied Shay's prone form then leaned closer for another look.

Something was shifting. He just didn't quite understand what. It was as if her form became less defined. Like he needed to put glasses on to see her better. The air fairly crackled, adding to the weird effect.

The hairs rose on the back of his neck.

Damn he wanted her awake. To know she was fine...

Then he planned to rip into her. Give her hell for taking off the way she did.

Even as he sat there, hoping no one would notice him hunched over her, she stirred.

He breathed a sigh of relief. He wanted to haul her into his arms, and at the same time, he was afraid to touch her. Something about doing so felt wrong. But damn. Should he take the risk? Would it hurt her?

It would make *him* feel much better. So would calling his brother...

Updating Ronin took only a moment. That his brother was more in tune with this stuff pissed Roman off. He hated to think all this had been going on around him and he hadn't known anything about it, for his whole life. It just made him all that more aware of how much he had to catch up on. And he would.

It also made him realize how little he really understood about security. Sure, he'd checked Shay's website completely, set up a security system that would make the computer very hard to access, and he had installers coming to tighten up security on Shay's apartment... But what good was any of that without a way to keep her safe from the dangers they couldn't see?

The damn twin was still at large, and they both hated the latest in developments.

Ronin rang off, saying, "Whatever you do, don't touch her. Apparently that's really bad for her."

Roman glared at the phone, then down at Shay. *Damn.* He'd already done that when he'd checked her over to make sure she wasn't injured. His phone rang. *Stefan this time.* Why didn't he use telepathy at moments like this? Shrugging, he answered.

DALE MAYER

"I burn through more energy using telepathy. I'm working on Shay. She should come around in a few moments. I can't have you disturbing her."

"That's why you called…?" he said. "To make sure I don't touch her?"

"You were thinking it. I'm holding you back and can't afford the energy drain. So leave us for a few moments."

"When do I know to call for help?"

Stefan's voice was hard and dry. "You'll know." And he hung up.

Roman had to be satisfied with that. He dropped the bough to hide Shay's form once again and then stood up. He checked to make sure no one was watching.

Whoever had attacked Shay had taken the time to hide her. Roman would have found her a good five minutes earlier if they hadn't. As it was, those five minutes were enough for the attacker to get away.

Chapter 21

Shay walked alone in the darkness. She didn't know why she was here. She could talk and think, but nothing made any sense. She even wondered if she might be injured and lost in her consciousness. Perhaps she was in a coma.

She tried to see into her memories. Tried to remember the last thing she'd done.

Her past was blank. That bothered her.

There should be something there. People. Scenes. Sounds. Actions on her part. Things she'd done. Plans, hopes, wishes, dreams.

The complete absence of all was the worst.

She felt alone in a way she didn't recognize. Like something important, something she'd just found, was missing.

She turned around, hating the blackness. Where was the light? Where was the natural light of day? There was no change in the depth of the blackness.

She wandered around in a circle. With nothing to ground her in place, she had a hard time seeing where she was. Fearing that she was losing her mind, she sat down and pulled her knees up to her chest. With her forehead resting on her knees she rocked gently in place.

Maybe if she sat quietly and waited, someone would come.

Shay.

Her head came up. She twisted, searching through the darkness. *Hello?*

Shay? Are you there?

Yes, she shouted. *I'm over here.*

Keep talking. This energy is so thick it's hard to see through.

She laughed. *I know. That's why I stopped moving. I'm sitting in one place hoping someone will find me.*

I'm here. Stefan showed up, a big grin on his face.

She stood up and threw her arms around him.

Except he was only energy. She gasped, and then laughed for joy. *I'd forgotten. Everything. My memories were all gone. But this... Now that I see you. Hear you. I remember you. Remember this.*

Good. I'd hate to have to go through an explanation. You're a little too far advanced to catch you up on your past in a matter of seconds. We don't have much time.

As long as you are here to help me escape, I'm game.

He chuckled. *There's no need for you to escape. You're home. You need to kick your visitor out.*

She straightened. *Say what?*

Remember...black energy. Your cousin Marie and the blackness inside her. The dark feeling inside? His voice darkened. *That same energy is here. I can sense it. It's a mask hiding your feelings, your memories...*

Really? Then how do I get rid of it?

First step is realization. Second step is to stop being a victim. Get angry. See the energy for what it is. An attacker. You can get free of this by reasserting who you are.

She blinked. Why was it so hard to understand what he was saying? But it was. His suggestions seemed to come from a distance. The information was out of her grasp. Even though she heard the words, they didn't compute.

They should. She wasn't stupid. According to Stefan, she was extremely capable in...whatever this stuff was. That meant something was stopping her from seeing it. Realizing it.

Something – or someone.

And that realization brought her that much closer to clarity. She was a victim here. And victim mentality was fear-based. She couldn't seat herself in fear. It made it impossible to fight back. Victims reacted. She had to act, not react.

As she went over these things, the blackness was shoved a little further back.

Now warm your inner light. Burn fiercely...brightly...from the inside. Where there is light, there can be no darkness.

Right.

Lightness. Love. Always the answer to the darkness. The negativity and the blackness that surrounded anyone. And everyone. She knew that. Somehow. And if she knew that much...

She closed her eyes, searching for the light. There was so much emptiness inside. But that couldn't be right. She wasn't empty. She was full of life and love and laughter. Sure, there would be pain inside, but she lived in the world of joy. Only she couldn't remember what she did for a living. If she did anything. She knew that she did something that helped others. Somehow.

Money. That's right. She helped others with money. The Foundation!

The darkness retreated a little more again.

And with memories of the Foundation came Bernice. Pappy. Roman. She smiled and her life came back in focus.

Memories flooded back. The blackness dissipated instantly.

Color surged at her from all areas. Noises filled her brain. Her thoughts, other people's thoughts. So much hit her all at once, she was on overload.

Easy. Stefan's voice surged through her, an anchor she could hold on to in the sea of sensation that tossed her from side to side. *Glad to have you back.*

She watched as the waves washed around her, pushing up against her legs and splashing high on her body. As with all waves, the onslaught eased, slipping back to rock gently in place and to allow her to settle into her old comfortable self.

Peace. The word meant everything to her.

Good. Now is it possible to wake up, please? Roman is beyond worried, and we're going to attract attention soon.

She studied him. *I don't understand.*

I know. That's why you need to wake up. You weren't just a victim inside. Your body was attacked as well.

She blinked. She spun around and then looked down at her body. She wasn't in her body? *Say what?*

Stefan spoke again. *You're almost there. Just not back enough. You need to come all the way home.* He sighed, reached out a hand, and squeezed her shoulder. *You're caught in your own mind. But you need to come back into your body.*

She looked down at her toes. She lifted a questioning look in his direction and raised an eyebrow. She pointed to her toes and wiggled them. "I'm in my body."

He snickered.

Both her eyebrows shot up.

He grinned and shook his head. His hand squeezed hers again, and then, as she watched him, he placed the palm of his hand on the center of her forehead. He gazed deep into her eyes and whispered, *Go home.*

She felt a shot of heat go through her forehead and down her back, circling at the base of her spine. As if she had an elastic band connecting her to something else, the elastic sprang back and pulled her through a tunnel of darkness.

There was an odd tension, as if she were connected to something else. Something she didn't understand, but it was important.

Her head snapped back, and she smacked into awareness.

She opened her eyes and groaned.

"Shay?"

She blinked and tried to turn her head. A sledgehammer pounded on the inside of her skull.

She groaned again.

"Easy. Don't try to move just yet."

She blinked, heard the voice, and recognized it, but the words didn't quite register. She pushed herself up on her forearms. And then lifted her head. Tree boughs brushed the top of her head. She tried to push up more, only to realize someone, probably Roman, had grabbed her by the arms and was lifting her free of the tree.

Hitting the vertical so fast was tough on her head. Another groan slipped free.

Roman tucked her in close to his chest and held her tight.

She slowly became aware that he was saying something over and over again. "Thank you, God. Thank you."

She must have scared him pretty well. Then again, she'd scared herself too.

Feeling stronger, her head no longer sounding the alarm of imminent destruction, she pulled back a little and said, "Let's go home."

He tugged her in closer, hugged her tight, and then released her. "If you're sure you're okay. Otherwise it's to the hospital for you."

"No hospital," she murmured. "I just need rest."

"Then you can rest at home, where I can keep an eye on you, while you explain just what the hell you were doing taking off on me like that."

She'd have laughed if she could have. But in truth, she was too damn glad to be back in his arms to be worried. She deserved to get chewed out by him. How could she explain that she thought she'd recognized the killer's energy, and that given a chance to track down the person, she'd taken it.

Had she seen who the energy was attached to? No.

And that confused her even more.

Had she been given a trail of bread crumbs to lead her into a trap? A trap she'd fallen into without a second thought. She'd been so focused on the killer, she'd even left Roman behind.

She shook her head as she realized how far from the car she'd gone. It so didn't make any sense. Why would someone try to lure her into a trap?

And why knock her out when she arrived?

Why hadn't they killed her?

***

Roman was silent as he drove the car through the traffic. He gripped the steering wheel so tightly his fingers turned white. Every turn was sharp, every braking movement hard. Shay studied his profile and watched the muscle pulse on his jaw line.

She had some explaining to do.

And she had only five minutes left in the car to come up with a plausible story. Every time she reached for an explanation, her reasoning dissolved under scrutiny. She didn't know what to tell him. Had she run after that energy of her own volition?

Yes. At least she thought so.

She'd hadn't been following a person but, rather, an energy trail.

That's the thing – she'd been alone. So who had attacked her? Had someone lain in wait for her? Directed her there? Or did someone have the ability to knock her out from a distance by psychic means?

Not nice if they had.

And if so, from how far away could they do this? She'd checked out the area before they'd left the park, but the energy had already been overlaid and dissipated with many other energy trails. She needed to go back to her memory and take another look around as she ran through the trees and away from Roman.

She straightened. It wasn't much, but it was a plan.

And she might learn something she could use to redirect Roman away from chewing her out.

Roman pulled into the parking lot, turned off the engine, and then turned to look at her. "Home."

"Good. I have something I need to do. There's a trick I can try, to figure out who attacked me."

His gaze narrowed, locking on her face. "What kind of trick?"

With a wave of her hand to the surrounding area, she said, "I can't really explain it but I need privacy and preferably peace and quiet to do this."

"Then we'd better get at it." He exited the vehicle and came around to her side to help her out. "Although you shouldn't be doing too much of anything right now."

"And being attacked is why I have to do this." She gave him a wry smile. "I don't want to give this person another chance."

He kept a supportive arm around her shoulders as they entered the lobby. She smiled at Thomas, her doorman. "Long day, and it's not even noon yet."

He smiled as he stepped to the elevator and pushed the button. "Some days are like that."

At her apartment, Roman opened the door wide, and waited for her to enter. She took two steps in and stopped. Shifting her vision, she searched the air, looking for any signs of an intruder. It appeared normal.

She took another few steps inside and collapsed on her couch.

"Everything good?"

"Yes." She sighed. "I'm fine, but could use some caffeine."

She closed her eyes and let herself relax. Her mind wandered over the mess of the last few days.

Had someone been tracking her? How would they know about the funerals? About the deaths? Perhaps they were involved. Yet, if they'd been involved, how had they known to target those people?

Her files. All that information was in her files.

But who had access? Jordan, Rose of course, and herself. Anyone who had a key to her office. Who else? The board members, maybe. But that was her brother and Pappy. They'd all approved the initial projects. And none of them took more than a passing interest in them.

And anyone who could hack into her files. But Roman had checked and said that there hadn't been any unusual access to system.

Then again, she'd attended the last two funerals; it would be expected that she'd attend the third as well. In fact, the killer had probably planned for her to be there.

Given what happened so far today, she needed to update Ronin. But if she could find out anything more solid, something that might help him put a stop to this, she needed to find it quickly.

"Caffeine?"

Startled, she looked over to see a cup of something hot being placed on the coffee table. She smiled. Before she could thank him, he bent down and kissed her hard. Heat spread through her, igniting flames she'd thought slaked. Her toes curled as she sighed against his breath. "Nice."

"Just a reminder that you're no longer alone."

Warmth filled her heart. "Thanks. I'd forgotten."

His beautiful warm eyes smiled down on her. "Don't forget again."

He lowered his head once more, warming up the hidden spots deep inside Shay. A curious sense of connection filled her heart. It felt wonderful. Comforting. Blissful. To share her good days and her bad days. And boy, did today count as one of the worst.

"I was thinking I needed to phone your brother and give him an update," said Shay.

"That's the most sensible thing you've said today. Except I called him while I waited for you to wake up." He sat down beside her and tugged her onto his lap. "Now, what were you talking about in the car?"

She snuggled close and explained her technique.

"Absolutely amazing," he murmured. "To think something like that is even possible."

"Hmm. There is so much that goes on below the surface." She sighed. "You have no idea the things I've seen. What Stefan has seen."

"It has to be difficult to know so much about everyone. To see their secrets. To know information you'd probably rather not know." He looked slightly uncomfortable.

"Absolutely. Which is why I try to block so much. It makes it easier on me." Not wanting to hold back anymore, she added, "Which is why it's important we don't have any secrets between us." She turned to look up at him. "I can find them out. I'd rather be told, up front."

He stared down at her, something immobile in his gaze. "A warning?" he asked lightly, but something had shifted in his tone. But then, to find out he couldn't hide a secret from her had to be disconcerting. At the same time, it was damn near impossible for her to not wonder about the secret he kept to himself.

She'd like to say, fine, she didn't really want to know. But she also knew it would be impossible for her to love, on that level, if she didn't have an open and completely trusting relationship. She might never know if Roman had the ability to hide his true self like Darren had, but she couldn't imagine he would. His artwork was too passionate. To open. He gave it his all.

And then she realized it must be his artwork, his model, that he wanted to keep close to his heart.

And she could understand that. Not that she liked it, but she didn't exactly want to share her past about Darren either. So, good enough. Time to change the subject. Hopefully, when Roman was more comfortable, he'd share what he could. And that had to be enough.

At least for now.

"No, not a warning. Just letting you know some things can't be changed. I wouldn't go looking for answers." Still, she might under certain circumstances, and so she added, "Unless it was a life or death circumstance."

She grimaced at the memory. How many times had psychics been forced to cross that line and go deeper into their partner's psyche for just that reason?

"Well, I hope there'll be no life and death circumstances in our relationship." His gaze narrowed and he added slowly, "However, after today that thought is a little unnerving."

"Are you saying you'd like to back off?" Shay withdrew slightly to see his face more clearly.

He snatched her back into his arms. "No," he said forcefully. "That is not what I'm saying. I'm acknowledging that sometimes things are beyond our control."

"Oh. Good," she mumbled as she slumped against him."

"I don't have the same skills you do or that Stefan does." His voice deepened. "Is that a problem?"

"Stefan is a good friend. A great one in fact. He's also a terrific artist...and a good man." She smiled gently. "I love him. But like a friend. A brother."

He tugged her into his arms and covered her mouth with his. "I heard you the first time."

She kissed him back, and then gently retreated. "Good. Now, let me do what I need to do. Then we can put this morning behind us."

He stood up. "Am I in the way here?" He motioned to the kitchen. "I can sit further back. But I'm not leaving."

She shook her head. "Not necessary. While I'm under, just don't touch me. It will affect my energy and could snap me back too fast. And that's not good."

With that, she stretched out on the couch and closed her eyes.

***

Tuesday afternoon...

Roman stepped back, unable to leave. He'd watched her do some weird stuff lately, but he had no idea what to expect from this. She appeared to be sleeping. Except...there was an eerie stillness he didn't understand. He didn't think he'd seen anything like it before.

Her face was devoid of all expression, but there was something animated about her. No one looking at her would believe she was asleep or unconscious, yet her facial features were slack as if she were.

Whatever that meant.

He gave a quick glance around the room, realizing everything was normal looking. Needing to do something, he headed to the kitchen. Surely, he could rustle up something for her to eat when she came back. She'd had a rough morning and needed her strength.

He opened the fridge but then heard something...off. He closed the door and tiptoed back into the living room. She was still on the couch, in the same position as when he'd left her. But if so, what had he heard? Or thought he'd heard? Feeling ridiculous, he headed back and was just about to step on the tiled kitchen floor, when he thought he heard it again.

Spinning around, he searched the room.

And saw nothing unusual.

A whiff of something passed across his nose. He turned as a faint trail of...cinnamon...passed by. Or maybe that was nutmeg? He didn't know. It was there and then gone.

He spun around and studied Shay. She was still the same. Except different. And whatever caused that difference, he didn't like it one bit.

He pulled up the armchair and sat down, keeping his gaze on her. He sensed she was in danger. He had to watch over her. Only he felt helpless. He didn't know how to handle this woohoo stuff. *Who did?*

Stefan.

He straightened. Grabbed for his phone and called Stefan.

"What's wrong?" came the question. No formalities. Stefan had gone straight to the point.

"I don't know." Roman growled. "She's lying on the couch. She said she had a way to see what happened to her this morning. And she seemed normal." Roman stopped, not knowing how to continue, what to say. "And then it changed."

"Right. What do you mean 'it'?" Stefan's voice went brisk. "In what way has she changed since you were in the room last?"

"There was no smell, then there was a cinnamon scent...or maybe nutmeg." He ran his hands through his hair. "I don't know. I can't explain it. Before she looked lifeless, now there is life, but it's not nice. Like she's scared?"

"I'll take a look." Stefan hung up.

Roman stared down at Shay, the dead phone cold in his hands. "I hoped you'd say so."

The air in the apartment chilled. Goosebumps rose on his arms. He rubbed his hands up and down his arms. He searched the room. It's not like he expected to see Stefan appear in front of him. But he hoped Stefan arrived quickly.

He shivered.

What the hell? Everything was the same except the air temperature. He could almost see his breath. He blew out a full breath and stared in amazement. He *could* see his breath. *What was going on?* He was a plain talker, and this was not normal. He stood and walked over to the thermostat. It registered 72 degrees. A normal temperature for inside on your average sunny day.

And definitely wrong. There is no way this could be right. It had to be broken.

He turned around, wanting desperately to give Shay a good shake and wake her up. Get her the hell out of here. He wanted her at his place...where she belonged.

Chapter 22

Shay strode confidently forward across the park-like setting of the cemetery. She'd had no problem finding her way. The funeral was in progress. She studied the energy as she had before. Because she was looking for a killer she had to open herself to the private dark energy of all these people, look under the surface at who they really were, to see what they didn't want anyone to see.

Horrible things. Often things that people didn't let others, even themselves, know about. Their deepest, darkest secrets were hanging like dirty laundry for her to see.

And as much as she didn't want to look, she had to. Lives depended on it.

So she did. Yet nothing triggered any alarms.

She followed her old path back toward the car with Roman at her side. She paused, caught that same whiff of energy, and stretched out, searching for the source. She thought the energy came from a cluster of people talking with heads bent together, in front of her, but when she moved toward them, they headed to their vehicles and took off. She watched as her body raced down the path toward the trees, only now she'd lost the trail. Damn it. *How could that be?* She ran to catch up to the energy before she lost it altogether.

Ahead and slightly off to the side, she thought she caught a glimpse of the same energy that she'd followed earlier. It was moving down the parking lot, parallel to the path she'd taken this morning.

That made total sense. She hadn't seen it earlier because she assumed she'd been following it. But she'd been following only one strand of that energy – as if the person had walked back and forth along the same path. That had allowed the person to keep track of her...somehow, and they'd circled around to catch her by surprise.

She ran faster. And came around the trees to find another group of people in her way. *Damn it.* Why were there so many people here? She was ready to scream. Had she been so focused this morning that she hadn't taken note of them? She whipped around the tree.

And ground to a stop just in time to watch her body fall. It appeared to be dragged under a tree bough. By itself.

She stared in shock. She couldn't see the person who was doing the dragging. She saw a weird, pinkish energy, as in her own energy distorted. As she couldn't see the other person, she had to assume they were either invisible, God she hoped not, or like Stefan had suggested, they were using her energy to hide themselves.

Maybe wrapping her aura around their body.

She stood in shock, watching. Her energy chilled, yet kept her rooted to the spot.

Only barely understanding, she studied the energy around her body, hoping her attacker would show himself. The pink vision was dispelling, the energy fraying at the edges. She concentrated, pulling more of her own energy into the vision to try and see something useful. As she stood there, desperate for anything meaningful to be revealed, she reached out a hand, and watched in horror as a hand reached toward her.

Oh God.

Stefan.

Shocked, she stared up at her best friend's face.

"Shay." His hand reached out and touched her. "Time to go home."

"No. I haven't found what I need to find."

"And you can't. Not now."

"I have to." She reached further, spreading her fingers and clutched at a wisp of the distorted energy, sucking the very essence into her space, hoping to examine it later.

He shook his head. And with an odd flick of his fingers, Shay was snapped back through time to land with a heavy groan into her body on the couch.

She opened her eyes to find Stefan, in astral form, leaning over her. "Are you okay?"

She blinked. Confused and disoriented, she murmured, "What happened?"

"That's what I'd like to know." Roman leaned over her. His energy blended with Stefan's. *What the hell?* She blinked and tried to clear her vision. Then Stefan moved. And she could see them both.

Thank God.

✳✳✳

"Would you like to explain what the hell happened just now?" Roman carried Shay's full mug of coffee into the living room and set it down on the coffee table. "I don't understand that...but I want to."

Shay sat up in a movement reminiscent of his grandmother's before she passed away. Slow and sluggish, like every muscle had to work overtime to make her body do what she wanted it to do. Eventually Shay reached forward to accept her coffee then slumped back into the corner.

"Is it always like this?"

She looked up in surprise. "Uhm, no. Usually I recover much faster. But I was pushing the limit this time, got confused, and didn't exactly have an easy homecoming."

"Why not?"

"Stefan sent me home, actually. And that was probably a good thing. I seemed to have been frozen there – as in, locked in place and unable to move."

"There?" Roman took a deep breath. "Please, tell me – what is *there?*"

She stared at him with a hypnotic expression in her eyes that made him want to reach out, snag her up, and hold her close. Yet he'd been warned not to touch her while she did energy work and when she was recovering.

And the sharing of her experiences was all new to him. He suspected Stefan was a special friend *because* he understood her and what she went through. To do the stuff she was doing and to be alone, with no one to talk to about it, couldn't be easy.

He wanted to be one that she could talk to. Open communication was important to him. *Or was it?*

Inside, he winced as he thought about his paintings and what he kept from her.

✳✳✳

Shay wondered if a washing machine felt as worn out after a busy wash weekend as she did after this trip. She hadn't even had a chance to sort through what happened. She'd been paralyzed on the spot. Hadn't been able to move, was barely able to think, and had been getting colder by the second.

The first attack had been on her body, but the attack while she'd been looking for more information…that attack had been on her ethereal body.

Like how freaky was that?

And if she felt like she'd entered the twilight zone, she could only imagine how Roman would feel if she told him details of her experience.

He said he wanted to know. She just wasn't sure he could handle knowing.

And she wanted to know about that energy she'd tried to grasp. She'd caught a touch of it, enough to know something about it, but she needed to be sure. She stared at her closed fist and stalled…

The phone rang, giving her a chance to put off making a decision. She dragged her cell phone out of her pocket. "Stefan? What the hell happened?"

She gave Roman a reassuring smile. "Stefan, I'm going to put you on speaker phone. Roman needs to hear this, too."

His voice filled the room. "Except I don't have an answer. I found you frozen at the scene where you were hit. There was no one around. At least not any longer. Not on any plane that I could find, but your energy was draining off too fast for me to do anything to stop it, except to break your trance and send you home."

"And how did you know to find me?"

"Thank Roman for that." Stefan paused then added heavily, "I think whoever did this was related to Darren."

She gasped. "Are you sure?"

"Yes. Look at what you're holding in your hand. Like really look. Drop all your fears, your insecurities and see what is really there. You brought home a piece of that energy. The only way you could have done that was if you had some kind of connection. Darren."

Taking a deep breath she opened her mind and switched on her inner vision and looked. There was something there, but... Grabbing onto her fears, she breathed love and light into them, releasing the fears to the ethers. Then she went deeper than she'd gone before.

And saw it. She gasped as a familiar signature shimmered in her hand. Familiar...and yet not. This signature was similar to Darren's but wasn't his. It filled her palm, quivering in place. She whispered, "It is a family member."

"It's got to be the twin." Roman said. "There is no one else."

Oh God. She bowed her head. *Damn.* "Ronin needs to know what's going on. He needs to find the twin. He has to be in this vicinity. In the city, close to me."

"Ronin does know."

"Is there nothing to be done? It's hardly safe with this person running around." Roman put his coffee down very slowly, but Shay watched the temper building on his face.

"It's all right, Roman," Shay said. "This is the first time something like this has happened. It's bizarre enough that it's not likely to happen again."

"But it could. Right?" He stared, narrow-eyed, at her. She tried for that reassuring smile again and was about to speak, but Stefan beat her to it.

"Yes. It could," Stefan said. "Any time we do energy work, there is a chance of something going wrong. The same as you could have an accident any time you get behind the wheel of your car."

Roman frowned at the cell phone in Shay's hand.

She raised it higher and smiled grimly at him. "He's right. It's very unusual for us to have a problem, but nothing is without risk. And rarely are we fighting off attackers."

He sat back and glared at her. "But this time you are. And I don't like it."

She answered tartly, "No, and I understand that. But you have to let me do this. It's what I do."

She stared him down, watching resignation and then acceptance slip into his gaze.

Stefan added, "It's what I do, too."

And that seemed to settle Roman. He stared moodily up at the ceiling.

Shay felt for him. Talk about being pushed out of his comfort zone. And she knew he didn't really understand what they were talking about. Would it help for him to have a different type of demonstration?

Stefan spoke in her head. *Go ahead if you want to.*

She grinned, watching Roman's frown deepen. *I don't think Roman is ready for another one of those displays.*

"Maybe he needs it. How else can he understand?"

Again Roman's deep blue gaze fixed on her. "Need what?" Suspicion laced his voice.

"It doesn't matter." She shrugged. "You don't need a demonstration right now, and I'm too tired for one anyway."

"What kind of demonstration? Stefan already gave me one." Roman leaned forward. "And how invasive would it be?"

"Not. And this would be what I can do." She said with a smile. "I could just walk in your footsteps today and tell you what you did."

He shook his head. "Like that would help. I was with you all day."

She laughed. "Good point. Then I'll read your energy and tell you about where you spend it."

He tilted his head. "Spend it. What does that mean?"

She leaned forward until they were eye level. "I can tell where your energy goes on a daily basis. It doesn't have to be too personal. For example..." She paused and shifted her viewing angle. "You have a close relationship with Gerard, and even though you pretend not to worry, you generally call him several times a day."

He smiled. "Of course I do. Look at his age and the personal loss he's sustained lately."

She smiled. "But you didn't have that same relationship with your grandmother or your aunts and two uncles."

"Two uncles?" he shook his head. "I believe I have only one."

She studied his energy again. "Two males and one female on that level."

"One male and one female," he corrected. "But that's all right, what else?"

Wanting to avoid an argument, but knowing he'd ask his grandfather, she studied his energy again. "You enjoy your job, but for you it's a nine to five commitment." She frowned. "Your painting is your joy. And..."

"Again, that's all superficial and has been discussed before."

"And I'm not trying to invade. Remember? However, if you want more… I can see an incident in high school that badly affected you. You lost someone you were very close to."

He straightened, a look of surprise coming over his face. "You spoke to my grandfather about that," he accused.

"No," she said gently, "I can see you dedicate a certain amount of your energy to honoring her."

"Her?" his voice was hard, stiff. "How could you know that this person is female?"

"Because you funnel soft, gentle energy in that direction. Loving energy that goes way into your past. Not to a child. Not to an animal, and yes, I can see those, too. Like your golden lab you grew up with, called Rex."

He sat back. What else could she know? Did she know about his paintings of her? Damn he should have told her himself. He didn't want her to find out this way. And yet this so wasn't the time.

Or was it?

She smirked. "Convinced?"

And the moment passed. Relieved, he smiled. "Well, I certainly am convinced you can access information in my past. How accurately, I don't know. Rex was my dog – a wonderful dog. He died when I was fourteen. I thought my world had ripped apart back then."

"But nothing compared to the loss you sustained when you were seventeen." She couldn't help but soften her voice. His pain had been real, his honoring of that special person a daily fact. One he continued to expend energy on her every day. "I can tell she's still important to you."

He said starkly, simply, "She is. She was my sister."

***

Goddamn it, Shay. What the fuck were you doing there The walls glared back, providing no answers.

How had she been there – like that? In that form. It wasn't possible. I only went back to the area to see if you'd been found – and what did I find – you in astral form.

Try to follow me, would you? Not likely.

Not in any way. There were limitations to energy work. But there was no way Shay was anywhere close to them. It wasn't possible that she could be that good.

No way you did that on your own. It had to have been a fluke. I've tried to do something similar to shadow walking – and I failed. There's no way you're better than me. You had to have help.

There could be a few others who could do this energy work – maybe. But not Shay. Not like that. Never that bitch. Darren had explained about Shay's holier-than-thou attitude to life and money and how it pissed him off. He'd loved knowing how superior he was to her. Knowing that she had no idea how he fooled her. That his skills were strong and that knowledge gave him a sense of power.

A power that was somehow false. He'd died. Shay didn't.

And that had to be fixed. Shay couldn't be allowed to live.

Darren had planned on killing her. That he had died in her place was a wrong that had to be righted.

But how? There hadn't been enough time to kill her at the cemetery. Not with so many people around. So I went back to see if I could finish the job.

And saw Shay. On the ground where I left her...but standing up in astral form as well, now that had been...bizarre. Shay had been so clear. Easy to identify. How? What happened? There'd been another sort of energy there, too. But that wasn't recognizable either.

Another person? Part of Shay's energy, even though it looked different? It would be great to think Darren's ghost had been going after Shay, but it hadn't felt like him. No one else understood both the freedom and the sadness of living like this.

No one cared.

There had to be an outlet for this rage. Now.

Someone was going to die

Chapter 23

Tuesday evening…

Shay entered the hospital and walked to Pappy's room. Roman walked silently at her side. He'd been unapproachable since her demonstration earlier. She couldn't really blame him.

His energy didn't reach for her or slide or caress her energy any longer. No. His energy swirled as if he wore a glass jar around his body with the colorful energy inside. Yet it wasn't angry.

Whatever she'd stirred up, it had brought on a major deep-thinking session.

Her insights were obviously a very sensitive subject.

But one they'd need to broach sometime in the near future because the bond was growing, deepening between them.

He couldn't hide his feelings any more than she could avoid seeing how his energy slipped around hers and melded and blended them into one. She felt the little strokes, the little brushes of his essence constantly. Her own energy stretched eagerly, reaching for him.

Normally, his energy responded in kind. Except right now.

He was locked down, big time. She could understand. He needed to do something. He needed to be able to put a stop to this nightmare. But she didn't have any answers or any way to stop it.

They reached Pappy's door in silence. Roman stepped back to let Shay enter first. Gerard was already there. He looked up and smiled when they walked in.

"There you go, Charles. Look who finally got here."

Pappy smiled and Shay rushed over. She reached down and gently hugged him. "How are you feeling?"

She studied him intently; his face was pale and wan. "You didn't sleep well, did you?"

"I'm fine." He patted her hand. "Don't you worry."

"Well, I will regardless, so you might as well let me." She dropped a gentle kiss on his forehead. "What about the tests? Did the doctors get the results?"

He shook his head. "None that say anything. I didn't have a stroke. My heart seems fine. I just seemed to have blanked out."

Shay smiled. "I'll talk to them. See if they have any other concerns, tests they can do."

She stepped back, letting Roman in closer, and then walked into the hallway to see if she could find the doctor. Seeing no one, she headed to the nurses' station and asked about her grandfather's test results.

"Sorry. The doctor is here but hasn't gotten to your grandfather yet." The harried nurse paused her clicking on the keyboard long enough to look up and answer. "Everyone is running behind right now."

That was normal. Shay understood. "I'll wait for him then. Thanks." She turned and starting walking down the hallway. There were various carts and doors at this end of the floor. She passed a trolley full of folded laundry, and a hamper at the end of the trolley that held dirty laundry. She stopped and looked at the dirty hamper.

Something was wrong with the picture. She switched her vision on and studied the energy. A nasty black swirled up around the garments in the bin. Oozing, murderous black energy.

Oh shit. She whirled around, searching for the energy trail. The black *came* from the hallway that led toward Pappy's room. That energy hadn't been in his room earlier, and Pappy should be safe with both Roman and Gerard to keep watch. Should be...

Her heart sped up. She was almost running by the time she reached Pappy's room, only to realize the energy trail carried on past. But there was a large collection at the doorway where it must have wallowed for a moment, as if the person looked in and considered this room and then moved on.

She studied the doorway. The black had pulsed here, gathering tighter together. *In anger? In frustration?*

Then it had moved on.

That information stalled her. Shay *had* automatically surrounded her grandfather with healing, protective energy, but she hadn't done anything to the doorway.

But there was other residual energy there. Something had prevented entrance to the room. Could Stefan have…? She stepped back, opened her inner vision, and gasped.

Bernice. The doorway was outlined with the residual energy of Bernice's soul. Connected as always – to Pappy.

Her heart stalled, and then she smiled happily. The trio had a unique relationship, and no one could ever doubt the power of their bond. Now, when Pappy was in trouble, Bernice was still protecting him.

And as for that horrific energy… Shay walked slowly to the next room, where the energy entered and looped back out and turned down the hall again. She stood at the entrance and followed the trail with her eyes. The energy swelled with emotion. It tossed and roiled with the need for expression – and it had found it.

The elderly woman on the bed had half fallen to the floor. Even from where she stood, Shay understood it was too late to help her.

She studied the energy, knowing she had to go back to the nurses' station and report what she'd found. But she needed confirmation, if she could find it, evidence that this woman had died of something other than natural causes. In her heart she knew the autopsy would say she died of a heart attack. The black energy had entered the woman's body at the heart chakra and only the heart chakra. The angry entrance had slammed into that poor woman and given no quarter. From where she stood, Shay couldn't tell if the energy had drained from the woman or if she'd been given such a hard jolt that, in her weakened condition, the assault had finished her.

There was only one purpose for energy like that.

Murder.

✳✳✳

Over an hour later, Shay headed back to Pappy's room to say good-bye. She didn't know what the normal procedure was in these cases, but as she'd initially informed a policeman who'd been standing at the nurses' center, She'd been asked to give a statement, just in case. She had no problem giving her version of the event. She really had nothing to tell.

Nothing that she could tell law enforcement.

With Roman at her side, she gave her grandfather a gentle hug and kiss goodnight. "I hope you're feeling better in the morning."

She followed Roman to the door.

Pappy called out as they were leaving, "Shay, could I speak with you for just a moment?"

She rushed back over. "What's the matter; aren't you feeling well?"

"Oh, I'm fine. I just want you to know that I spoke to my lawyer today. Made a few changes to my will."

She grinned. "That's nothing new. You do that every few months or so."

He smiled gently. "I do, but that's because I never know when my old heart is going to give out. I want to make sure everything is taken care of."

"You're not dying, and when you do go, it won't matter anymore because you'll be gone." She chuckled.

"Don't be cheeky," he chided her gently with their old joke. "I'm not going any time soon. I know that. But I do want you taken care of before then. So my question is: how is the relationship with Roman?"

She flushed and laughed lightly. "Fine."

"He's a good man."

"I know." She didn't know where he was going with this, but she knew he had something to get off his chest.

"I thought you two would be good together."

"Are you matchmaking?"

"No. I need to tell you. I gave him a picture a long time ago. A couple of years ago at least. Of you. From some family gathering. Thought maybe he'd be interested in meeting you."

She tilted her head and frowned. *Interesting.* Roman hadn't mentioned it. Then why would he? Besides, for all she knew, Pappy had sent the picture after she and Roman had started chatting anyway. "Okay...I don't know why you would have, but that's fine."

Relief washed over his face. "Good. I've been worrying over that for a long time. I should have asked you before giving it to him, but..."

"But you forgot."

"And Bernice told me not to tell you."

Bernice? Shay laughed. "Now that figures. She was trying to match the two of us at the end too."

Pappy smiled. "Maybe this is one time you should listen to your elders."

Her grin widened. "And maybe it's not."

She brushed her lips against his papery cheek, hating that such a thing had been eating away at him. He was precious to her.

And she had to protect him.

***

Roman drove home through the busy streets in a deeply contemplative mood. Finally, needing to understand, he asked, "How do you know it's the same energy?"

She gave a long, heavy sigh. "Energy is like DNA. Individual to each person. Once I see an energy signature, I can recognize the look, the feel of it again. There's a familiarity or sense of knowing that is hard to miss." She settled back. "In this case, as I not only saw it, but was touched by it, I know how this energy also feels. And the same person who attacked me at the cemetery killed that poor woman."

"And your cousin, Marie, and David, and possibly several other people? That can never be proven."

"Exactly. Look at what Stefan is up against. How can the police stop someone they can't see? How can they believe a crime was committed when there is no physical evidence?"

"There's a dead body," he countered.

She slid him a sideways look he caught from the corner of his eye. "A dead body that will show up in the autopsy as having had a heart attack – ergo, death by natural causes."

"How can so many people die of natural causes?"

"Thousands of people die every day from natural causes. And millions die every year from heart attacks. That's why an attack like this is so easy to get away with."

He couldn't argue with that, but he wanted to, damn it. How often did things like this happen in the world? With everyone oblivious, shaking their heads. "We have to do something."

She nodded, and then leaned her head back against the headrest and said, "We are."

"You and Stefan?"

"Yes."

Stefan again. "I want to help." He frowned. "What can I do?"

"I'm not sure there is anything you can do."

He drove the car around a corner. In a thoughtful voice, he said, "Can you trace this energy to a person?"

"We're trying to. Stefan picks up a thread of the energy on the ethers and then tracks it back, but he says in this case it's almost like the energy changes, morphs into something else, and then he loses it at that point. It's not a visual path in the way that you or I would think, but an inner vision, so the trail can be lost easily."

"And lost because someone is hiding?" He watched as she fumbled with her phone. "What are you doing?" he asked.

"Calling your brother." She moved it away from her head and turned on her speaker phone. "Hi Ronin, anything new?"

"Actually maybe. We've tracked the brother to Seattle, where we have a last known address. He had a girlfriend – on again, off again. Apparently, she was questioned about him today but said she hasn't seen him for a year or so."

"A year?" Shay's mind spun on the possibilities. Surely that timeframe was no coincidence?

"I'm working to track his movements from their point of departure. I'll keep you updated." He coughed. "How's my brother doing these days?"

Shay glanced over at Roman. "He's fine."

"And how are you and my brother?"

Shay coughed with obvious embarrassment. "All is well. Thanks, Ronin. Keep in touch."

Roman drove his BMW into his underground parking at home, stopping to key in the code to open the gate, then drove into his parking spot. He turned off his engine and turned to face her as she finished her call. She hopped out of the car and walked toward the elevators. Roman shook his head. Talk about determined.

He laughed, caught up and wrapped an arm around her shoulder. "I wanted to show you my place."

She raised an eyebrow. "Good. Have you got new paintings? I'd love to see them."

"Not the latest. Those are at the gallery."

He joined her at the elevator and punched in the number.

She watched, raised an eyebrow, and asked, "Penthouse?"

"I like my space." That's all he said as the elevator rose. The doors opened, and he led the way to a single door in front. He unlocked and pushed it open, letting her inside.

"Nice." She walked in, her eyes locking on the artwork covering the wall. "These are beautiful." He stood in the hallway and admired her as she wandered the large open space admiring the art.

"Some older pieces. Glad you like them."

She smiled, a look that lit her up from the inside. "It's spectacular."

"You're spectacular," he said softly. "Truly."

Her smiled warmed. She walked toward him. "Thank you." She reached up and placed a light kiss on his lips. He snatched her up and lowered his head to kiss her with the intensity he'd kept locked inside all day.

She purred in his arms. He deepened the kiss, shifting her slightly to allow better possession of her mouth. He could never get enough of this woman. She was so special. So his.

***

Shay stepped closer, wanting to be inside his mind and body. She needed this man like no other. It didn't matter that she'd said 'never again.' They were words spoken before she'd understood what was waiting for her. She'd have raced toward her future if she'd known. Roman was her future. She just needed him to be comfortable with his present, and with her.

And one perfect way to do that was right here and now.

She stepped back and smiled up at him. And her fingers went to her blue cotton shirt. She undid the buttons as he watched – a gleam lighting his eyes. His hands hurriedly unbuttoned, unhooked, and undid his clothing, tossing clothes from where he stood. Minutes later, they were both nude in the living room. Standing, staring at each other, with enough heat steaming from their bodies to make her skin glow.

He was a magnificent animal. Tall, muscled, so masculine. She didn't think he worked out but rather thought he was blessed with a natural grace and form that most men would die to have. She reached up and unclipped her long hair, shaking it free around her shoulders, then took one step closer. She reached out a finger and stroked over the lean muscles of his chest, her finger running a long, teasing stroke that ended at a nasty ragged scar over his ribs. His bullet wound. She couldn't resist; she leaned forward and dropped a kiss on the hardened center. He hissed.

"You're going to have to tell me about that sometime," she murmured.

She pulled back slightly, a smile on her face.

"Later." He opened his arms and she stepped into them.

***

Early Wednesday morning...

Hours later, Shay woke up refreshed and energized. Roman slumbered, face down beside her. His arm was flung across her belly. What time was it? She couldn't see a clock from her position. There was a gray light to the room, so she guessed it was probably early morning. She wiggled upright and slipped out from under him. She needed a drink and was too wired to go back to sleep.

A couple of folded t-shirts lay on Roman's dresser. She tossed one over her head, almost laughing when it came to mid-thigh on her. She gave a curious glance around.

She'd never seen his place and she was wanted to take a peek. The walls in the bedroom were a light, soothing mocha with sharp white trim. His bedding, so similar to hers included a huge duvet in a rich deep chocolate with lighter stripes, now rumpled into a ball at the bottom of his massive bed.

The atmosphere was light and breezy and satisfaction oozed from the bedroom. And she smiled. She loved being with Roman, and she was seriously thinking that she might be in love with him – maybe even past thinking about it.

She walked through to the kitchen and poured herself a glass of water from the tap, loving the open spacious feeling and the bright tiles on the floor. As she sipped, she wandered around his penthouse. She'd never considered what type of home he'd have, but appreciated that this suited him perfectly.

There was a large solarium that opened up on the left that appeared to be part workroom and part sitting room. The art on the walls there, sprawled into another room that was filled with paints and easels. She wandered through the large room, loving the pictures. The half light added shadows to the images, highlighting various parts and hiding others. And there she was. That they were all the same model only reaffirmed her belief. She hoped one day Roman would share who this woman was that had grabbed his passion and held on so tightly.

And explain the relationship he had with her.

She was stunning. But his skill made her even more so. He expressed so much in so few strokes. Her profile, shoulders, everything created with minimal paint.

The blue accents on some of the pictures intrigued her.

On some of the paintings there was almost a sheen, a blue air around the central figure. Like an aura? Unusual and intriguing.

And yet the painting sitting off to the side was thick and almost three-dimensional. It held so much paint. She wouldn't have been surprised to hear that he'd carved it instead of painted it.

Fascinated. She stood back and paused. Tilted her head again. Backed up as far as she could go.

She gasped.

Inside, her heart jolted, stilled for a long moment, and then raced forward.

No. The lines were so familiar. But it couldn't be. Wasn't possible.

A soft laugh filled the air. She spun around. But she was alone. Turning back around, she caught a glimpse of something.

A fragrance…cinnamon, maybe whispered through the room. *Of course it is. Do you really not know?*

She gasped. "Bernice?"

That same warm laughter.

Shay laughed too. "Aren't you supposed to be off in the light, doing things that dead people do?"

I will soon. When I know Charles is fine. Until then, I'm here. Then again, as he hasn't got long anyway, I might just stick around. Bernice laughed. *He'd like that.*

Even though Shay hated the thought of her grandfather dying, she had to smile at the thought of Bernice staying close until then. Pappy would be tickled. "I'm glad to hear he has a guardian angel. Thank you for helping him."

I love him, Bernice said simply. *How can I do any less? Now, look at the paintings. Are you really so blind?*

Shaking her head, Shay studied several paintings again.

And then she knew.

Indeed, how could she *not* have known? Tears crept into her eyes. Warm shivers rode down her spine, and her heart swelled.

Finally, Bernice said; then she disappeared, leaving Shay to face the truth.

The model was *her.*

Chapter 24

Shay couldn't move. Her mind froze long before the rest of her body, which was still trying to move forward. This wasn't possible. There's no way. Yet, no matter what she did, the fact was irrefutable. She was staring at portraits of her.

The how eluded her, and the why... Well that just blew her away. Helpless to do anything but obey her instinctive need to see more, she walked quietly forward and stared at the closest canvas directly in front of her. Unfinished, it resembled many of the others she'd seen at the gallery, but this time the face was turned coquettishly with just the jawline complete. Her jawline. Her hand instinctively lifted to touch her smooth chin that he'd captured so easily with a single stroke. She wouldn't have believed it if she wasn't seeing it.

Fascinated, she walked around the studio, stopping to shift a canvas to look at the ones hidden behind it. So many. She could see a few, discarded in a pile at the back. She reached forward to pull the canvas that had been tucked the furthest away. It was a struggle, but she finally managed to pull it into the light.

There was more of her showing than in the ones she'd recently looked at. Her face was more defined, less of a hint and more of a sketch. She looked back over at the others. He'd used less detail in those and gave more of an impression of her features. His skill had improved.

Amazing.

As she studied the paintings her mind flitted from conversation to conversation. To ones that offered uncomfortable insights about his muse, his passion. His discomfort with the many conversations. It all made so much sense.

And made her feel foolish. She'd been jealous – of herself.

269

She crouched down and flicked through a stack on the floor.

Studying another one, she barely heard a noise behind her. She spun around to find Roman leaning against the open doorway. His only clothing was a pair of snug boxers molding to his muscled thighs.

"Like what you see?"

She gazed at him, a tic pulsing in his cheek. Her mind so full, her heart on overload, she could hardly speak. She took a deep breath and answered honestly. "I'm not sure, to be honest."

"Oh?" He frowned, straightened and walked closer. As his gaze went to the canvas in her hand, he grimaced. "Ugh. That's an old piece."

"Why are there no other models? No landscapes or still lifes?"

She replaced the canvas in the stack before crossing the room to stand in front of him. "Is it only me that you paint?"

His whimsical smile tugged at her heart. "In a way. I've been fascinated with you for a very long time." He studied her face as if waiting for a reaction.

In truth she didn't have a reaction to give. She was too stunned. So he'd been painting her longer than they'd been communicating? Longer than he'd known her? Really? Was that possible?

When she continued to stare at him, a gentleness spread in her heart. As if sensing her acceptance, he continued. "Your Pappy gave me the original picture. Although I think Bernice sent me a couple around the same time. I thought at first that I could paint you out of my system. That if I did just one more, if I got the line of your shoulder...just right...you'd leave me in peace." His gaze roamed her face, as if memorizing the slight nuances of the real thing to compare to his artwork.

She arched a brow. "And? Did it work?"

He shook his head, a curious light coming into his eyes. "It had the reverse effect. I became obsessed. I couldn't get enough.

You dominated my thoughts and my days. I couldn't wait to get home so I could paint you again, this time with the draping of a sheet, or a dress or...nothing."

She shook her head at the thought of this man, someone she hadn't even met, going through his day, eager to put her image on a canvas. It blew her away. And in a little way...it kind of creeped her out.

She studied the proud man in front of her and realized something important.

No. She wasn't creeped out and the reason it didn't creep her out...was because it was *this* man. If any other man had done this, yes. *That* would have been all wrong. But not Roman. In some way, perhaps his need to paint her every day had kept her alive in his mind – she almost understood it. To paint her had become an obsession. His passion. There'd never been any doubt about that. She knew it. Had noticed it right from the beginning.

She'd even told Stefan at the gallery.

She just hadn't understood who he was obsessed with.

Now she realized where the difficulty lay and why. And how personal this whole thing was. And why he had put up his walls. His obsession to paint her, and only her, had been his guilty secret. The reason for the distance she'd felt. And he hadn't known how she'd react.

She checked his energy now. It no longer felt invasive. The wall had been there to protect his secret and now that was out, the wall was crumbling. Not completely gone yet, though... The wall was lighter, thinner. Still there, but no longer as solid, and it was collapsing even as she watched. He'd opened up, become vulnerable. She sensed he waited...for a judgment to come. From her.

Then she remembered Pappy's confession at the hospital. Old matchmaking Pappy with Bernice as a willing accomplice. He'd given Roman pictures of her. Not nudes, just casual pictures from one of the many events in the last few years.

Roman had taken it from there.

She walked around the small room and studied the paintings. Every picture was at an angle of some sort. There were no full-on paintings of her face or a front view.

"Why are there no pictures of my face?"

"Because I couldn't get it right." He walked to a cupboard at the back of the room and pulled out several sketchbooks. He turned to face her and held out the smaller one to her. She accepted it. Turning it around, she flicked it open and walked a few feet away, engrossed in looking over all the different images. Several pages in, she glanced at the cover again, looking for a date. "When did you draw these?"

"When I first got the pictures, maybe two years ago now. I was hoping to do your face, and I tried." He motioned to the book in her hand. "But I could never get it right. Eventually I gave up."

"And why do you think you couldn't get it right?" She turned the page to see another attempt – this one looked really close.

He took a deep breath. "A couple of reasons. I didn't know you, and I was doing this without you knowing. In essence…I couldn't paint your face because I hadn't faced you about this. I felt…guilty."

Startled, she gazed up at him, her attention diverted. A man with a conscience? She didn't know what to say, so she focused on the question she needed to ask. "What is with the blue?"

Silence. Roman gave a short laugh. "I don't know what to say to that, except to say I have to add it. I don't know why." He shrugged and gave her a lopsided grin. "I gave up trying to change it a long time ago. It doesn't help that Stefan said he knew the reason for the blue…but wouldn't tell me."

She widened her eyes. If it had been a soft pink, she'd have wondered if he'd seen her aura, but blue…? "Interesting, and so typical of Stefan."

"It bothered me in the beginning, but it became one more thing to accept. Just like I used to do abstracts…but from the first time I saw a picture of you...there were no more abstracts." He shrugged helplessly.

"You've done no other type of picture since you started to work on paintings of me?"

"Well, I tried." He gave a short, self-conscious laugh. "But none of them worked. I tried for a few months to change... Only as long as I could paint you, then I could paint. But once I tried to change the subject, then I was lost. And I could do no more."

She shook her head. She handed the sketchbook back. "I don't know what to say."

"Are you...upset?"

That answer was easy. The rest *so* not. She remembered all the things she'd instinctively known about his relationship with his model. Feeling her way through, she answered slowly, "No. Not upset. Surprised. Confused. Stunned actually. And uncertain."

"Uncertain?" He jumped on that.

She winced. "I didn't mean to say that."

"But you did."

She took a deep sigh. "I'm wondering...with all this...what you really feel for *me*." At the surprised and shuttered look on his face, she rushed to explain. "Are we together now because of this?" She waved her arm around the studio. "Is this what I am to you? Your muse? Do you worry that you can't paint... Are you afraid that without me, you won't be able to paint anymore?"

Once she started, the words poured out. She hadn't realized they'd been churning inside. Or even that they'd demanded voice, until the torrent had started.

"And am I only here so you can fill in the pieces of your painting, the pieces that you haven't been able to, until now?"

The silence was absolute.

She glanced over at him nervously.

273

He stood as if slammed by a bullet. He barely moved. Not even a breath gusted free.

She had to finish. She had to get it all out. Then she'd leave. But she needed to know the answer first. Then she could go home and sort this out. She took a deep breath and continued.

"I guess I'm afraid that I'm only here because of your obsession. Not because I'm *me*."

***

He couldn't breathe. He couldn't formulate a thought. And words strung into a comprehensive sentence seemed impossible. This is what he'd been afraid of. That she'd find out and misconstrue what she saw.

Hell, he couldn't have foreseen *this* worry of hers. It never occurred to him that she'd doubt his feelings for *her*.

But he hadn't known how to handle telling her, so he hadn't.

And that had been a mistake. If he'd only brought up the issue first.

But he'd woken up alone. And had freaked. He'd thrown on boxers and raced through the apartment searching for her. He'd been so sure she'd left to go home that when he'd found her in his studio, his first thought had been only relief because for that instant his secret was forgotten.

It had taken minutes for him to relax enough to lean against the wall and watch her. She'd been so intent, so curious, he'd quickly fallen into artist mode, watching the expressions ripple across her face. She was so expressive. He'd actually reached for a pencil and sketchbook. That's when she'd heard him.

Even now his finger itched for his pencil. To sketch out that long hair as it brush over her shoulder with her every movement.

Except he wouldn't be able to hold anything. He was frozen. What he said now would decide the course of his future.

A crossroad.

What could he say?

He opened his mouth as if to speak, but no words came out.

***

Roman tried again, watching her as she studied him. Shay stepped toward him.

"Tell me." She narrowed her gaze, willing him to step up and speak. To tell her what she wanted him to say. What she needed to hear.

What he needed to verbalize.

That she was his model, was both stunning and gratifying, but she wanted that reaction to be about *her*, in the flesh, not her image on a canvas.

She took another step closer to him, and stood on tiptoe so she could stare into his eyes. Her gaze locked with his, probing, urging him to speak up. His eyes warmed, deepened. She offered a tiny smile in response.

His gaze burned as fire ignited deep inside. The flame dancing in his eyes, grew stronger, brighter. That intense look caused a conflagration deep inside her belly. An answering prayer of joy rolling up through her insides, carrying a song as old as time.

"Tell me," she whispered.

A tiny smile played at the corner of his mouth. He leaned closer, intent on kissing her.

She shook her head, insisting, "Tell me."

His head lowered even more.

"Tell me," she insisted, her breath brushing up gently against his lips.

He stilled. His mouth inches from hers. His warm breath played over her eyes and face. She closed her eyes, letting his closeness warm her soul and soothe her thundering heart as she waited to be released from this prison of doubt. She knew it could happen. Would happen. If he was ready.

If he meant all that his pictures said he did. If he *was* true to his passion.

Then he'd be true to her.

But she knew, first he had to be true to himself.

"Tell me."

Shay kept her eyes closed. She felt his energy surge toward her, wrapping around her, caressing her shoulders, her hips, her head. Light gentle strokes caressed and soothed even as they whispered through on a promise.

She needed to hear the words.

He needed to voice them.

"Tell me," she whispered, keeping her voice soft and delicate, yet offering him hope and a future together like none other.

He lowered his head to rest his forehead on hers. She opened her eyes to see him close his. An almost imperceptible shudder worked down his body and his shoulders lowered and relaxed. She sensed his energy sink deep into her own, blending and melding to join with hers, as one.

As calm and sure as she'd ever heard his voice, his words came as a benediction. Releasing her from her prison and giving her the strength to fly free.

She let her heart energy cross the small divide to crawl into his heart chakra and curl up inside.

So quiet, more impression than sound, he whispered, "I love you."

***

Wednesday, at dawn…

Ronin loved working the night shift. Although it was closer to breakfast time, there was something magical about the city at dawn. That more crimes were committed, and there were more predators to hunt at night made his working life that much more interesting. He understood the predator mindset and he did some of his best police work at night.

His twin brother Roman often did his best work at night too. Even growing up, Roman could be found, well after bedtime, with a pencil scribbling over every square inch of his textbooks. He'd gotten hell for that many times.

Instead of art, Ronin had music in his soul. He played the trumpet and favored jazz. That both brothers had gone into law enforcement said much about who they were as men, but having a creative outlet meant they survived the rigors of the brutal world they worked in better than many others.

He had worried about his brother for years. After that bullet, Roman could have taken a desk job. Instead he'd walked away and set up his own company. And he had proved to be damn good at it. Ronin had used his services many times.

He knew that while Roman checked over Shay's site and said that there'd been nothing obviously amiss, he'd also worried that the door to the office was essentially one any two-bit burglar could break if they wanted to get inside. That just meant they couldn't narrow the field at all that way.

And Roman had gone a step further with the new security system he'd ordered for Shay's apartment *and* her office. Last Ronin heard, they were both still arguing over who would get to pay.

There were many people involved in the Foundation. Any one of them could access the information needed to identify people associated with it. But none of that explained how these people had been killed recently. He understood about the energy – well as much as any non-psychic could – but, like Stefan said, the person doing this could be anyone, anywhere and have skills they hadn't run across before.

And how scary was that?

He didn't understand Stefan's explanation about Tabitha hiding on the ethers. Like who could?

Ronin had spoken to several of Stefan's friends about other cases involving psychic criminals, trying to get a handle on how they dealt with these sorts of things, but the information wasn't helpful. Some had been enlightening in the scope of the crimes and the people who committed them, but it didn't shed light on Shay's issue right now.

His brother was playing watchdog, and Ronin knew it would take a tank to pry him away from Shay's side. Good thing; as it seemed her attacker could appear and disappear at will. He needed to brush up on his skills if criminals were taking to the ethers.

Just then his email signaled a new message. He clicked on the link and bent his head to read.

Finally. They'd found Darren's twin. He read, then reread the message. *Shit.*

He reached for the phone.

"Stefan," he began, "I found Darren's twin. He's in Seattle. In the morgue. He was a John Doe and has only been recently identified. Cause of death...as far as they can tell, heart attack. He's been there for a year."

Silence.

"Stefan?"

"I'm here." Fatigue whispered through the phone line. "I didn't see that coming."

"No one did. And if he isn't the one causing all this havoc, who the hell is?"

"I don't know, but we have to find out, and fast. There's an edge of instability here. I don't like it. In fact, I'm working at the children's hospital right now. Trying to strengthen the walls. Just in case."

"Is it working?" Ronin asked. He'd love to think something like that was doable, but he highly doubted it. He knew Shay's foundation had contributed heavily to the new wing at the hospital and that definitely made it and those who worked there, potential targets. He winced as he thought of the damage that could be done.

"I hope so. I'd planned to go home and rest, then do more tomorrow. Now I'm not so sure. It's one thing to have a villain you think you know, but it's quite another to have a nasty piece of work that is also aggressive and faceless. While we thought it was Darren's twin, I understood the potential capabilities of this person, now... Now, it's a whole new game."

Crap. Ronin hung up the phone slowly. "A whole new ballgame? Why is nothing ever easy?"

He bent over his keyboard and got to work.

***

Enough was enough...

Too bad Darren was no longer here. They could play his favorite pastime. Murder. The hospital wasn't the best place for games. At least right now. It was however, the right place for real get-away-with-it murder. Everyone there was dying anyway. So who would notice one more?

And that was the pissy part of tonight. It had been too easy. The old woman hadn't even been scared. It's as if she'd waited for her maker to come. And if that didn't beat all.

The old woman had started praying as soon as the process had started. And how could she have known that her time had come? And not just praying, but almost chanting. Bizarre. There'd been nothing to it. The old woman had given up on life almost immediately. Almost grateful to end her existence.

Peaceful. As if she'd been happy to go. And damn, that wasn't the intention at all. The children's ward would have been better.

And it's not like the plan had been to take out the old woman. She'd just been the closest target to vent my anger after not being able to enter Shay's grandfather's room. The old woman had been the closest target.

But had Shay gotten the message? Not likely. It wasn't personal enough. She didn't know the old woman. She wouldn't care. She wouldn't suffer from the woman's death.

That was the whole purpose here. To make Shay suffer. To make her afraid, looking over her shoulder to see if anyone else she loved might die or when she would become the target.

There was no fun to this game if there wasn't pain caused to someone else. And fear.

Shay needed to be afraid…because she was going to get hers. And soon.

Or maybe not soon…

Maybe now…

Chapter 25

Stefan closed his phone and closed his eyes. Damn and double damn. At what point did life get simpler? When did the number of bad guys decline? He'd thought for sure they were dealing with Darren's brother, Danny. Had to be. It made perfect sense. But he'd been dead a year. A whole year. Had died around the same time as Darren. And of a heart attack. Like Darren, like the recent victims.

A coincidence? *Not.*

Stefan knew he was missing something.

What?

There was a definite familiarity to the energy, and if it wasn't Darren's twin's, then whose was it? A parent? A child? But then it would have to be a young child. And few children hated with the degree of intensity required to kill, and kill again.

Darren hadn't been old. Twenty-eight, maybe twenty-nine and he'd died a year ago. It's possible he'd fathered a child when he was as young as sixteen, but not likely. Still it *could* mean there might be an eleven- or twelve-year-old out there with his abilities. But it was unlikely a child that age would be a killer.

It wasn't impossible for the psychic skills to develop that young, but they usually showed up at puberty. Who knows with this family? But even if they did show earlier, the pattern was they didn't develop the required strength and endurance for several more years.

More likely the killer was a sibling or a parent.

Lissa, his ghost friend, appeared in front of him. Gone was the joyous soul he'd come to appreciate. Instead a sense of gravity, of sorrow, emanated from her. She never said a word. Just sat there.

Waiting. Hoping to help, but like him, not knowing what to do.

So like her sister Alex…

Sister? Could Darren have a sister? Or another brother? Damn. He leaned forward and stared out into the dark night beyond his bedroom window. Was that it? Was there any chance there was *another* sibling? A sibling who might have had lost both their siblings at the same time. Was that possible? And if so, would that be enough to cause such a reaction? To compel him to extract revenge for the deaths of his brothers? Maybe all the family he had in the world.

Thanks, Lissa.

She smiled hopefully. *I didn't help, but if you have an idea of what to do – good.*

Sometimes you don't have to do anything. Just being you, is great. He smiled at his visitor even as his mind worried on the problem.

But why focus on connections to Shay?

Unless this person believed Shay was responsible. And the only way this person could know that is if they knew what happened that night?

And understood what had gone wrong.

In that case, were they after revenge? To kill Shay. Destroy her life. Or to make her lose what was important to her?

Anyone who knew Shay, knew people were more important to her than even her projects, but Darren had always had a major problem with Shay's projects. Shay had shared how much Darren complained when he thought she cared more about them than about him. He'd been right, but that's because he must have realized Shay's heart hadn't been engaged the way Darren wanted it to be.

Stefan had been able to see that. But Shay hadn't been willing to see it.

But what about the last victim, the elderly lady in the hospital? She hadn't been associated with one of Shay's projects. Who knew why that target had been chosen? So close to Pappy but not an attack against him.

Or was the old woman a target for any number of other reasons?

If the attacker had gone after the old woman out of rage, that meant their anger was unstable. The person unbalanced. When one focused on using negative energy long term it had the effect of destabilizing the energy at the core. That could be what happened. And it would make the attacker *very* dangerous.

But now what? What or who would this person target next? Stefan had already considered the children's ward. Was there another vulnerable spot? One that held more meaning for Shay? She'd funded thousands of projects over the last decade through the Foundation. She had many friends with only a few family members to target.

More of Shay's projects? More of Shay's family? Friends?

The field was pretty open.

Stefan?

He frowned, not recognizing the voice. Lissa had left, so it wasn't her. And this voice was so faint as to be hardly distinguishable.

Stefan? Help me. Something bizarre is going on here.

He shook his head, trying to clear it and focused on the voice. *Tabitha?*

Yes! I had an ethereal visitor. When it couldn't get in my room it got pissed. Went down the hall. I followed, but they've gone into the children's ward.

"Shit." Not there. *Please not there.* He hadn't finished reinforcing the shell. It took longer than a few hours. Could take days.

Help. I need help, Stefan! Tabitha screamed.

He couldn't do this alone. He sent out a massive panicked call to anyone who could help and then he jumped free of his body.

Shay bolted upright, her mind screaming awake. A film of fear slid over her skin. She brushed hair back off her face even as she studied Roman's bedroom, looking to find what was wrong.

And found nothing. She took a deep breath and tried to reassess. At her side, Roman rolled over, snuggling closer. Her heart still pounded with fright, but the sight of the sleeping giant beside her made her smile. He slept like an infant with such peace on his face, his body open and relaxed with sexual surfeit. Just the way he should be.

So what was wrong?

The nudge came again. She sent out a questioning response.

And something exploded in her mind.

Oh God.

The hospital. Stefan was calling her to the hospital.

She jumped free to race through the ethers, her body collapsing, limp on the bed.

***

Stefan took a direct hit. He'd have groaned if he had a voice. Instead, he was so focused on his astral form and keeping a protective bubble over the kids on the ward, a trick that Dr. Maddy had been helping him work out, that that attack blindsided him. Again.

He was getting damn tired of this. In his world, there was always evil. Working with the police as he did, he'd seen so much, but no one could keep his guard up all the time. And tonight he'd been so far past tired, he'd let it drop.

And he just hadn't been aware of the attack early enough.

And he'd been alone. Weakened. Unprotected.

At his panicked cry, so many friends had come to help – none prepared for what they found.

Energy blasts.

Stefan, go stop the attacks. I'll protect the children. Dr. Maddy's voice filtered through his awareness. *Send Tabitha my way. She's advanced enough with energy to help.*

I'm here. Tabitha's strained voice arrived ahead of her teal energy. *Stefan, if you can, get this bastard.*

Even Lissa's energy moved frantically at his side, trying to send Stefan away.

Maddy was already protecting the children. Her powerful healing energy was a bulletproof casing around the little ones in the room. It's not as if the attacker could get through that. But they'd seen so many people capable of so many horrible things, Stefan no longer believed in certainties.

Others were there to receive the black energy, sucking it out of the ward. The person they sought appeared to have connected to the universal energy – it wasn't possible to run out of that. And right now, that was majorly bad news.

Stefan could sense the chaos on the earthly reality too, as people panicked, searching for answers to what they could only sense, but not clarify. They tried to contact him, looking for help. But he couldn't help anyone.

Stefan could only hope they were doing what they could.

Because whoever this asshole was, he had serious skills.

And serious mental issues.

This wasn't a cold, calculated act. This was murderous rage.

With the flavor of revenge.

And there was no end to this attack in sight.

Stefan needed Shay. Where the hell was she?

✳✳✳

Panicked, Shay arrived at Dr Maddy's hospital in astral form to see...energy... God, she didn't know what was going on...but thick turbulence filled the space. More than one person, more than one fight. At the center of it all – Stefan in a battle of wills. Only she couldn't tell with whom...or what.

The large, open communal space was dark and silent – as in the aftermath of a grenade going off. There should be noise, voices, conversation. Instead there was a complete absence of sound.

Shay spun in a slow circle, trying to sort through the impressions bombarding her. Silence. Shock. Pain and destruction. Her view was filtered through a smoky, charcoal-smelling haze. Tables were overturned, chairs tossed, toys strewn on the floor and paper floated through the air to land gently on the ground like leaves falling in the wind.

Her arrival *had* come in the aftermath of a massive blast.

An energy grenade.

She'd heard of them. Had never seen one.

And she was grateful to have missed this one too.

The energy listed and shook as the particles came together. The blast had disturbed time – making everything move in slow motion. She searched through the oddities, her instincts more useful than her eyes. She had to see through the wrongness to what was really happening.

Deep, dark colors bombarded her as wave upon wave of energy slammed into her. *Waves from the energy bomb?* Surely not?

A psychic attack? At this magnitude?

She couldn't make sense of anything. She was also too busy protecting herself. The more walls she put up, the more the waves increased. She was forced to throw walls higher and higher in an effort to keep safe. Someone incredibly powerful was blasting her. And with their continuous waves, she couldn't gain the upper hand; she couldn't find her footing in this horrific reality.

She was losing the battle.

Another wave slammed into her, lifting her off the floor. She would have dropped to the ground, but she floated in a world with no gravity – no ground.

No longer in the physical plane, the rules were different here. No physical senses, no physical touch, no Newton's laws. Nothing she could use to re-center herself.

In her mind's eye she could see the destroyed center of the room. But she could see a deep, dark black off to the left, and opposing it off to the right, a deep midnight blue. She'd landed in the middle of some kind of war.

And she had to pick a side and fast.

But who was where?

Shay, duck!

She ducked. But too slowly. The blast lifted and tossed her on her virtual butt.

Again.

There would have been a trickle of laughter, but it arrived on Stefan's panicked cry, *Another one's coming your way.*

She gasped as the blast hit at the tail end of Stefan's warning. This wave was weaker. Barely skimming over her body. Better.

Thanks for the warning, and what the hell is going on?

The ward is under attack.

She snorted. *I got that much. But who's doing this? And why?*

I don't know! I can't spare the energy to find out. I need your help. I need everyone's help. This is bad, Shay. I'm trying to protect the kids at the same time. There are too many of them for me to guard. Maddy's also protecting them now as I'm spread too thin. Help. I can't spread out any more, that's your specialty, not mine. We never got to you teaching me that trick, remember.

Damn it. What trick? What do you want me to do?

Disperse completely. Become one with the universe!

Shit. Ask for something easy why don't you?

Taking a deep nonexistent breath, Shay thinned her energy down to a misty vapor. It helped her disappear into the ether as she dealt with the waves of energy still pouring her way. *And now she was harder to target.*

Following the success of her first attempt, she thinned her energy further, and was no longer solid enough to be hit by the energy attacks. Instead, she filled the room with her very essence. She spread out to the far corners, including the ceiling. She could see other energies in the battle, and the children's energies. They were silent, still, but she could see their energies pulsing in strong healthy waves as they slept.

Nice. Dr. Maddy was full of cool tricks apparently if she could keep their consciousnesses and their bodies protected while the war raged.

Leaving the others – and God only knew who all was here – to protect the children, Shay thinned her energy even further. Within seconds she'd become little more than mist in the room, a fragrance, a mere sensation.

Surrounding her attacker. Above, behind, on her attacker – the vibrating dark purple-black ball at the side of the room.

Shay closed in on the person so bent on destruction that they didn't care who was destroyed. Anger, frustration and a horrible madness poured from this person's energy – this person, bent on maximum destruction. Emotions, thoughts, words fired from this person in an endless vent. Shay couldn't help but hear the refrain that poured through the night.

She struggled to make the words clear.

Then she heard the disembodied voice.

Hurt them all.

Make them suffer.

Make them pay.

***

Ronin grabbed his phone and dialed Stefan.

No answer. *Damn it.* He tried again, then again. Switching tactics, he tried to call Shay. And it rang and rang. *Shit.* Someone needed to answer, damn it.

"Hello." A deep, dangerous voice growled into the phone.

Ronin reared back. "Roman? Is that you?"

"Yes. What the fuck is going on?"

With stomach churning, Ronin asked, "Why? What's the matter?"

"Shay has collapsed in bed like a coma victim, and there's a weird buzz going on in the air. I've tried calling everyone I know, and no one answers. Hell, Stefan's not answering telepathically either."

Telepathically? "Roman, can you talk that way too?" Jesus, if only. It would make life so much easier for him. The concept blew him away.

"No, but Stefan can talk to me that way. In theory that means I can learn, too. But these people have skills I'd never imagined. I want to know what the hell is going on," Roman roared.

"I'm trying to get a hold of Stefan and Shay. Wait, did you say she was in a coma?" Ronin tried, but couldn't stop his voice from rising at the end. He closed his eyes and took a calming breath. Damn this case was weird and getting weirder.

"A psychic coma or some damn thing. I can't touch her. Can only sit here and watch over her. Helpless. I fucking hate that." Roman's voice calmed somewhat. "Why are you calling?"

"Darren had another sibling. Younger by several years. Apparently she adored her brothers and they adored her." Ronin stared at the screen in front of him. "I have a photo. It's fuzzy but I thought maybe they'd recognize her. I don't know her."

"Send me the picture. Maybe I will be able to."

"Sending..." Ronin zapped the image to his brother's cell phone. "You should have it now." He waited. And waited.

"Roman? Are you there?"

"Hell. Yes," His brother snapped in fury. "And I know exactly who this is."

***

No.

Anger screamed through her mind, blackening her thoughts into molten rage.

How could these people do this? She'd come here for an outlet and found a fight. Well if they wanted a fight, they could have one.

There was a lot of anger to get rid of. A lot of payback to deliver. "And damn it, I refuse to be cheated. I need my vengeance. I deserve justice." The anger soared outward, blackening all thoughts into molten rage.

How could there be so many people here? And how could so many understand energy?

Until now, she'd believed her and her siblings were special. Above the others. Believed they'd been the only ones with such skills. That the world was their playground – to do with as they wished.

What a rush that had been.

She'd loved that sense of uniqueness. That sense of superiority over the rest of the world. That power to play God. And boy, had they played. Together and apart they'd done what they wanted with who they'd wanted, believing it was their right as superior beings. That no one would ever know.

How wrong could they have been?

They weren't the only ones who could do this. The only ones that played in both realities.

Disbelief fired the rage all over again and she blasted off more grenades. Barely satisfied she realized now how Shay had beaten her brothers. Not just one, but both of them.

Shay and her helper. Or many helpers. She'd known Shay couldn't have done this alone.

Then, Darren had Danny to help him. That Shay most likely had never even known about Danny's existence, hurt. Darren rarely told anyone about his twin. And he'd never tell a mark like Shay. It was private. Danny had been the other half of Darren. The two of them were identical in so many ways. But when Darren had hesitated to kill Shay, it had been Danny that had stepped in and made sure it happened.

Made sure Darren didn't change his mind.

Only something had gone wrong. She remembered their panicked cries for help as she raced toward them. Their agonized screams as they died. Both of them – at the same time. When the energy had taken one brother, it had also taken the second. Connected as always.

She'd come to their aid, entering the fight at the end – just that one instant too late. She'd seen the two energies, Shay's and this asshole's here in the children's ward. She recognized him here. He'd die tonight as well.

But there'd also been something else there at the end. Or someone else. A blue energy. Even now, she couldn't place it. It had jumped into the battle just ahead of her attempt.

And when combined with the other energies, had blown a hole through her siblings' heart chakras.

If only she'd been earlier. She could have saved her brothers. She could have killed Shay. Only she'd been too late.

Now, a year later, she would get her revenge.

Or was trying to.

No! she screamed to the ethers. You won't beat me. I am too strong. I'm stronger than my brothers ever were.

Her brothers had always said she was the strongest person they'd ever seen. Often snapped the words out in a jealous rage. She'd have grinned if she were in her physical form. Laughed out loud if she could have. She was the damn strongest. No one could beat her.

No one. And no group could either.

She closed her eyes and focused on pulling in as much energy as she could handle. She'd see this place blow, and herself with it, before she'd let these bastards win.

More. Pull more. Using techniques she'd learned a long time ago, she opened up her energy chakras and pulled at the atmosphere.

She'd show them.

Chapter 26

Pain whipped through Shay. Followed by heat and anger in a steady one-two punch as energy rattled through her, separating her misty form even further.

Whoever this person was, they had some serious power behind them. And they were seriously demented.

Shay struggled amongst the blasts, the energy that she was both assimilating and blending with.

Stay strong, Shay, Stefan's voice whispered through to her.

I am. I'm trying to envelop the energy. Wrap it up so it can't get any bigger.

No! Don't. It could blow you up. You have to jump inside and power it down.

I am so not able to do that.

Yes, you can. Blend with the energy, find the source, become a part of it then shut down the chakra from the inside.

That will kill the person.

An awkward silence ensued as she realized how foolish her comment was. Then Stefan's gentle voice filtered through her consciousness. *I know. But if you don't, we're all going to die. We can't keep this up.*

Damn. She shuddered. *I'm on it.*

Go quietly. Hide your tracks.

Hide her tracks? That made her pause. It meant technically no longer existing as herself, but becoming one with everything around her. She'd heard about it. Hadn't tried it yet. Supposedly it came with a dangerous hook – becoming permanently lost on the ethers. She'd have to have help to return. More help than Stefan would likely be able to provide.

Becoming one with everything, meant losing her individuality, her identity. That's where the problem lay. If she did what Stefan asked, she'd cease to exist.

Still, she had to try. If it was a one-way trip, then so be it. Better that than to have this asshole take out dozens of lives. These were her friends. And the children were innocent victims. Someone needed to stop this. To save them.

If she was the only one that could – so be it.

With a last loving regret for Roman and what they might have had together, knowing that taking the next step was the riskiest thing she'd ever done, she took a deep breath and dropped her consciousness another level.

She became one with the broken floor. One with the destroyed furniture. She became one with the very air. The very essence that made her who she was, melded and blended to become one with the black power that was filling the room. Her fragments, so tiny, so light, could attach her to the attacker and not have them know it. She'd feel familiar to the person's energy. She'd feel like she was one particle of the many.

That's because she was. She'd become *one* with everything.

And there was the danger.

If she destroyed this other person, there was a good chance she would destroy herself.

And yet there was no choice.

She separated herself further from life, from the physical reality as she knew it. With another breath of air, she slipped further away, yet again. Becoming one with the universe. One with her past.

And she became one with all.

The emotions of her attacker poured through her, filling her, hooking her, sucking her into its existence.

Memories overwhelmed her. Of children laughing. Adults crying. A barrage of images flew past, of cars. Schools. Classes. Men. Old. Young. Lovers. Haters. And then one face that made Shay gasp as hurt and betrayal threatened to swamp her.

Darren.

This person *was* connected to Darren. To the man who'd tried to kill her.

Tidbits of conversation streamed through her new awareness with emotions attached. Another face. A similar face. *Twins?* Darren and his brother. But still he was not this person she'd joined. This threat was another of Darren's sibling. A third sibling connected to the twin brothers. Another brother? No. A sister. A sister Shay had never known about. A sister that Darren had never wanted her to know about.

Because, in the end, Darren hadn't intended for Shay to survive to meet her.

But Shay had. And now, as part of everything, she understood it all. Most of all, the hate Darren's sister felt for her.

And that's why Shay had been targeted. That's why her projects had been hit. Why suspicion had been thrown on her. Why the children's hospital – her special project that even Darren had been jealous of – had been targeted. And it explained why no one had recognized the energy. As Darren had been able to hide his energy, his true person, so too had his sister hid hers.

Like Darren, his sister could mask what she was doing, keeping a completely false front in place for others to view. Yet inside, she'd been scheming and planning to destroy Shay and all Shay held dear.

To avenge her brothers' deaths by murdering innocent people…

Like Bernice. Like David. Like Robert. Like Tabitha, Marie, that elderly lady beside Pappy's room.

Shay's heart cracked, causing pain like she'd never felt before. So many victims. So many unnecessary deaths. So many families destroyed.

Stay focused. Stay in the light. Stefan's voice whispered through her essence. *We have to stop her.*

She couldn't speak. She was too full of this other person's agenda that tried to take her over. To control her. To keep her and contain her.

Careful, Stefan warned.

Shay swallowed hard. *I'm trying.*

Don't try. Do.

***

Roman raced to the address his brother had given him over the phone – after he identified the woman in the photo. His brother and a team met him there.

Such a small unassuming townhouse on the edge of town. Made of unassuming bricks and mortar…and filled with evil. He swore he could almost see the oozing clouds of wrongness coming off the front of the building. A couple of neighbors sat on their porches reaching for the cool night air.

The cop cars arrived with screeching brakes but no sirens. If anything, the lack of sirens sent out a stronger message that scared the hell out of those enjoying the peace and quiet of the night.

Roman motioned for the old guy sitting next to the townhouse to come down to the street level. The man scrambled in his direction. The others, realizing something was wrong, joined him. Motioning everyone to silence, the cops emptied the homes on either side of the one they needed to access.

With Ronin in the lead, they snuck up to the front door.

***

Yes. Shay understood. She had to go inside the blackness. Beneath the memories and the emotions. She had to go deeper into the physical being. Wherever that person was. The woman wasn't here physically at the hospital. Like Stefan and Shay, she was out of her body – fighting in astral form. Now Shay had to find this person's body. Find her physical form.

And shut her down.

Struggling to keep her thoughts pure, her energy golden and warming, she allowed her own consciousness to join with her attacker's. And she sank deeper into the woman's psyche to hunt for and find the woman's silver cord. There was so much pulsing and surging energy around her that she couldn't see it. She searched the light, the dark, the nonexistent…and then she saw it. Relief washed through her. At least this person had a cord. Shay admitted to herself that she'd been worried about what specific abilities this person had and whether they truly *were* earthbound.

With the silver grey cord winking in and out of the blackness, she slid along the lit pathway, racing faster and faster, hating the panic threatening to overwhelm her. She didn't dare stop now. She couldn't fail. This was too important. Too necessary for these kids. For Stefan. And all the other souls that had come to help.

And Roman. If her attacker beat her and survived this would destroy him. They'd just found each other. To lose him now…

And just like that, she came to the end of the cord and fell into the body of Darren's sister.

And realized who this person was. With access to all her thoughts, memories, motivations. Shay stood in silence, filled with more pain than she thought possible, a greater sense of betrayal than she'd have thought there could be, and evidence of more damage than any trio of siblings had a right to inflict.

This was *Jordan.* Her assistant. With access to all of Shay's files. With inner knowledge of all of Shay's projects. With a connection to, and information about, Shay's personal life through her brother Darren.

Who had access to Bernice. To Bernice's emails. And even to the Foundation function that night.

Even though Ronin had run a check on her, she'd managed to hide who she truly was.

Jordan who was aware of her relationship with Roman. Had commented on it. Was he her next target? And then there was Pappy, Tabitha, her cousin Marie…

Her assistant knew all the pain and fear Shay had been through this last year. And all the while she'd been twisting the screw tighter and tighter. Had she been the one who sent those threatening letters to Bernice? Those horrible emails? She'd had access to all Shay's contacts as well as her computer.

And she'd been a blackmailer who went after payouts from Bernice, before she'd agree to just go away. Greedy like Darren. Wanting more and more. Only Bernice, though she'd agreed to pay, hadn't agreed to an amount. Jordan had considered her offers too low to be bothered backing down.

So this then was Bernice's deal with the devil. She'd been scared by the threats and the promise of the evil behind those letters. She'd offered to pay to make it all go away. Only her offer was too low and so Jordan had only twisted the knife harder. Demanding more and more. Why? To torment Bernice, and thus torment Shay. Jordan had known how close the two of them were.

There'd been no way out for Bernice.

Shay now knew why there'd been no stopping the emails – because money wasn't the only object of the game. Just a nice side benefit.

Vengeance had been the goal.

And Bernice had nothing to do with any of this but she was someone Shay loved. Bernice had been an innocent victim. Just like David. Like Robert… Like so many others.

For years, Bernice'd been the closest thing to a mother Shay had. Why Shay's brother hadn't been targeted too, Shay didn't know. Unless Jordan thought Shay wasn't close to him because he'd spent the bulk of the last year on various continents around the world whereas everyone else she cared about was here. Close by. Available. Visible.

Anger spiked through Shay as she realized how she'd been manipulated. How she'd been played. Not once, but twice. By Darren and now his sister. Struggling for control, she tamped down the anger slightly, not wanting to bring attention to her presence. She didn't dare risk exposure at this stage.

But she acknowledged the anger, honed it to precision accuracy. She zeroed in on the chakras and raced through

Jordan's body to the heart. There she waffled, though she understood what was needed.

She knew that to use deadly force was going to take her to a place she didn't want to go. Again.

Don't use deadly force. Use love as the force. Don't direct your anger and pain at her. Instead, shine your love – for all these children and for those of us helping...indeed for the rest of all that's good and true in the world – through her heart chakra. There can only be one of two outcomes. One, the deadly blackness will dissipate under the love; or two, she won't be able to withstand the influx of energy. Remember...love conquers al.l

Shay lifted her face to the light and let her love pour through. She smiled as the warmth and joy filled her. She wasn't made of anger and pain. She lived a life of love and grace. She believed in it. Chose to live her life by it. At that moment, she was in the perfect state...*of grace.*

She closed her eyes and pulled the small, vapor-sized pieces of herself toward her, glowing with love for her fellow man. For freedom to walk the path she needed to walk. She called the basic elements of her essence home.

In a wash of golden goodness.

Her energy swelled with joy. Shay's form grew as the tiny parts of her raced home. One by one, they collected to become one whole astral soul. *Hers.* All the while, she sent out strong, loving energy, healing energy, warm caring energy. Forgiving energy. She forgave Darren for his betrayal. She forgave the twin brother.

And hardest of all – she forgave Jordan.

Her heart swelled with her own joy as hurts of the last year dropped away. She released herself from the bondage of pain she'd locked herself into this last year.

Her astral form continued to grow, and her energy continued to glow. What a weight she'd carried this last year. And now, she just let it go. She felt it release, felt the emotions and memories, energy hooks, all the negative energy fall away. She let it all go.

She realized she really was thankful to Jordan for this opportunity. Shay could grow through this. And Shay could cleanse her soul.

Jordan would have to make peace in her own way on her own time.

But it wouldn't be in this lifetime.

Even as the words flew through her thoughts, the last of her astral form came home – swiftly, silently and secretively – so quickly Jordan didn't see Shay's arrival.

Until it was too late.

Shay witnessed when Jordan suddenly understood that something had changed. Something in her world had gone wrong. Shay could feel Jordan's disbelief, her anger, then her realization.

That she had a visitor. On the inside.

In a featherlight movement, Shay whispered, "Knock, knock. Guess who's here?"

"*Noooo...!*" The scream ripped from Jordan's throat in one long anguished torrent.

Distant sounds barely filtered through Shay's consciousness. Yells, pounding, splintering wood, more screaming.

Then...it all stopped...and Shay heard...nothing.

And the internal pressure, the force from too much energy contained in one confined space – burst through in an explosion.

Shay cried out as the space she was in – shattered, sending her astral form spiraling back out to the universe, in a million infinitesimal fragments.

✳✳✳

Friday morning...

"You need to rest," Stefan urged Roman. "You can't help her if you can't look after yourself."

Roman stared at him, knowing the pain of the last few days would never truly go away. Shay was comatose before him, still lying on his bed as she had when he'd woken up that fateful morning.

Dr. Maddy was still trying. And so was Stefan.

Shay wasn't just lost in the ethers, but her fragments were spread so thin, the pieces flung so far apart, they couldn't call her home.

"I can't sleep," he said simply. "I have to help."

What could he do? He wasn't like them. He had no psychic abilities. He couldn't track her down like they were attempting to do. Or track all the lost pieces that made up the Shay he knew and loved. Talk about a mind-boggling concept.

He shuddered and closed his eyes. "But I don't know how. Tell me what *I* can do to bring her back. I'm not like you."

Stefan's smile was tired but held real amusement. "You, more than anyone, should be able to help. You know her better physically than I do. Than anyone does." Stefan gave a short laugh. "This might not be the best time but...maybe there is none better. You are likely the only one that *can* help."

Roman shook his head, but Stefan continued to speak. "Though you aren't aware...you are a dream walker. You called it inspiration. And true, that's how you started on this journey, but one painting, one photo was never enough. You had to have more. You had to see more. You dreamed of her. Of knowing more. Of being more with her. You don't remember but in your dreams you traveled to her, so you could see her in greater detail. You walked with her in your dreams. And then you painted her."

Roman stared at him. Shock rippling through him. "*Say what?* All I've ever done is paint pictures of her. Sure, sometimes I close my eyes to pull an image into tighter clarity, but that's all." He tried to shrug it off. The rest of what Stefan said was just too bizarre.

"And that's how you've been doing what you're doing. The first picture peaked your interest, but it can't account for the visual images you've been drawing on these last couple of years. You've been accessing the images that you have stored from walking with her in your dreams. That's how you have seen her in such clarity – in such detail. In so doing, she became a part of your psyche. A part of you. A part of your soul. It's a connection that can't be severed. You are now her safety line. Or her ground, as we call it. You are the one that can show her the way home."

There were no words. Roman could only stare, as he remembered the many tormented nights and happy mornings when he'd woken up with his thoughts full of Shay. He'd felt foolish. Like a lovestruck teenager. All the while he'd been developing a skill called dream walking? To become Shay's lifeline?

He loved that idea. Wanted to be what Shay needed. But surely Stefan was wrong? Talking about someone else? Someone with psychic abilities. Someone like Stefan.

"I think you're wrong. But I hope you aren't. *If* you're right, I still don't know how to help."

Stefan walked closer. "How, you ask?" He smiled, realization dawning on his own face. "By doing what you do best. By painting her. Your love for her is in every line. Every brushstroke. I saw it. She saw it."

Roman stared at Stefan. "She did?"

"Absolutely. She said as much at your showing that night. She understood, even then, the power of the connection you had." He smiled gently. "She just hadn't recognized the connection was to her."

"I don't understand that."

Stefan, so tired that his voice cracked, said, "There's nothing to understand. You love her. Now go paint her. All of her. You no longer need a photo of her. You know her so well. You could paint her with your eyes closed." His face lighted. "And from your expression I can see you already have done that. So do it again now. Paint every inch of her. Show her the way here. The way home. Help her to pull her energy back to become whole in her astral self. If you can do that, the shift to her body will be easy."

Roman was too scared to answer him right away. What if he couldn't do what Stefan said he could? What if he could, but he screwed it up? What if by his actions, he lost Shay forever?

He walked over to the bed to stare down at his beloved Shay. "You're crazy. It's ridiculous to say I can do any of that stuff you talked about."

"What you don't understand is that Shay is here," Stefan said. "Right now." He waved his arm around the room. "She's everywhere. But she's fragmented. She's so small she's in the very air we breathe. But she can't find her way home – or else she'd be here. You are her home. You are her other half. Now paint exactly what you see in your mind and guide her back. Ground her here."

Roman narrowed his gaze at something he couldn't quite detect in Stefan's voice. His heart sank as he thought he understood. "You don't think I *can* do this."

"I'm hoping you can." Stefan ran his fingers through his hair and down the back of his head, then admitted, "But I'm afraid that what you'll paint won't be what you're expecting." Stefan pointed to the door. "Your studio is there. Go. Close your eyes and paint Shay as you see her in your mind, right now."

With that command, Roman bolted for his studio. He picked up a blank canvas and removed the unfinished picture on his favorite easel. Not allowing himself to second-guess, he allowed himself to begin without thinking about what he'd paint.

At his paint counter, he instinctively opened red and white tubes. In a slapdash methodology he never used, he squeezed paint onto his palate and started mixing. As always, the feel of a brush in his hand calmed him. Made him feel more in control. As if what he would put on the canvas was important. Meaningful – at least it would be to him.

Nervous tension gripped his stomach. He was so afraid Stefan was wrong. Roman wanted him to be right, but... Roman was not like Stefan, or Maddy. Or Shay. Yes, Roman could paint, but his talent was nothing compared to the stuff they did...

But if there were anything he could do to help Shay...Roman would do it.

He walked back to the blank canvas and went to place a long stroke of her arm, when he realized he couldn't. His hand couldn't make the stroke. He tried again, the effort breaking a sweat out on his brow.

Stefan spoke from behind him. "Relinquish control. Let the brush tell you what to paint."

His back stiffened. Realizing Stefan could guide him, he nodded.

"Close your eyes, and let your brush speak for you."

Such an odd suggestion. But it felt right. And that was even odder still. Aware of not having painted Shay since they'd become lovers, he closed his eyes and let his hand – his brush – do as it willed. He'd been aware of every line of Shay's body for a long time and now he knew her at a physically intimate level. He dreamt of her. In that Stefan was right. Had he really travelled to see her, too? He cast his mind back. Seeing the times he stopped a painting to stare off into space. Accessing images from...somewhere.

When his arm dipped and dabbed, he was astonished, wanting to look, but he was scared to stop the magic. When his brush no longer moved, he realized someone behind him was taking a deep breath. "Well, you got that much right."

Roman opened his eyes to see he'd painted a woman's form lying on a bed. She was barely discernible in white. More like a ghosted image on the canvas.

But covering the entire form were thousands of red dots.

"What the hell is *that*?"

"That is Shay as she is now." Stefan studied the painting, and then apparently satisfied, nodded. "Now call to her in your mind. Tell her how much you love her. And need her. Call her home."

Stefan wandered the space. Spying a stack of blank canvases, he replaced the one Roman had just painted with a new, blank one. "Here. Now paint her again. We'll see if there is a change."

Thinking he was crazy, but willing to try anything if it would help, Roman closed his eyes and let his need pour forth.

Shay. Please come home to me. I love you. I need you. Don't make me live this way. Without you. I was lost until I found you, and now, you are lost to me. Please. Find me here. Come to me. Let's live our lives together. Be with me until we grow old, together. Please. Come home.

He closed his eyes and bowed his head as the litany played over and over again in his mind. He barely registered when his arm lifted and the brush started moving rapidly across the canvas. He could feel pressure inside his chest. Feel the pain of his loss and the agony of his need to have her returned to him. He'd never been much of a verbal communicator, preferring to use a canvas for his expression. And he found an odd sense of freedom in giving that expression free rein.

"Now open your eyes." Stefan's warm voice sounded at his shoulder.

Roman opened his eyes and studied the painting. The same white image lay quietly in the bed, only now it was more defined. Was it more lively than the first image?

He raced back to his first canvas and checked. He frowned. There might be a tiny change in her expression? And then again, maybe not. He returned to his canvas. The red dots had collected more closely together. In the shape of a woman's body. Not a definable solid line, but they were representative of Shay's body, as if he had used a stippling technique. Interesting. He never used that style. "But what does it mean?"

"It means she's hearing you." Stefan smacked him on his back, "Good. Now – do it again."

Obediently, Roman closed his eyes and started all over on yet another blank canvas. He explained how he'd loved her long before he'd met her. How he'd been ashamed to tell her. How he hadn't been able to explain for fear of chasing her away. And he'd do anything to keep her in his life.

Anything.

Before he really understood how much he'd done or the time that had passed, he realized a fatigue like he'd never known before had settled deep into his soul.

"Open your eyes."

Roman gazed at the more collected, but still undefined, form of a woman hovering over the slack woman in white. He checked on Shay. This time he could see the change. The stillness was gone. She wasn't back, but she no longer looked like the living dead.

"Again."

This time, Roman knew what to do. Seeing the change, knowing his efforts were working, he closed his eyes, and with determination and a hint of anger in his voice he called out to her while his arm worked at a furious pace – with a surety to it's strokes. If she was listening, then she could damn well come home.

"Shay. Get yourself back home and into my bed where you belong," he roared. "I love you. I always have. God damn it, I won't sleep with your ghost for the rest of my life. Get your beautiful ass home – now."

He could sense Stefan's surprise. Felt his bated breath as he waited to see what would happen next. Roman opened his eyes and couldn't believe the image on his canvas. "Wow."

"I'll say."

The red polka dot form had lain down over top of the white still form, injecting existence and blood into the woman on the canvas. The red became pink, giving the impression of life and a spark to her image.

He threw down the paintbrush and raced back to his bed.

And cried out in pain.

Shay didn't look any different.

His heart dropped. He'd been so sure he'd actually be able to make his paintings create truth in real life. Panic set in.

Ignoring the rules he'd been told, not to touch, and with Stefan making no move to stop him, Roman dropped to her side, lowered his head and kissed her. Gently. Tenderly. Afraid to hurt her.

He pulled back, studied her for a long moment. Then spoke forcefully, lovingly, but giving no quarter. "Enough, damn it. Come home, Shay. Please."

And he dropped his head again and kissed her. Hard.

It took a few seconds to realize that the cool lips were warming beneath his, that the arms crushed against his chest were hanging on to his shirt, and that she really was responding.

He pulled back to stare into that beloved, half-lidded gaze. Tears formed in the corner of his eyes. "Shay? Oh thank God. I love you," he whispered. "Thank you for coming back."

"Thank you," she answered simply, "for showing me the way."

He dropped his forehead to rest on hers. "Good thing you came home or I'd have found a way to cross over and drag you back."

"You won't have to." She smiled, tears pooling in the corner of her eyes to slide down her face. "Just do what you did tonight. Use love and I'll always find my way back to you."

The two gazed at each other in exhaustion and hope, and then Roman lowered his head once again.

Chapter 27

It was much later, after a shower and some food, that Shay pushed her chair back and walked over to the studio to stare at the pictures Roman had created to bring her home. As she studied the last one Roman picked up his palette and quickly created a last painting of Shay at home and whole. "Just to make sure."

She laughed. But she waited willingly. She asked Stefan and Roman all the questions that burned inside. "What happened to Jordan?"

"She's dead, for starters," Stefan said, an arm around her shoulders. "I'm not sure what the coroner will say is the cause of her death though. Her heart, the actual organ, exploded inside her chest." He grimaced. "I didn't know that could happen."

"Good thing," Roman muttered, as he focused on his painting. "Saved me from having to kill her."

Shay reached a hand up and squeezed his shoulder. "I'm going to have to overhaul my hiring policies. I could have saved myself a lot of heartache if I'd known she was Darren's sister."

"You and me both," said Stefan. "But there was no indication that Darren had any family living. He was adopted. They all were and to different families. Remember? The three of them found each other somehow. Their unique abilities may have facilitated that as they became young adults." He frowned. "According to Ronin, Darren and his twin Danny appeared to have been running scams together. I don't know if Jordan was as well. That's for the police to follow up on. If they ever do."

"Not likely," she scoffed. "This is difficult for them to understand."

"Difficult for anyone who wasn't there," murmured Roman, his gaze on his canvas. "As it is, I can't imagine the explanation they gave the public for the destruction in that hospital wing and as to how the kids all survived. Some kind of explosion I believe the media said."

"They had to say something. The public doesn't want to know about people like us."

"Roman's brother is looking into Jordan's history for us." Stefan rubbed his forehead and yawned. "I think I called in everyone I knew last night. Just to keep Jordan in check."

"I hope we never find anyone that strong or that crazy again." Shay shivered, so grateful to be home whole and healthy. It had been a close call and she knew who to thank for her safe return. Hopefully she'd be given a long and healthy life to thank him.

"You and me both," Stefan said.

"Why was she so strong at the hospital? I don't understand that." Shay had puzzled over that while in a hot shower. She hadn't been able to come up with an answer.

"I think she was drawing the energy from the protective bubble Maddy and I put over the children to keep them safe. Once she recognized how strong it was, she stopped trying to damage it. Instead, she started to use it to amplify her abilities."

Shay shivered. "Smart. And nasty."

Roman wiped his hands and reached out to squeeze hers. "But she's dead. So that's no longer an issue."

"She caused so much damage. She killed Bernice. For fun, I think." Shay already explained the bits and pieces she'd found in Jordan's mind. "And the others. Poor Pappy. I'm so glad he's doing fine. I don't know if I should tell him about Bernice or not."

With a snort, Roman said, "I'd want to know my beloved was standing over me as a guardian angel until it was my time to join her."

"Good point." Shay laughed. "I'll tell him tomorrow when we take him home to his apartment."

Stefan smiled down at her. "You did good tonight, Shay. You'll have to teach me that trick."

"Not any time in the near future." She shuddered. "The trip into Jordan's mind was not pleasant. So many people. Jordan treated so many victims as toys. How wrong is that?"

"We always believe the unbelievable can't happen – until someone proves us wrong." Stefan smiled at her. "Let's hope it will be a long time before we come up against someone else like this."

Shay nodded. "I'm just hoping that is the end of their family." Shay glanced over at Stefan. "I won't sleep well until I know I'm not going to be under attack from anyone else looking for payback because I killed off their family."

"That is one of the primary issues Ronin is looking into." Stefan paused when Roman stepped back from his painting. "We will find out."

"Wow." Shay stared at the picture on the canvas.

With a self-conscious shrug, Roman said, "Not good enough for the gallery, but it certainly should do the job for tonight's mess."

"It's beautiful," Stefan said sincerely. And it was. It was also the only painting with Shay's face. She still lay in bed, the covers up tight, but there was a calm serenity to the sleeping form. So few strokes but the painting glowed with life...and love.

Roman walked to his sideboard and picked up a tube of blue paint.

She laughed. "What are you doing with that color?"

He hunched his shoulders and said almost defensively, "Damned if I know. But I have to add it."

Shay glanced over at Stefan, one eyebrow raised. The smirk on his face had her tilting her head. "Stefan?"

His gaze deepened, the smile shining from the chocolate depths. "Listen."

She frowned. "I can't hear anything."

But Stefan's grin said there was something she should be hearing.

With a start, Roman said, "I'm hearing something. Like an engine. But... *What the hell...?*"

Shay gasped. "Morris!" She spun around searching for the glowing ball. "Surely it can't be?"

Stefan laughed. "It is indeed your beloved pet. His soul scattered in the craziness of Darren's death, but he stayed with you all this time. As Roman brought you back..." Stefan nodded to the painting now sporting a ball of blue curled up on the woman's sleeping shoulder. "Roman also showed Morris the way to return in one piece. Or in as many pieces as the ghost of Morris contains."

Tears formed in Shay's eyes, to trickle down her cheeks as the truth, and the purr of her best feline friend, wrapped around her heart and hugged her close.

"So Roman saved not just one of us tonight – he saved us both." She walked over and wrapped her arms around Roman.

His arms closed tightly, holding her against his heart.

She whispered, "Thank you."

"You're both welcome," Roman said. The distant sound, like a warm, happy engine, kicked up a notch. "Although I'm not sure how to get used to a ghost cat."

Shay smiled. "No problem. After what you've been through, Morris will be easy."

"But I'm going home now." Stefan rose. "I'm way too tired to do anything but sleep for a few days." He hesitated. "I'm beyond tired actually. Must be the fallout from all those energy blasts. Hope my abilities aren't going to change over this mess."

"And mine." Shay smiled. "I don't imagine the others would be happy either."

"Happy or not, it's the life." Stefan smiled. "We will adapt, if need be."

"And speaking of those other people that stepped in and helped..." Roman said as they walked to the front door. "Thank them for me."

"Actually, I think it might be better if you two say it yourself." Stefan smiled at Shay. "Shay knows them all. Not well, but she knows them a whole lot better now than she did before. Don't forget to connect with Tabitha. She's just been released from hospital and is home now."

"And Pappy. Thank heavens." There'd been so much uncertainty, so much danger, and now it was over. Hard to believe.

Stefan reached out and gave her a hug. "I'm so glad you survived."

Tears pooled again. She sniffled them back and beamed a teary smile up at him. "Me too. Thanks for pointing Roman in the right direction and saving my life again."

His grin widened. "So we're even." He dropped a kiss on her forehead before he turned to face Roman. "Thank you for helping bring her home."

Roman smiled down at Shay, tucking her close under his arm. "And that's where she belongs."

They watched the elevator close behind Stefan. "Does it bother you that you might never have the same abilities that I do?" Shay asked, not wanting him to be envious, but showing she understood if he were.

"No. I might not like you disappearing like you have this scary tendency to do, but I'm sure I'll get used to it. Besides, I might not have *your* talents, but I have enough of my own."

"That you do." Shay realized he spoke the truth as he led her to his studio, where he'd placed the weird collection of paintings that had helped call her home. "Are you going to ever put these on display?"

"In a gallery? Oh no. Never."

"Not good enough, huh?" She laughed as she studied the weird paintings in order – from red splattered paint to the one with a hint of blue Morris.

"I don't know how I feel about so many paintings of just me," she admitted. "It's a little odd."

"Get used to it," he said cheerfully, "because now that I have you at my side, I have so much more to work with."

He tugged her into his arms and kissed her soundly.

About the author:

Dale Mayer is a prolific multi-published writer. She's best known for her Psychic Visions series. Besides her romantic suspense/thrillers, Dale also writes paranormal romance and crossover young adult books in several different genres. To go with her fiction, she also writes nonfiction in many different fields with books available on resume writing, companion gardening and the US mortgage system. She has recently published her Career Essentials Series. All her books are available in digital and print formats.

Published Young Adult books:

Vampire in Denial

Vampire in Distress

Vampire in Design

Book 4 (winter 2013)

Dangerous Designs

Deadly Design

Deceptive Designs (fall 2013)

In Cassie's Corner

Gem Stone Mystery

Published Adult Books:

By Death Series

Touched by Death

Haunted by Death (fall 2013)

Psychic Vision Series:

Tuesday's Child

Hide'n Go Seek,

Maddy's Floor

Garden of Sorrow

Knock, knock…

Book 6 (tentatively titled Rare Find)

Book 7 (tentatively titled The Wish List – Stefan's story)

Bound and Determined…to find love series

Unbound

Undone (winter 2013)

Other Adult novellas/short stories:

It's a Dog's Life

Riana's Revenge

Sian's Solution – part of Family Blood Ties

Non Fiction books

Career Essentials: The Resume

Career Essentials: The Cover Letter

Career Essentials: The Interview

Connect with Dale Mayer Online:

Dale's Website – www.dalemayer.com

Twitter – http://twitter.com/#!/DaleMayer

Facebook – http://www.facebook.com/DaleMayer.author